HE'S THE DEVIL

HE'S THE DEVIL

TOBI COVENTRY

4th ESTATE • *London*

4th Estate
An imprint of HarperCollins*Publishers*
1 London Bridge Street
London SE1 9GF

www.4thestate.co.uk

HarperCollins*Publishers*
Macken House, 39/40 Mayor Street Upper
Dublin 1, D01 C9W8, Ireland

First published in Great Britain in 2026 by 4th Estate

1

A catalogue record for this book is available from the British Library

ISBN 978-0-00-873286-8 (hardback)
ISBN 978-0-00-873287-5 (trade paperback)

Set in Stempel Garamond LT Std by HarperCollins*Publishers* India

Printed and bound in the UK using 100% Renewable Electricity at CPI Group (UK) Ltd

FSC
www.fsc.org
MIX
Paper | Supporting responsible forestry
FSC® C013604

For Christoffer.

'We are each our own devil and we make this world our hell'

– Oscar Wilde

He's in there.

In the room next door.

I can feel him through the breeze-blocks. Breathing heavy, sweating, turning over in the thin cotton sheets that I bought.

Pulling a wedgie out from between those melon-tight cheeks. He's right there, eating something wet. Picking stringy strands from a molar. Inspecting what he finds on the end of a long, thick nail, cracked right down the middle.

He keeps the windows closed. Stinking up the square footage with his unholy morning breath. Bags unpacked in my flat, T-shirts folded in the wardrobe. Body lotion rubbed in deep, into the arms, the abs, the thighs, second layer of skin good and moist. Everything smells like patchouli, earth, sticky old blood.

He's bringing back guys, all sorts of guys. Tall and

ginger, scruffy. Small guy, quiet; then loud. Young, white-blond, expensive shoes. Big dick I reckon, from the sound of it. Smashed a wine glass, left soon after.

I'm in my room, listening through the wall as he's gulping pint after pint of water but not pissing for hours. Burping gently. I hear his throat expanding and retracting when I listen closer. I listen so close that I crush my ear hot red. We're separated by nothing but a wall, not nearly thick enough.

He's crying, he's laughing, he's gone out then come back again. He's sleeping, he's reading, he's showering for the third time today. He's wanking, he's chewing. He's about my age, I think.

He's making my skin crawl.

There's something else too. In there with him, in here with me, in the flat with us. A hot horny creature climbing slowly from the depths, carrying a lantern to lead the way out, to show me more. A faint light burning, a thin flame flickering.

There's something else.

Yeah, there's something else.

CHAPTER ONE

You're not going to believe this, by the way. Any of it. But it did happen. I'm just telling you so you know.

It began the night I first heard his name, like a weather report promising a bed-rocking storm, whispered in my ear. The first night I knew he existed. That's where it started.

The flat felt hollow that evening because, just the day before, my best friend Josh had moved out. He'd taken some good things with him – the armchair that was his, the wine rack that wasn't. I let it slide. I didn't have enough money to replace this stuff, but I'd get used to their absence. He'd left the toaster, which was shit, but still just about toasted the bread.

He'd left other things too: a bin bag full of DVDs I'd already looked through. I found some really good ones. I'd spent an hour elbow-deep inside a cardboard box full of his old clothes.

He was coming back for them soon. They sat in the corner like toads, watching me make my toast.

I was ready for work. My uniform was clean – white shirt, black trousers, little jumper, all ironed and steamed. My shoes were polished, an old pair of Josh's brogues that I clicked together. No place like home. The rooms of the flat felt larger, but they weren't, and I felt smaller, but I wasn't.

I left the flat on time as always. Turned around like clockwork on the street, looking up to check the windows were closed, the handles down. Nothing stirred. It was empty. Josh had gone, remember. He'd moved out. But the building stood as it always did. Large, red-brick and concrete, as square as its windows. Once a tyre factory, it still sometimes smelled like rubber when the wind blew just right. But now, it's where I had lived for five wonderful years. Home. The empty glass eyes in their steel frames watching me leave, blinking with the reflection of a passing Ford Transit. The kind people are put in before they're never seen again.

The evening called me onwards. Past the red fire station hunching beneath the monkey-puzzle tree, avoiding the sharp branches. Past the ambulance depot, two doors down, still and silent for now. The church crouched a little way down the road, behind its tombstones, a fat grey cake with a cross on top that wobbled in the wind.

Fire, Ambulance, God. The holy trinity. As good a place as any for a story like this to begin.

Most nights, sex workers crept through the graveyard and

crowed about twenties and fifties. *BeeJay. He asked me for a BeeJay! The dirty bastard.* Then a long loud cackle. They fucked, farted, ate crisps. I was fond of them, they lulled me to sleep on long nights with their screeching, held my hand and stilled it when it hung swinging over the bedside.

I looked back at the flat, briefly, once more. It waved me off, down the road. *Get on with it, Simon, hurry up.* Past the wide, concrete stairway that led to the canals, past a little man with dirty feet, playing with something in his pocket.

This city's huge. You could walk for hours and never bump the edges; tonight was no different, though the autumn air was particularly thick. With each footstep, it felt like every streetlamp behind me, every curving car headlight, every cosy living-room fireplace was snuffed out as I passed, one by one. A city will do that, you can't stop it. It'll make you feel massive and tiny, all at once. A great wobbling shadow grew larger behind me, the night gathering at my back. I swished it, long and cloaky.

I got to work an hour early, as usual. I had things to do. The restaurant had recently been featured in three online buzz lists. Three! We had standards to uphold, tables to set. I polished the lamps. I polished the *bulbs*. I put the bins out.

I broke down brown boxes, cutting through the tape with the little yellow box cutter I keep on my keyring. Tiny particles of cardboard puffed upwards. I took a moment and watched an old brown dog, blind, eyes white like poppable cysts, licking the fishy brickwork under the Biffas. I liked the way it cocked its head when I tapped my foot; I gave it a little smile it couldn't see and some cheese from my apron.

Something on the street called for my attention, a flash of white in my periphery. I turned quickly and scanned the night, the empty alleyway around me, the wooden fencing with its peepholes. I had felt, for a moment, naughty eyes on me. Not canine, the dog was already walking away. I watched him piss against a pushbike before I went back inside to set the tables.

This was a really nice restaurant, as I said. Fancy, lots of wood and glass; I could see myself in the tabletops when I was finished. Bulbous blue eyes, looking back at me. Lana folded her arms across the chest of her white shirt, turned her nose up at my efforts. My supervisor. She puffed out her pink cheeks, chuffed and chuffed like a bulldog chewing a wasp then looked at her watch, a reminder of our standards. I did not need reminding.

People came here to eat well. We served soft brown bread that pulled apart like an accordion, salted butter, natural wines the colour of morning piss. Steak tartare. That's raw meat that's pretty much already been chewed. And people eat that, they pay for it through the nose. They book in advance. Outside, it could be dark and thundering, filthy rainwater flooding the storm drains, but inside the candles would be lit, and all was anchovies, radishes, spatchcocked little birds.

I did an excellent job that evening. *Excellent*. Perfectly presented the prawns when the chef had been sloppy. Stroked their spiky heads as they bathed in paprika. Refolded a pristine napkin. Made a baby laugh when I really did not want to. Although I had skipped dinner to be thrifty, I ignored the spare plate of hot fries in the kitchen. I did not try the untouched tuna that a diner had returned. Or the meaty dumplings. I downed a pint of ice water instead, to stop the gurgling in my stomach.

I checked on the customers regularly, watched their eyebrows, how they touched my gleaming cutlery. They were happy with my work.

The Regular was there, of course. A woman in her fifties, dark-red coat, dark-brown bob flicking out. Orange glasses. She came in three times a week, ordered a small glass of red wine and a bowl of French fries. Mustard, mayo. She ordered another small glass of red, then another. Sometimes another. Never a bottle, ever, although I always smiled sweetly and suggested she would save money that way. *And my time.* She didn't care. She watched a different film on her iPad every night and laughed like a lamb. And I looked her in the eye and giggled back. That night she finally paid her bill, didn't tip, and left, wobbling into the street.

Midnight. Everyone had gone. I turned the music off, wiped down the surfaces with a sickly little cloth that stank of vinegar. Mopped up the cod slime that leaked from the fridge. Picked up the green strawberry stars from under the counters and flicked them like bogies into the rubbish grinder. Pressed the button and let the steel teeth get to chewing.

It was Saturday and the restaurant had been full. I was dog-tired. For a moment, I had pressed my forehead to the broom handle, wiggled the bristles with my brogues until I felt an indent forming on my frown line. I stopped when Lana came through from the back. What a face on her.

'Did you take the bins out?' she said. I stood tall and straight.

'Oh yes,' I said. 'Twice.'

She sighed, so small that you would hardly notice, but I like to keep an eye on these things.

'And the bathroom? Clean?'

'Sparkling.' I grinned extra chimpy, felt my dimples burn.

I waited carefully for my next instruction.

'You got employee of the month again,' she hissed through closed teeth, handing me a laminated photo of my face. It was not a question. She didn't choose these things. She was not the manager, who I had only met once, when he'd bothered to turn up. Lana liked to think she was in charge – she was full of ideas above her station.

'I did?!' I smiled back, my own teeth almost the same colour as the polished white bricks I'd cleaned chunks of chard from an hour before. She watched me Blu Tack the photo to the wall, while I avoided making eye-contact with myself.

'Nice work,' she said, but she didn't mean it. I was ten years younger than her. And she was a bitch. I told her I would take her apron home and wash it for her, if she wanted. We locked up and parted ways.

Around me, the dark, empty streets were silent. I felt suddenly alone; the only living boy in the whole city. Invisible. I texted Josh, pausing on the pavement. *How was the move?*

I waited. No reply. Nothing from nobody, but it was late, I suppose.

I walked a while up the road to a distant bus stop, which felt remote on this lone stretch of tree-lined road, lit by the moon. The buildings nearby seemed to have been slurped down into the earth, leaving nothing but open scrubland.

Was this the place? I hoped so. Once more, I opened the app I had been checking for the last few hours. I sat on the red plastic bench of the bus shelter and waited patiently, listening for sounds from the streets beyond while three buses went past, goosebumps prickling where my socks reached upwards for my trouser legs. I was practically glowing in the white light of the lamps above. I wondered how many creatures were watching me, hiding in the undergrowth. After twenty minutes, I heard sounds coming from the trees across the road. Footsteps, quiet belching. Something emerging onto the pavement.

A boy. Fingering chips from a box with one hand, texting with the other. It was Josh.

I was so pleased to see him, it burned like a birthday. He looked up to cross the road, right at me. I thought I'd cry. It felt like it was coming.

Josh stopped on the dotted yellow line and squinted one eye.

'Josh?' I called. His head moved at the sound of my voice, but he said nothing.

'Josh! It's me Simon.' He just looked at me.

He must have been pretty drunk, because he couldn't seem to process my presence. I watched him blinking, squeezing both eyes. Finally, he moved, approaching across the road, wobbling. He sat down very carefully, looked straight ahead.

'Simon, what are you doing here?'

'Waiting for a bus. You?'

He pointed through the trees, down the street, towards the bars and restaurants.

'Been out. To a party.'

I nodded. 'Where are you going?'

'Mum's.' He pointed up the road. 'Most of my stuff is there. Remember. Where are *you* going?'

He wasn't smiling much. I said nothing about the texts I'd sent him.

'Home,' I said, and he frowned.

'The flat's that way, Simon.' He gestured in the opposite direction with his head. He was clearly wasted; I could smell the tequila as he moved his head to look at the timetable. 'Does this bus even go there?'

I shuffled on the seat.

'How's the new place then?'

'Not in yet. Couple of days.' He gestured to the world out there, then looked down at his phone.

'Exciting.' I kicked my feet.

'End of an era, five years!' He whooped like a jungle bird. Like he was glad.

'I'll have to come and visit soon,' I said, ignoring the lump in my throat. He turned to raise an eyebrow.

'OK, Simon. Sure.'

Five years together, best friends I thought, and then he fancied something leafier, so his Mum bought him a place somewhere leafier. *'I'm paying some of the mortgage, though. So really it's mine.'*

I wanted to stay in the flat, I had told him, I didn't want to leave. It all happened so fast.

Josh licked sauce off his fingers. 'Have you spoken to the landlady? To sort things out?'

The landlady. This was a woman I only heard from when she wanted me to like a social media post about her new holistic pottery venture, or ask me at seven in the morning whether anyone had accidentally delivered a spicy pizza to the flat, instead of to one of her residences in Singapore. She was not a woman who sorted anything out, ever, and that was fine with me. I did not need sorting.

'Yes,' I said.

I looked over at the chips. I reached out a hand and took three, putting them in my mouth and chewing carefully.

Josh watched me, eyes wide. I swallowed hard, and sucked my fingers.

Across the street, some way along, a man was walking his terrier, the brown kind. The dog trotted alongside him, looking up longingly every five seconds to make sure the man was still there; they appeared and disappeared under the streetlights until they got closer to us.

I slid across the bench, nudged Josh. 'Pretty good one,' I said. He seemed to flinch slightly, as if I frightened him.

'The dog.' I pointed. That was one of our games. He looked across the street, frowned hard, and tried to lean forward onto his elbow, which dug into the flesh of his thigh before slipping off. His curly brown hair wobbled as he righted himself.

'No, Simon.'

'What?!' I shook my head. 'Look at the loyalty, the sweetness! That actually is a really good one, Josh.'

Josh watched the man and his dog pass under the next streetlamp, the terrier padding carefully, the man eyeing us.

'Simon. Those are the kind of dogs who find their owners dead in a chair.'

I considered this.

'And then eat them.' He stabbed the air with a chip.

Josh looked me in the eye. 'You might think it would be an Alsatian,' he said. 'Or even a Great Dane. But you'd be wrong.' He ate the chip. 'It's one of those.' He nodded back towards the terrier.

'OK. Fine. It's not a good one.'

'Simon.' He grabbed my arm hard and squeezed. I shivered. 'Maybe you should get one.'

He laughed, and I took the box from him before he dropped it. I put on a smile.

'Josh, I tried to call. I wanted to ask you about a roommate. I'm going to start looking.'

'Oh, I've just found someone.' He ate a chip from the box I now held.

'What?'

'A guy. Friend of a friend I think.' He wiped ketchup off his wrist.

You think?

Deep in my gut, an ice pick twisted at this news. I felt it turning, looking for a soft gap in my stomach lining.

'Wow, that's so good! That's seriously good. Who?'

'I think he's Spanish. I'll remember to send you his number.'

Spanish.

'I met him tonight,' he said, and burped. It sounded wet.

Slowly, I took another chip, for something to do with my fingers. Josh was lighting a cigarette. He didn't offer me one, just took a long drag and looked at the sky. I think he was thinking about something else entirely, like he'd forgotten I was there. I coughed gently, for his attention.

'I sort of had some people in mind,' I said. I hadn't.

He turned to me.

'Who?'

I shrugged. He kept talking.

'This guy is *super* keen. And the rent is due soon. I need that rent to pay the new mortgage.' He laughed. 'You know the drill.' I nodded. I did not know the drill.

'I would really like to just look around a bit. For someone nice,' I said, but Josh just sighed.

'Simon. I've sorted it out for you. I've already given him a key.'

I thought this was the worst part, but the bell was to toll once more.

'He's moving in tomorrow.' He was grinning at me, his teeth shining. He flicked his cigarette into the road. 'I think you'll really like him.'

The pick slid deeper. I did not vomit, although it rose thickly in my throat. I swallowed it down instead.

'What's his name?'

'Who?'

'The guy. The roommate.'

'Oh. Massimo, I think.'

He looked up at the moon that was now sidling out from behind thick cloud. He nodded, as if it had brought him clarity.

'Yeah, Massimo.'

CHAPTER TWO

Massimo.

There it was. Spoken out loud like something on a menu.

Josh turned to me, one last time, as I tried not to grind my teeth.

'Simon, how did you know I'd be here?'

'Find my Friends.' I smiled at him, and was trying to work out the look on his face when suddenly his bus arrived, bearing down on us red and hissing. Josh stood up quickly and moved toward the opening doors, but then stopped. He turned, seeming conflicted, and looked back at me.

'Night, Simon,' he said, then turned away again. I watched him board the bus, lurching up the steps and falling into a seat before getting out his phone. I checked the app once more to see his dot moving away incrementally, before, in a flash, it disappeared. *Inactive.*

'Goodnight,' I said to the bus as it slowly gathered speed and disappeared down the moonlit road.

I stood alone again. I didn't want to go home now, not to the flat which felt occupied already, like right now a prowler was sniffing my shampoos. Fuck this, I deserved a drink. I turned down past the fancy bottle-shop where two hairless cats sat in the window, staring out like golems. I watched the three women behind the counter, the Turkish Kardashians, hair glossed like spit. One ran her hand over a third cat, also naked, and I could practically hear the sound of skin scraping on skin. I kept walking; I'm not paying those prices; seven pounds extra for a bit of paper around the bottle and a face like a smacked arse. A trio of women who can't even look at you, their eyes are so firmly glued to the security camera monitor, in case something terrible begins to happen on the street and moves its way inside.

I hit up the corner shop instead, and bought a cheap white and a packet of cigarettes from the ugly shopkeeper. 'I love your hair clip, and your teeth,' I told her, as she smiled at me from behind a wall of protective glass. On the street, I unscrewed the bottle, took a long, deep, swig. I felt the liquid trickle down into my gut; it prickled just right. I clutched the bottle tight by the neck as I moved into the night, eyes peering for danger. I swung it twice, an adequate weapon. I'd never brained anyone but it felt good to know I could, if it came to that. You never know when the jump is coming.

I drank and drank. Then I dropped the empty bottle in a large black bin and admired the clang.

The wine buzzed deep, my fingers itched. I was still thirsty, so I went to the only open bar in the area, where the wait-staff and police officers went to unwind after work. The place was busy, and I prowled the sticky edges of the room, avoiding eye contact with the drinkers. I ordered a white wine, and took it to the corner, where I laughed like a drain at a podcast for thirty minutes. On my way back to the bar, I accidentally bumped into someone I sort of knew. I put on a smile. He said, 'Hello, it's Sean, right?' I did not correct him. He asked me was I coming from work? Yes, I told him, and it had been a good shift, thank you. There's a new dish on the menu going down a storm! It's got tomatoes in it. His eyebrows disappeared beneath his fringe, and he said something I couldn't hear above the music, then sidestepped away towards his friends.

I drank more white wine with ice in it, and sat outside under a heater, smoking. A stranger offered me poppers which seemed to burst the blood vessels behind my eyes. I was really pissed but pretended not to be.

I only realised how drunk I actually was as I swayed in the bathroom stall, struggling to read the graffiti on the wall. *Laura's a cunt.* Well, that's just one opinion. I fingered a really good drawing of a dolphin in green sharpie to see if it was fresh. A scribble of a fried egg. A piggy face. I realised I was in danger of missing the toilet. I steadied myself, found some balance, placing one palm flat on the wall, my hand sliding a little on the cold sweat of the tiles.

I pissed like that, perfectly straight, and for a moment after I'd finished I just stayed there. Then I let myself cry, with my dick still out, dripping into the bowl, both of us crying together. I stood there and cried for about one minute, really hard, heaving sobs. And then I stopped and gulped a breath.

I stood back from the wall and zipped my jeans up. I left the stall, washed my hands, dried my eyes by swivelling the nozzle on the hand dryer up into my face and made my way back down the corridor. Only now, as I looked ahead at the lights through the frosted glass in the door with its stencilled signage, did I notice how good the music was. My hips wanted to jiggle.

I stepped through the door, and observed the people on the dance floor. They were really letting loose! The same guy from before noticed me from within the throng, and waved a hand, grinning. He looked a bit high. I widened my eyes and grinned back, wondering as I sometimes did, how hard I would have to clench my teeth in order to snap them off in my mouth. He gestured that he was dancing, was I coming? I gestured back, jiggling my full glass at him like a little Christmas bell. He was only being polite. I slunk back against the wall to watch the room heave.

I lasted one song before I hit the road.

Back at home, in the dark kitchen, I swayed in the emptiness of the flat and let it run its fingers over me. The blinds were open, and moonlight shone in, creating chunky rectangles on the bare floorboards where only weeks before, me and Josh had danced like children to girly pop, drinking vodka so cold it gave us the judders.

I stepped through the memory, toward the window, and looked out at the city, sprawled and winking. I stood in a patch of light and watched the ghostly shapes of bodies moving in the dim lights of the fire station.

The wind rustled the spiked branches of the monkey-puzzle tree. I heard the sounds of the night outside that I had just walked through, bin lids being lifted and slammed about, the thudded shunt of a car door. A flute *peep-peeping* in the gloom.

I opened the window, and whispered to the streets.

'Please, bring my friend back.'

Then louder, long and mournful.

'Please. Bring me a friend!'

CHAPTER THREE

How to be a good boy?

Make your bed every morning. Stack the pillows and fold the sheets in tight. Brush off any crumbs and hide any wankstains. Wet the corner of a T-shirt in your water cup and dab them off. Better yet, change your sheets, you little pig.

Offer everyone tea or coffee even though they can make it themselves. Ask how they slept. Pretend you really care. Listen to them talk about their REM cycle, and a dream they had about their dad. Try not to recall your night terrors in vivid detail as an offering in return.

Wash up *immediately* after breakfast. Do not leave your shit in the sink. Wash everyone else's stuff too.

Laugh at people's jokes. All of them. Every single one. Tell them how much you liked that one joke next time you meet. Lie through your teeth.

Wait your turn for the shower. Keep waiting. Do not knock! When it's your turn, wait for the water to run hot. Realise it will not. Do not scream. A cold shower is no big deal. People are dying in this world.

Reply to all your texts if you get any, don't miss a single one. Even the spam.

Give the dregs of your bank account to the charity hawker on the corner; the bread and milk you came out for can wait. Smile nicely. Give them your email address. The real one. I mean it.

Make lists of all the things you need to do. Buy flowers for people you hardly know. Congratulate them online. Rinse and repeat.

Dress well. Spend money you do not have on good shoes. Wash your underwear. Iron and press, darn and sew; nobody wants to see your manky toe peeping through your sock. Check your outfits twice. Polish the shoes.

Arrive early to work. Bring your best attitude. Toe the line. Do *not* be tempted to speak your mind. Focus on the tasks at hand. Finish your shifts with gusto; another good job well done.

Take care of your home, which actually belongs to someone else. Pay your rent on time, if not a week ahead. Scrub the walls and windows, and buy the good bleach every time. Real clean isn't cheap. If something is broken, find a way to make it work again. Do *not* be late with rent.

Defrost your freezer. Clean out your cupboards every weekend. Don't be concerned about the crazy neighbour who threatens daily to burn down the building, just replace the batteries in your smoke alarm.

Put up with the damp, even if it kills you.

Scream only inwardly, not outwardly unless you are truly alone. Scream long and hard and do it in your head. Or into a pillow if you *must*.

Wish everyone an amazing fucking day. Please don't say fucking, though.

Good boy.

CHAPTER FOUR

Today was a big day.

The ice pick had woken me, still lingering in my gut. I'd slept heavily, and was, miraculously, not so hungover, but anxious. I checked my phone, and found a message from an unknown number.

'I'll be there later. Six p.m.'

I looked for the accompanying photo. I couldn't make out what it was; it looked like something made of wood. I put the number into Google. Nothing. I put the phone down and looked at the bedroom around me, with its faux wood floors and large desk. My lovely room, impossibly tidy some might say. But it was possible. Look at it. Anything is possible.

I got out of the bed and stood in the hallway. With Josh gone, the flat felt more precious than ever – a physical reminder of our friendship. That it had all been real. *Simon,*

I'm all you've got, the flat was saying to me. And it was right. I had my job too, I suppose. I worked so I could sleep, then slept so I could work.

I was growing restless, and I took one last look around me, at the floorboards soon to be trodden by a stranger. The thought of sharing this home with someone other than Josh was so alarming, I wanted time to sit with it, but the clock was ticking. Time to make this place shine.

I strode to the kitchen in my pants and put on rubber gloves. Their synthetic insides felt disgusting on my hands, but I was used to it. I began by wiping down the sink, the splashback, and the cupboards. I scraped dried milk from the back of the fridge and sniffed my bleachy plastic fingers before scraping again, harder. I finally threw out Josh's yoghurts that were growing black and leaky. Next, I took out Goblin, the shiny green hoover, from where I kept him in the triangular cupboard near the windows. I plugged him in, turned him on, swirled him through the flat; Goblin screamed with pleasure as he snorted a line of dead flies. I rolled him quickly past the sealed vault of Josh's bedroom.

I hoovered under the sofa, and behind the TV. I sucked out the dust from the speakers and watched Goblin grow fat and happy, before I took him to the bathroom to hunt for pubes.

On the way back I put a quick hand to Josh's door, almost opened it. Almost. Instead I cleaned the living-room windows with newspaper and a bowl of vinegar. Job done, I looked through them at the wide balcony of sorts that stuck out from the wall. A flat bit of roof covering the entrance to the building below. I climbed onto it, to reach the outside of the windows. Standing in my underwear, looking down for a moment at the street sixty feet below, I let the freezing wind tickle the downy hairs on my back; the feeling of my body meeting the cold city was electric. I kept buffing for as long as I could bear. The vinegar made me gag but the windows looked incredible.

When I started to clean the light switches with a toothbrush, I knew I could delay it no longer. *Do it, Simon.* In one clean motion I walked to Josh's bedroom, opened the door and looked inside. The hollow space stared back at me, and I blinked hard in return, as if squeezing back tears. The very emptiness of the room was physical, its lack of Joshness throbbing like a burn.

I took a deep breath, and began by hoovering each of the four corners, throwing away empty baggies, feeding Goblin hard tissues from under the bed, picking larger items up carefully in turn and housing them safely in a bin bag. Socks, headphones, an old phone that still worked. Discarded, upgraded. I found a gram of coke in a folded lottery ticket under the mattress and stuck it in my waistband, in case Josh wondered where it was when he came back for the rest of his things. I studied the bare patches on the walls, where his beloved prints and posters had been hanging, before he'd taken them away.

I scrubbed at the sooty spot where Josh had left a candle burning on the floorboards, one magical midnight I had spent reading aloud to him. I wiped down the surfaces and watered the skeletal fern we had carried home together from the market. I started to sweat, so I lifted the thin white blinds covering the windows that looked out onto the filthy alleyway. Josh always used to say it sounded like Kesha when the wind howled down it. I opened the window so the chill wind blew my fringe from my face.

I turned around. What was left? A nice wooden bed with a mattress, where I had often sat barefoot and cross-legged, staring up at Josh as he tried on sexy new outfits and told jokes, making me howl with laughter. My hands cupped under my shuddering chin as he danced in something sleek and funky, Celine Dion megamix on the laptop, both of us sparking from little coke bumps and vodka tonics until we realised it was two in the morning. Then we'd lie down on the bed to watch *Blackfish* for the fortieth time until he fell asleep, Josh crying at the inhumanity, me agreeing it was so cruel, that poor marine mammal. His room around us cosy and dim while he slept soundly, before it began to brighten again with the warm morning sun touching every pillow, every poster, every pair of pants.

I filled a bucket with warm water and bleach and mopped the floors, removing the tiny traces of my best friend with every twist of brown water. The droplets of sweat from his home workouts that I had sat and watched, the coffee spills he had ignored, the spots of blood from a finger sliced and sucked, before I had gone running for a plaster. All washed away.

I dressed the bed in fresh blue ticking-striped sheets. On the bedside table I placed a little glass of Josh's favourite yellow flowers, ready for the new arrival. I observed the space. Josh's red wardrobe in the corner, his stack of *National Geographic* magazines, the old rug in the centre, frayed at the edges. All changed now. This room? It could be anyone's.

But soon, it would be Massimo's.

Finishing the kitchen, I put the TV on in the background for some light company. At noon I heard glimpses of the news as I was on my knees scrubbing a secret stain off the skirting board.

'You're saying this is part of a string of similar deaths?'

'Third so far. This guy's teeth were rolling around on the kitchen floor. Next to his head.'

I looked up. The tiny reporter was interviewing someone in a big yellow hi-vis whose thick hair was blowing in the wind, partly covering their face.

'The last bloke's spine was snapped in two, under his skin. Hard slime coming out his mouth.'

The news reporter had their little doll hands over their mouth, staring at the person they were interviewing.

'It fucking stank in there. Sorry, can I swear?'

Outside, the light was dimming. I turned off the TV.

I inspected the room. Satisfied, I removed my gloves and rewarded myself with one hour of kitchen dancing to a K-pop song I was addicted to. It had a very serious beat that made me think of running around a gorgeous

European city, wearing sunglasses, smiling brilliantly at everyone I met, hot-stepping over bridges and smoking long cigarettes. I was still in my underwear but I'd put on socks so I could move my feet in a cool way on the hard floor, and I wiggled my hands like bird beaks, two birds elegantly laughing. I moved my hips in a rhythm that I hadn't tried before and it was good, it was really good!

I bopped my head to my own reflection in the glass of the framed poster of Björk that hung above the sofa. A birthday present from Josh. I think she approved of my hard work, but she did not bop back. I pursed my lips in a pout.

After all this, I needed a shower. Standing in the needles, washing my body, I ignored the bubbles of anticipation bursting in my gut. Would he like his room? Had I done enough? I stamped my foot. Was this really happening? Me and Josh had made this place our haven *together*, over months and years. This new inhabitant was simply prising off the lid and climbing inside. What had he done to deserve it? He had not signed a contract.

My beautiful clean flat! To him, it would just be another dwelling. I did not *want* to live with a stranger, who knew nothing behind the scratches on the ceiling, the crooked cupboard door, the secrets that made this place a home.

Weeks later, down the line, I would laugh at this memory, understand how much more uneasy I should have felt. I should have *taken a moment to enjoy* the scarcity of true bone-cracking horror, at that time. But who was I to know? I scrubbed my body 'til it stung, and practised my welcome smile before I turned off the water.

All clean, I put on a shirt and green wool jumper, jeans and socks. I put white trainers on, took them off. Took the jumper off, put a lovely red sweatshirt on instead. Put the trainers back on.

I did one last sweep of the flat. Straightened his pillows, adjusted the plants. Lit a lemon candle that cost more than a weekly food shop. Checked the time.

He was coming. I went into the large, white, square kitchen-cum-lounge, sat on the sofa, and waited for him to arrive.

CHAPTER FIVE

A car door slammed at seven. I heard the sound of movement on the street, so I stepped over to the window and looked through the glass, pushing my face right up against it to see around the side of the building where a boy was climbing out of a small red convertible, lit from above by a streetlamp. He was a man, really, just slightly older than me. I could only see a glimpse – a black jacket, maybe leather, and dark hair – before he disappeared, walking towards the front of our building. I walked quickly to the hob for some reason, and then to the fridge, and finally down the hallway to the intercom. He was an hour late.

The buzzer rang close to my face, a yowl so shrill I put my fingers in my ears. I took a breath and pressed the button.

'Hello?'

'Hi. It's me,' said a thickly accented voice, muffled by street sounds.

'Come on in.' I said this like I worked in a hotel, and pressed the other button. I could hear the thud of the heavy steel door downstairs, despite the fact I was breathing like a pony. I listened for every footstep, deep in the belly of the hallway downstairs, as someone ascended.

A pause, and then a heavy knocking on the door. I took a huge breath, put on my best smile, and opened the blue steel door to let him in.

Now, a change. This part was hard to put my finger on, but the moment that blue door opened, the second the steel parted from the concrete, there was a movement of something else. Another door whining open somewhere at the same time, in another city, or on a distant hillside. I felt suddenly alert, eyes wide open, every sense tingling.

As the stranger backed his way through the door, entering the flat for the very first time, I noticed how much crap he was carrying into my home. And then I saw – properly – how he looked. Tallish, tanned, his short hair a sort of rusty brown. A young Richard Ramirez. I saw the freckles on his face as he turned, which made him seem at once sparky and weathered. Like a deep-sea fisherman who has just ridden the darkest of soul-engulfing storms and had the time of his life. Not exactly smiling, but a smile crawling somewhere on his face, and he faced me, he looked me dead in the eye for a long time before speaking. I felt like I had just arrived in his house, and not the other way around. His eyes were bright, grape-green and glimmering. The jacket was leather.

'*Ciao. Simone*. Yes?'

He put down the suitcase.

Not Spanish. Italian.

'Massimo,' he said, putting a hand to his breast. His left eye twitched, and a strange pool of saliva filled my mouth. I swallowed it down.

'Hi. Yeah. Yes. Simon,' I said, taking a small breath between each word, remembering to smile. I didn't flinch when he put his hand out, instead I felt the warmth of his outstretched palm when I took it and shook it. His long fingers gripped the small round bone on the back of my wrist in a way I loathed, but I shook for as long as I could. It was my home, remember.

'So many bags,' he said, gesturing to the hallway behind us. 'I'm sorry for the inconvenience, Simon.'

He pronounced it again like 'Simone', on purpose I thought, which was a bit sexy. But from the manner in which he carried his bags and placed them dead in the centre of the hallway, like a tomcat delivering a blood-soaked bunny, it seemed clear that he wasn't sorry for the inconvenience at all.

He looked me in the eye, and his left eye twitched again. Once, twice, the flicker of a moth on a lightbulb. I was staring. Where were my perfect manners?

'I'll give you the tour.'

'Please.' He put a hand on the paintwork and I worked hard not to flinch at the thought of sticky fingerprints.

I led him down the corridor with a sweep of my arm. I was trying to look hostly, but wondered if it gave a touch of magician.

'This is Josh's room. Well, it's your room. This is your room.' Was I stammering, was I sweating?

He simply nodded, and took off his jacket, revealing a black T-shirt and leanly muscled arms. Tattoos peeking from his short sleeves. He didn't thank me for the clean sheets, but then I hadn't told him it was me who put them there. I watched the muscles working in his back as he moved the cases along the far wall, stacking them up. I pointed to the one remaining framed poster, a man in rollerskates holding red balloons, head tilted back, screaming.

'Do you like that, do you want to keep it? It's Josh's. It comes with the room.'

I showed him the kitchen, which he looked at without turning his head, his eyeballs roaming the confines of their sockets. I offered him wine, which he refused, and I wondered if he was hungry, so I held out a packet of wafer-thin ham. It was all I had.

'Do you want some?'

He blinked back at me, long lashes meeting.

'I'm vegetarian.'

I put the ham away while he opened a cupboard and looked inside.

'Well, this is the space.' I gestured to the living area and laughed. Apparently it was funny to me, but he just smiled and nodded, stepping around the room as if he were trying to avoid holes in ice. Was he shy? I sat down carefully on the edge of the sofa and figured out where to put my hands while Massimo inspected the ferns.

'So, what are your interests, Massimo?' I asked, looking up at him.

He turned carefully, and brought himself to the other side of the couch. I heard every shift of denim fibre in his jeans as he sat down.

'Well. I like food. Walking. Holidays,' he said. Good start.

'OK. Very nice, where?'

'Portugal?' he asked me, unlocking his phone. He showed me a photo; him and three other extraordinarily handsome men, all in black linen shirts. Tanned in a restaurant, teeth twinkling through the Aperols they raised. I tried not to stare too long.

We sat for a moment, listening to each other breathing, and I looked around the room as if it were my first time visiting.

'It's cold out there,' he said eventually, meaning the streets. 'It's nice and warm in here.'

I made a gesture, rubbing my arms with both hands, all cosy.

'What do you think of the area?' I asked. 'What do you know of it?' One hand lifting to the windows upon each question. Massimo put a finger to his lower lip, tilted his head and smiled at me.

'Up and coming,' he said, and then he yawned, stretching. I heard the tiny knots of muscle pop like corn in the ropes of his arms, which I was deliberately *not* looking at.

'I'm really happy to be here,' he said, and I think he meant it.

'Good. Great. Me too,' I replied. 'To roommates!' I put my hand up in a high-five.

He simply blinked both eyes, hard. 'I'm going to take a nap,' he said. I lingered on the sofa as he slipped away, first to the bathroom where I heard him piss, and then to his room. I gritted my teeth. The air in the room felt different, like something had been plugged in.

Later, when I brushed my teeth, the bathroom had a new smell to it, like fresh soil, though I kept no plants in there. *I live with him now, in this flat*; I tried to let the fact settle but it curdled, milky and sour. I padded carefully past his closed door. *It's not Josh in there, it's a stranger.* Unfathomable.

Perhaps, in time, we could become good friends? I felt for the sweet stir of comfort, at the thought of a companion, of not being alone, and there it was. But with it came a sting of panic, as I imagined what could be done to me while I slept, by this flatmate forced on me, shoved into my home. I knew nothing of Massimo yet.

Standing in my bedroom I thought about locking the door, but reckoned he would hear it click. I began to notice new sounds; little scratches, footsteps that changed direction. I pressed my ear to the outer wall, and heard what I thought was a laugh. Grunting. It must be the neighbours, or people shooting up in the alleyway. Or a stray dog. Or him.

Something about that boy in the room next door made my skin crawl. The more I thought of him, the more it crawled, crawling and crawling until I imagined it would crawl all the way off me, and out the window, falling down into the street, where nightbirds could peck the goose-bumps off my baggy neck, and gulp them for their dinner.

Something is burning my eyes.

I wake to find the room washed with a blinding brightness that renders the cheap blinds almost useless. I get up and walk to the window, looking for the source of the light. I pull up the blinds.

The sun is glowing hot in the sky outside, a truly gorgeous day. From my vantage point up in my room, I see movement below, and I look down to see Massimo's red convertible pull out of the side-street, the roof down, cool. Massimo is in the car with a boy, both of them with cartoonishly large sunglasses on. The boy has curly brown hair, and he's cackling at something that Massimo is saying. Massimo's wearing tiny shorts and, even from up in my room, I can see that the boy is stroking his hairy muscled thigh. I can see each hair bending to the boy's gentle touch. And then, just at that moment, Massimo isn't concentrating, he's looking in the wrong direction, and something huge thunders into the car with an enormous sound.

A lorry ploughs the vehicle right into the churchyard opposite, snapping the gravestones like teeth until the car is crunched flat against the front of the church. The bonnet bursts into flames, and then the car is slowly engulfed in bright yellow fire. I feel the sizzle of it, from all the way up here. I feel the delicious thrill of something hot waking up in my belly, warming me from the inside. The fire rages on.

Dramatic, yes, but beautiful too.

Through the steam and smoke that rises from the crush, Massimo crawls out, his arms and legs even longer and more muscular than before in his little shorts and vest top, everything soaked in blood. He turns to pull the boy out of the mess, as if the twisted molten metal is merely brambles, and starts to pick bits of scorched leather seat from his friend's new sideways face. He wipes the smears of blood from the boy's eyes so he can see. Strokes his soft head. Turns it by the neck towards me so I can see too, keeps turning until it might snap. I strain, suddenly struggling now from this angle to get a clear view of the charred face in Massimo's large, muscular hands.

The boy seems panicked, down there in the rubble, but Massimo soothes him, smoothing the hair which comes away in singed handfuls from his chewed bubblegum-pink scalp, and then they're both *grinning*, Massimo's teeth sharp as the glass that litters the road, and the boy's face an unrecognisable pulp that Massimo starts licking off in cat-food chunks. They begin to laugh at this in a sexy way and then both turn together and look up at the window, right at me where I stand watching in my boxers, my erection growing. They wave me over, call me to come down, to step over the decapitated lorry driver in the road and come close.

I watch, for a moment, and then I open the window, before I wake up.

CHAPTER SIX

Day one with Massimo.

I had woken even earlier than usual, and I was a little trepidatious as I walked to the bedroom door and opened it, listening hard for any small signs of movement. The flat beyond hummed like a string barely plucked.

I put on trousers over my best blue boxers, tucked in my T-shirt, and stepped into the corridor. Silence. Down the hall, I could see Massimo's bedroom door was open, and when I walked past to the bathroom, I twisted my head gently to look inside. The room was empty. No Massimo. I stopped. The bed looked like it hadn't been slept in, its sheets spread taut by me.

I left the flat. I was starving, so I stopped at a bakery before work. I never order a croissant, because I don't want to say it with a French accent and I don't want to say *crossunt* either, so I ordered banana bread. Really I wanted a soft, buttery, almond croissant. They toasted the banana bread which was kind of them. I took a fat coin from the tip jar when nobody was looking, and paid with it.

My shift was fine, mostly. I served a huge table for a birthday lunch with six girls and three boys, a lot of red shirts and corduroy. Nice leather handbags and a cute little clutch. Three rounds of martinis. I found myself wanting to sit with them and celebrate, even though they talked like babies.

'Is the choccy pud any good?'

'It's yummy!'

I stayed perfectly in place, fixed my collar, and got a nice cash tip for it, which I tucked into my shoe, safe from Lana. Around four, I headed home.

I had imagined maybe we would eat our dinner together, me and Massimo. I spent the tip on a mid-range red wine and some ready-to-cook tortellini from the corner shop, along with some milk and a bar of chocolate for bedtime, and took them home.

I looked up at the living-room window, and suddenly blushed, wondering if Massimo would think I had chosen pasta to impress him, something Italian to get his attention. I thought about going back to the shop to swap it, but I talked myself out of it. I braced myself and went upstairs.

But he was still missing, and I felt myself deflate slightly. The flat was empty, and I wondered if he had been out all day. Though when I looked around the kitchen, I was sure that items had been moved from where I'd left them, like something had been walking around, touching my things.

In my still-clean shirt, I ate my hot pasta at the table and opened the wine to breathe. Eating alone, I felt Josh's absence more strongly than ever, without his braying laugh and long legs swinging under the table. On the evenings he was home, we would often watch telly in the candle-light, whatever series Josh was in the middle of, and he'd tickle me with the simplest of stories. I'd be laughing for most of the evening, safe in our sanctuary from the stress of the world outside, from all those *people*. Trying hard for the sweetest bite of the apple, the moment when I could make Josh laugh back. I wanted him here so badly, to see him smiling, but all that was gone now, so I just sat still, waiting, ready to greet his replacement.

It got late, and Massimo never came. I re-corked the wine and checked the windows were locked before brushing my teeth and getting into bed. I got up again and locked my bedroom door, before sliding back under the covers, and rolling over to plug in my phone. It wouldn't connect. No lightning bolt appeared. I plugged it in again, removed the charger, plugged it in again five times. *Piece of shit.* I held the phone to the light, and looked inside the hole.

One long leg poked out, wiggling slightly. A spider had crawled inside the cavity and I had stabbed it almost to death with the charging prong. Poor creature. It was half-turned to mush by now, but I stabbed it twice more until the leg stilled. When I removed its body with a bent paper clip from my bedside drawer, it slid out, dark and glistening with spider juice, eight eyes unseeing. Now the phone would charge, so I closed my own eyes and rubbed my feet against each other until I finally fell asleep.

A screaming whine woke me. I felt the mattress depress, then rise, like something large had stepped off the bed, but there was nobody there. Another screech. At first I thought it was a blast of a siren from the fire station, and I waited for the familiar rumbling of the machines as they unsheathed themselves and veered off into the city, to someone in real danger, but it didn't come. I lay there, eyes wide, teeth chattering for a moment. The screech rang out again, echoing through the corridors of the flat. Someone was buzzing to come in.

I got out of bed in my boxers and T-shirt and unlocked the bedroom door, opened it and stared into the dark.

'Massimo?' I called out, softly. 'Is that you?' A mumble. I called again. 'I think someone is here.' I did not mention how insanely late it was for visitors.

I pressed the switch, and the light above me flickered on, but the lamp at the entrance did not. Scuffling sounds down the corridor, in the darkness. Another screech of the buzzer that cut right through me, made me clutch my balls. I made myself walk closer to the shadowed place near the bathroom where the intercom clung to the wall. A figure was stood there.

'Massimo?' I said again, and was met with a gentle

grunt, like something nestled in zoo straw. I could see it was him, now, huddled near the wall, dressed in boxers and a long-sleeved T-shirt. I could not see his expression, or the movement of his hands, just his nice back, but he turned suddenly when I was close, and his eyes were bright, staring, almost vacant.

The buzzer rang again, and Massimo looked me in the eye.

'Simone. Can you show me the buzzer?' He said it like I'd been there the whole time. 'I can't do it.'

What was *wrong* with this guy?

'Of course!' I nodded keenly and stepped closer. Released my breath from Tupperware lungs.

'It's janky. You have to jimmy it,' I said, as I showed him the sticky buttons.

I could smell his mouth as he breathed over my shoulder, a strange odour that prickled me. Like the smell in the bathroom, earthy and sweet. The hairs on my arms rose, as if summoned. I licked my teeth.

'Janky. Jimmy. OK.' He nodded.

'Are you expecting someone?'

'Yes.' His staring eye twitched.

I watched him press the plastic button, and heard the clang of iron deep below as someone entered the building. Massimo rocked on his heels, but said nothing more, so I said goodnight and walked quickly back to bed, listening to the interloper arrive.

I heard the sound of a man laughing, the blur of something

in French, a voice much deeper than Massimo's. I listened to silence for a minute or two, my eyes wide in the darkness of my room.

Suddenly there came a scream of something like pain, through the wall. I turned on the bedside light, then quickly turned it off. A few thuds, and then more moaning. I got out of bed, and put my ear to the wall.

The moan rang out again, now like a bull calf trapped in a ditch. A man in pain? I rose onto tiptoe, and then back to flat feet. Something awful was happening to the visitor. I found my keys on their tray, on the desk, felt for the little yellow box cutter on its keyring and slid the blade out with a well-practised thumb.

Another groan. I caught my face in the mirror, as I shifted my head to hear more clearly. My brow furrowed, eyes fiercely dark, lips taut in a squirm of a smile. I looked frightened, confused. Aroused. More harsh breathing. Gravel in a blender.

What was happening in there, through the wall? I put a hand on it again like I would feel something thundering through it. Maybe I could, a slight tremor just there. Now, a moan of pleasure.

Ah. They were *fucking*.

I had heard this before of course. From that room. Josh's nightly activities had kept me awake more than a few times. I might have listened, once or twice, just to check if he was enjoying himself. I thought of Josh. I wondered what he would do with Massimo, if he were here right now. Would he put him in his place? Would he be bitchy, or would they get along like a house on fire? Maybe Josh would lean right in for a hot kiss, without hesitation. Confident. One thing was certain, he would not be silently quivering against this wall, alone. He would be in that bedroom right now, bucking with Massimo.

Who would be on top? What would they whisper to each other, if they spoke at all? Where would their fingers go? Would they use protection? Lube, or just spit? I noticed I had opened my bedroom door, stepped through it. Whose spit was slicker? I wondered what Massimo looked like naked, trying to imagine the shape of his body in motion, whether his torso was hairy or trimmed. I'd seen a line of hair when he had lifted a suitcase, leaned back to steady himself. A delicate snail-trail I'd wanted to pluck a hair from with my fingernails.

Who would be louder? Was there fuzz on his arse, or was it shaved silky smooth in every direction? What would Massimo say in that rhythmic, purring accent? Right up close. How would it feel to see those knife-bright eyes from below, glinting in the dark? To watch his biceps strain. To smell his hot breath. To feel his wet tongue enter a cavity. I was moving down the hallway, bare feet sweaty on the pale wood.

Would there be choking? Now I was at Massimo's closed door. The grunts loud and deep, a hot bull being milked, slapped flank quivering. Massimo's dick must be hard as a rock. Boy-cries rang out, like a fox mounted in the street, head tilted to the moon. Josh rarely made sounds like *that*. I should be in bed with my earplugs in, eye mask on, but I was transfixed by their voices, blending in harmony. My ear was to the door, and was that my hand moving to the handle? My fingers brushing the shining metal of it with a crackle of static? My hand hot and closing on the cool steel, listening closer, thinking about the rocking rhythm of it, the heavy smell. The image of teeth biting down on veined flesh. Pearlescent splatters on his sculpted chest. My fingers tensing slightly and something stiffening in my loose boxers, a red-and-white-striped circus tent being lifted skyward at the sound of their excited fucking. The other hand pressing down on the handle.

It ended like a thunderclap. Both men together, a raucous cry that was mostly the stranger, with a deep low growl from Massimo. I was frozen to the door for a moment, but then I drew myself back, heard my knees crack. I went back to bed, marching quickstep. As I passed back along the hallway, the bulb above me flickered. Once, twice. I needed to fix that.

I lay in the quiet, breathing hard, and thought I heard the man leave. Doors opening but not closing. I tossed and turned, imagined something coming in off the street through a door left carelessly open. Imagined screaming at Massimo that this was *not safe*, I did not want to be brutally murdered in clean sheets. Imagined more sounds from behind the wall, where my head lay inches away. The chirp of crickets climbing through the wall cavity, the lowing of a baby cow wanting Mummy. A rapid bleating. Furniture shifting. A throaty sigh. I heard it all as if through a curtain, like the sound of footsteps on the roof was a roiling, boiling fantasy and not in fact happening at all. I drifted in and out, until a new sound permeated the fog, and woke me sharp.

Click.

Thick branches cracked across a muscled knee. A sound like dragging chainwork echoing through the flat as the sky outside unstitched itself. A sharp noise that made me think of teeth snapped out of a skull, and then the unmistakable sound of crying.

Click.

It rang through the hallway and my heart felt like it was rolling over, a tiny rotisserie chicken in my chest cavity.

CHAPTER SEVEN

I woke to four missed calls and a voicemail. None from Josh.

All from my landlady, who was really my landlord's daughter, and three years younger than me. She was very small and very thin and permanently abroad, moving through time zones buying and selling something. I always forgot what. Livestock? Timeshares? Cannabis? When her calls came, they were deep in the night. I listened to the garbled message. She always sounded like she was on the bow of a ship, or calling from a concert.

'Hi Samuel, it's Anna, I'm . . . . . can't quite get there this month, so call me . . . . . probs going to have to up the rent soon ugh sorry babe . . . . . quite a lot more really this time . . . . . ghastly I know but . . . . . can you check under the stairs for . . . . . in that ugly box on the wall . . . . . send those bills again in January? Sorry, darling, thanks Samuel.'

I deleted the message.

Outside, it was still just about dark, the sky slowly warming as it pressed at the glass. In the soft orange glow, I could make out the familiar items of my room. I tried to shake off the fact that the desk was out of place. Like something had moved it.

I opened the blinds to greet the day, but something on the street surprised me. A figure, down beside a streetlamp, backlit into silhouette. Someone was watching the windows, staring up. I could see a hot red cherry burning bright, before white smoke plumed upward from their opening mouth. They kept staring as they took another drag on the cigarette. The figure suddenly seemed to notice me, because after a moment they turned and walked into the dawn, thick strings of long hair flickering in the wind behind them. The streetlamp went out to signal the new morning.

I took a sharp breath, and made sure the watcher had disappeared from view before turning away from the window. It took me a while to feel at ease – *I* was the one who watched.

For thirty minutes I sat at my desk drinking water from a plastic bottle while hunting for Massimo online. I found his profile, looked at him smiling kindly from his bubble in the corner, but it was private. I didn't request an invitation.

My heart ticked uncomfortably. I put a hand to my chest. It *murmured*. The sound a cat makes when you listen close to its tiny mouth. I was exhausted. All night, I'd tossed and turned, those sharp sounds piercing my sleep. Clicking, snapping, cracking. My body was furious, adjusting to the boy through the wall, who was feeling more and more like an intruder than anything else.

Outside, the city was waking. I thought about eight million first deep breaths, each opening eye, every long dark sigh released to another new day. People wishing flatmates a good morning in huge unclean houses and tiny shared studios, hearing others stirring in the bowels of their buildings and smiling. Waiting for the bathroom. Sharing paper-thin walls, sharing coffee, sharing gossip, opening blinds and curtains to look out together upon the crush of the city that waited patiently for them to join it in another day.

As a boy, I'd lived in a small town, near the woods. In the mornings, I would wake and clean my room before dawn, feed the dog, wash my face and hands. I would dust off the TV and line up the dishcloths by the sink. I brought in the milk bottles, took out the wine bottles, and collected the cat shit steaming in the flowerbeds. I got busy being good. I emptied bins and waved to the postman, the milkman, the surly neighbours. Sometimes they waved back. I made breakfast, cleaned the kitchen, and listened to the house stir quietly, soaking up the glory of a fully ticked list so early in the day. Often, nobody was home to witness my deeds, but I did them anyway, in case one of my parents returned to the house by surprise at lunchtime, and saw my hard work. But they rarely did. They stayed out, as if they were avoiding the small, strange boy who lived in their home. As if they had looked inside his head, and shuddered at what they saw.

So, I just kept working, filling up the small hours before school. Lining things up, wiping things down, getting things in order. Being good.

Often I would stare up at the hillside through the kitchen window, at the dotted treeline where I knew the dirt and the deer were waiting. The second I got the chance, I would pedal hard along the main road away from the house, eventually taking the right turn that led up the hill, my feet pushing and pushing towards the woods. Trees would appear as I reached the crest, and I'd press harder, gasping for breath as I flew along the track, slamming the pedals, almost there. My yellow bike was alive, spitting up small stones and spraying mulch and dirt from the track, before thumping down onto the wooden bridge, the tick-a-tick-a-tick over the ruts. My rubber wheels on the grooves of the decking were a clear, triumphant signal to the dog walkers and the birdwatchers and the body-buriers and the mice squeaking in the undergrowth, that now I was safe, and now I was Simon.

I would ride my bike for hours through ancient wood-land, or leave it sleeping in a bush and trek through fields eating jam sandwiches I'd shoved in my pockets. I could sit for a day and just watch the trees shifting in the breeze, or practise my screaming. All that space, full of creatures;

the enormous highland cows that made no sense here with their blond fringes and handlebar horns, the kestrels that defied the winds. I watched the foxes chewing the hind legs off a rabbit from a field away, caught the curve of trout as they slipped through the stream. All these beings, free to bite.

I was yet to make proper friends, but what boy needs friends? It's a myth. I taught myself to make small fires once or twice and, when I'd finished with it, burnt the old porn I'd found behind the supermarket, then went home to scrub the soot from my fingernails.

These woods are where I'd come later, with a guy, in his silver Nissan at night, looking for a safe lane to park. We sucked each other off inside the car, but we never fucked, *never* kissed. He 'wasn't gay, just horny', he reminded me every time without looking me in the eye. It was no skin off my nose, what he was or wasn't.

I got semen on my sweatshirt once, and only noticed when I was back home. I'd fingered the stain, and thought of the smell of the pine air freshener in his car mingling with his cigarettes. One time, the Nissan got stuck in a shallow ditch in the pouring rain, and the boy said he might have to call his dad, or the AA, but that was his dad's account, so it meant the same thing. We'd be found out. I walked home alone in the downpour, so he would be found alone in the white glare of the tow-truck's headlights. I would sit in the spotless, empty house, or make dinner, waiting for a parent to come home. He'd be fine.

Out in the woods it was another dimension. The flock of geese spearheading the sky don't give a damn what I've googled, what I've written down and burned. My bed was the fallen oak I passed on the way through, rotten wet and hollow, and for breakfast I could creep down to the edge of the lake and slip out a minnow, or rummage for a worm to slurp. I would lie back then, and watch the sky through the gap in the trees for a while, listening to my bird friends call to each other above my head, before I took a run through the horse paddock, and they'd thunder along beside me. I would whoop and call among the horses, both invisible and seen. They might let me pick off a flea or two, comb through their tails, and together we would shudder with delight when the rain fell on our skin beneath the pylons, or panic at a passing truck. But they don't want to know about my wet dreams, how many times I've seen *that* video, the dark ideas, the things that come knocking for me in the night.

The city streets were silent that October morning, as the dawn broke. I had gone back to bed, and was enjoying the brand-new model on a popular underwear site when I heard a gentle rapping at my door. Tentative, like someone practising how to enter. I sat up straight. Surely Massimo was not awake. I listened hard for five minutes, but it did not come again. I really had to eat. I put on fresh trousers and a clean T-shirt and checked my hair in the mirror. My eyes looked a little too blue, but I couldn't help that.

I walked to the kitchen with purpose, a strut. The door was ajar, and I could hear movement behind it. The blinds were closed, the room was dark. I widened the gap.

I walked into the gloom to find Massimo eating a tongue in his underwear. He was hunched by the sink in small pants and another tight, long-sleeved T-shirt, with his head tilted back and one hand gripping the edge of the counter, the other hand dangling a tongue the size of my palm over his mouth which was wide and waiting. I was looking at him side on, with the blue light of the open fridge illuminating him, casting him half in shadow. With that strange angle – the forward curve of his back, the bend of his knees, his muscled thighs, and the scythe of his throat gleaming upwards – he looked gargoyle-esque.

The heating was on high, the room stifling.

He held the tongue, ribbon red, and lowered it down, sliding it between his lips so he could suck off the juice. He took a bite, and I heard his teeth meet between the meat. I stared, transfixed as the large bulge of his throat contracted, swallowing the chunk down into his belly, before he took another bite, standing up a little now as if the effort required a firmer stance. He turned his body fully toward me, and I saw his abs contracting through the thin fabric as that chunk descended.

The tongue was huge. Far too big to be human, far too red, I promised myself. I moved my own fat tongue inside my mouth, just to check. It must be animal. The surface of Massimo's meat was smooth, glistening in the neon backlights under the cupboards, and almost blackened in places like he'd held it, stretched flat over an open flame. That smell in the room, wet moss and matches. I watched him peel a long strip off the muscle now, and slurp it down.

I shifted my weight and he heard me, as I knew he already had. He turned fast, chewing, blinking hard.

'Good morning, Massimo.'

'I'm eating,' he said, pointing to the tongue in his fist.

Fucking hell he's insane.

'I thought you were vegetarian,' I said politely from the doorway.

'Yes,' he said, and took another bite of tongue.

The room was seriously hot, and Massimo was covered in a sheen of sweat, his damp hair flicking across his forehead in little spikes. I felt sweat beginning to prickle my own back.

'You look like you're enjoying that . . .' I didn't want to say it. 'Is it a tongue?'

'Tongue?' He looked at the ragged meat in his hand, then at me, incredulous.

'What is it then?' I flushed. 'If it's not a tongue.'

He stared harder, right into my eyes across the kitchen.

'It's a . . . fucking pepper.' He turned to pick up something I hadn't seen, sitting in the sink.

A jar.

'*Rrrroasted* red peppers,' he read aloud, rolling each R. 'Taste the sunshine.'

I was embarrassed.

'Go on, *Simone*,' he said, holding out the jar. 'Taste the sunshine.'

'Oh. Wow. Looks good! I'm alright, thank you though.' I shuffled backwards, almost into the hall behind me.

The peal of an ambulance outside suddenly. It startled me, but not him, as if he'd made it happen. Massimo stepped forward, pulling out a fat wet pepper, which up close looked even more like something corpsey. A kidney, or a spleen. He squeezed it gently between his fingers, and then held it out on his hand. It was, somehow, impossible to say no.

'Come on. Eat. It's good. Taste the sunshine.' He waited for me.

I walked to him. I ate the pepper from his outstretched palm, like an animal, trying not to choke on each briny bite. Satisfied, Massimo put the jar down on the counter.

I could feel myself turning red hot, both from the heat and the experience, so I walked to the fridge and opened it, focusing on its contents, which were meagre. I had not been paid yet. I noticed that somehow the top three shelves were full of pale-green containers that had not been there before, all marked in indecipherable black marker pen. Well, it was his fridge too now, I realised. Inside, through the condensation, the contents looked meaty, like the cow brains on sale at the market, and I stared at the wet flesh pressing against the plastic sides for a moment, perplexed. Then I got it.

Mushrooms. Different colours, textures and sizes, stacked in the boxes. Maybe it was for a recipe he was preparing, something decadent for him and a boy. A romantic and delicate dish that would take hours to simmer and fill the flat with a rich, heady aroma, topped with chopped parsley and accompanied with something cold and dry to drink. I heard the gurgling of my stomach in the silence of the room. I took out the butter, though I didn't have a plan for it.

'Do you want some toast, Massimo?' I said, in a tone I thought felt confident and clear. I brushed sweat from my brow in a secret motion.

He was still standing by the sink, and he looked at me steadily before answering.

'I don't like it, Simone.' The smile slipped from his face.

He said it hard and flat, his mood turning fast.

I decided to try again. I had to live with this person, he was not going away.

'I guess you like mushrooms, though?' I gestured towards the open fridge. The pause was too long. I sounded crazy.

But he just nodded, very serious.

'Yes, I like mushrooms,' and then he grinned. 'When picked by hand. By me.'

'Where do you pick them?' I hated the sound of my voice, wanted to burn it.

'You cannot ask that,' he said, moving toward me. 'Important rule.' He was not happy.

'Oh, sorry. I didn't know that.' I took a half-step back. I wanted to close the fridge, but for some reason I was afraid to turn away from him.

'It's my secret. It's easy to find what you need, when you know.' He said this glassily, his accent turning his T's into soft bullets.

'Here, in the city?'

'Sometimes.'

I was intrigued.

'Do you know which ones are safe? Aren't lots of them poisonous?'

He shrugged his shoulders, poked his lip out, but all the while standing rock still, illuminated by the open fridge. Was I staring?

'I know the ones to choose,' he said. He stretched his long, glossy arms above his head and walked towards me again, quite fast, got close to me as he started to name the types of mushroom that could be found, with strange names that bounced like spells through the kitchen.

'. . . bay bolete, stinkhorn, fly agaric.'

As he spoke, he became more animated, moved his arms almost grandly. He was looking at me, stepping into my space, going into great detail now, and his eye started to twitch again. Flickering as he spoke. I was staring, imagining him digging through mud, biting into the pale flesh of an unwashed mushroom, his lips stained with dirt. His pink tongue sliding out from his mouth, to catch a lump of something too delicious to miss.

'. . . collared earthstar, inkcap, puffball, shaggy parasol.'

The jar of jam I didn't remember taking from the fridge fell from my hand and landed on my foot, before thudding to the floor. I looked down at the jar, and my pale foot now blushing. It fucking hurt, but I didn't flinch or cry out.

'You OK, Simone?' Massimo asked me, smiling, a dark look on his face now. A bead of sweat ran from his brow to his chin before falling to the floor. I followed it, swore I heard it sizzle. He was watching me with a deep new curiosity, solving silent maths.

'Yep, I'm OK. Just . . . dropped the jam.' I bent to pick it up, fumbling, incredibly aware of how close I was to his crotch, the meaty smell of his sweat. He cocked his head down at me. I wanted to tell him to *fuck off*, to stop looking at me like that. Instead I stood up and spoke gently.

'Better get back . . . there.' I pointed to the door. 'Get ready for work.'

'Tell me. What did you think about? Just now?' he says, and continues looking at me in that strange way.

'Work. I was thinking about work,' I say, and I flick my finger again back towards the door.

'But, you work in a restaurant,' he said.

I was tensing up. I found myself suddenly wanting to press his hand into the hot toaster, or slam the fridge door repeatedly onto his head, so I decided to leave, fuck breakfast, but then he gave his sweaty head a small shake, a half smile for me, a shrug of the shoulders. He left the kitchen, and soon I heard the shower running. Shaking slightly, I closed the fridge and turned back to the room.

For a moment, I stared at the spot where he had been standing. I looked down at the floor, and noticed several droplets of sweat that had dripped from his hair, his back, his face, onto the boards. What a mess. I walked over and reached down, smearing one drop with a finger and then bringing it gently to my nose, then to my tongue which was already sticking out in anticipation. Salt, a tang of spice. Something old.

I took one more taste before I got the cloth.

CHAPTER EIGHT

The bathroom. The things I did in there. What a horribly intimate space to share with a stranger.

I thought maybe the room would have physically changed since Massimo had arrived, he was in there so much. I had often found Josh's wet chaos quite sweet; the drawings he left me in the steamed mirror were never wiped away, but I couldn't bear the thought of Massimo's bare feet on the tiles, or his loose hairs in the sink. His long toes touching my towel. The places he had put my soap. Maybe now it would resemble some lair, a cave behind a waterfall. Would the bath be filled with rocks and fishes? Would the cistern be froggy?

In the last house I lived in, the bathroom was revolting. The tiles were cracked, the grouting was sprouting. I would hold my breath as I showered, fixing my eyes on a corner of the ceiling to avoid seeing other things. I won't even tell you about the toilet. The other people who lived there, they didn't seem to mind washing in grime. I had once watched a worm crawl out of the shower drain.

This bathroom, however, it was beautifully done, white and sparkling. Practically holy. Private. Until now.

I held my breath when I opened the door, careful and slow. I steeled myself for horror. But I was shocked to find it was clean, and I blinked a little. The towels were folded, toilet seat down, bathroom cabinet closed. His long green toothbrush did not smell of carrion, as I had thought it might. It smelled of peppermint. I was almost disappointed.

I confess, I felt a little sad that morning. I got into the bathtub, and stood there naked. I smelled my armpits. I pinched a soft bunch of fat above my hip a little too hard. Eventually I turned on the shower, and let it soak me. Held my arms around myself in a gentle cuddle. When I washed my hair I did it lovingly, and I used the shampoo that ran down my body to clean my pits, my groin, my legs. I blasted myself with cold water until I forgot my name.

I was stepping out of the bath when a sudden sharp pain, like a bee sting, shocked my right foot. I jolted, almost slipping with a squeak on the tub floor, then froze, holding on to the wall rock climber-style.

I turned to sit on the edge of the bath, and lifted my foot to inspect it, angling myself awkwardly to get a proper look. The pain was in the front pad of my foot, and now I could see a bright bloom of blood, spreading fast and red, filling the cracks and crevices of my skin. It looked like a crimson weather map, and there in the centre, at the eye of the storm, a thick slice of ivory jutted out from my flesh. *How curious.* I was dripping blood over the shower floor; I turned on the tap and it *Psycho*-swirled down the drain. It's amazing how much blood comes out of hands and feet.

I took the object from my foot, wincing as it slid from the flesh. The soles of my feet were fairly tough, I'd been a barefoot child, but this had been sharp enough to cut deep. I held it to the light. Was it a shard of glass, maybe a slither of enamel from the bath itself?

It was a toenail. I turned it in the light. A slim, perfect crescent moon, the colour of pale granite. Big toe for sure. Slightly pointed. I pincered my fingers tighter around it. The nail sliced deeply into my finger, more blood running first down my finger, then to my arm, where it lingered. I stared at the toenail, held it so close to my eyeball – its sharpness was incredible. Carefully, I picked up the sponge that was nestled behind the shampoo bottles, and sliced into it. It cut a line straight through, opening a soft wound in the meat of the sponge without hesitation.

Well.

CHAPTER NINE

Our cohabitation was not going well.

However I tried, I could not get used to him, and the next few days passed by uneasily, a heavy atmosphere growing like a blister that I couldn't seem to burst. He ignored the messages I sent him, in an attempt to bridge our gap. A polite offer for a pint, a photo of a bird outside the kitchen window. Left on *read*.

The flat was always too warm; I noticed my T-shirt sticking to my shoulders and a dry scratch in my throat. I had already checked the thermostat, convinced Massimo had been fucking with it, only to find it was not even on. Something was clearly wrong with the boiler, so I spent half an hour with my arms deep inside it, playing with its small taps. I followed a YouTube tutorial by a man with enormous shoulders who talked me through it.

I could *never* call the landlady about a problem like this;

that would remind her too much of my existence. So I keep the flat in order myself. I have replaced cupboard doors and even soldered wiring in my time. Once I was electrocuted in the hallway by a light switch. Josh stood and watched, grateful; he could barely change a bulb. He had doubled over in laughter when the voltage thumped my arm, causing my hair to stand on end. So I did it again.

I was uncomfortable, no matter how cosy I made my bedroom, or how I plumped the cushions on the sofa. Just knowing he lived there, that he had a key, that we *shared* the place, it was too much. I dimmed the lights, lit a candle, but still felt rigid, stiff as a board. The snapping sounds that filled the flat at night echoed in my ears throughout the day and set me on edge; the boiling of the kettle was enough to make me scream.

I found myself avoiding Massimo. I went to work, did an excellent job but had to work a little harder to be my nicest. I performed with great gusto, bowed to Lana, holding down the digs and spiky remarks that rose quickly in my throat, drowning them with cold water. I took deep breaths in the freezer, rubbing my face against rock-solid sides of beef and venison to bring me back to myself. I re-emerged, Mary Poppins with a tiny notepad. But even when I would get home late, as late as possible, I could feel Massimo's presence in the flat, whether he was there or not, and it would undo the charm I had worked so hard on.

Where *was* he? Did he have a job? I had so many questions. I considered the idea of hiding myself in his wardrobe, just to get a better sense of his movements. But the thought of what I might see in his room, for some reason it frightened me. I still had not been inside. Besides, that would be crossing a line. *Behave, Simon, just ride it out*, I told myself, and mostly, I did.

His things were *everywhere*. Josh had always spread his crap around the flat, but I had enjoyed picking up his jeans and T-shirts, breathing in their familiar smell and folding them properly. Massimo's belongings were a constant spook. One evening, something beneath the sofa caught my eye. It was lying there in the dark, where I often found things he had dropped. Books or Rizlas or little black pants. This was something chunky and bone white, with what looked like deep hollows for eyes, horizontal ladders of teeth. Like a face staring out. A passing car washed the room softly aglow, and it looked even more like a face. Eyes rolling toward me. A long thick neck. The headlights disappeared, but the thing was still there. I turned on the big light to see one of his sporty little trainers lying on its side, discarded without a care in the world. I thought about shoving it down his throat.

My ire for him grew. But so did my curiosity.

Sometimes Massimo would be home when I returned. I'd prepare myself, count to ten by the door. He might be working out in the kitchen, shirtless in a tight plank while the veins throbbed in his forearms, his glutes twitching with the strain. Showing off. He knew how he looked. Sometimes I watched, tried to figure out his tattoos. I took a photo of him once, when he couldn't see me. On my phone, as he lunged in the living room. To study later. It wasn't very good; I had been too quick, and the bright kitchen lights had warped the image, so I was left with a blurry photo of Massimo in a sweat, a spear of light protruding from either side of his head, his face stretched in a grimace. Terrible. I felt immediately naughty and deleted it.

So far, I had been good. Once or twice I was tempted to peek, when he was in the shower. The door open just a crack, leaking steam. I almost opened it, I wanted to see what he got up to in there. What he looked like with the water running off him. A man like that in my house, a free show, it would be fair enough. Might as well get something out of this partnership. I caught a flash of pink before I stopped myself. *Boundaries, Simon!* I nearly broke my neck running back to my room, and scolded myself for misbehaving so brazenly. He was bringing out the bad in me.

Of course, he was attractive, nice to look at, that was one thing. However, I also found his appearance darkly ominous; the way he held his long neck, how his face seemed always in shadow, his muscled hands so awkward as he turned the kitchen tap. It was hard to look away from.

Often he was slinking down the corridor towards me as I opened the blue steel front door, so I would have to linger at the end of the hall, looking at his face, or squeeze past him and grin, hold my breath. Try not to growl. Try not to whimper. That haunted, faraway look he sometimes had, and at other times so pleased to see me, like he had been waiting. Clothes filthy, one green eye twitching in the gloom, exhausted from whatever he'd been up to. My obsession festered. What did he *do* out there? Who was he *with*? Maybe he just skulked the city alone, disappearing down holes and watching from wall-tops like a hungry crow. Like me.

Day by day I grew more restless, as the flat felt less homely, less secure. I was sure he'd been in my room, though I locked it when I left, and triple-checked. Pulled down the handle three times, made a small barking noise so I would remember. I noticed things had been moved, my pillows not exactly as I left them. The rug shifted by two inches. He used my spoons in the kitchen, I heard him crunching ice from the freezer. Goblin looked startled when I took him out. A smell that I assumed was Massimo appeared and disappeared, a stink like flowers left in water to rot, sweet and almost meaty. The flat was clearly unhappy too; a patch of mould bloomed in the kitchen. I painted over it so hard I fucked up the bristles on the brush.

My mood darkened by the day, stuffing me from the inside. It was getting harder to be good. I browsed the aisles of the local shops. All the way at the back of the Costcutter I saw myself in the anti-theft mirror on the ceiling, watched my pale hands shoving a Pot Noodle into my coat pocket, and three rolls of sellotape. I froze, waiting for the shopkeeper's startled call, but none came, so I took a packet of wet salami too. She did not see me, behind the counter; she was watching yoga on her phone. I ground my teeth and threw some of the items over the wall as I walked home, hearing them splash gently into the filthy water of the canal. I kept the noodles. Just a little badness, peeking out. It hardly helped at all.

Why did I have to live with him? I fantasised about throwing his bags out the window into the alley, and changing the locks. I would put my headphones in as Massimo banged on the door. I hadn't wished for him, or even vetted him! I imagined living all alone, and giggled at the idea – dancing naked beneath Björk, crying with my bedroom door wide open. But with these thoughts came a pang of something sad, and I realised I was glad to have the company, as unsettling as it was. I missed Josh desperately. Besides, my bank account was a black hole. Only recently I had summoned the courage to ask for a raise, and been laughed out to the bins.

Perhaps he could be replaced. I could hold auditions, letting a stream of people into the flat one by one, and chatting politely with them, holding open conversation until I found the perfect match . . . *Hideous*. I crashed that train of thought immediately.

The truth was, I needed Massimo, and this infuriated me.

I felt usurped. On edge. And most of all, challenged. I was distracted at work. I paused, hungry, just a beat too long over an unfinished sirloin, and had to drag myself away. I got a wine order wrong; a woman in tiny pearls tutted at me and asked me if I needed a moment. But I did not pour warm red Beaujolais over her bitchy little waistcoat like I wanted to, or slip kippers into her Birkin, instead I offered her more bread and sang out the specials like a bright canary, before secretly licking the rim of her glass.

'Enjoy, madam, it's on the house!'

There was a new man working at the pot-wash, which helped ease some of my tension. Handsome. Early forties, quite muscular, not the usual type here. He looked like a young dad. I observed his big broad back and shoulders from the kitchen-edge as he scraped grime off a steel tray. When I dropped the fork I had been holding, the muscles in his neck strained as he turned to catch my eye.

On my break I downloaded Grindr again. I looked at the squares of flesh and ate half a Bounty bar. A few nice beards, round brown eyes. An activist. A doctor! I checked a message from a hedge fund manager I'd been teasing. 'Hey Solomon been enough dirty chat on here why don't you finally come over and sit on this . . .'

No. Nope. I deleted the app after I'd saved the image to my camera roll.

I washed my hands; the lavender soap in the dish was so enormous I had to pet it like a cow before I returned to a restaurant full of fussy mothers, fat children, buggies the size of Land Rovers.

My thoughts turned dark. Things were not in order. Something was afoot. As I crept through the city, I couldn't help but feel haunted, hunted, dragged out, toe-punted.

Full beams seemed to wash me bright from behind with every passing night-car. Blinded me from the front. I had always felt like the follower, the lurker, lichen creeping up a rock. But now, there was something in my rear view. The shutter-snap of an eye, the scuff of a boot. The twist of something heavy quick-dragged behind a doorway. Something was there.

Massimo was following me.

CHAPTER TEN

The first time, I thought I saw him at work, in a party of nine on table three, among the crowd baying for booze. Tanned skin, tattoo on a wrist, long fingers reaching for a fish knife. But no, when I took the order for *more chablis and maybe some chorizo*, it was not him. Not even close.

But that was him, right, breathing by the bins? No, it was just the wind. Or there, peering from a taxi that was circling the block.

One shift, I saw someone on the other side of the street, standing for a while, watching me through the glass. That could be him. But it was just a girl in a yellow coat, with enormous hair, boots, wild eyes. Chain-smoking. Not the usual kind of customer. Probably lost.

Was *that* him? Crossing at the traffic lights, dodging a scooter to keep up as I made my way home. Right *there*! Peeking at me through the cornflakes in the corner shop.

I travelled deeper into the city than I was comfortable with, further from home, just to stay away. I took the overground train, a terrifying place, and sat next to a glass partition between seats. Someone's pink puffer jacket pressed against the other side of the glass like wet meat, and I stared while the train took us all, the whole carriage, from one station to the next. I kindly gave up my seat to a witchy little woman on double crutches, and slid to the end of the carriage, where a man with oily stains on his jumper screamed at a woman who did not scream back. I hid behind a boy with a cowlick sharp enough to draw blood, and looked for glimpses of a slim Italian through the crush of bodies.

Getting off near the parks, the doors opened and a gust of wind blew a person's long black hair deep inside my mouth. I stepped off the escalator before it turned me to mincemeat, and I walked and walked.

Stopping for a snack, I loitered near a parked police car, its window down, hunky officer taking a nap with his hat angled over his face. I got close enough to hear the crackle of the radio coming to life. '*Come in Unit 9C. Dispatch to Unit 9C. Come in. Got another dead one, Steve. Small flat, Barnsley road. Silk rugs all over the place. Fancy art! Thirty-seven-year-old male. Architect, six foot two, great cheekbones. No signs of forced entry, but his heart seems to have stopped. Gaping wound on the left thigh. Left eyeball has burst. Front tooth missing, presumed swallowed. Watch the Ming vase on the way out.*'

The officer sat up and cleared his throat. He saw me creeping and looked me in the eye.

'Alright there, sir?' he growled.

'I'm perfect!' I replied.

I went for a swim to drown my thoughts. The lido was quiet, thin steam pouring off the water, the one or two figures already in the water rising and submerging, rising and submerging. I had promised myself a hot chocolate afterwards as a treat, and it kept me going. Sitting shivering on the concrete, preparing to enter the water, I had watched a man, athletic and tall, naked in the outdoor showers, washing his body, soaping himself excessively. I peeked and peeked.

I did three laps, four. It's fucking hard work, swimming in a large circle, so it took some time. Then I saw him there, sitting on top of the lifeguard tower, watching me. Back hunched, legs straight, peering down with a squinted eye. Tracking me with tiny movements of his head. Wrapped in his large black coat. Massimo.

I did not know he worked as a lifeguard. In fact I did not know he had a job at all. I was baffled at the idea of him caring about anyone enough to enter the water fully clothed. I trod water. I could get out and walk around the pool, to say hello, and surprise him. I would decide how I felt about the experience by the time I got there but I would be, as ever, polite.

I didn't want him to see me awkwardly heave myself out of the water like a seal and roll wetly onto my side, my knees, my feet. I would prefer to swim gracefully to the shallow end, doing my best work, and then rise gently from the water, shake my hair and towel off, tense my stomach. I gulped air and went under, lifted an arm, scythed it. Came up. Gulped air, went under, scythed. But when I got to the shallow end, he was gone. The chair was empty, and a teenager in a yellow polo was climbing the ladder to start her shift.

At home that evening, I sat quietly in the kitchen and ate a bowl of tomato soup. I dipped in corners of buttered toast and sucked them clean. The sun went down outside and took with it the light until I was sitting in the dark. Massimo was out again, at least I thought he was; I hadn't knocked on his door.

I looked at Björk on the wall, frowning from the shadows. Until recently, I could have recited every blemish, every hairline crack, every squeak of the washing machine in this flat. Now, it didn't feel much like home.

The buzzer rang, and startled me. He must have lost his keys, leaving them out there in the city for a rapist to find. I left my soup and hurried down the corridor, towards the intercom. I lifted the handset and held it to my ear, but heard only static, and the distant blare of a car-horn.

'Hello?' I said.

Nothing replied, and the static intensified, before I heard a sound like breathing that soon turned so heavy it began to groan. It unnerved me, I was *this close* to swearing out loud, into the machine.

'Massimo?' I whispered instead.

The groaning intensified. It might have been something

wrong with the line, but it sounded deep and bodily. The static swirled as the groan transformed into frightening, guttural speech, and I pressed the receiver hard to my ear, until I heard clear words coming through. It was warped and distorted, the line was fucked, the voice mangled and maimed by traffic and white noise so it came out like an inhuman death rattle.

'Heeeello. I found you.'

I slammed the handset down.

I heard the heavy clicking of the main door, before its familiar opening screech as something let itself in, somehow. Had I pressed the button? Then nothing for a moment, until heavy feet came treading up the stairs, along with the thick clanking of metal, a chain-like noise echoing through the concrete atrium. Far too big to be a boy. Far too loud to be Massimo.

I waited as the thudding grew closer to the flat. But then it stopped. All was silent. Who had come inside? I padded to the door, put the chain on, and opened it slowly onto darkness. My eyes adjusted, and there he was, through the gap, just Massimo. A little unsteady on his feet, his hair sticking up in tufts, hands fucking *filthy* and holding out the keys that he had taken from his open rucksack.

'Found them.' He looked me in the eye and grinned.

I did not sleep a wink that night.

I grew tired in a way I'd never been before. My exhaustion became almost physical, a separate being to myself. One evening I could take it no longer. Without sleep, I am at risk. Presentation requires energy, a smile must be fully charged. My tiredness was affecting my work, my ability to be *good*. I crept around the restaurant with Lana on my back, a criticism permanently rolling like gum in her mouth. I was reaching my limit, restless and highly irritable after another endless night of loud snapping, and Massimo's footsteps echoing through the flat. I smiled through it, of course, but my lips ached from the effort, as if they might start bleeding at any moment.

As usual, the manager had not bothered to turn up; yet again Lana had snatched the gauntlet of running the restaurant to within an inch of its life. I watched her fat head swinging back and forth.

'Simon, you forgot a spoon on table nine. Oh, what on earth is this tray doing *here*?'

She put her hands on her hips, like she was looking out to sea.

'That was not good enough. Tomorrow I want you on better form, I want you perfect!'

'Aye, aye, captain.' I gave her a sharp salute instead of a karate chop to the forehead.

I'd reached boiling point. At the end of the shift I stormed out of the restaurant muttering through a gnashing smile. *Walk it off, walk it off, walk it off.* I stomped past a bright young couple moving a velvet sofa into a crack den; I walked for an hour in the wrong direction to keep this feeling at bay. It was not working. My head was thumping, my heart was beating again in that irregular way, like a tiny creature spooked and shuddering. I looked left and right, sure there was someone in the vicinity, peeking at me. But there was nobody there, so I turned quickly down the street and hurried on towards a line of parked cars, away from the lamps that lined the street.

I have *always* been good. It is who I am – a good boy who, in any situation, knows what to say and how to say it to present the best possible image of myself; this keeps me moving through the world. It works like a charm. I have no choice; if I am not good, it will be clear just how bad I really am. People will discover the grime within me. Because it's there, wriggling through me, whole strings of filthy rotten boy coiled up and squirming. Long, terrible fingers of things that I keep folded away at all times. Pushed down. And it must stay there. Because dirt gets scrubbed out. Because everyone is afraid of the dark.

You put a fresh tablecloth over a filthy piece of furniture. You saddle a sad, scrawny horse in leather so shiny you can see your face in it. Slap extra lipstick on that pig. Keep slim, keep smiling, keep up the good work. Be *good*, Simon, I told myself there on the street. You must be very good! But the rotten fingers were flexing, itching to scratch me deeply from the inside, to rise up through me, ready to unfurl into the big dark night and grab it by the fistful. I had reached my limit.

Black Ford, Blue Honda, Black BMW, Red Fiat, Black Ford.

I put my hand into my coat pocket and took out my keys, rifling fast through the bunch with one hand, looking for the mini box cutter. In one movement, I released the blade and pressed one finger from the other hand hard against its tip. I drew blood, a fat red bead.

I moved onwards, down the road, before carving a beautiful thin line with the blade straight across three cars. I watched the tiny particles of paint blow through the air and I blew after them, my breath smoke-white in the night. Dragon boy. Felt *good*. Before I reached the end of the line, I turned around and looped back to the main road, on the other side of the cars. I sliced another line, *much* deeper this time. I pressed down with all my might. Better. More satisfying. Deep and angry enough to set an alarm screaming on a shiny new Peugeot. So hard the metal squealed. That felt *really* good. I echoed the sound with my voice, howling to the sleeping streets. *Woo-woo. Woo-woo.*

That release, all those days of tension let go for a wicked little moment – it felt fantastic. But the following flush of shame came creeping fast, and I was angry at my slippage. I shook myself off, stood straight and tall. Opened my eyes wide and smiled. I told myself *enough*! Time to stop this satellite dance, I won't live like this. When I got home, he would be there, waiting for me, and we would pour a glass of wine and chat. We would be friends. Maybe not best friends like me and Josh, but perhaps something like it, in time. Something good. I girded my loins for it, felt something like excitement. Almost kicked through leaves.

But the flat was empty yet again, and I slunk through the rooms, disappointed. I closed my door and stood against it, chewed the hairs on the back of my knuckles, coming down slowly. I pulled each hair gently with my teeth until it tugged free with a thin, sharp pain, before trying the next hair, trying to ignore the sensation that something was in the hallway, pressing against the wood on the other side of the door. I got into bed and put in earplugs, bright-orange like lifejackets. I turned out the light. I put a hand to my chest, felt my heart thudding, stumbling.

When I woke again it was because something had been walking around the bed while I was sleeping.

CHAPTER ELEVEN

When I first came to the city I barely knew where to start. I moved around like a ghost, watching groups of friends who all seemed to know each other already. I didn't understand how this was possible, that every person in this place had gone to school together. They all had interesting jobs, good connections. I could not find a groove to slot into.

I did not want to be locked inside an office, so I temped. I worked for a month as a runner on music videos, after one day walking past a shoot taking place in a warehouse, and simply stepping onto the set. Making coffee, taping up blackout blinds to windows, tricking day for night. Once I sat on a pleather sofa that was spilling its green stuffing, and looked after a pop star's hairy greyhound for six hours. It smelled of cheese and looked like it was crying. I just sat there, in case the dog needed anything.

These were places where I could be useful, and get by

mostly unnoticed. I thought it was my calling. I took the food orders, waited for hours in the cold, smiled through my teeth. Loving everyone. Hating everyone. I flexed my charms, my goodness, and it got me paid.

I know a hard day's work as much as anyone, I love to work. It was the people that I loathed. Still, I faked it brilliantly. For a while. But I slipped up once or twice, and kept getting hired, forgotten, hired, forgotten. Something didn't quite stick. I had to try *harder*, do *better*. Once, when I was really broke, I tried webcamming. I created a profile, FuckPig95. I put a pillowcase on my head while I performed in the privacy of my room. I made almost a hundred in three hours. But the next day, at the pool, a man was staring at me too hard for too long. Like he recognised me. Like he knew what I'd done, from my nipples or that freckle on my back. Like he'd been watching. I deleted the account and found a new lido.

I got a job at a shoe shop in the centre of the city. It was upmarket, smelled good. My customer service was amazing, I really stepped it up. I became an even better liar, and people remembered my name.

'Who were you served by?' I would hear my manager ask at the till, and they would look back at me, and point. *Simon*, they would say. *I was served by Simon.* I would smile back, give a wave, and as they left the shop I would think about them stepping into oncoming traffic.

I was renting a basement room in a house with six middle-aged women and I hated it. I would sit on my bed, looking up through the bars as the rain fell, at the friends screaming with joy, dodging the puddles. I began to notice a wary longing.

I was angry. Sometimes, at the end of a shift, I'd mix up the shoe sizes in the stockroom. Something for the morning team. Then I would take the rubbish out, cradling piles of cardboard through the concrete alleyways. That's where I met Josh.

I had been squashing a pile of delivery boxes for dainty little loafers, and I had finished the job by jumping down hard in a series of furious stamps. I'd heard a gasp behind me, a sound of exaggerated anguish, and I turned around fast. There stood a tall boy, a look of shock on his handsome face, his curly hair a stark silhouette against the backlit doorway. His hands were gently pulling a cigarette from a packet, and he looked like someone I had seen in a magazine, or on a billboard.

'There was a baby cat under those,' he said, his brown eyes round and bright.

'What?'

He pointed at the flattened boxes with his cigarette.

'A baby cat made its home under those boxes this morning. A stray one. I was bringing it a sandwich.'

I stared at him, then down at the boxes.

'But now you've killed it.'

I watched his face as he sparked up, all nonchalant.

'You don't have a sandwich,' I said, finally.

'Then I was coming to give it a cigarette.' His wide,

brilliant grin. I laughed, how could I help it? When he offered me a cigarette, I took one, though I never smoked.

He worked above the shop, at a fashion agency. I was exhausted – the city had been slowly eating me, taking whole chunks that I tended to alone each night, before stepping out into the streets again.

I became curious about this boy who seemed to notice me. I practised the smoking, and I found myself waiting for him, burning through three in a row until he appeared at the top of the staircase, his shadow leaping up the walls. We got to know each other there, in that back alley, chatting. Josh's arm cutting the air to drive a point home, whatever he was most excited about that day, and me chuckling carefully at whatever he said.

One evening, he invited me for a drink, and I had looked him in the eye hard, seeking a motive. 'Come on, Simon, I'm gasping.' He had looked right back and touched my arm, the section between wristwatch and rolled sleeve. The skin had tingled momentarily. I'd cleared my throat, licked my lips, and said yes please.

It had just been a beer, maybe two. I sat quietly while he talked about his job, and showed me photos on his phone of a celebrity he'd done a fitting for. He had leaned back in his chair, watching the room around us, grinning that grin. I saw the way people looked at him, men and women, their gazes snagged by his rolling shoulders, his boyish guffaw. He talked a lot, and sometimes asked me questions, but mostly I was just happy to listen, to be seen sitting next to him.

I waited for him to get bored of me, but he never did. We started going for drinks regularly after work, or to gallery openings, album launches, anything with a free bar. He always had the next move planned. I could tell he enjoyed the way I followed his lead, said yes to any suggestion – a keen disciple at his service.

Once, after a white wine ceremony, I had to jump off the train and vomit onto the tracks. He stroked my back and bought me a bottle of water. As he looked down at the free crisps turned to yellow mush on the steel below, I wondered if I was meant to kiss him in thanks.

Josh wiggled into events with ease, squeezing us through the cracks of the city like tiny worms. Fashion week, magazine launch, pop-up restaurant. He was connected, and firmly believed in exploiting those connections to have a good time, sharing his charm with entire industries. I knew how to crack a smile, but I was nothing on Josh. I didn't have the stamina.

He was not all sunshine, he could bite; I once saw a woman steal his taxi. 'She's a *fat bitch*. She can eat shit and die choking on it!' But it always balanced out – when his boss screamed at him in front of the whole team for a mislaid invoice, he shrugged it off. He said, 'She's getting a divorce. It wasn't personal.' He lived for uncertainty, so I did not have to, excited to eat the world around him, eyes bigger than his stomach.

One day when he called me, his voice was electric through the phone. 'Simon. I've found the best flat in the world. It's a two-bed, I need someone else. Two besties living together! Say you'll do it. Say yes!'

Besties. I assumed it was a prank, but I was wrong. We moved in quickly to the unfurnished flat, which was indeed the best flat in the world. The contract was dodgy as fuck, but it hardly mattered; it was clean, the rooms were large, the light was amazing. The location was terrifying enough to keep the rent just the right side of affordable. 'It's up and coming,' Josh said, as we skipped down a violent high street, the wind blowing us onwards to the big blue steel doors, through the atrium and up the stairs, where Josh let us in with brand-new keys.

I practically exploded my overdraft buying a bed, a desk, new towels. Paying the first month's rent. Had to pull in some favours I'd rather forget. Some Sundays I resorted to stealing smaller pieces from the flea market on the edge of the playing fields. A lamp, a painting, a pillowcase. The bits that make a house a home.

I could not believe it – the idea that someone like Josh would see me as a best friend, and then as someone to share a home with. I wasn't even sure I knew *how* to be a best friend, but I decided I was prepared to try. No longer would I have to survive in this city alone, I had someone to share it with. And somewhere safe to hide. I would lie awake in bed and hear him moving around, or taking a midnight bath, and have to pinch myself, trying to burst this cosy bubble just to prove it was a lie. But it was *real*.

I got fired from the shoe shop not long after moving in,

for reasons that are private and unfair. I almost choked to death on panic for a week while I tried to find temp work, but it seemed my name had a dark smudge against it, and every door was closed in my face. Eventually, I told Josh.

'I have to leave, I've run out of money.' I was trying hard not to cry because nobody wants to look at that. He stopped me, put an arm out. 'Don't worry, Si, I've got you. Pay me back later, if you can.' He ruffled my hair with a long-fingered hand, and it was glorious to feel that way, like he had my back. The dynamic worked well. If Josh was a glorious white whale, gliding through the city, I was the little fish nipping at his belly, coming along for the ride. There's nothing wrong with that.

Yes, I was sometimes sat alone, waiting for him to come home from nights out with his other friends, and yes he brought up the money, once or twice, when he needed a favour doing. No, he did not often attempt to dig deep into the inner workings of my soul, but as it might be clear by now, that is how I liked it.

The flat became our sanctuary against the churning chaos of the city and I kept it that way, clean as a whistle. I had never loved a place like I loved our home, and I was always on the hunt for new blue vases, bowls I could not afford, fresh techniques to make the oven shine. We slipped into a routine. Every third weekend or so became wine and lines night. I got high for the first time in my life. Josh performed his infamous Kate Bush routine without fail and I, chemically ecstatic, would warm up to the idea of twirling around, using a blanket to shroud myself in my own jerky Katy Perry pop performance. I had moments then, of understanding how it felt to be smiled upon by Josh; pure magic. But I could not reach his princely heights, he never laughed as loud at me as I did at him.

There were chinks in his armour, though, and sometimes, after a bottle of wine, he exposed them to me. His genuine need for advice and validation crept through. '*Does this really look good, Simon? Honestly? Do you really think that guy was checking me out? My dad didn't mean it like that, did he?*' I saw real worry in his eyes, and it touched me. I told him what he needed to hear, over and over, until he smiled and opened another bottle, satisfied. Grateful for my kind ear, my eager reassurance, my friendship. He would hug me tight.'*You're a good guy, Simon.*'

Once or twice, high as a kite, I shared my own secrets with him, spittling out things I had never told anyone, private little snacks that made his eyes go wide. I would pour him another drink, before giving him another snippet of a story, a morsel of a dark little dream that wriggled into the candelight between us. He would nod sagely and, as he shared something in return, the bond was further braided.

In the morning I would wake sweaty with dread at the things I had told him, preparing to pack my bags, or find him packing them for me, now that he knew what Simon *really* says. But the shoe didn't drop, and he never mentioned it. *Oh.* Maybe this was a place I could slip up, occasionally. A couple of times I wondered if he'd even been listening. Still, to atone, I would make the flat look amazing again. Everything back to normal but now better, cleaner, sparkling with a flash of pink peonies, or a new coffee-table book about Georgian princes.

In the evenings, Josh would bring stories from work. I would be anxious about being late for a shift at the cocktail bar where Josh had pulled a string to get me a job, but was dutifully enraptured by the words coming from beneath his Cupid's bow. Even if over time, in his excitement, he had forgotten to notice how the fridge magnets were perfectly aligned, or the TV screen sparkled in the spotlights, he was still letting me be his best friend. He was giving me permission.

We almost got together, but only once, accidentally. High on whatever, drunk again, the lights down low. Both of us unblinking as I shifted along the sofa to where he sat. Me leaning in toward him for a kiss, mostly to see what it might be like. Josh coming to his senses just in time, swerving away hard. Laughing it off, not looking me in the eye. Never speaking of it ever again.

Actually that's enough. I don't want to think about Josh any more right now.

CHAPTER TWELVE

I sat up in bed, wet with sweat. My earplugs had been removed, twisted and slid from my ears. There was a soft hissing, a breathy grunt of sorts, like something had been moaning from within my pillow itself.

I breathed deeply and looked around the soft darkness. It was 4 a.m.; I can always tell. I was desperate to piss, but I could still feel a strong presence in the room; something was here, I had heard it walking. I sensed it in the corner, and at first I turned away, not able to look directly at it. I forced myself to turn back, to where the soft light from the streetlight slid through the gaps at the side of the blinds, illuminating my clothes that hung on their cheap steel rack. Shirts to the left, white first, then grey, then blue. My eyes slid along the rail, full of clean clothes. I heard a heavy foot press down, the creak of a floorboard in the corner.

'Massimo?' No reply.

I did not even know if he'd come home earlier, but when I sniffed the air, I found that unmistakable, now familiar tang of stagnation. And then the shirts began to move and I heard the harsh screech of the metal hangers moving across the steel of the bar, quiet at first and getting louder as the hangers collected against each other and moved as one. I watched the shirts move aside, just a little further, one final sharp screech, and then they stopped, and swung gently. I sat in terrified silence for what seemed like forever, until another sound reached my ears.

The shower was running. No more sounds in my room. I crept from the bed, unlocked my door and peered out; the bathroom door was slightly open. But Massimo's room was dark.

'Massimo? Were you in my room?' I wanted to call out, louder than the water. *How did you get in?* But then I heard a sharp noise, coming from the bathroom.

Snap.

The hallway was extra dark, dimly lit from the yellow light in the bathroom. I could see a light fog building, as shower steam buffed from the doorway. A shape moving. He was in there.

How to describe it, this feeling, the lure of that partially open door?

Snap.

A choice. Back to bed, curled up tight till morning? Or onward down the hall. A familiar voice. *Come on now, Simon, be good.* I ignored it. My feet were moving forward on the floor, skin unpeeling and resticking to the wood with each step. The terror I had felt just moments before leaking away, replaced with something more furious, more urgent, more dangerous.

Snap.

That sound of clicking. Those snaps.

A moment of revelation. *He's cutting his fucking nails.*

I kept walking. I really, really needed to piss now. And I was suddenly desperate to catch him in the act, where he could not slip away. To find out why he cut his nails in the middle of every fucking night. To demand outright, with him standing undressed before me, the truth behind *all* of his dark little mysteries. To find out where he went in the day, why his eye twitched like crazy. Why he smelled like that. If he had been following me. Had he been in my room? How the fuck had he got in? I had waited long enough for answers.

Already I pictured him, his hard muscles wet from the shower, his mouth open in surprise. His towel on the floor. *Tell me everything!* I would scream, until all of his sordid secrets were exposed to me, and I could rummage through every inch of them with my bare hands. Turn him around and check for more. I kept walking; I couldn't stop myself.

This was *bad*. Forcing myself on Massimo in his nakedness was a line I should not be crossing. But here I was, marching forward, eyes trained on that door. Hairs standing on end. Not being a good boy at all. Irresistibly drawn to the image of him, in there, the terrible things he might be doing.

Another *snap*, unbelievably loud, and then a shadow

moved fast across the light on the floor. I flinched, so startled I almost turned and ran, but then the shadow was gone. Another click, and a low, angry growl that sent a shudder right through me. I stood there, staring at the triangle of light on the floor, waiting for movement. Less certain now about opening that door, not wanting to enter. *Snap.* Then another sound, a sharp bark of pain, a sigh of frustration.

He wasn't finished yet. I still wanted to see. I was close now, and the door was open in such a way that I could peer through the narrow space between the hinges, so I looked. Massimo was naked, sitting on the closed toilet seat. He was hunched over and twisted away from me, toward the wall, so that I could only see him side on, his buttocks and broad back, his face in profile. Everything wreathed in steam. He had tattoos everywhere, and they were stretched into beautiful shapes, like grooves and faces in a great bed of rock. An animal of some sort on his shoulder, a castle beneath his neck. Just visible on his side was the largest, an outline drawing of two men kissing.

He lifted one hand, put a ragged finger in his mouth, and began sucking on it. Even from here I could see him moving it around, his tongue working around the digit like a slug on a tomato, the muscles of his face twitching. He removed the cleanly clipped finger from his mouth and studied it, turning it in the light. From the hand that rested in his lap, the clippers glinted. I couldn't tell if they were mine.

Above the running of the tap I heard a small growl of vexation, and then he said something, in a voice that was gruffer, frighteningly thicker than usual. The finger was lifted into the light, for a better look. It displayed a slick, dark nail, an inch long, where only moments before it had been clipped down to the quick.

I saw what I thought might be a tear fall from that wickedly bright eye, down his cheek, before he turned suddenly and looked towards the door. I drew back, fast. I listened for his voice, but nothing came. He had not seen me. I waited. After a breathless moment, I heard him stepping into the bath, his feet squeaking on the tub.

I stepped around the door, a little closer, just tapping it with my bare foot to nudge it a little wider, incrementally, peering fully round now. I could see the mirrored cabinet, slightly open, reflecting the bathtub back at me. The mirror was fogged up so much that all I saw was a pink blur. Just a little more, I told myself. I nudged the door more, and now I could see the bath clearer, and Massimo standing in it, hot steam billowing around him. He hadn't pulled the curtain across properly, and a corner of it stuck to his bare, round buttock. He reached round to peel it off.

He was just standing there, head bowed, letting the hot water rain down onto the back of his neck, his tattooed back. I should've turned on my heel, closed the door and left. But just as I stepped back to go, I saw something that stopped me. With his back to me and his body turned just so, I could see the kissing men on the side of his torso clearly, looped together in bold black lines. They were holding each other with long fingers, mouths locked, their hair detailed with great skill, flopping over eyes that closed, complete with flicking eyelashes. It was truly beautiful. I kept looking at it, telling myself I would shut the door in one second, I would not look any lower.

But I could not unpeel my eyes. Because the tattoo had started to move.

The lines were sliding against one another, and the men kissed deeper, then moved apart. Massimo's golden skin now had a large blank space where there had been ink, one man stepping to his front, the other onto his back. As the lines separated, the skin between them slowly split, and began to open up. A thin, dark stream of blood was trickling down his side, to his hip, then his thigh, and as the skin opened the stream grew thicker and I could see shining red muscle, and maybe bone, something winking white within. Other things too, what looked like the inside of an amethyst, jagged and gleaming.

Now Massimo moved, twisting to examine his wound with a scowl. His eyes too were now darker, even greener, much larger than they'd been before. He opened his mouth in a grimace, and inside that pink hole, every tooth was neatly daggered, razor-sharp. He hissed loud in pain, before reaching down and placing his longest finger, with its sharpest nail, deep into the hole. I gasped, and he turned toward me, mouth wide open. He pulled the finger out, and started to inspect what was on the end of it, that sparkling rot.

I ran in terror, quickly to my room, much too noisily, slipping on the wood with panic, panting hard. I locked the door, and doubled down with a chair under the handle. Around me, the walls seemed to vibrate, the very concrete rolling against itself, sharp rappings under the floorboards like something testing for a hollow. I thought my bladder would burst. I scattered the pens from a large cup on my desk, and pissed into it, a thick frothing stream.

Something that must be Massimo, but sounded so much larger, was pounding down the corridor to my room. I could hear him panting behind the locked door. Impossibly, he was squeezing through the keyhole, the gaps around the wood, that sliver underneath. Coming right in. My heart beat dangerously fast.

I felt a sharp pain, hot scratches on my back and I dropped the cup of piss, watched it splash all over the rug. Felt the warm liquid on my bare foot. My instinct was to mop it up, but I could barely move, there was agony in my chest now, jabbing at my lungs, my little beating heart. I heard it murmur, I swear to God I heard it murmur. Creaking like a galleon in the wind. I held my hand over my heart. It felt like it might be breaking. I wanted to cry, but I did not, instead I tilted my head back and let out a sharp, rasping gasp.

A flickering whine in my head. A soft hiss in my ears.

That flute *peeping*.

A thumping in my chest.

Darkness.

CHAPTER THIRTEEN

I know exactly how I'll die.

I'll get hit by a bus crossing the street, distracted by a man with a beard and a bubble butt. Or maybe it'll be some teenage twink with razor-sharp cheekbones, boarding an overground train one carriage down from me. I'll miss my footing and fall on the rails, my gaze attached to his eyelashes, and underneath the train I'll be sliced in two like a cheap tomato.

I could be staring at the long bulge beneath the towel of a Daddy at the lido. I'll slip on the crisscross tiles and crack my head open, big red gash at the back leaking head juice and mingling with the chlorine like a dirty brain-martini. Children staring down at me, asking Mummy if I'm dead.

Yes, sweet boy, I am dead. I've actually died. A gory paint-stripe on the tarmac, a lone eyeball skidding down the drain to peek into the mulch up close. A cracked-up, snapped-up bag of meat in the footwell of a smouldering Prius. A bloated corpse bubbling up gas for the fish and frogs to swim through. And you can blame it on the boys.

Boys with tans, boys pale as ghosts, ginger boys, Asian boys, Brown boys, Black boys, tall and lean and surly queens and men so buff you think they might burst. The curve of a large buttock on a bike seat, that dude looking over his shoulder to take a turn and the sunlight hitting him just *so* over the brow, sparkling in his eyes. Boys in bookshops browsing seventies sci-fi, carrying little dogs in jackets. Boys with massive arms and dark twinkles in their eyes. Boys in parks stretched like cats over each other, smoking, yawning, burping, groping. Football boys so terrifyingly straight and fit and rugby boys with thighs and butts and grins that make you want to cave under and die beneath the huddle, mouth wide open for gulping and teeth chewing on every ounce of meat. Boys with swan necks and curly hair, boys that look like Josh. Boys that are not mine. All those boys, boys everywhere.

I'm a looker. A looking-atter. And I've always got a sentence, in case I'm caught. *Oh, I thought we used to work together. Have I seen you on TV?*

But I'm never caught.

Sometimes, I wish I did more touching. Being touched. Being kissed. Cuddled and curled into armpits and the backs of taxis, snout-full of the smell of another. Suffocating. I can imagine the feeling, of hands on my body, hands holding mine, turning my face inward for a whisper or a kiss. One day, maybe, I'll get there.

But for now, I'm just looking.

I sat down in front of the doctor and watched him yawn.

He was staring at me, then blinking hard behind his glasses like a stupid little mole. *Honestly how these cunts ever get through medical school . . .*

'I'm sorry to waste your time,' I said, and smiled a straight line earlobe to earlobe. I was feeling a little off.

I still had my coat on, and he gestured for me to remove it, then performed a give-me-a-minute nod and turned to his computer, where he was typing something, very slowly with two long fingers. He was dressed in a shirt and tie, glasses with red frames. Mid-fifties. Quite handsome, quite nice. A photo of children on his desk. His, I presumed. I blinked at him with one eye, then the other. It's called winking.

In the waiting room, where I had sat for ninety minutes, I had watched a man in a wheelchair vomit onto the floor before the police who had wheeled him in finally took him to the toilet. Everyone in the room had black eyes and broken arms. I stared. Nobody watched me back. For a second I'd wondered if I was actually there, so I scraped my chair back hard, and made it screech. The only person I surprised was myself.

The doctor drank something from a mug and turned to address me; I shifted, alert.

'What can we take a look at . . . Simon?' he said, and had to check my name on his screen.

'I've got a heart murmur.'

He nodded, sort of gravely. 'Do you know what a heart murmur is?'

I looked him dead in the eye. 'It's my heart. Murmuring.'

'Mm-hmm. Is it painful? Tight in the chest?'

I shuffled in my seat.

'No,' I said, and he raised his eyebrows. 'OK, yes.' I looked away from his gaze.

His tone softened now, ever so slightly.

'Any stress, new worries or anxieties? Any changes to lifestyle?'

My flatmate wants to eat me.

'Not really.' I shrug.

'OK. Shall we have a listen, then?'

I breathed in deep as he took the stethoscope that was coiled around his neck, and lifted it, inserting the buds into his ears.

'Should I take this off?' I asked, chest pushed forward keenly towards him.

'No. No. Just undo the top buttons there.'

The doctor warmed the round end of the stethoscope in his hand, then placed it against my chest. I held the top of my shirt open carefully, stretched open like the belly of a cat in surgery. The metal wasn't as cold as I expected; I didn't gasp. I looked up at the ceiling and around the room and the doctor listened.

He frowned, just a little at first, then a little deeper, adjusted the instrument, listened again. For a moment, he was deep in thought, and then he jerked his neck back in a strange way, like a garden hose left unattended. I listened to the clock ticking as now, news-reporter style, he pressed a finger to his left ear, to push the bud in deeper and get a clearer sound. His eyes widened.

I broke the silence.

'Is it murmuring?' I said, startling him.

He removed the buds from his ears.

'Is it murmuring? Or can't you find it?' I joked. 'My heart.'

The doctor gave a small laugh. It seemed fake.

'I think it's this stethoscope. There's something wrong with the seal, maybe.'

He put the instrument down and stood up, his eyes fixed on my diamond of exposed skin.

'Sorry about this . . . Simon, just . . . give me a minute,' he said with his hands up apologetically, and he edged out of the room like a crab.

I looked at the stethoscope on the desk, and its one round Cyclops eye winking up at me, the green rubber tubing a tail across the doctor's paperwork. I picked it up and, angling the metal stalks that glinted in the ceiling lights, pressed the two black buds into my ears. The room became immediately muffled, the sound of the clock no longer audible. I turned the silver disc in my hand, and heard the sound of the air moving through it. I opened my shirt again with one hand and, with the other, pressed the circle to my chest.

After half a second, there it was, the steady *whump-whump* of my heart. Deep in the darkest of my depths, calling out to me. *Whump-whump. Whump-whump.* I moved the disc around a little, like the doctor had, and the sound of my heart moved with it. No murmuring, no stopping, no creaking. The rhythm was steady, the beat clear. I frowned, and listened harder to my blood. Then I heard another sound, creeping through the *whump*. I couldn't quite place it: short, sharp sounds, as if coming from behind a thick door, but coming closer.

Footsteps.

I turned, removing a bud, expecting to see the doctor walking in. He wasn't there, and I couldn't hear any footsteps coming from the room, or the corridor beyond. Only through the stethoscope.

I put the other bud back in, and pressed the disc down hard on my chest. There. Footsteps again, echoing faintly but heavy, like work boots on wood. There, a new sound. A scratching. Something was *in there*.

Then: a knock. Followed by two more. Three sharp thuds delivered on my inner door by something huge, pounding to come in, and a word, from the caves of my innards.

'Sssssimon.' A hideous rolling groan of my name, thick in each ear.

'That's not real,' I whispered. 'No way.'

'Simon . . .?' That was clearest of all. In the room, something moved. I screamed, and pulled the stethoscope from my ears.

The doctor stood in the doorway, holding up two brand-new stethoscopes like a pair of pheasants he had just shot, their bright-red tubing stark against his white coat. His expression was one of pure bafflement.

'Are you OK, Simon?' he asked me, and I could tell my eyes were bursting. So I composed myself, and sat back in the chair. I nodded. Everything was fine. Everything was *fine*.

He watched me closely as he tried again, listening to my haunted heart. He nodded, shifted the new stethoscope. I prepared myself.

'You can release your breath now,' he said. 'I think you're OK. Nothing to worry about.'

'No murmur?' I said, gripping the seat.

'Not that I can hear.'

'Call yourself a fucking doctor?!' We both blinked at each other in surprise at my furious voice.

He leaned back in his chair. 'Well, Simon, I can prescribe you something to take the edge off, if you'd like?'

There was a warm burning in my brain and belly, my balls. It was not unpleasant.

Outside, I took a little beat, sitting in golden sunshine on a bench opposite a housing estate. That was very out of character, to behave so rudely to such an upstanding member of society. Not my usual style of public interaction. I felt edgy, a little embarrassed. If I thought about it too much, I might have started to panic, so instead I sat very still, watching the building in front of me.

Eighties brick brutalism, stunning colour palette, red and yellow. I watched an ambulance pull up, and two paramedics, a tall man and a younger lady, emerged from the vehicle. They fussed with the main door's buzzer until someone let them in. I heard a tiny voice.

The lift is fucked again. You'll have to walk.

I heard the girl swear, she was very loud. I watched the neon green of their hi-vis jackets and little bobbing heads float round and round the stairwell like limey bubbles in a drink. I ate some of a Yorkie bar I found in my pocket, followed by a chunk of whatever the doctor had given me, white and chalky like Xanax.

They shouldered open a door on the third floor and entered the flat. On the wind I heard a strange sort of gasp as they stepped inside – *Oh no no no* – before one of the team re-emerged, the young woman's pale startled face with a little round mouth, lighting up a cigarette. Hair wild, unbrushed and absolutely massive. Unprofessional.

A neighbour came out from two doors down, dressing gown covered in sauce. Hands clasped to her throat. Edging towards the darkness of that open front door, and the smoking paramedic stationed there.

'Oh, God, someone's died in there, haven't they?' I could hear her clearly.

'Clear the way please, can you go back inside? I need to get past!' The man ran out, pushing past the neighbour. He leant over the balcony and vomited a hot river down three storeys. I watched the steam rise from the chilled concrete. Saw what he'd had for breakfast. The neighbour heaved, crept closer.

'Is it bad? Is it a mess, in there?'

The paramedic wiped his mouth.

'Madam, it's absolutely revolting.'

CHAPTER FOURTEEN

There's a place I know. A good place to go. When I'm startled, star-sparkled, thrown off course.

You wouldn't know what this place was, passing it on the street. Just a dirty doorway round the side of a building where the wind blows crooked. Next to a Chinese restaurant I've never eaten at. Sacks of rubbish spilling open, rivers of slime in the gutters. There's no neon sign, no clear wording above the door. You need to know it's there.

I'd only ever come here alone; this was private, and not a place I wanted to share, especially not with Josh. This was just for me. It's not often, it's not a big deal. I'm allowed a bit of fun.

I had called ahead to make my appointment, but it was pretty dead when I arrived. I was feeling hazy; the Xanax I'd popped was indeed taking some of this morning's edge right off.

I wasn't surprised at the lack of a queue for entry; it was still fairly early for this kind of thing. The lights were dim, the enormous bare bulbs hanging from the ceiling turned low. TV screens flashing on every wall. Some just playing static. There was a new girl on the desk, one I had not met before – it had been a while since I had treated myself. I gave her my name quietly, and she checked my booking on her screen. My eye twitched and she pretended not to stare.

'One hour.' She held a finger up, the other hand playing with her curiously long ponytail.

She asked me if I wanted a drink and I said yes – large white wine please. House wine is fine. Put it on the tab. I asked for ice, please, and she added a couple of cubes. I took a sip and shuddered deliciously. Lethal. Pure Bitch Diesel.

I followed her down the corridor, which smelled of bleach and something stranger, almost sweet. The ice cubes tinkling in my wine glass. Her high heels clacking, long ponytail swishing as she jiggled a key attached to a large, flat piece of round purple plastic, a number etched onto it. Number sixteen.

My usual.

We walked past several doors, each with a meshed rectangular window, and I peered inside, but they were all empty, cleaned out and ready for the next punter. Above us, the lights flickered faintly as we headed deeper into the building. We descended a staircase, as I knew we would, and I began to hear faint sounds. A thin, high-pitched wail, cut off abruptly. The sound came again, followed by a longer scream of sorts, still muffled and distant. It sounded male, but it can be hard to tell down here.

We were deep in the belly now, far beneath the city. The girl stopped at a door and held the key aloft, double-checking the number before letting us in. Some rooms allowed up to ten people. I find that difficult to imagine. My room was a tiny purple pod, perfect for one, maybe two. The place needed a touch-up; I noticed dark stains on the walls, scuff marks and spotting on the padded bench that ran the length of the back wall. The wipe-clean leather was a sickly green.

Ponytail turned to me. 'I know you've been here before but I'm going to talk you through it anyway. It's protocol.'

I nodded, trying to be polite. She was keen to do a good job, but I was itching to get going.

'You know how to use the monitor, right?' she said, pointing to a sticky screen on the wall.

'Yep, yep, I've got it. Thank you,' I said, teeth on display, the Xanax-wine combo working a treat.

She nodded. Bob-bob. I took a huge sip of wine, felt cold liquid creeping down my gullet.

She pointed to a switch on the wall. 'You can change the lights there. They're on dimmers.'

She looked quite pleased with that.

'And there are . . . props. There, in that box. If you need them.' She looked at me with a raised eyebrow. I shuffled my feet.

'You can order drinks directly from here. Someone will bring them along.' She pulled up a menu on the screen.

I reached right past her and ordered another glass via the icon on the screen, to show her who she was dealing with. I was in the mood for a good time now. She smirked.

'Dutch courage?'

'I guess so!' I said too loudly, and she peered at me.

'Well. Enjoy.' She gestured to the room with a swish of her head, ponytail flashing behind her.

'The timer will start as soon as you begin.'

I listened to the door click shut as she left me. Alone at last.

The monitor was warm to the touch and buzzed beneath my finger as I began to scroll through endless names, endless choices. Different styles, ages, images. Some just faces, others more obscure. Just for a moment, the ice pick. My gut shuddering. I felt myself twitching in anticipation. I was ready for this.

There was a knock at the door, and it startled me from my scrolling. Ponytail was holding a goblet of wine on a non-slip tray.

'It's plastic, so you don't hurt yourself.'

'Or anyone else!' I barked, but she didn't find this funny. I was getting a little nervous.

I smiled my thanks, she smiled back thinly.

'Spill it and you'll get a fine.' She swished away.

I took a gulp and squinted back at the screen. This was the crucial choice; I would kill the mood for myself if I got this wrong. Then I found it – it just came to me.

I took a look towards the door, girded my loins and touched the icon.

I lifted the microphone to my mouth, and began to sing.

Sugababes. 'Push the Button'.

The song was familiar, comforting, sexy; I could really get into it. I glanced at the door a couple of times, still easing into the freedom of this soundproofed room, but by the end of the song, my glass was half-empty, and I was rocking my hips, banana boat-style. I was having fun.

I padded all catty up to the screen, singing my heart out like someone seriously mad. Britney's 'Stronger' than yesterday thanks very much and I'm a majestic horse, a prancing pony girl in a padded cell. I stabbed the screen – more wine please!

I felt woozy, and was thrilled to remember the fold of Josh's coke I had found in my clean-up. It was tucked into my wallet, and I took a mean little bump from my key, which really got me jumping.

Ponytail delivered. I leaned back against the door to sing out the chorus to Cher's 'Believe'. I felt so *good*. I squeaked a figure of eight with my bum.

Yes, Cher, I do believe. I do!

Jason Derulo, Nirvana, Girls Aloud, keep the hits coming. I lay down on the floor and sang to the ceiling, pouring it out for the tiny security camera in the corner of the room. 'Oh baby! Oh baby baby.'

I crooned like a witch to the moon as the last of the wine slid down. Oh this was fun. A shudder in my chest, a big smile on my lips. I felt the sweat pooling above my boxers too, and reached a hand around to feel the damp patch, sticky and warm, where something had scratched at me last night.

I needed something loud and raucous. Alanis. What a woman. A dark, friendly, tingling sensation was creeping over my body, my mind. I can't lie, it felt amazing. I surrendered, I went out to pasture, and I could hear my voice ringing out wild and true and buttered with something terrible, a sound drawn deep from a stinking well that mingled with my voice and was loud, undeniably loud, undeniably *there*.

OK, you're real. Fair enough.

Whatever it was, I let it sing.

A banging. Deep thuds.

Rhythmic, but not part of the song. I opened my eyes.

A face stared in at me, through the small window. Ponytail? The handle was juddering like she was trying to open it but couldn't. I blinked at her wide-eyed face. At last the handle jolted down, and the door swung open far more forcefully than she had intended. She righted herself, and looked at me hard.

'How did you lock this door?'

I climbed to my feet, the room spinning as I rose. In the corridor, over her shoulder, I could see two men and three women, all holding plastic flutes of booze, their faces contorted behind enormous novelty sunglasses and wearing top hats from the dressing-up box. One of the girls held a shiny black dachshund.

Ponytail was looking at me, unsure. The song finished, the last in the queue. I stood and shivered.

'How did you make it so loud?' she said.

I suddenly felt a little defensive, blinked slow cokey-Xanax blinks.

'It was the same the whole time,' I said, perhaps slurred. 'The room's meant to be soundproofed?'

She was trying to work this out. Keeping both feet behind the threshold, and watching me like a bird eyeing a snake.

From the corridor, one of the men piped up in a high Scottish lilt. 'Why the hell were you screaming like that?!'

The girl with the dog was peering around. 'Have you got a dog in there?' she said, cuddling her little pet. 'She's not good with other dogs.'

I was starting to feel attacked. I barked out a sound, I couldn't help it.

'No! And who the fuck brings a dog to karaoke?!' I jerked my head at the dachshund, which seemed to be choking on a bit of green wig.

'Actually, it sounded more like a cat,' mumbled the guy, and one of the other girls snorted.

'In a washing machine.' But even she looked a little unnerved, clutching her sunglasses as they slid down her nose, avoiding eye contact. They were all afraid. Of me. That was new.

Ponytail wiggled her shoulders, puffed up her chest.

'Have you got someone in there with you?' she said.

'Perhaps a piglet?' said the guy.

'There are no animals in here!' I shouted, but I could feel that familiar blush of shame creeping from somewhere within, my neck turning red. I'm not the best singer in the world, but this place is fucking *soundproofed*. That's the whole *point*.

Ponytail fidgeted with the lanyard around her neck.

'We had a complaint. You were screaming. People were scared.'

I blushed.

'I wasn't screaming,' I said, quietly. 'I was singing.'

She continued. 'I heard it too. All the way from the desk. What song was it? I've never heard it here.'

I opened my mouth, then closed it. 'The door was shut, the whole time,' I said.

'Is it a prank?' she said, looking for a hidden camera crew. 'How do you do that with your voice?'

'Do what?!'

'Make it so . . . loud. And deep. Is it like a heavy metal thing?'

'I like pop.'

She was getting stressed, wiggling about all over the place.

'It was actually quite frightening.'

She paused, sniffing the air. I watched her eyes glow.

'Have you been smoking in here?' she said. 'What type of cigarette is *that*?'

I felt myself move backwards in surprise. 'No,' I said.

'And . . . farting? It smells like smoke and farts in here. Have you smoked? Have you farted?'

She sniffed the air again, her head tilting back, going for a full whiff, squeezing her eyes tight.

'Yes, you have.' She was almost smiling, a sharp blade of steel in each eye under the glare of the hallway lights. I thought maybe her ponytail would come to life and slash the room, her head was shaking so hard. 'That's an automatic ban. We don't have the insurance!'

'A *ban*?!' I said.

'It's company policy.'

'I don't even have cigarettes! Where would the butt be?'

'In your pocket. Your shoe. Or your stomach. Maybe you ate it. I don't know.'

I grabbed at my pockets, grabbed at my coat. Emptied them all out into my sweating hands. Wallet, keys, phone, lip-balm.

'Can't you *smell it*?' she hissed.

I sniffed the air. Oh, shit. There, *that tang*, right there. The faint reek of smoke, acrid and toasty. Almost sulphurous, like fresh swamp.

Time to go.

I scooped up my things and tried to push past her into the corridor. She wasn't finished.

'And what is *that*? Oh my God!' She was pointing at something now, and I turned to see the three deep gouges in the green pleather bench, slits from end to end with the chunky foam stuffing, yellow like bad teeth, peeking out from within. The same stuffing under my fingernails.

I couldn't get past her, so I shoved her, quite hard. I was surprised to have done it, but also that I'd loved it. The thrill of violent contact was strangely delicious. She tottered on her heels. I ran.

Behind me, I heard the shouting. 'You know you haven't paid your fucking tab, right?!'

A tiny inner voice was screaming to turn around and pay the damn bill. I didn't want to. 'Turn around, get out your debit card. Say sorry. Hey, pay for everyone!' I was running out of corridor. A louder voice was laughing. *Go on. Pull that ponytail right off her head.*

More faces in round windows, peering out, eyes agog.

'We've got your address on file!'

I climbed the stairs to more tunnels. I could see an exit sign.

'Check your fucking cameras!' I yelled back over my shoulder, and something warm sizzled through me. I wanted to know what they would see when they did.

I ran to the door, the green box above it filling the corridor with a venomous light. Rushing forward, slamming into the release bar and opening the door, before falling into the night, exhilarated, slightly frightened, but free.

The night air shocked me back to myself. *Calm down, Simon.* I walked home, slowly. *Stop gnashing your teeth! People are staring. Calm down.* It took an hour but I needed to unwind. Once or twice I sang quietly, looking for the voice, the thing that had been inside me, but it was just me, mostly. I weaved my way through people laughing, fighting, prowling for the next pub. I followed the canal, a straight line; almost home.

My street. I passed the ambulance depot, where a sooty vehicle was parked with its back doors swinging open. Pale smoke puffed outwards from the cavity, followed by a low voice. I edged carefully along the side of the ambulance, front to back, until I could hear every word.

'So I had to crawl through the bastard dog door to get inside. Fucking glass everywhere. Mm. She was a squatter. I actually sort of knew her. I'd bought her a couple of teas . . . There was shit all up the walls. Found her on the third floor, staircase almost killed me, rotten as fuck . . . Um, she was like nineteen or twenty? Yeah I was doing overtime, as per fucking . . . Teenagers called it in, trying to have a party . . . The girl? Oh she was unrecognisable. Split into nine pieces. Both her hands in different corners. I've never seen so much blood! Like a Jackson Pollock in there . . . Fourth this month. Worse than the others. No, no way – not natural. No, I haven't slept. Yeah, I'm starting to think I wanna come home.'

Her voice was trembling hard, like she might cry. I looked around the edge of the door, and saw a girl in an oversized yellow hi-vis, phone to her ear, other hand holding a cigarette. She looked exhausted, hunched and unblinking, eyes rubbed red. Her hair was huge, piled messily in a bun on her head, and when she caught my eye, she squinted and jerked her head back in surprise, before giving me the finger with the cigarette hand. I put my head down and hurried on.

Behind me I heard the ambulance doors closing, ringing out like iron bells.

CHAPTER FIFTEEN

The next day I had a hangover like a drum, but no shift, and the flat to myself. I was slowly coming down from yesterday.

I had woken from a dream of Massimo turning inside out. Glimpes of his bleeding body in the shower crept through my head. That horrible grimace. The teeth. I rejected these thoughts, pushed them away as I lay in bed. Then, little flashes of the day before, my public misbehaviours. *No, thank you*. These were also dismissed. I allowed myself to write it all off.

I listened, for a moment, for any voices. I checked for a funky heartbeat. All seemed well.

Massimo was out. I ate a banana while I pissed with the bathroom door open. I farted into the sofa three times in a row and read a *Hello!* magazine. So bad! But nobody would ever know. I did all this and more, ate lemon curd from the jar and watched the spillage drip down my bare thigh.

I had always seized these moments of solitude when Josh was away, out for the night or the weekend. It could be hard sometimes, to be so good for so long, and alone I could melt into a version of myself that required no effort. It was a relief. But then, I always knew he was coming home.

I'd messaged Josh twice that morning, to see how he was. Asked for a photo of his new place. I was keen to see all his things in their new habitat, how he had styled it, the curtains he had chosen. No response yet.

I was determined to relax, release some of the unease chest-nesting inside me. I kitchen-danced for twenty minutes, finishing with an Irish jig of sorts. It helped a little.

I'd decided to give Massimo a chance, the poor boy. A clean slate. It wouldn't be the first time I'd misjudged someone. The things I'd heard, the things I'd seen in the past few days. Odd behaviour. Well, I can be dramatic. I can turn nothing into something.

Perhaps I should have legged it by now. But please, it's *my* home. And out there, it's a battlefield. People are paying thousands for a bed in a wet shoebox. I'd never find this square footage again. Besides, I'm made of harder stuff than that. There are things that frighten me more than a boy with a gammy eye and fucked-up tattoos. Or something playing with my body.

I'm not afraid of being hit by a bus and shamed by

skidmarks in my pants when the paramedics peel me off the street. Just don't check my search history. Please. I see the young mummy picking up my phone where it lies cracked on the pavement, scrolling through, eyes wide and eyebrows raised. Looking at my broken body and shaking her head. Giving me a hard kick for good measure. Holding out the screen to the gathering crowds. *Jesus Christ in all of heaven look at this. 'Charles Manson naked.'*

Filthy pervert. And the rest.

I can kill an entire afternoon online with a hangover like this, stalking the dark web. Quality time. There's nothing sweeter.

'What does a dead body smell like?'

'Worst crime scenes Germany. Worst crime scenes France.'

'Myra Hindley's Holiday.'

'How to survive a plane crash.'

'Worst crime scenes ever. Photos please.'

Terrifying 999 calls. Crime scene walkthroughs. 'Two Men One Hammer.' Then the finale, the best bit. The animal attacks.

'Man attacked by lion.'

'Man attacked by bear.'

'Brothers attacked by piranhas.'

'Woman's face eaten by chimp.'

'Woman v snake.'

But there's a balance for when I've truly reached depravity. There's an upswing. I'm not a monster.

'Soldier returns from war.'

'Pony's last day on earth.'

'Rescued kitten loves first fish.'

'Foster child given big green birthday cake.'

A whole day indulged on video clips, interviews, mean pranks. Recordings and videos and threads. And then on to porn, for another hour or so. Pornhub, Xtube. Only-Fans. I had subscribed to an account, just for a month. A straight man, totally buff with a perfect uncut penis. His whole library was bizarre; videos of him in a loose, over-sized T-shirt and no underwear, reaching up to get tins of beans from a kitchen cupboard, exposing his peach. I would select a video, then spend half an hour with it, like a leopard with a buck, dragging it into a tree and working until slick drips of gore fall to the leaves below.

This particular man also collaborated with other straight men. Gym bunnies with haircuts and huge tattoos who did everything but penetrate each other, or kiss. A lot of butt slapping and jerking off next to each other on white corner sofas. You could hear the skin of their backs peeling off the leather as they reached for lube, helped each other use a dildo. Gay for Pay, the absolute worst.

I couldn't get enough.

But today, nothing was working. I could not enjoy it. I had done my kitchen dancing, and dug into the deepest corners of First Responder Radio. I had scrolled through recent news reports of missing children, a knife fight in the north of the city, the usual burglaries. I checked my email. Spam, scam, spam, scam. A couple of alerts from the Neighbourhood Watch app: *Anyone know what happened in Mersey Way this afternoon? Busy busy! Fire engines police and ambulance. I saw them breaking into someone's home and there's been a horrible smell. Did someone die in their flat? So sad! I saw a severed head last week this city's not safe xoxo.*

I had finally chosen a sexy video, and I was lying on the couch half naked, restless and distracted; I kept looking away from the gang of shaved jocks on my computer screen and around the empty room, leaning back and staring down the corridor. Something was calling to me.

I put my shorts on, got up, and opened the fridge to drink some juice from the bottle. I eyed the collection of memorabilia stuck to the fridge. A letter from the council pinned beneath a black and white magnet of Whitney Houston in a feather boa. A Thank You note from Josh's sister. A drawing I loved by one of Josh's nephews, of a cat that looked like its mouth was full of blood. He had left these things here, when he moved, as if they meant more to me than to him.

Josh still hadn't messaged back. The ticks weren't turning blue; he must have changed his settings.

Dead in the centre of the fridge, pinned by a magnetic clip in the shape of a pterodactyl, was a photograph I had seen a thousand times. I took it from the door. Me and Josh, on a stony beach at the start of our friendship, the sky baby-blue behind us. A proper friends' day out, a truly amazing experience. Josh's idea, of course. We had eaten fish and chips and watched the men swimming. Bonding. Josh had got a number from a guy who cleaned the boats.

There I was, slightly hunched in a grey hoody, holding a bottle of white wine between my legs, trying to get it open. A splatter of dried Bolognese on my shoulder. I'm half-grinning, half-grimacing as Josh appears to be trying to vault over me. Both so happy. My eyes are staring at something in the distance. His hands are gripping my shoulders, legs spread out into the air, his mouth open in a screech that I could hear now if I closed my eyes. I remembered that feeling, the disbelief at such intimacy. Me and my best friend, paddling in the ocean. I put the photo back, snapping the pterodactyl into place. It looked like it was hooking its clawed feet into Josh's shoulders and carrying him away. Leaving me there alone on the shore. I removed the photo again and put it into a drawer on the way out of the room.

Massimo's door was open, just a crack. In one way, it felt sweetly familiar to hover here, memories of waiting for Josh to be dressed and ready for the night, to call me in and say *Simon, my babe, it's time for a drink*. Excited to be invited. But it also felt wrong, because with Josh, I always knew the rules of our cohabitation, and now I did not.

I nudged the door with a toe, and peered at the darkness beyond. The blinds were closed, and thicker than mine. I could hear the traffic from where I stood, louder than I should be able to. He must have left his window open.

I had still not been inside the room since Massimo had moved in, though I'd often thought about it. I'd caught glimpses of bed through the crack, but little else. The memory of what I'd seen in the shower came back fast and strong now. Worse than anything on the internet. Blood and bone, that jagged slit in his skin, opening up. I had tried to ignore it, but it was impossible. I had an itch that needed to be scratched. I opened the door further.

What would I find in there? I reached in through the gap and turned on the light. No movement, no scurry of bugs. I pushed the door wide open.

This room was twice the size of mine, and had one extra window along the back wall that looked onto the alleyway beside the building. That had been the deal with Josh; I got the street view and the chorus of traffic noise, he got the space. But now the room was changed, and I did not recognise it. I am a clean freak, Josh is a pig. It's what I was used to. For some reason I had imagined, or hoped, that Massimo would have strewn his belongings everywhere, blowing his case wide open and rolling in the detritus.

The room I found was not a pit, it was quite nice. Not as tidy as I had made it, but not revolting. The made bed, the paperback books stacked with their curled yellow edges. A few stray socks and cups, but not much more. Usually the wardrobe burped its Joshy innards halfway across the room, but now it was closed. I put a foot over the threshold. The room still *smelled* different, though. That unique scent, earthy and sweet, like the smell of saliva on skin, dried then sniffed. Massimo. I would not say that smell was bad.

What was this feeling, forming in the bowl of my stomach? Not the ice pick, a hard stone, like the pit of a peach.

I placed another bare foot into the room. Now, I could hear the tyres on the road outside, wet from the recent rainfall, some of which still clung to the windows on the outer panes. I looked to the bed where one of Massimo's T-shirts was folded under the pillow, the blue corner peeking out. The water glass sealed with a kiss of lip balm on the rim. Another breeze blew through the open window, the chain tapped again.

I crossed the room and fingered the blinds, looking through the window at the sun-filled alleyway beyond. The same white Toyota rusting in its bay, the same skip piled with debris; dishwashers, traffic cones, a large, curious stain on a pile of breeze-blocks, dried to the colour of Pepsi.

I looked at the building opposite for any movement, but found none. A huge, pebble-dashed structure studded with frosted windows, as if every room was a bathroom. Sometimes, I'd seen shapes moving through the milk. Pinky-white blobs emerging then disappearing. We had laughed once or twice, me and Josh, sure we had seen a blowjob occurring, someone shaving their pubes. Today, the surface of the building was calm. Nothing looked back at me.

I turned to the room behind me, sensing something. A creeping. I followed it. *Let's find out what we're working with.*

Against the far wall was Massimo's stack of luggage. God he was neat, his belongings lined up like that. The cases seemed slightly expensive. I'd seen them before, helped him put them in here. I don't know why I expected a hessian sack perhaps, a rusted trunk covered in chains and border control stickers; it was just two small rucksacks and a wheeled suitcase, slightly scuffed with use. Not locked.

A severed foot, a sawn-off head, a nail bomb. There could be anything in those bags. If I unbuckled the yellow rucksack, and lifted the flap, would a long black snake slither out, eyes like gemstones? Would it coil up my leg, around my arm, and begin wetly tonguing my ear, whispering Massimo's secrets? Telling me everything I needed to know. Outside, a car sped past, a song I knew blaring. The shuffling of wings on the roof. That horrible flute.

I slid the suitcase out from under the rucksacks, which thudded softly to the floor. I unzipped the case and it smiled open, both sides now equally flat. On one side, a netted compartment was zipped shut. I unzipped it.

The hairs on my arms rose, and I turned around to check the doorway, and the empty space of the room, before returning to my work. I peeled the netting away. Two pairs of jeans, and a pair of trainers. Nothing in the pockets, or tucked inside the shoes, where Massimo's feet usually lived. On the other side, a stack of comics, and a plain-sheeted sketchbook. I flicked through it, and found some beautiful doodles. Beaches, fruit, olive trees, winding highways. Nothing too strange. I was both disappointed and relieved.

I put everything back, meticulously, and zipped up the case. Next, I opened a rucksack, lifting the flap and rummaging inside, cautiously at first like I might get pricked with something, but then a little more thoroughly. Pairs of shorts, another sweatshirt, purple lighters clicking together in the bottom. A debit card, and an ID from a graphic design agency, Massimo grinning in the corner. An old packet of tobacco in the front pocket, some keys and an empty notebook. Three condoms.

I fingered these, feeling them slide around in their own slime inside the thin plastic. I thought about Massimo putting one on his dick. I thought about putting one on mine. That peach pit rolled in my stomach, the sharp end of it grating against my insides, scratching the lining. I picked up the second rucksack. This one was a bit smaller but the same design – flap and buckle. Inside I felt several small bundles. Socks. Nothing tucked inside them, not even drugs. Six neatly rolled pairs – white and sporty, the kind that reach the calf.

In a pocket I found polaroids. It was difficult to work out exactly what I was looking at. Three pictures the same; it looked like a row of fuzzy blocks in a semicircle, and I turned the photo around and around. Teeth. This was a photograph of teeth, very close up, almost like an X-ray from the dentist, but in a greenish hue that made me feel sick. Perplexed, I picked up another beneath it, which was just as bizarre, almost like the buds on a tongue covered in a film of spit. I leafed through the pile of squares that slid like fish in a bucket against each other. Each stranger than the next. A bulging green eyeball, a bleeding fingernail, the small humps of a spine. In one, a patch of mushrooms, in another a line of knobbled tree trunks. They made me think of dry scabs, ready to be picked.

I felt like I might be getting close to something. Did I know what it would look like when I found it, when I pressed my itching finger upon it?

Two more plain T-shirts in the bag. Soft to the touch, worn and comfortable, washed dozens of times. I lifted a white V-neck to my nose, inhaled. So clean, almost minty, delicious fresh boy. I breathed in again. Tried another T-shirt. An odd bass note that I couldn't put my finger on, but didn't hate.

He could come home at any moment.

I reached in and found his underwear. Ten pairs, folded, all white briefs. I saw Massimo clear as a road, putting them on after a shower, his skin still slightly damp. Or taking them off after a workout. Something stirred in my shorts.

Then, I'm sure something spoke. I'm sure the blind lifted, and a voice was in the room. *'You again.'* But nothing stood over my shoulder, so I ran my fingers around the waistband of his briefs, and then, like the T-shirt before, I lifted them to my nose. Deep breath in. That same scent, clean and delicious. Green apples with an earthy twang of Massimo. A touch of rot, a deeper breath.

Now my shorts were tenting, and I didn't even think about it, I just took it out with my free hand and started working. Each in-breath pulled that smell down into my body, up into my head. The thoughts came next, images of a shoulder rolling, hot beads of sweat sizzling on the wood floor, the veins of an arm joining the lines of muscle as it stretches to retrieve a fork dropped beneath the sofa. Those ragged nails being bitten down by long teeth.

I heard myself panting a little, kept working at the job in hand, kept breathing. More images, a wet tongue catching a drop of milk at the corner of a mouth. Massimo growling in the bathroom. Lips closing then parting to reveal the tiny chip on the corner of a sharp incisor. Skin splitting, that sticky shining blackness inside. Water running from the showerhead, deep into his insides. His twisted face.

The feeling got better, no longer a peach stone but the whole peach, growing rounder and fatter around its pip, juicier. The fuzz on the bubble, soft beneath a thumb, tiny fronds bending to the touch. I reached up for a moment to slide a hand beneath my T-shirt, brush my nipple, then went back to my shorts, which were now stretched lower, taught around my thighs.

I was almost there now, I was letting go of something heavy. One more deep breath in and I was on the edge. One more vision of Massimo, teeth impossibly sharp, his gnarled finger sliding inside flesh. A new image forming in my mind too, coming to the surface as I reached the humming finish line. As the peach split open, released its stone, I saw a flat bed of rock, cracking down the middle and splitting wider. Something huge coming out of the hole, thick brown stone splintering and an indescribable feeling of dread as an eye appeared, like a reptile but huge, looking at me, and the putrid stink of wet earth everywhere as stones are falling, skin is unzipped, a terrible leg steps through a crack toward me.

I gasped as the explosion hit me. I rocked there, for a sweet second, then opened my eyes and looked down at the mess I had made. Taking my T-shirt off as I caught my breath, I wiped fast at the puddle, then threw the filthy rag into the corridor. I put it all back. Not a bag out of place, not a line changed. Zips hanging like tiny gallows. I watched them swinging.

I closed the window, then opened it again. Lowered the blinds. I went to the kitchen, took the wipes and the surface cleaner and came back, scrubbed the floor, wiped it over and over until my fingers squeaked.

It was then that I noticed something, a faint crack in the wood that I was sure hadn't been there before; the length of my forearm, but fine. A fracture in the pine, running towards another twisted shape, a knothole that could have been a peering eye. One more, inches from it, half closed. Winky. A jagged little gap with splinters sharp as teeth. A wicked little face, if you looked at the right angle. I moved the rug over it, just a couple of inches to the left.

I stood quietly in his room, clutching the floor polish, while two thrilling thoughts danced in my head, holding hands of cracked leather and spinning in a circle.

One, the image of Massimo, creeping through the city,

out there somewhere right now with his green eyes flashing in headlights. Climbing rooftops flat and vaulted, for better vantage. Watching me right now from the fire station.

Two, that very real image of the rock splitting open, deep in forested mountains. The movement beneath. A shape emerging. A pair of horns. That churning, hissing sound that could so easily be my name.

The idea that something is coming.

The idea that something has come.

CHAPTER SIXTEEN

I learnt things about people. From a young age. I was not popular at school, though not bullied.

A chameleon. I observed the boys, and the girls. Oh, those boys. The funny ones, the smart ones, all in between. Their mannerisms, their style, the humour they enjoyed. Biceps and abs I could only dream of growing. I was a lingerer; I got good at switching roles, trying to find the right one. Catch me with the sports boys and I'm making jokes about a fat kid to get a laugh. With the girls who love to read, I'm reading too. I'm helping the girl who smells strange, discussing fantasy films she's seen for her homework. Sometimes, I'm recognised in the corridors, a glancing high five. But I never get invited to parties. I play alone instead. Once or twice I tried. I went jogging with the quiet boy, he wants to show me a baby frog. He's calm and friendly. When I whispered one of my innermost thoughts he faked a phone call from his mum, turned the other way, told me he'd see me later. I did not see him later. I went up to the forest instead.

I reassessed. I put those dark parts of myself in a box and squished them down with a mud-brown Converse. I circled hallways and playing fields. I ate a sandwich I made for myself at home, some salami and a strawberry. I found the art teacher who was going through a divorce and we had the best chat in weeks. Her words not mine.

I learnt to never get too deep, I never stayed too long. When that sixth-form bell rang for the last time, I was remembered as kind, polite, playful but never a trouble-maker. *That boy, that loner, you know, what was his name . . .?*

The world got bigger and my frame of reference grew with it, but only slightly. I took a gap year, and got a job in the nearby town selling clothes I didn't like. I sold *a lot* of ugly jeans. Manners will get you everywhere, it seems. I'd see some of the people I went to school with and they'd smile and wave, try to place me. I'd wave back, alive and kicking, but dead behind the eyes if they looked close enough. They did not; they had boyfriends and girlfriends, they had tattoos, they'd put on vodka weight. I'd burn hot, but wouldn't blush. I kept the lid on the box.

I didn't go to the pub with the team, they forgot to invite me to the office party. Despite the denim sales.

When I did go to university, in a suburban campus establishment that accepted my perfectly good grades, it could have been a new start, but I floated. I felt bad, at first, for leaving my parents to fend for themselves. But they didn't seem to mind. I ate bagged popcorn in my room with the curtains closed. I turned in my essays, perfectly on time of course. I went to the gym and ran for an hour beside the hunks, stole glances, slivers of cake then bigger slices, whole chunks until I'm simply staring. I had a favourite, he noticed me. He stopped his machine, came over.

'Are you OK? Do you need me to get the nurse?'

I stopped going to the gym. I drank too much at the club. Not used to it, I threw up in someone else's saucepan. Kept it hidden under my bed. I watched box-sets of comedies and horror movies with the girl in my hall who smoked too much weed. She told me about her Alsatian at home and her mean sister. I told her a made-up story about my family, where I'm from, what I like to do. I kept it up for three years. It's not like I'll ever see her again.

I completed all my coursework. I was so good. I got so *bored*. I gatecrashed a party and sat carefully in the corner, helping to choose the perfect tracks to keep the vibe bumping. The room heaved; nobody ever saw me dance. In a stranger's dorm room, I fucked a guy who was visiting his brother and stole a sweatshirt that matches my eyes. Cracked the lid on the box.

I created a glory hole in the back of the sports hall and filmed the guys that went looking for it. I released a rumour about one of the male cheerleaders, who *might* have been arrested for GBH. On a child. I stole a mean professor's car and burnt it on an airstrip, forty miles away. I was almost caught, chased by a security guard through fields and underpasses. I got away, felt bad, cringed beneath the covers for days. But I promised myself I was just trying to find myself. That's what university is *for*.

I attended graduation. I won a prize, top results in my year. I grinned on the stage when I knew I was meant to grin, I cried on cue. I did so good, and that feels great.

I decide not to return home, to leave my parents be. They do not challenge me. So, I'm burped out, into the city; I head straight from campus on an overnight, overground train into the belly of this enormous concrete beast. *Open the box, go on, try*, I tell myself, and I do. I crack it open, slightly, and let things breathe. They stir like babies waking too early in the morning. I smile down at these horrible little parts of me and take them out on short trips, just to see how they get on.

So many men in the city! I have sex with some of them. They are very attractive. It's fun. I'm not a virgin. I get sperm in my eye and think I might go blind. I don't, it just turns red and leaks for a day. Sometimes the sex tries to lead to more. One sweet man invites me to Spain to meet his family at Christmas. He wants to look inside the box. I delete his number, hide from him behind a pillar at the train station.

The city grows bigger by the day and I have nobody to talk to. Two girls from a temp job invite me to a rave and I go along, but they watch my dancing with narrowed eyes so I disappear, spend the night hiding from them under a trestle table. They don't talk to me again, but I hear them talking about me at the printer.

I check my hair, my teeth, my eyes. Grimace and do it again. I slap my skin quietly and pinch trimmings of fat. I punch a mirror repeatedly once and my knuckle splits and scars. If anyone's asking, it was a wasp.

I put the lid back on tight, and the things howl. I think maybe I'm twelve feet tall down there, in the box. Folded up like a lawn chair gathering rust. When I flex my fingers and toes, crack a vertebra, I hear it pop like bullets into the summer air, the winter chill.

I become so good. Then, even better. I choose music, cheap white wine, porn. I read books, get jobs, get a flat. I meet Josh. We're best friends. He takes care of me. I take care of him back. It's all good. It's all *great*.

I survive.

CHAPTER SEVENTEEN

I was starting to panic.

Massimo had not been home for almost a week, and he'd taken his car. At first, I had grown restless. The idea of him never returning filled me with a surprising sense of dread which I suspected was more than financial. I should be pleased, I told myself, to have the space, but somehow waiting for his return was worse than his presence. I looked inside his room, underneath his bed. I found myself waiting by the door, opening and closing it, as if he would appear. There I was, pacing the hallway one early morning, checking my phone. I was considering calling him.

Instead I made myself put on new black shorts, white socks, bright-green trainers. My nicest long-sleeved T-shirt. I was stretching my calves when the buzzer rang by the door, startling me.

Who the fuck is that?

'Hellooo?' I asked nicely, almost cooing.

'Hi, can you come down?' A woman's voice.

'Who is it, please?'

'Quickly, it's important.'

You can't tell me what to do.

'I'll be right there!'

I descended the stairs and double-checked I had my keys. I opened the entrance door to a flash of bright yellow and sporty sunglasses.

It was the paramedic who had flipped me the finger from the ambulance a few nights before. She stood and waited for the door to fully open before she spoke.

'Hi, is that your car?' She pointed at a vehicle down the street and kicked a boot against the doorstep.

Massimo's car? A tiny bright glimmer in my gut. *He's home.*

I stared at the car. It was large, gold and rusting. Not his.

'No.'

'It's in an ambulance bay and that's fucked up. It needs moving.'

I knew I should offer to move it for her, somehow. She was staring at my face, and then peering behind me, and up the stairs. Then back at my face.

'Do you live here?' she said.

'Yes.' I shuffled on the thick spread of post beneath my trainers.

'Who with?' Her eyes kept flickering from my face to the space behind me.

'My . . . flatmate.'

She breathed in deep through her nose. That big hair was up in a bun and she reached up to pull it tight. I saw my face in her sunglasses, wide-eyed. She took a step forward and I took a step back.

'Can I come in and have a look around?'

Absolutely not, you nosy bitch.

'Can I ask why?' I said.

She removed her sunglasses and squinted into the gloom of the atrium.

'I'm thirsty. Cup of tea?' Her eyes peered deep into mine.

I squirmed in place, tried to think of a reply to this bizarre suggestion.

'You good?' she asked, and I nodded.

'You can't come in, I'm not supposed to talk to strangers.' I laughed at my own joke. 'Not really. No, I'm running late. I'm so sorry.' I was garbling. I flashed my chops to show I wasn't crazy.

She raised an eyebrow and watched my jittery body, summing me up, before sighing and stepping back.

'OK, well, thanks.' She put a hand up and moved away, crossing the road. She turned one final time to stare at me, and then up at the windows of the flat. So strange. I did not like her vibe at all. She stood outside a shop and lit a cigarette. I lingered for a moment, unsure if she was going to try and break into my flat. I watched her giving a homeless man a coin before I started to run.

I parted the mists settling along the canals with my sweaty body. My feet rang out loud and persistent under the brown brick tunnels. Right there I made a decision. When Massimo finally came home, everything would change. I'd had enough. Of the selfishness, the uncertainty, the endless anticipation, the way it made me behave. Not knowing whether he would be clanging the steel doors at 3 a.m., climbing the stairs. Or through my window. Mass-i-mo. Mass-i-mo. Mass-i-mo. I heard it on my breath as it turned ragged, and I used this wild energy. The moment he came home, we'd have it out, begin to pave our way to friendship. No more of this rotten nausea, no more creeping about!

Look here, mate, young man, Mass. I know you're a bit . . . out of sorts. But that's OK. We're gonna live together, in my gorgeous flat, and we're gonna be friends. Maybe even best friends. Or you're out. So you're gonna chill the fuck out and stop doing . . . whatever . . . you're . . . doing . . . to . . . me.

He would smile and nod, and make us a delicious hot meal before suggesting we go to a bar. Or perhaps he would be surly, a bit scary, in which case I'd bring out some charm sharp as lightning. Or I might have to get a bit rude. It could go that far. I imagined myself holding Massimo down with strong arms, telling him to get a grip. My mouth close to his, wide open, pulling at his protruding tongue with my teeth, pulling it out ribbon-like, yards and yards of it coming wetly from his throat, his innards, all the way out, something on the end of it.

I shook my head like a fly-fussed bullock. I had made my decision and now I was excited, eager to finish the loop and get home. Surely he would have returned by now. I picked up speed. A stream of runners headed towards me, one after the other. I ducked back as they thudded by. All twelve of them. 'No, no, it's fine, girls, take your time, take your time.' I wanted to push each one into the hazardous waters, but instead I took a sort of elegant bow and stepped right back against the wetness of the walls until finally they cleared and I could run onward, into a tunnel. *I swear to God if one more fucker gets in my way . . .*

I picked up speed. The tunnel never seemed to end and I relished the darkness, how cold and quiet. A bell rang out, I skidded fast to dodge a speeding cyclist. *No fucking light on.* Squeezed my fists, nodded at nobody, kept running through the dark. *That's it now, just run and run and the way is clear, it's all clear for running home.*

When I got there, it was to find that Massimo was back, and he'd changed the locks.

My key seemed to hit something soft before sliding all the way. Like it had pierced a membrane. And then it stuck and would not turn. I took a breath, tried to withdraw it, but it was caught firm. I wiped my brow, and tried again. It kept catching on something and I couldn't get it out.

I had been evicted.

'Massimo. *Massimo!*' I called, my whole body trembling, sounding more urgent and secretarial than I would have ever liked to sound. I heard movement in my flat, behind the closed door.

I pounded on the door in pure panic. I slammed on the metal and called out his name. I put a foot on the steel of the door and pulled at the key, almost losing my balance. My eyes began to burn, hot tears rinsing my eyeballs red. I was going to cry. Or vomit.

'Massimo. Have you . . . have you changed the locks? Have you changed the fucking locks?!' I couldn't breathe. I pulled harder, grabbed with two hands and felt my fingers sliding on the slippery key-head.

'Massimo. Open this fucking door, Massimo, I swear to God and Jesus let me in this flat before I cut your fucking *dick off*! Massimo!' Now I really was losing my shit. I was screaming, not thinking of neighbours or niceties or being a good boy. Just getting inside my flat and getting my hands on him and punching his face to pulp until my knuckles met the concrete.

I let fly on that door, screaming out days of frustration, nights of unease. I said bad things, the worst I could think of. I could hold them in no longer. I banged and banged; I would beat on that door until my fists bled.

The door opened. I stumbled back, hitting the steel

railing that barely stopped me from tumbling down the concrete stairs and splitting my head open like a cocktail lime. Massimo was frowning out at me through the doorway. I lay panting on the ground, and he studied me curiously before turning to the open door.

He looked at the key in the lock, and slid it out. 'It's janky, Simone. You have to jimmy.' He smiled. The way he said it, like *jeeemy* – it was quite charming. And he looked friendly, like he meant it. Maybe he did.

'Are you OK?' he asked.

The burning embarrassment of me huddled on the floor, stressed and shaking, looking up at him. It was unbearable. I released it. The venom left me, trickled down the stairs.

'I'm fine.' I smiled to prove it, got to my knees in front of him, tried to look normal. 'I'm really fine.' He reached out a hand to pull me up and I took it, his grip furiously tight. I noticed now that he was wearing one of the white T-shirts I had unfolded from his suitcase, damp moons under his arms. I could smell the sweat and laundry powder, and the triangle of bare chest beneath his throat glinted softly, like a spearhead pointing down. I realised I was actually happy to see him.

I put the key in my pocket, stepped fast into the flat towards him so he had to step away. I closed the door behind me.

'What are you doing tomorrow, Massimo?' I asked, and he shone like glass.

CHAPTER EIGHTEEN

Massimo went out that night and did not return. Me, I slept like the dead.

I woke to embrace the morning with open arms. It was a special day.

Halloween, my favourite.

I was busy all that morning rifling through Goblin's cupboard. I found boots, a jacket, a huge thermos that I filled with coffee. I had washed six Tupperwares and put them in a bag as I waited for Massimo to come home.

When he walked into the flat at 8 a.m., I was sitting at the kitchen table. I felt a faint flicker in my left eye, and rubbed it. He looked gaunt, dark circles under his eyes. I didn't bother to ask him where he had been; nothing he said would match my violent fantasies.

'*Ciao*. Simone.' He took off his wool hat, and I watched the tips of his ears blush pink. He rubbed the fibres of the beanie with his filthy fingertips. I saw the brownish stains on his jeans. The glassiness of his eyes, like he was trying to recall something. The funky smell. He gave me a dirty look, just for a second, as if his exhaustion was my fault. And then he turned and drank water from the tap.

I ignored all of these things.

'Massimo. Good morning. Are you ready for your surprise?'

He cocked his head, nodded. I cleared my throat.

'Please take me picking.'

He lifted his head to its original position. 'Picking?'

'Mushrooms.'

His eyes lit up with the wham of floodlights. I thought he was about to crow, or kick his heels.

'I thought you'd never ask.'

He rolled his shoulders, and put his hat back on his head. I stood up and put on Josh's old wax jacket, enjoyed its oily smell, found one of his hairs clinging to the collar. What we needed was a good day out; I had everything I needed. I checked my pockets. Left pocket, phone and wallet.

In my right, my shiny little box cutter, hanging off my keys. Biting at my finger.

I was folded into Massimo's car, which smelled a bit skanky, like cannabis and old banana. I'd watched him close the door and creep around the bonnet, his hands in his leather jacket pockets, looking for something. He was, as always, furtive, on the prowl. He got into the driver's seat and turned to look me in the eye.

'Wear this, please.' He had something in his hands.

I looked down at a silky green eye mask I'd never seen before.

'Is that a joke?'

'It's not a joke.' He looked gravely serious. 'It's important. I told you. Where I pick my mushrooms, it's private.'

I faltered.

'Please,' he said.

I looked into Massimo's eyes, at that wicked earnestness, and beneath it a boyish pleading. Two boys, flickering over one face. I let him put the mask over my eyes, and it slid over my skin like melted butter. The gentle ritualism of the act stirred something in my belly.

The car thrummed beneath us as Massimo put the roof and windows down. We drove in silence, I swear the city made not a peep. I heard only my breath, felt only the wind in my hair, licking its way along my jawline, but little else. I reached a hand out. Like a stream the air flowed through my fingertips. I dipped each finger into it.

There is something about a car that's even more intimate than a bedroom, and I enjoyed being in his personal space. I imagined him next to me, his hands hovering close to my face like small ghosts, but I knew surely they were on the wheel, getting us to where we were going.

The sun was shining, I felt it warming my hair, tilted my covered eyes towards it. Instead of asking for the radio, I listened to the tickle in my brain and bones that seemed to be slowly growing in volume. I felt bile rising in my chest, but it passed. Once or twice, I sensed the electricity of something brushing my leg. I leaned into the cracked leather of the seat and enjoyed the ride. Relaxed. I closed my eyes and let my mind wander to dark, soft places, breathing in sync with the purr of the engine. Slipping into warmth and drifting there . . .

I woke up from a deep sleep I didn't realise I'd entered, panicking for a moment in the darkness until I remembered where I was. The car had stopped. I waited for Massimo's voice, instructing me to remove my blindfold. Instead, I felt the band rub past my ears and saw the morning sunshine. There was Massimo, grinning at me, fixing my hair, backlit by white light.

'We're here.'

Trees around us: birch, fir, elder, they watched us unfold ourselves from the car. Where I had taken in concrete and used condoms before, now everything was green, golden, wet and dripping. I stretched, rubbed my temples where the elastic had pinched, winced at the bright spears of sun thrown down through the canopy above.

We had parked on a gravel track alongside a long brick wall. I noticed a withered sign, buckling under ivy.

'Massimo, this is ten minutes from home.' I laughed uncertainly as he collected items from the boot. I did not tell him this was a popular dogging spot, in case it ruined the moment.

He nodded, serious.

'But we drove for ages!'

'I let you sleep. Come,' said Massimo. He was slinking away, smiling at the mud beneath his boots. My feet were pulled down by the unfamiliar weight of my footwear, sinking into the dirt as I followed him.

Such impossible silence here, nothing but the worms turning in their tunnels, a bird making sweet peeps somewhere like little sips of wine. *Peep-peep. Peep-peep.* I watched Massimo, his jacketed back straight. Jerking his head, gesturing for me to keep up. I thought we were headed for the wooden stile up ahead, but suddenly Massimo turned right and disappeared into the bushes. I parted leaves with my skinny fingers, looking for him, staying close behind. He was pointing. Up ahead, a huge wall of graffitied stone. A large hole like a mouth, crossed with iron bars, foliage hanging in thick fronds. A tunnel.

One bar was missing, and he went through it. I followed, stepping into thick brown water, sloppy mud, damp stink all around us. Light snatched away. The sound of our footsteps went out and returned to us, bouncing off the wet walls. My chest tightening with unease, feet stepping gently through the muddy ooze. Massimo pressed on, needing no torch. If I'd heard him stop suddenly, I would have cried out, but he was moving closer to a circle of light up ahead and so was I, until suddenly I let go of the breath I'd held and emerged through a bright hole into deep green woods.

Massimo was smiling at me, almost juddering in the vegetation. Then he was off again, up a slope thickly carpeted with orange leaves. Here and there a rusty red Coke can, thin blue pages from a slimy magazine. He was quicker than me, a net bag strung over his shoulder, and I had to hurry to keep up. I watched him pause for a moment as he bent down to pick up a long, thick stick which he snapped with serious ease over his bent leg. He pushed on with his new striding cane, and I hurried to stay close.

I breathed in the gravy. Saturated earth beneath my feet, the must of mulch and rotting leaves, the air fresh and sweet. The familiar, oaky smells of Massimo that filled my mouth with sticky spit. There he was loping up ahead, turning to check on me once or twice. The jut of his chin. His eyes like brand-new acorns. He seemed different here, a little taller, a little more muscular perhaps. His hair glinting before my eyes in the clean sunlight. His feet on the ground were certain in their stride, no need to check where he was going. He knew the way.

These woods almost felt like a dirty secret, a furred mole on the skin of the city. I was sure if I climbed the right hill, I'd see our house from here. Thin mist still hung in the air, breaking in a steady swirl as we pushed through it, leaving patches of moss on the trees spongy and swollen. I saw the forest in golden summer sun, branches bursting with greenery, blueberries underfoot, and saw the dead of winter too, when all seems a breath away from death, but really it's waiting, it's just waiting. Such peace here; only the gentlest siren-scream reached our ears. The last wisp of my unease curled away. I was *excited*.

'This is amazing!' I called to Massimo, but he didn't reply. Instead, he was crouching suddenly in the bushes.

It took me by surprise, and I slowed down, almost called out, to ask what he was doing. He tilted his head to look at me with that secret look in his eye, a strange smile on his lips. He had a slightly crooked tooth, at the front, and sometimes the hood of his lip caught on it, before concealing the enamel. He was looking at something.

I inhaled, fast, when I saw it.

'Shit. Dead fox,' I said.

It was lying at a strange sort of angle, like it had laid down comfortably to sleep among the leaves before slumping its shoulders to one side, its beautiful rusty head and ears turned up towards us. It was massive and glossy, like it had enjoyed a healthy diet of alley cats and fresh kebabs before it died. Blood on its snout. One black ear scarred, chunks torn from it. One large round eye staring up, slick with resin, as if the fox had only seconds ago blinked its last blink.

'It's huge,' I said. 'Beautiful.'

'Yes,' Massimo said. 'A really big one.'

'Should we eat it?'

He didn't reply. I was only trying to make him laugh.

One eye, sultana bright, was angled straight back up at him. I heard him exhale as he leant down towards the animal's body. He leaned closer, and tilted his head, his left eye now trained on the beast's eye – a connection of two satellites flashing back at each other, only one was full of life, blinking lights, and the other was cold and flat.

Until it glimmered.

I saw a twitch of fox leg; it was moving. The silence gathered itself around us like sheets. The forest watched the scene. Me staring at Massimo. Massimo staring down at the fox. Then he reached forward and touched one downy ear, ran his finger along the scarred velvet crease.

The fox exploded away; I grasped on to a tree as it hurtled from its position and crashed through the fallen leaves. A bushy burst of white disappearing into bracken.

'Fucking hell,' I whispered.

'Not dead,' Massimo said. 'He was waiting.'

'Waiting for what?'

He shrugged. 'For me.'

CHAPTER NINETEEN

Massimo was howling. He had found what he was looking for.

He'd stopped in a small clearing, where the moss was fat on the ground. He stilled me with a warm hand to my arm. 'This a good place to start,' he said, and put his bag down. 'You've never done this before, right, Simone?'

'I know my way around the woods,' I replied, shrugging.

'You know these ones?' he said, pointing to something at the base of a huge tree. A pair of brown mushrooms, their skin mottled like the breast of a thrush. I shook my head.

'It's called the prince. Quite common. But can look similar to a young death cap, which is very poisonous. So be careful.' He whispered so closely it raised the hairs on the back of my neck. I could feel his breath on me again, and something hot filled the chunky channels of my spine.

Massimo began crouching down, retrieving something from his sock. Something yellow, slim and clicking; as I watched he pressed a button and unsheathed a triangular tooth in one clean motion. With his bare fingers, he snapped off the blade, and fresh steel was born beneath. Was that . . . ?

My box cutter. I felt for it in my pocket, on my keys. It was gone. Amongst it all, the fresh air, the adventure, sunlight glinting on dew, I had fucked up. I had forgotten to be vigilant.

'Where did you get that?' I demanded, breaking the silence that still hung thick around us.

I could feel my breath catching in my lungs; they held the air tight, in case I might need it. He smiled, then turned to the larger of the two mushrooms, and sliced neatly through the stem.

'I found it on the ground, back there,' he pointed. 'So *cool*. Better than mine. Very sharp!' he said, and slid another knife from his pocket, small and hooked like a tiny bird.

'This one is very blunt.' He pulled a sad face that I did not believe.

A thick fear came creeping toward me, over the carpet of leaves. I was frozen, speechless. Would I be murdered by my own knife? I had often wondered if the box cutter was sharp enough to kill. I was about to find out.

'You want to use mine?' he asked, offering his knife. Looking directly at me. I wanted to snatch my knife back, but I could not overpower him; he was definitely much stronger than me. I had seen his muscles. I held very still, and waited to see if he would strike.

He did not. I took his small knife, carefully, and kept my eyes locked on his.

We stood there, holding our knives towards each other. Both in boots, jackets and scarves, hair blown about like surf, wicked daggers sticking out, glinting in the sun. A duel. The oddest little knights you ever saw. His eyes narrowed.

'It's very quiet here today. Nobody would hear you screaming,' he said, his voice low. He started to smile.

As the wind blew around us, I began to panic.

I'd invited Massimo here to bring us closer together, well aware that I could not trust him. Aware that there was something undeniably horrifying about him; I'd seen it with my own eyes. Wanting to see more, I had put myself right in its path. Well, curiosity killed the cat, so they say. My time was up. He would have the flat all to himself now. He could do whatever he wanted, uninterrupted. With his time. With the space. With my corpse. With my things.

He took a step toward me and I faltered back, hardly breathing. His eyes roamed my body, looking for the best place to stab first. I summoned courage. I might as well ask him outright before I died.

'OK, Massimo. What's your deal then?' I stammered, knife protruding. 'What have you been doing?' Louder now, blunt knife in my grip, trying not to let it shake. He looked at it and grinned.

'Eat, sometimes sleep, watch TV. Fuck.' He arched an eyebrow, stepped forward even further.

I stepped back again. 'No, there's something else,' I said. 'Weird stuff.'

'You don't like me living with you?' He looked hurt.

'You want me to move out?' he asked, and I swear his eyes filled. It looked genuine.

I didn't expect this, it stung me, cut through the fear. I shook my head fast, surprising myself. I looked at the box cutter glinting in his hand.

'No. I didn't say that. I just—'

I don't want to die.

'Don't you want to be friends?' he asked, and put one hand on his stomach, like that's where friends lived. '*I* do.'

I made an odd squeaking sound. Had I heard him properly? Friends. Warmth spread all over, like I'd pissed myself. *Friends.* I ran my finger round the rim of the word. Heard it squeal out.

'Oh. Well, yes. I do want to be friends. Please,' I said finally, tentatively, and felt the blush on my throat. That is what I wanted. If he meant it.

'*Bene*,' he said, and blinked hard. He lowered the box cutter. 'We are friends.'

I had been disarmed.

'I just wanted to know what might be happening, back at the flat. To me. I just wanted a couple of answers.' I said these last words quietly, but he wasn't listening now anyway. He was doing something down on the ground instead, talking up at me, grinning. His face was so open, so excited, the panic melted away.

'You want to taste?'

He sliced off a triangle of mushroom. For a moment, I thought he was going to put it in my mouth, but he just held it there, so I took it and chewed it up, cheesy and sweet.

'It's good,' I said. I wanted more.

'Yes, very good.'

He held the net bag out to me, and I took it from him in agreement. He would slice, I would hold the bag. I let him keep the cutter.

We found ourselves. Massimo silent in concentration, focused on the task in hand. Me hunting, finding more mushrooms. One, two, three, four, five. Clumped on trees, peeking through leaves, shimmering up from the wet of log-wood. White, yellow, sausage-brown, huddled together or standing brightly alone as if spotlit.

I realised I was enjoying his company. I was having a lovely day. I watched him stalk among the leaves, eyes bright. I watched him scuttle, his filthy fingers rummaging in tree-holes, and I followed suit. The smell was intoxicating, rich and dank, and I was soothed. I was drooling, actually, and I wiped it away, before it spattered down my coat.

The bag grew heavier with milky globes, brown, fleshy pads, chalky stalks. He was an expert.

'Got a favourite?' I asked him.

He paused in thought, his tongue came out. 'Destroying angel.'

'Can you eat it?'

'Yes.' He smiled at me. 'But you will die.'

I laughed, but he became very serious.

'And, Simone. I don't want you to die.' He smiled a huge smile for me.

He was funny. His eyes shining like beetles, tiny puffs of steam coming from his mouth even though I couldn't really feel the chill anymore.

'Did you grow up near the woods, in the countryside?' I asked.

He shrugged. 'I come from somewhere like this,' he said, tapping a foot on the ground.

'In Italy, yes?' I asked.

Another sort of shrug, head tilt, a grunt. He didn't want to go there. OK, I get it, I really do. I turned the conversation back. Baby steps.

'Is that where you learnt to do this?' I asked.

He stopped cutting mushrooms, and turned to me, my neat little blade smiling in his hand.

'Why buy, when you can take, Simone?' he said, his voice a low murmur, almost hypnotic. A little deeper than usual, like I'd heard in the bathroom. He looked for my gaze, found it, held it.

'If you know what you're looking for. What you want. It's about the *selection*, to make sure you find what you really want, and then you *take it*. With respect. You know?' He stood up, and moved very close to me, his eyes still flashing on mine. He put a hand on my arm, and my skin tingled beneath the layers of fabric. Electric. I could not pull away.

'Sometimes you have to pull a little harder, dig a bit deeper, but you *can* take it if you want it. It's beautiful. Things don't grow just to rot and die, Simone. It's OK to take them, I think they would be happy. They should be happy to nourish me. They should *want it*.'

He did not blink as he spoke, his eyes darting between my mouth, my throat. Then fixed on my eyes. I could only nod in agreement. Then he pointed at something on the ground.

'It's a big one,' he whispered, kneeling down to inspect a mushroom the size of a hubcap. It was beautiful, like a swollen human brain, dropped from a great height to land here in the forest. Massimo was holding my knife out now, and I knelt down next to him. I held the blade underneath the mushroom cautiously, struggling to find a good angle to start the cut. I crouched a little lower and reached my other hand around to hold it steady. I heard him sniff behind me.

I was sweating. Could he smell it, my new friend?

'Here, let me help,' he said, and crouched down close to me, moving his hands around the giant fungus to hold it with me, our knuckles touching.

I looked at his face, focused on mine, and tried to regulate my breathing. His freckles seemed to be dancing, as a cloud passed over the sun, covering us in shade. With it, his features seemed to wobble a little, grow waxy and frightening. I looked into neon eyes, and mine widened in response.

'I've got a good secret,' he whispered close to my face, and goosebumps sprung up through the skin of my back.

'What is it?' I whispered back.

'I don't want to scare you.'

I took a tight breath, the pressure in my hands felt too much. I slipped, and felt the sharp point of the blade slitting its way deep into the side of my other hand.

'Fuck!'

Blood was already welling from the deep incision, but before I could move Massimo took my hand and put it to his mouth, where I felt the muscles of his tongue and cheeks feasting, drawing my blood into his mouth. From inside me, a slow gasp was building.

Something came, crept over me, there in the bracken, a steady pressure that seemed to wake all the dark and dirty things within me. The same thing that had scratched at my back, and raged from my mouth at karaoke. I felt woozy, that itch in my spine running thick. I felt like I could lie down and sleep, right there in the forest, or I could pull every tree from the ground and dash them to the hills like javelins. I could *let something in*.

Massimo's mouth on my skin, drawing in fluid . . . I waxed and waned, the desire so strong it would take me, pluck me quick, and I said I would let it. Sure, do your worst, baby. Don't stop. Come on in.

I let the heavy-horned fog come for me, felt it billowing

from Massimo to swallow me whole. It nearly did. A beautiful voice sucking a raspy gasp. More pressure on my body, hard and thick. *'So delicious. So terribly tasty.'*

But then no, no, I didn't like it. It was too much, too awful. So I fought it. I kicked back down. Hard. I wrenched my hand back in shock, staring at Massimo, waiting for him to swallow. Blood on his lips. He looked furious, staring me down. I thought he would come for me again, but instead he spat, a frothy pink mix of spitty bubbles and blood splattering onto dry leaves. We both looked at it.

'Just in case,' he said. 'Knife is dirty.' He wiped a trickle of my blood from his mouth, and handed me back the box cutter. It was only when I took it from him that I noticed the wound on my hand; it was growing, getting bigger in front of my eyes, splitting with a bright flashing sting towards my wrist. And then it stopped.

Back at the car, I wrapped my throbbing hand in gauze from the first-aid kit I had packed. I looked over at Massimo, his work done, leaning against the fabric of the roof and tilting back his face to the sun, closing his eyes. Sighing heavily. Frustrated at something.

In the car, buckled in tight, Massimo turned to me. He removed something from his pocket, its toffee surface gleaming slightly. A beautiful mushroom. When Massimo ran a thumb over the gilled underside, it flickered at his touch.

'Wavy cap,' he said. 'Gets you wavy.'

I gave a nervous little laugh, and he started the car.

'Small bite,' he said.

I looked at the mushroom. Tested it in my mouth, just front teeth. The waxy white stem bruised blue where my fingertips held, no matter how gently I grasped it.

Fuck it. I took a bite.

CHAPTER TWENTY

Vampire.

Werewolf.

Zombie.

Slutty cat.

Naughty prawn.

I'd had an idea.

'Let's have a Halloween party. Tonight,' I said to Massimo in the car as we drove through tree-lined streets. The soft buzz of mushroom pressed against my vision.

'Halloween,' he said, nodding.

'Like a housewarming, for you. New tradition.'

'Very short notice,' he said, gravely.

'I think people will come.'

He considered the idea.

'OK,' he said, nodding slowly, turning down a side street. 'I am free.'

'Do you want to invite people?'

He thought for a moment. Flicker-tic on his eyelid. We were driving through city grime now and I could feel the difference, the hot grey crush of it on the windscreen, bearing down so hard I thought it might crack.

'All my friends are busy,' he said.

'Well, I'll invite extra,' I said, not sure if I seemed manic or gentle. 'People will be around. I mean, it's Halloween, not the Met Gala!' I laughed and it bounced back off the glass.

I knew people would come, people came to parties! I was feeling positive. I think the mushroom helped. When they came, I would charm them, let them be who they wanted to be, bring who they wanted to bring. Listen to their stories, tell them what they wanted to hear. I remember a girl once told me, at one of the house parties Josh had thrown: 'You really see people, Simon, you make people feel seen. You're always looking.'

'Like a detective,' I'd replied.

I sat in the passenger seat and sent out messages. *SOS. Emergency! It's time to party. Bring whoever. I'm making the punch!*

Some texts came back.

Sorry who is this?

Massimo drove us home.

This part of the city, where I live, it's always been eerie.

The autumn is cold, but in the summer it's fucking

roasting. Last year it was 42 degrees for nine days. The air was like custard, people went mad with it; a stabbing a day, so it seemed. Bodies on the street. The concrete so hot you'd think it might vaporise blood, and expect to see pink steam rising above the police tape.

Boys shirtless, everywhere, summer sausages bouncing. Me and Josh at the lido, all eyes on him flexing his brown biceps at the poolside, my skin burning even in the shade as I watched him swim with grace. I had tried to dive once, in the hopes of matching his mystique, or even impressing him, but I had belly-flopped, split my elbow on the tiles, and crawled away to get dressed.

The air in Eastern Park filled with ritual smoke. Chicken spit and halloumi melted onto barbecue coals, mingling with the smell of piss from the toilet block. Even further east, there was a scrubby wetland ringed with trees, a dollop of wiry countryside full of small white birds. It was cooler there, but not much.

When I first arrived, I went there often. On a sweltering summer afternoon when the grass was bleached blond, I had disturbed the tree-shadows and noticed men crawling in the undergrowth at the edge of the forest. Like I had lifted a stone. I found a man in nothing but work boots and swimming shorts, his orange waistband tucked under fat purple-plum balls, looking me dead in the eye. Challenging me.

I had avoided that park since then, the shrouded lust of it. It was too exposed; I'd always felt that, crossing its great dry plain, it was a perfect place to be snipered.

Violent fights would break out in the pubs, outside the bars. They got worse every year. I once watched two teenage girls pull each other into the canal, screaming and biting until they tipped over the edge. Their faces opening in surprise as they fell, their friends filming them from the safety of the towpath. The *screaming*. I hovered behind Josh, holding back until I thought it was safe. One of the girls had pond weed all down her back as she climbed onto a trolley in the water and stood there, wobbling triumphantly. The other tried desperately to climb out, gasping, half-submerged as blood gushed down her neck from a ragged earlobe. The other girl held up the earring she had torn from it, a trophy. I'd warned Josh not to get involved as he gave the ringleader a high-five, but he just laughed. In fact, all the girls were laughing too, even the bloodsoaked girl shoved back into the canal by her friends, slipping down like a rat in a toilet bowl.

'Simon!' he'd said, elbowing me beneath the ribs. 'They're *friends*! Take a chill pill.'

I had slowly gotten used to it, the strangeness around me. The woman who clapped at every passing taxi. The long haired man in his pyjamas, taking his house rabbit for a walk down the street, letting it lead the way, calling it back. *Not too far! Not too far, my baby.*

I got used to the violence of the city too, in time. Once, watching a man on the bus apply pressure to an arterial wound, I had thought of picking up the phone, dialling my parents' landline. Hoping someone would answer. '*Hello?*

I'm coming back home.' Other times, waking alone in a furious midnight storm, walls and windows shaking, the same urge. But I never did. I never made the call.

Every season became a little stranger around the city. Something to do with the buildings – the reformed factories and glassy new developments mirroring the murky grey canal water. Shards of glass stuck into mud. Art deco buildings, some torn down, some left to crumble. Winter comes. The streets get emptier, a bone-deep coldness arrives with the wind that blows across the playing fields, heading for the houses. Over the flat ground there, the empty library hulks, a fifties gem boarded up, thin people climbing into its broken back. The wind blows through it, nudging the needles and waking anyone who might be sleeping, before moving onwards and blowing harder, making its way along the pavements and under the fences, toward the street where I live.

That Halloween night I'd left the building and paused to watch the shadows creeping their way down the sides of flats and pavements, reaching the gutters, shimmering, licking the drains. I picked up the vitals – plastic skeletons, Lambrini for the punch, coke, a bit of MDMA. A costume for Massimo, who had nothing to wear.

It was freezing; I hadn't brought my coat. I rubbed the goosebumps on my neck, the stinging wound on my hand. Through the wobble of mushroom-vision, I checked my phone. More replies came pinging in. A temp girl from work who I didn't like, contacts from various circles, various past jobs. Some of Josh's old fashion crowd – I'd found their numbers on the old phone of his I'd been keeping safe. I'd invited the neighbours downstairs, which always seemed like the right thing to do. They didn't reply, thank God. They were never home anyway.

I'd asked Josh. He hadn't replied either.

In the corner shop looking for face paint I saw the paramedic again, her hi-vis buttoned up and those Oakleys on even though the sun outside was dwindling. She was standing by the Twixes, half-pretending to read a *Busty Babes* magazine but really she was watching me. I didn't like that, it spooked my buzz. I looked back at her and almost laughed in surprise, but she seemed like she was going to forget the chocolate and say something to me, maybe ask me a question. Her mouth was opening, but I paid in record time, did not need a bag, and was dashing out the door in seconds, back out onto the streets, heading home again as the darkening sky gently rippled above me.

I took a shortcut down a street of Victorian houses, dodging children. A woman exiting a house looked distressed, dressed as a scarecrow, straw peeking out her sleeves. On the phone to someone, walking into the road, her voice shaky, make-up ruined from crying. Little hat threatening to fall off.

'. . . Yes, he's very old, he lives alone, I hadn't seen him for about a month so I just came to check, I thought he might be frightened by all the kids and . . . I mean, Jesus

Christ, you'll have to see for yourself, it's like something from a film.'

I stopped. I peered at the open doorway behind her, a nice dark green. I saw one lone eyeball winking on the doormat. A thick streak of blood down the hallway herringbone. Something made me walk up the cracked path, and step through the door, over the dried-up eyeball.

A fusty stink, though I'd smelled worse. The echo of something that made me want to go deeper into the house. A line pulling.

I took a few steps forward, the lights twinkling above me, walls wobbling.

Blood on the wooden floor, dark red. Blood up the bannisters as I passed the stairs. Blood up the walls in what I could see of the kitchen, down the hall before me. A purple hand, on its own, just in sight near the oven, nub of wrist-bone winking. I stopped and stared, transfixed, looking at the hand, shuddering, before the woman's sobs shook me from the daze.

Very realistic! Very good. I wanted to applaud the designer. But there was no time to admire decorations. It was time to party. I turned and left.

I marched past the church, which throbbed in my periphery, its doors shut tight, barricaded. Lights snuffed out inside. Small children were out already, running through alleyways and knocking hard on the doors of houses I wouldn't dream of approaching. A tiny robot, a bleeding bride and the Creature from the Black Lagoon passed closely by me through the graves and I had to edge out of the way, carrier bags clinking. A little witch hissed at me, her teeth bared and already stained with brown chocolate, lips leaking. A miniature crack whore. I hissed back.

I heard baying, barking, the sound of claws on concrete. Three dogs ran through the misty churchyard, following the children, and I got closer to take a look. From the sound, I had expected mange, scabs, fur hanging off in sheets but instead they looked healthy and clean, glossy among the graves. I was just in time to see the leader of the pack, a large Dalmatian, licking a gravestone. She stared into my eyes as her tongue slapped the grooves of a long-dead name. She was beautiful, that black-and-white dog, squatting to shit on the dead orange leaves that littered the grave. I crouched down next to her and took a bump of something off my keys. Floated home. The mushroom was really doing its thing.

Upstairs, I unloaded onto the kitchen table and watched the items wiggle slightly. The Lambrini. Vodka. Juice. I pre-made the infamous spooky punch. Cranberry juice, pineapple juice, Lambrini, lemonade. Two bags of MDMA. I mixed it in a bowl and it went in the fridge, lemon slices swimming like sharks.

Don't misunderstand me. I was not fully relaxed. I kept a beady blue eye on Massimo at all times. But the mushroom and the Halloween glee had further snapped the tension, like a rubber band projected from thumb and forefinger, it twanged loose between us. The bump helped too.

My gut was churning, trying to warn me, but I ignored it, told it to settle. The night would be *fun*.

I should always trust my gut.

CHAPTER TWENTY-ONE

I was fucked.

I had nothing to wear. Consumed with shopping for Massimo, I had neglected to choose something for myself, and decided to find something at home. But as I rummaged through my wardrobe, I began to panic. Cheap pin-striped suit? Useless. An itchy wool V-neck. Pointless.

I'd never known how to dress. I watched people, looked at photos online, tried to emulate their styles, but in the summer I ended up as either Young Dad on a Camping Trip or French Exchange Student. Shorts, trainers, cagoule, rucksack. In the winter at least I could cover up, hide myself in coats and scarves. Most days I wore a uniform for work, thank God.

So, a spontaneous costume? That would require an actual wardrobe.

Josh always looked incredible on Halloween. We're

talking next level. A matador, the Tin Man, a glistening merman complete with faux garnet tail. I'd wheeled him round the streets in a wheelbarrow. It was always out of this world. He would set a competition, knowing full well he would win the prize – a handful of ecstasy pills.

Standing there, staring at myself, I remembered the boxes of his old clothes that now lurked in Goblin's cupboard. He had still not come back for them; I was sure he would not mind a loan. I lifted things into the light. Black cashmere rollneck with embellished sleeves? That might do. Strange, wide-legged grey wool trousers that I'd never seen him wear? OK. Silver boots that might cut off circulation? You only live once.

I took a sip of vodka, iced and brutal, from my favourite mug, and studied myself in the mirror. I turned different angles, rocked on my heels. A transformation of sorts, but really it wasn't a costume, and I didn't look like Josh. But I didn't look like me, either.

Something was watching me.

Massimo was standing at my bedroom door, staring through the gap. He had begun the process of wrapping himself in the bandages I had bought him from the pharmacy, but not finished the job. One arm and one leg were bound, the rest was bare but for white briefs that I avoided inspecting.

'Are you going to wear the cape?' he asked quietly.

I turned rigid.

'Excuse me?'

He pointed towards the foot of the bed.

'Your mum's. It's perfect,' he said, and nodded deeply.

'How the fuck . . . how do you know about that? Josh told you?' I stammered back.

He pushed the door open.

'It will look great, I think,' he said.

'How many times did you meet Josh? What did he say?'

He shrugged, not interested. 'Just once. Tall boy.' He nodded again towards the bed. 'Cape. Yes? That won't look good without it.'

I looked over at the dark gap between the bed and the floor. He had a valid point.

'If you insist.'

I got down on my hands and knees, moving quickly and dragging out the only box unlabelled. No dust bunnies. Goblin was fat and fed.

My mum's cape, the only thing I'd taken from home. Precious, vintage, from the 1980s, when nurses would wear thick wool capes over their uniforms on the ward. Navy-blue, and the lining was crimson; you secured it with two black woollen belts that crossed over the front and then buttoned in the back, which gave it a sort of kinky bondage feel, made more so by its high collar. It was almost magical. If she missed it, she never said.

I stroked it. He was right. It was perfect.

I'd worn it around my room, once or twice, over the years. I'd neck a gin and tonic, a couple more, lean out the window to smoke, swishing the fabric with my spare hand. Shirtless beneath the wool.

I put it on now, and it completed the look of someone I didn't recognise. Dark, brooding, vampiric. I puffed out my chest.

I turned to Massimo, who watched me carefully. It felt almost like the old days, getting ready with Josh, the buzz of anticipation for the night ahead.

He stared. '*Perfetto*. Now you help me.'

In the kitchen Massimo climbed onto a chair and gripped the edges with his long toes. I watched the veins in his arm as he held the ceiling for support, passing me the roll of bandages. I eyed his tattoos. A small cat on his upper arm, some sort of sword on one of his fingers, tiny and delicate. A coin-sized heart, filled in black and beating, on his ribs. A snake wrapped around a carton of Ribena, drinking from a straw. It was hard to imagine this boy lying down, letting someone ink a winking kitten, sweet and mischievous, into his skin.

On his left side, I found the lovers I had seen part and crack open. *Move, come on move.* I studied it closely for signs of scarring, but found none. I kept binding. Something wet landed on my hand, and I looked up. A drop of saliva had fallen from Massimo's mouth, slick off the tongue that poked out in concentration. I let it dry on my skin.

This was the most intimate I had been in a long time. I let myself wonder, just for a moment as I bound him, if we could ever be more than flatmates. Soulmates? I squashed it fast. *Don't shit where you eat, Simon.* Besides, I knew someone like him would never look twice at someone like me.

I had reached his neck, and could feel his hot breath on my arms. I had the sudden urge to tie the bandage tight, way too tight over his Adam's apple. Keep pulling. Instead I wound my way back down, and pinned the last bandage in place, right above his perfectly cuppable arse cheek, strode over to the speaker, and put on Britney.

Toxic.

CHAPTER TWENTY-TWO

'I've got drugs! If you want them.'

I was pissed by ten. And high, almost ready for a good time. Everyone seemed happy to see me upon arrival, thanked me for throwing another party. Couldn't remember my name, but still they greeted me warmly. 'Hey, where's Josh?'

Everyone admired the ambience, the strobe light I'd plugged in, the cheap smoke machine. A crude pumpkin I'd taken from outside the estate agents, its toothy face sending yellow chunks of light up the walls. The room had a swampy feel. A werewolf with tight gold trousers and pecs the size of my head put a hand on my shoulder, whispered in my ear.

'Is there punch?'

Standing in my bedroom, I had picked up the black rollneck from the bed, ready to stretch it over my head, my bare chest. But then I stopped. Shirtless, I'd watched the goosebumps form as I put the cape round my shoulders, straps across the waist and chest, collar high beneath my chin. I was not buff, not even muscular, but the slightest suggestion of abs showed themselves against the straps. Hair dark and slicked. Some white paste and eyeliner, Josh's silver boots numbing my pinkies. Was this cool? Something close to sexy? The wool straps rubbed against my nipples and they hardened in response.

When I'd revealed myself to Massimo, I got a double thumbs-up. A firm twitch of the eye. I swear his tongue came out to wet his lips.

Now, as the party filled, I turned on the restaurant charm, cloak swishing as I offered drinks, and chirped otter-like at in-jokes I couldn't understand. Smiling all the way. I slid over to Massimo, my co-host, my team mate. My friend.

'Having fun?' I gently bumped his hip, gave him a little wink. But he stood rigid, just watching the crowd form, a little aloof. I was doing all the work. No big deal, though. That was fine.

The room filled quickly, so people spilled out a little onto the shallow, flat bit of roof, climbing through the kitchen windows. Stressful. I didn't want to watch someone fall and break a leg, or seven vertebrae, so I went downstairs for a smoke.

A tall skeleton was arriving, getting out of a taxi with Fred and Rose West. It looked at me.

'Do you know where the buzzer is?'

'I've got a key!'

'Who are you?' the skeleton said behind its mask.

'Simon!' I said, though I felt a bit like someone else.

His eyes burnt through the holes in his mask, right into mine.

'Cool. I like your cape.' He reached out to touch it.

I stared back at him.

'I like your bones.'

The music inside was louder now. Japanese electro pop pulse-pulsing. I gave the skeleton a bump through his mask, took one myself. He had a great bum, a nice voice. He was very lean. Was it Josh? Almost everyone was dancing, and the green light flashed. The room rolled. I had made a playlist with some of my favourite songs, choosing those with the best beats and some real pop classics. I reckoned people liked those. Some of it was maybe a bit manic, but nobody had complained so far. They were having fun!

The room was filled with people, some of whom I'd never seen before, others I half-recognised from the local barstaff clique I had texted. A couple of past chefs from the restaurant. A few of Josh's old crowd. People patting me on the back. Skeleton poured me a drink, cheersed me with a grin. I marvelled at the scene, at the crowd I had drawn to my flat. The party I had somehow dared to throw. I clinked glasses with Jeffrey Dahmer in a jockstrap and felt almost confident. Almost cool. I smiled, buzzed, and found that it was genuine. I couldn't find Massimo anywhere, so I took another bump and felt euphoric.

The costumes were gorgeous. Some were outrageous, full-blown devils covered head to toe in red paint, tits out, thongs tucked in tight. And the boys. The beefcake werewolf, the beautiful couple kissing in the corner, both in leather harnesses and little black police hats, their hands lovingly on each other's thighs, their muscled backs. The tiny man covered in spiders' webs, with the longest eyelashes I'd ever seen. Skinny little thing. Pet Shop Boys blasting, everyone rocking. One girl wore simply a bra and fishnets and she'd painted her shaved head luminous gold. Two enormous bears were dressed as murdered twins in blue dresses, *covered* in fake blood. 'Come and play with us!' they screamed over the music. Massimo must have been out on the roof, smoking, or making friends.

I had not expected so many wet outfits, and I worried about the paintwork. I could not lose my deposit. But it did not kill my vibe. I was hosting a party! With my new friend Massimo. I took long gulps of punch as the buzzer kept yowling in the hall.

When I finally found Massimo again, he was leaning against the far wall and staring around the room. Several people giving him the eye. I waved to him, gestured to our party. *Isn't this great?!* He ignored me. One of his bandages had slipped and a brown nipple was peeking out; I wanted to walk right over and bite it off, chew it down like Haribo. I tried for his attention once more.

He was watching the skeleton instead, who danced around the kitchen like a sexy monkey. The skeleton had noticed, and was watching him back. Transfixed. Neither of them looking at me. I felt suddenly queasy.

I yelled in the skeleton's ear when he got close enough. 'That's my roommate! My friend.'

He nodded behind his mask.

'He lives with me!'

'OK.' He looked over my shoulder at something.

'We're hosting this party together!'

Another nod.

'None of his friends came!'

'Maybe they had another . . .' The rest of his sentence was swallowed by the song.

'A WHAT?'

'ANOTHER PARTY!'

I laughed really hard, though it wasn't a joke.'Wanna bone?!' I yelled, and touched his back, but the music was too loud, and he wiggled his hips to the beat, danced away towards one of the Manson girls, blue denim dresses down to their knees, hair touching their boobs. Left me alone. I saw Skeleton looking over at Massimo briefly. Wiggling his arse.

Someone took over the playlist and put on a song with a thick heavy beat, and Skeleton's glow-in-the-dark bones were electric, that excellent bum gathering a crowd with its moves. The haze had risen, and the cheap lights flashed on, the glow of the candles like hot little orbs around him.

Everyone was watching this naughty skeleton roll his hips, his head flying back like a thing possessed, gnashing his teeth.

I thought about pushing through the crowd, shimmying right up to the skeleton, dancing right there with him. Showing him how I could move. Showing Massimo. I stayed where I was, and just watched him dance.

Massimo stared, looking at him like a snack, cocking his head. Skeleton snapped his fingers and approached him, flashed his hands back up to his face, a leg out to the side winding in a circle. *Real* confidence. All eyes on the bones. Massimo nodding his head to the huge fat cake of a beat that wobbled against the walls. I watched Massimo take a mushroom, the special stash he had fed me from, and slide it under Skeleton's mask, into his mouth. I felt the party slipping from my fingers, along with the version of myself that, for a moment, had felt so good. I saw Massimo's strong hand reaching down to touch Skeleton's round arse through polyester. No. This was all wrong. I began to burn.

For the first time in my life I prepared to punch someone. Arm pulling back, fist curling, tongue slick between teeth. Feet marching towards them, trying to figure out who I hated more in that moment. Skeleton, who had shone his light on me for a moment and then found something more exciting? Or Massimo, who had done the same. And worse. Telling me we were friends, dropping me like a stone. I made my choice.

Skeleton. I'd snap his spine into three pieces and clean

up the mess immediately. I felt something hissing at the back of my throat, that murmur in my heart; I was seconds away from violence, inches from the Bones.

I felt the room stop. All eyes on me, not in a good way. The host of the party gone mad, losing his mind on the dance floor, spittle on his lips. Everyone turning. The enormous Werewolf frowned, put his drink down. Would somebody restrain me, if I went truly apeshit? Should I find out?

I stopped, right in front of Skeleton. I lifted my outstretched arm, and patted his head gently, then turned and left the room.

I locked myself in the bathroom. I would not unleash myself; nobody likes a party pooper. Had I really thought I stood a chance, with a skeleton who'd crawled straight out of Studio 54?

I took three deep anxious breaths in front of the mirror. Blue eyes peering out from chalk. My make-up was smudged along my jawline, where I had been rubbing it. My nipples were chafing now, sore. The plastic teeth in my mouth were cutting into my gums and lips, and I took them out, watching the slick of pink spit that dripped onto the floor. The sadness of it all. I touched my bare chest and hated it.

I took out my phone and downloaded Grindr. I had to squint, my vision was off, hands a little shaky. A blurred gallery of tracksuit bottoms and sausages. Over the thud of music, little chimes for me. *Klook. Klook.*

Hey Mr

Hey hows U?

A long dick peeking out of briefs.

Hey U

Smaller dick perfectly formed and glossy.

Hiya ;) Can you host tonight?

No! No, I cannot host, I'm hosting a party. I am forming a friendship! *Simon, try harder! Don't give up.* I took another breath and then a big bump, which got me moving. Felt my rage and frustration turning into a rush of bubbles as I left the bathroom and went back to the party. But as I marched down the hallway, I noticed a pink glow coming from Massimo's bedroom.

Oh but this was private! This was out of bounds. I looked down the long corridor, and could see a glimpse of Skeleton, grinding against Massimo in the kitchen.

I put my head around the bedroom door, and quickly wished I hadn't.

CHAPTER TWENTY-THREE

Something horrible was on the bed.

A creature, large and muscular, oddly tall, hunched uncomfortably near the headboard, and wearing some kind of horned headdress. A devil of sorts. Its face was in shadow; I could only see glimpses of mottled skin, wide eyes. The costume was so terrifying that, along with the bump that buzzed through me, it had almost stopped my heart.

It was not alone. There were two others on the mattress, Rose West and a dead priest. The room was dark, but I think they were huffing balloons.

The sweet smell of weed mingled with the spiral of incense rising from a joss stick in the soil of the spider plant. Something else too, thick, like rotting pine, Christmas trees stagnating in water. The lights were low, a thin pink scarf draped over the bedside lamp creating that hue I had seen from the corridor. That's a fire hazard.

The fourth person in the room was rummaging through the wardrobe, chucking away shirts that flew spectrally through the air. As I entered, she stopped to turn and watch me. This girl was dressed as a witch, black dress skimming the floorboards, a thick purple cloak hooding her head, her boobs spilling out of a corset like a cake baked in a bucket. A small silver pentagram winked from her cleavage, and I could just about see her heavily lined eyes peering through dark hair that fell all over the place. She was incredibly striking. She also looked a little manic.

'Well? Coming in?' asked the witch, slightly irritably, and the party down the corridor seemed to disappear. She was a little unsteady on her feet, and sat down heavily on the chair next to the bedside table, before lighting a cigarette she took from a packet in her bra. On the table was a purple plasma lamp, and she stroked it with a finger so that the electric snakes inside wiggled to her touch. In her other hand, she ashed the cigarette into her lap. I itched to clean it up.

I edged into the room, smiling at the gang on the bed who were engrossed in their own party of three. The tall, terrifying person stretched out a little and I heard the headdress scrape the ceiling.

'Having fun?' the witch asked. She sounded accusatory; something in her voice stirred a feeling. I knew her from somewhere.

'I live here. This is *my* party.'

'Oooh!' she breathed out spookily, now putting both

hands on the plasma ball and tapping. The rings on her hands flashed, bejewelled with stones that clicked on the glass.

From the bed, Rose West cackled. 'You should have known that already, Mystic Meg.'

'I knew,' she snapped. 'Do you want your palm read?' she asked me.

'Can you do that?'

'Fuck off, can she!' the priest screamed, and let go of his balloon.

The tall, horned man said nothing.

The witch bit back. 'Fuck off yourself.' She was pretty drunk, like a frazzled Nigella about to read my fortune, pouting her lips and rolling her long-lashed eyes. Suddenly, I was eager to learn more. Clearly everything I had put into my body that night was dismantling my guard.

'Sit down then,' she said. I obeyed.

'Now give me your hand.'

'Which one?'

She paused for a beat, looked into my eyes. The mood flickered ever so slightly, a faint line forming between us.

'Which hand do you wank with?'

I placed my right hand flat on the table. The wound from Massimo's knife had begun to throb.

'Does that make a difference?'

'No.' She smiled. 'Oh, what happened to your hand?'

'Knife,' I said, and she tutted.

'People should be more careful out there,' she wagged

her finger towards the windows, then stared me down, a pencilled eyebrow raised. 'It's not safe.'

I eyed her back. 'I didn't see you arrive with your friends,' I said.

'They're not my friends.'

'Oh. Then who do you know here?'

'Nobody. Hand please.' *Why* was she so familiar?

When she touched my hand, lifting it gently between her palms, I was surprised to feel a strange surge of raw emotion, as if three hard blinks would push tears from my eyes. That moment of contact, almost tenderness, stung. I wondered when I had last held someone's hand.

I watched her rolling her thumbs over my palm, a smile tingling on her lips. She looked into my eyes, before turning my hand over in the pink light, looking for something I couldn't see.

'What's your name?' asked the witch.

'Simon.'

'That's what I thought.'

From the bed, Rose West snorted. 'You're so full of shit.'

The witch flipped her the finger, ruby gemstone winking, then put her hand back on mine.

'Well,' she said. 'I can see from this line here that you've never ridden a motorbike.'

I nodded. I started to wonder if she was also very high, like me. Where did I know her from? It was driving me mad.

'Yes, you have, or yes, you haven't?' she said.

'You tell me.' I raised an eyebrow. The priest enjoyed that.

Now she was silent for a moment, deep in thought, then suddenly she looked into my eyes as she traced a line on my ring finger.

'This here says that you will live a very long life, and you'll have much fun, but right now there is sadness.' She started to stroke the soft pad of flesh at the bottom of my thumb. 'You're lonely.'

Was she mocking me? Her eyes were fixed on mine, as she stroked my hand. Eyes so brown, and she looked genuinely moved, as if my feelings had crept from my hand, into hers, and burrowed deeper into her bosom. Her hood slipped back, and I saw more of her face, the small frown formed on her brow.

How dare she speak my secrets to a room of strangers? I wanted to pull away. And then I realised who she was.

'I know you. You're that paramedic that came here.' Now I snatched my hand away.

She smirked.

'I saw something, in your window,' she said, her voice very low.

'Pardon?' I whispered.

'I came to find it.'

My skin prickled with goosebumps, head to toe.

'What did you see?'

I realised the room had gone silent. The gang on the bed were not making a sound, though I noticed the tall, stooped man cocking his head to listen closer. He was smiling at me. The only sound, a gentle clinking of metal on metal.

She noticed the silence too, cleared her throat, raised her voice again for the room.

'Well. Am I right?'

'About?' I asked, a little defensive, choking up.

'That you are lonely.' She tilted her head, but I said nothing.

'Give me back your hand.'

I felt that warmth envelop me again as she took my palm into the smooth clamshell of her hands. There was movement on the bed as the trio seemed to loom closer in the shadows, their attention caught. The large devil-man hunched in the dark, and I noticed his eyes flashing like flints in that deep, waxy face that edged forward. It was sickening, actually.

Suddenly she flinched, like she'd been pricked.

'Fuck. There it is,' she murmured. I could smell sambuca on her breath. The devil stretched on the bed, catching my eye. He was slowly moving out of shadow, and looking directly at me, opening his mouth. He was so big.

'Christ, that costume. It's so fucking real,' I said, but the witch dismissed the bed-dwellers with a wave, and I looked back at her busy hands.

'Someone new has come into your life. Or . . . they're coming.'

She looked distressed. Her hands moved faster, searching for something.

'It's both here, *and* it's coming. It's . . . Ugh, it's horrible!' She squeezed my hand like a vice, her nails digging into my flesh. 'I *know* it's here. Whatever it is . . . it has its *eye on you*.'

Behind her, the devil-man was leaning forward, getting closer. Grinning. The room suddenly *stank*. He stared at me, awful mouth open, reaching out a pale hand. It brushed her shoulder, and she shuddered violently, turned, gasped.

I snatched my hand away, knocking the plasma lamp to the floor by accident. It didn't smash, just thudded, and went dim.

'What the fuck's your problem?' I said.

I saw she was almost shaking, turning back, her eyes on me, flitting around my face, then back to the bed.

The main light flashed on. The girl with the golden head was in the corridor outside the room, her hand on the light switch.

'What are you guys *doing* in here?' she said, one eyebrow raised.

Rose West got up and spun round.

'I think Professor Trelawney's on shrooms.'

I turned to look at Rose West. She was pulling the priest off the bed, and he was trying to light a cigarette, and now they were both laughing like crazy.

Gold-head groaned and stepped into the room. 'You've all had the punch.' She reached into her bra. 'Who wants a line?'

Rose West and the priest followed her to the desk in the

corner, near the wardrobe, but the witch stayed where she was, standing next to me. I waited for that huge, revolting, horned man to brush past me, following them. But nobody moved.

I turned around, and looked for him on the bed. There was nobody there. I spun, looking in every corner, what the fuck.

'Where's your friend?' I said, and the priest turned round, rolled note sticking from nostril.

'Who?'

'Tall guy, big horns. On the bed,' I stammered.

Rose West rubbed her nose and frowned. 'It was just us.'

Gold-head was staring at me. 'You OK, babe?'

I just blinked back at her, my head starting to spin. The trio left the room, stifling laughter. It was just me and the witch, alone in the bedroom. She was staring at me.

'What did you see?' Her voice came out deep and wobbly, the look in her eye was too much.

'I'm off my tits,' I said, and went scurrying back to the rest of the party. To reclaim the night. I almost danced, but I was too far gone. I noticed Massimo's hand clutching Skeleton's bicep, the other reaching down to grab his arse.

I wanted everyone to leave now. I smoked a bit of someone's spliff so my feet and tongue grew heavy and I swayed for a couple of songs. The flat warped around me; I noticed cupboard doors seeming to open by themselves, the toaster turning on and spitting out rancid smoke. The entry buzzer shrieked and shrieked. Was that man from the bed in here?

I thought I saw glimpses of him too, that pale face rising up above the crush and looking at me, his huge hand tugging on a horn, standing on the roof outside and peering in through the window. Eyes like coal.

The paramedic witch stalked the edge of the party, sometimes watching me with a wide-eyed look. I watched her back. She was getting drunker, higher by the minute, and with every drink she downed, I saw that bolshy, bossy girl slipping away, and something a little sadder, a little wilder began to emerge. She lost full control of her hair, her eyes, everything. I saw her minesweeping glasses of punch, knocking them back like she was trying to extinguish something, but instead she was only stoking it, making it burn.

I watched her through the small crowd. Dancing with strangers for a moment or two, then rocking on her feet, off balance. I heard her talking to a Manson girl, stabbing the glass of the window with a finger. 'Mate, mate, this city is *fucked*. Something is *fucking* it! I'll swap jobs with you any day. Give me your job! Do you wanna stay at mine tonight?'

I watched her take two bumps of god-knows-what off someone's fingernail, and then open Goblin's cupboard and half-crawl inside.

Then she came to find me.

'It's fucking *here*, it's here at your party, I know it. It's fucking here, I saw it in the bedroom and so did you,' she whispered wetly in my ear, and then she was off, smoking out the window, running her hands over the wall again and again.

'What's here, what do you know?' I wanted to say, but I didn't think I could form the words if I tried. If I'd been sober she would be driving me fucking crazy, touching all my stuff like that. But I watched her movements play out like little videos, frantic glimpses of a mad girl on a mission.

At 4 a.m., I was standing by the washing machine, watching the room. I'd popped a square of Xanax to help with the wind-down, and I felt its waves lapping at my edges. The witch was a mess, and she howled from where she'd been smoking a spliff on the sofa, an animal sound escaping from her open throat. Mascara like engine-oil running down her cheeks. The sounds she was making were so piercing, they almost cut through my high. I'd made those sounds before.

She was shaking her head and looking furious, terrified, eyes fixed on the doorway. 'It's fucking there! For fuck's sake, *I can't take it anymore!*' The gold-headed girl took her by the arm.

'OK, babe, home time. It's OK. You can come with me.' The witch looked exhausted, and gave me one last intense stare before Goldy led her out, sobbing into the hallway and away on shaky legs. The last few people nodded, took this as a sign. The party was over.

I breathed out, a deep sigh of jittery relief.

I really should have gone to bed then.

CHAPTER TWENTY-FOUR

It was just me, Massimo and fucking Skeleton left in the flat. The last boys standing.

I was sky high. I floated to the sofa and sank into it, my fingers massaging the threads of the cushion as Massimo put on a record. The room was very dark; I'm not sure they even noticed I was there.

Skeleton still had his mask on, pulled just above his mouth. I could see his square teeth as they danced, the music like the swell of the ocean building and building. The Xanax did its thing. My body pulsed. I was going somewhere.

I was a tiny fish in the surf being lifted and rolled, rocked back and forth, unaware of the coastline coming closer. Massimo was dark and sharky cruising through the body of water, cutting through it no-nonsense, a direct line to find blood among the currents. I guess Bones was a surfer, if he had to be there at all. Hope the shark bites.

My mind was a glittering, chemical mix, collecting ideas and turning them over gently, noticing sweet spikes of panic in the hazy rumble of pleasure.

Massimo was getting really into it, hips bucking, his hand lifting up the boy's costume to stroke his stomach, his palm separated from his organs by mere centimetres of muscle and skin. Massimo turned suddenly, and looked at me. He saw me sitting and watching, and he opened his mouth to show me his teeth that were now in fact shark's teeth, ragged triangles, parting to reveal a fat brown tongue. Well, that's a new trick.

He shimmered strangely, shook his head. I watched as small spikes began jutting from his temples, slowly tenting and then piercing the skin, long ropes of bone twisting themselves out into cruel horns. One jagged-sharp tooth split the tongue at the tip when he pushed it through, forking it, and I blinked at the blood running down his chin, blooming bright-red onto his bandages, though it felt like the room blinked before I did.

Massimo was still watching me with his pupils huge, whites veiny green, gnashing his teeth, moving his body tight against the boy. Everything so *woozy*. Our eyes met, he wanted me to see this. The skin on his face was waxy and shining, like clingfilm stretched over meat. More blood dripping from his long split tongue, spattering down the boy. Skeleton not noticing or not caring. I heard thunder break outside, then a flash of lightning, a strange phenomena I gave little attention. The cheap ferns were briefly illuminated, staccato fronds of shadow everywhere. The green of the strobe, the white of another lightning flash, Massimo ghoulish.

I tracked his hands, still inside the boy's costume, lifting up stencilled bones higher to reveal even more firm freckled flesh, his face now pressed tight to the side of the boy's stomach that flexed, tight as a drum.

Massimo opened his sharp-toothed mouth wide and bit deeply into the boy's belly, his eyes fixed on me. I almost expected to hear a pop, like the pierced skin of a ready meal, but the sound was wet and gushy, barely audible over the techno drumbeat. The boy fell to his knees, but his head was tipped back and he still swayed his hips as Massimo remained latched to him, the blood now pouring from his stomach and onto the rug. Massimo raised his head, face dripping with gore as he swallowed the chunk.

A scream was rising in my chest, my lungs like bellows working to push it out and it was almost there through my lips but it was also choking me, coating my tongue, my fingers gripping to tear holes in the sofa, and Massimo burrowed his face deeper into the boy, the rug beneath them *soaked* in blood and the boy's eyes rolling in his skull, almost in ecstasy. Massimo patted the rug with a palm as he chewed, small splashes of blood and bits of boy flying up onto the wall.

He was done, because now he was crawling over the body, sliding it aside and coming to me, his face unbelievable, monstrous and transformed, bulbous tongue lolling out wet and wolfy. Body huge, chunked with muscle. Horns heavy on his head. The strobe flashing, shining upon him as he grew bigger, changing by the second.

Looking like that devil from the bed.

Another strobe flash. Or was it more lightning? My boots squeaked on the floor as I felt my feet pushing for a grip but failing, and he was leaving the chewed body on the rug, coming past the filthy coffee table, a big slimed hand reaching out to streak gore on my boot, pushing himself closer with his other arm, grinning, reaching up towards my groin, my stomach. His face was opening, mouth widening, skin rippling in the flash, flash, flash of the strobe. Eyes turning massive and teeth turning sharper still and all I could do was watch him, or whatever he was now, climbing up, up, up the sofa, towering over me, hard hands on my thighs, my chest, my skull, leaning in for a kiss or something worse, leaning in to rock my world.

Deep inside me, something pounded on a door.

CHAPTER TWENTY-FIVE

I think I've died.

I opened my eyes, and laid still for a second, listening to the squeal of the fridge. Everything hurt, every bone in my body. The cape straps chafed my chest, and I stank of sour sweat and cigarettes. Slowly through the clouds, flashes of horror began coming back to me, small teeth, large bites of boy. So much blood, the sound of splashing. Massimo there on the rug, horned and gory. My heart beat like crazy, rocking on its axis.

I sat up and looked around the dark room, the strobe weakly winking. I managed to get up from the sofa and turn on the standing lamp, which did little. It was still very early. Outside, I heard heavy rain falling into the street. I felt like dogshit, a thick fog in my head that settled and swirled, settled and swirled at the slightest movement.

An aching pain in my right hand, a tenderness that bloomed when I flexed the fingers there.

I looked down to the rug, which was not there, the wooden floor clean and shining. No blood. I realised my boots had been removed from my feet, but I could not find them.

The *state* of the room. Empty bottles on every surface, long black strands of wig hair scudding in the breeze from the open window. Streaks of rubber across the floor from so many dark leather boots. The stink of cheap booze, ash, human breath. But the centre of the room was spotless.

I staggered to the tap, gulping water that got colder as it ran, trickling into my empty belly. I felt a terrible pain in my right shoulder, lifted the cape to inspect it, and found a deep red bruise, from my collarbone to my upper arm, dried blood around a gash. I winced. There seemed to be another large cut on my thigh, leaking clear liquid through my trousers.

I was shaking, struggling to stand upright. I had the sudden urge to call Josh, to ask him what to do. For someone to intervene. But I was alone. Where was my phone?

I stood breathing in the kitchen for a moment, walking the tightrope between dream and reality. The skeleton. Massimo. That monstrous thing.

I walked into the hallway. His door was closed. I didn't care, I was too fucked up for pleasantries. I opened it all the way, my hand shaking on the handle. Lumps under the striped covers, a hairy leg sticking out. That disgusting smell. The room was hot. I looked closer and saw a pair of eyes, watching me from the duvet.

'Simone. Are you OK?' Massimo whispered.

'Where is the boy?'

'Gone.'

'What did you do? Is he OK?'

'Simone, are *you* OK?' He shifted, swinging his legs over the edge of the mattress, the duvet sliding off him, so that I could see his bare torso in the dim light from the corridor. His naked body. He looked like himself. Massimo.

On the floor, a skeleton mask.

I was trembling. 'Fuck *off*. I saw you. Did you . . . eat him?'

He grunted, got up from the bed, creeping towards me, reaching his hand out. His voice was quiet as he repeated his question.

'Simone, please . . . you OK?' He tilted his head with concern as he studied my face. 'How are you feeling?' I looked at his face in the shaft of light.

'Is he in there?' I asked.

His eye flickered.

'You want to come in and see?'

'I know you're . . . something,' I said, and his eyes narrowed, but only slightly.

'OK,' he said.

'I've seen all the things. Your nails. Your skin. *That* . . .' I pointed backwards to the kitchen. 'I think you should leave.' I knew this sounded pathetic.

He started to yawn, but didn't complete it. Put a finger in his open mouth instead, reaching back to hook something from a molar, inspect it, flick it away.

'No.' He said it so bluntly, so coldly, that I took a step back. He yawned, wide, and then he spoke again.

'Did it scare you? Seeing what you saw?' He whispered, his voice now terrible, changing. 'Did it . . . how you say . . . *disarm*?'

'What?' I wiped cold sweat from my brow.

He leaned toward me, holding the doorframe, his lean, naked body on full display. His abs tightening, dick dangling. It did nothing for me.

'Did it break you down, hm? Did it . . . lower your guard? Because it did not seem to. Did it scare you into *submission*? Not much at all. It was not *enough*.' He barked this last word, clean and sharp. I could not help but flinch; It sounded almost nothing like Massimo. He moved closer, into the light, and I noticed a dark bruise on his cheekbone, blooming towards his eye.

'Did I do that?' I asked, flexing my throbbing hand again.

He nodded. 'Mmhmmm. It was a good fight,' he purred. Something scuffled inside the bedroom.

'Why? Because you tried to eat me?'

He rolled his eyes. 'How can you be so clever, yet so slow to understand?'

'Understand what?'

'What I want.'

I let out a breath.

That fog in my head was going nowhere, that tingle in my balls. I wanted to shake my head furiously, remove the images that were rooted there. But I couldn't take my eyes off his. The one with the bruise.

'Where's the rug, Massimo?' I asked him, and he shifted in the doorframe.

'It's clean, Simone,' he said as he opened the door wider and stepped into the corridor, keeping his voice low. I could almost feel the heat of his body, rippling from his bare chest. I stepped back quickly while straining to see past him to the bed, where I thought I saw movement.

'Why did you clean it?' I managed.

For a moment, we locked eyes, and I wondered if he was about to bite me, as he licked his lips and parted them, his mouth thick with sleep. But then I thought maybe I heard something in the bedroom again, the sound of sheets moving, and Massimo moved to block the way.

'You were sick on it. Everywhere. So much puke. You had a lot of mushroom, a very bad trip. I cleaned the rug, and your shoes. They're in the bathroom. Go, look.' He nodded down the hall, eyes wide. I turned, towards the end of the corridor, and he spoke again.

'I helped you. That's what friends are for.' His horrible voice, rough and mocking. I made to turn away, but he reached out and touched my bare chest, stopping me.

'Simone, do not worry.' He was grinning. 'This is not the end. *So* much more to come.' I watched him press his face against the wood of the door as he closed it, so the last thing I saw was his round green eye before the latch clicked shut.

I ran to the bathroom. There was the rug hanging over the edge of the bath, dripping like a pancake into the tub. The water clear, not pink. Josh's boots, wiped clean, tucked into the corner. I inspected the bathtub . . . bleachy-clean. I looked in the plug for a lump of gristle, a molar, but found only tomato skin that I had probably thrown up.

Back in the kitchen I closed the door and leaned against it. I felt slightly safer near the cutlery. I heard sounds building in the corridor, muffled thuds. Heard the blue door slamming hard at the end of the corridor. Silence.

I counted to twenty, then twenty more. No more sounds. Certain he was gone, I did the only thing I could think of. I put on rubber gloves.

From under the kitchen sink I pulled out a roll of bin bags and snapped out five, laying them in a line on the floor where they rustled like snake skins. I surveyed the room. I could see every bottle and baggie and blim hole in hyperfocus. I began to fill the bags with whatever was closest to me. One of them blew against my bare chest in the breeze from the window and I almost had a panic attack. I took the cape off, wanted nothing to touch me. I turned to Goblin, and was grateful for his help.

I dressed my wounds clumsily; it was hard to concentrate. Every now and then I felt a bit dizzy, a bit sick. That fog trickling through me. I cleaned harder, and slowly got a grip.

Mopping the corridor, I felt something watching me, though Massimo had definitely left. I had checked his room. No sign of a corpse either. I looked through the flat for another presence. Something big, with horns and teeth and muscular limbs. A shape that might have stayed, curled under the sofa, towering behind a door. But nothing came to me. I sniffed the air for rot, found only bleach. I found that I was disappointed.

I don't know what's happening. I don't know what to do, I told Goblin, who stared back with cold plastic eyes. He knew it was a lie.

Don't you always know things, in the soft sewer of your gut?

Really. Don't you know what you want?

CHAPTER TWENTY-SIX

I knew several things.

That Massimo lived here now, and was not leaving. And things had begun to happen, not long after his arrival. Sounds, smells, dreams, small occurrences. A private horror show, creeping shoreward with each day.

I knew that Massimo was startling. Very strange indeed. A hunter in the home, a usurper in my ordered world, with nails that never seemed to stop growing, skin that split, an attitude that sometimes chilled me to the core, sometimes stoked a campfire in my chest and chucked on wood.

But now I knew that there was something else. Something bigger than him, scratching at my door, flashing through my mind. Wanting something. Taking my attention.

That terrible skull, two sizes too large, those horns. That *smell*. But how did that fit with Massimo? Did it live within him? I did not know where the line was drawn between the boy and the being.

After cleaning, I'd slept for a few hours. Then I'd taken a shower and properly dressed my throbbing wounds. Clean jeans on my legs, thick jumper on my body. I'd brushed my teeth, brushed my tongue. Gagged, almost puked and tried again. Looked at my weird face in the mirror. Furtive all the while, but with every lap of Goblin, I felt a little better. Sucking away at the horror. I cleaned my room twice more.

The buzzer went around four and startled me. I almost dropped the teaspoon I'd been polishing. I crept to the intercom as it buzzed again.

'Hello?' I whispered.

'Can you let me in? It's freezing!'

'Who *is* that? Who is it . . . I mean—'

'It's Kat.'

Who the fuck is Kat?

I stared at the blinking red light of the intercom as if it were the intruder's very eyeball. It buzzed again. I pressed the button hard, and heard the door clang deep through the building's small intestine. I heard footsteps scuffling, heavy footwear dragging on the concrete floor. Singing. The second buzzer sounded and I smoothed everything down, clothes, hair, monstrosities. I answered the door.

It was her, the paramedic.

'Those stairs. Are a bitch!' Kat huffed, like I had built them myself.

I stared at her like she'd crawled up through the toilet.

'Can I come in?' she said, but she was already coming in, through the door, edging past me so I had to squeeze against the doorframe.

I didn't know what first responders wore off duty, or out of costume. It turned out it was something like a brown corduroy skirt and a faded band T-shirt. Little rubbery boots and a chunky red cardigan. She was wearing her paramedic jacket as if it were the warmest thing she owned. A green tote bag clinked at her side. Eyeshadow, fresh lipstick on a smiling mouth. Like she hadn't gone mad at a stranger's party a few hours ago. She did still look a bit mad though, with some of the lipstick on her teeth.

She was staring down the sparkling corridor.

'Christ, it's clean.'

I nodded. 'That was me.'

She was impressed, I think. Stuck her lower lip out and nodded. That pleased me.

'I should have come earlier, given you a hand,' she said, and pushed past me again, pressing deeper into the flat. I followed her down the hallway, watching her inspecting the walls, the spotless skirting boards.

'Thanks for having me last night. I've got tonic if you've got gin,' she said as she walked into the kitchen, panting gently, patting her bag.

She adjusted her skirt and did not remove her wet boots. 'Hair of the beast!'

I did not want company, I wanted to be alone.

'What is it I can help you with please, Kat?' I said, keeping my voice nice and steady.

She turned and looked me in the eye. 'Are you OK? You're very pale.'

She was staring at me.

'You took a lot of drugs last night,' she said.

You can fucking talk.

The hangover was thundering back with the effort of speech.

'Lots of people took a lot of drugs last night.'

'Yeah, fair enough. Who's in?' She looked around the room, suspicious.

'Just me.' I crossed my arms.

'We'll see,' she replied, and began pulling her hair into a bun. I couldn't believe her neck could hold the weight of all that hair. I kept on trying very hard to be very nice.

'Kat? It's Kat, right?' I said, and she nodded. 'Tell me what you want. Please.'

She sighed. 'Make me a drink.' Like I worked for her.

I'll be honest, this kind of person was a particular weak spot for me. Loud, commandeering, effervescent. Such *purpose* was terrifying. I wanted to tell her to fuck off and let me get back into bed with three hours of disgusting porn, but instead I found myself taking down half a bottle of gin, the last of the party leftovers. Fixing a smile, looking for cucumber, a sprig of rosemary, some pink peppercorns to garnish her drink. I could only find half a lime, turning brown.

Outside the sun was already setting, and through the windows the sky was spread lip pink. Kat tapped the table-top with her hand, nervously.

'Listen, I'm sorry for being weird last night. It's been a lot.' She said this very quickly to get it out of the way, and didn't look me in the eye. I saw her lip tremble.

'What's been a lot?' I asked her, and she looked like she was trying to figure out if she could trust me.

'Life. Work. I'm a paramedic,' she said, like this explained everything.

I gave a small uncomfortable laugh, which was all I had in me.

'I think there's something really fucked up in this flat,' she said.

The hairs immediately stood up on the small of my back, along my shoulder blades. I saw flashes of that terrible chalky face on the bed, heard the clanking of chain. Massimo eating a hot boy on the rug.

'Last night you said you saw something in my window.' I put the sad little G&T in her outstretched hand. She took a sip as I sat down.

'Yeah. I think so.'

'When?'

'About a week ago.'

'Are you in the habit of looking into other people's homes?'

'That's rich!' She claps her hands together. 'I've seen you lurking around all over the shop.' She pointed to the street, which pissed me off. I live here! I could lurk wherever I wanted.

'What did you see?' I asked. 'In the window.'

She squeezed her eyes, like this was hard for her to talk about.

'Some *weird* shit's been happening out there.' She gestured to the city spread darkly outside the window.

I made a face. *Tell me.* She sat down.

'I'm not sure you're ready for this but OK. So, it's always rough out there, in this job, obviously, but recently the bodies have really been piling up. Few weeks ago I was on shift, in this old woman's house where her body was just . . . gross. Like a melted candle. Bits in the bath. She'd been in there a while. I thought I saw something weird, behind her shower curtain. Then the same week, some bloke in his bedroom, split into four pieces on the duvet. Smelled like cat food. And I saw it again, under the bed. A figure. That face . . .' She was staring into space above her drink now. 'I think it goes for people on their own. Lonely people.' She looked at me now, a little pointedly.

'Describe it,' I said, more eagerly than I meant to, and she took a gulp of G&T.

'Imagine something like from right at the end of a nightmare, the bit that makes you wake up. Massive thing. The face . . . Fucking terrifying.' Now she shuddered in a way that was mostly horror, but also slightly dramatic, like she was enjoying having an audience. I nodded along; that's what she wanted.

'Call-outs all over the place. Same sort of scene. I mean I've seen some shit in this job, but, babe, this is next level. And it's been getting worse. The other night, I was called to an empty old townhouse . . .'

She petered off, and I waited for a moment before I said her name, prompting her.

'Kat.'

She blinked hard and carried on.

'On this job, you meet all kinds. Lots of lonely types, waifs and strays, mad and sad. Friendless people. In that house was a girl I sort of knew. I'd bought her hot drinks once or twice, you know.' Was that a tear in her eye? 'That one hit me,' she said, and cleared her throat before continuing.

'She was sprayed all over the place. Like she'd *burst*. And it was *there*, in that room with me as I scooped up all the bits of her. I know it. I fucking saw it. Then, a week or so ago, I saw it right *there* a couple of times, from the street.' She points at the window behind us, almost excitedly now. Her energy was impressive, it took up space in the room. She met my eye.

'Although once it might just have been you.'

Rude.

'And now it's here. I swear I keep seeing it. I think it looks for lonely people. People like you.'

I swear if she calls me lonely one more time . . .

Kat took a long sip of her drink, looking me in the eye.

'I think maybe it . . . goes into people. And then it kills them.'

She could not be serious. I was trying to equate my recent experiences in the flat, with a city full of dismembered corpses. Surely she was pulling my leg. I let out a giggle.

'Like a demon?' I said.

But she didn't laugh. Instead she shuddered at the word.

'Fuck, it sounds scary when you say it. In your voice,' she replied. She lit a cigarette and I let her, getting up to open the window and sitting on the ledge, facing her.

'So what are you trying to do?'

She looked up from her drink, which she had been stirring with a finger. She was almost shaking now.

'I've got to get rid of it, 'cause I'm sick of finding people split in half like logs every night, splattered all round their homes, and nobody giving a fuck. I'm sick of rolling around this city where all this insane shit happens every day and it keeps happening 'cause nobody cares about stopping it. I can't take it anymore. People are *dying*! I'd like to get some *sleep*.'

There she was – a glimmer of that girl from last night who crumbled, sitting on the sofa and wailing in front of the entire party.

'Do you know what blood sounds like in a carpet, Simon? When you put a boot on it?'

'No.'

'I do. I know what it sounds like nine times.'

'OK.' Was she boasting?

'I couldn't live it down if it got you. If I had the chance

but did nothing. Do you want to end up with bits of you blown all over these nice white walls?'

Absolutely not.

'I don't know how to . . . kill it. But I need to try. Maybe we can get it out of here. I promise, I'm gonna stop it from getting you. I'm gonna find it. Right *now*.' She jabbed her finger towards me and drops of G&T landed on my cheek. I did not wipe them.

Kat leant back, a little spent. She closed her eyes and then opened them again.

'Your dressing is fucked. Want me to take a look before we start?' She was looking at my hand, where the brown-stained bandage had started unravelling. She reached out to take it.

I pulled back, suddenly uncomfortable.

'No, Kat. I'm very sorry but I actually have things to do. And that all sounds mad but I haven't seen a single thing like that. Thank you for checking on me though.'

'Simon.' She cut me off, grabbing my knee. 'You're telling me you have no idea what I'm talking about?' She pointed directly at my nose. 'You're lying.'

Suddenly here was a precipice, and I toyed with it, scuffed at its kerb. I looked down at the floor, where the rug should be. I thought about the events of the past few weeks, the lack of sleep. The terror of this morning. A boy being bitten into. That monstrous *thing*. Then I thought about that fun, fuzzy feeling. The push-pull of recent days, as something had toyed with me. The visit to the doctor, the trip to Karaoke. I imagined it all going away. I had to admit, the desire was strong, to meet this mischief-maker. Just *one more time*.

'Did you think Massimo was strange? My flatmate, when you met him last night?' I said.

She shrugged.

'Everyone's strange. You're strange. What's *he* done in particular?'

'I'm strange?' I blinked at her.

She just laughed. I continued, slowly unfolding my arms.

'There's a smell here sometimes. Since he moved in. Rotten. And something walks about. I have dreams. It's always when he's home.' I did not mention my recent bad behaviour. How it had felt. The lure of it all.

She was getting animated, excited.

'And . . . have you *seen* anything . . . physical?' Her eyes were narrowed, and she put a hand on her shoulder, unconsciously. Where I had seen it touch her.

'Did you see anything in the bedroom last night?' she whispered. 'I think you did.'

I crossed my arms again, feeling suddenly protective. I wasn't prepared to tell her all of my behaviours, my dark dabbles. The fun of it, the enjoyment. That was private.

My home, my demon.

All morning as I cleaned, I had found myself calling for the being. Searching. I had taken moments to pause, feeling for it in the silence. Hoping it might speak to me. I'd wanted to see it again, but it had not come. Kat was offering to find it, she sounded confident. I could use her, for one last look. Just to remember how it felt to set eyes upon it. After all she had just told me, you would think I should be running for the ring road. I conjured the weird things I had seen and heard, out there on the streets. The terrible little nuggets of death and dismemberment which were suddenly standing out, stranger and starker than the usual horrors of the city. That should have been enough to shut the whole thing down.

It only made me more excited.

'I don't know if it . . . lives here, or it's just . . . in him,' I said, and watched as Kat put up a triumphant fist.

'Shall we find out?'

CHAPTER TWENTY-SEVEN

An empty chair sat in the centre of the room.

'Put some music on,' said Kat. She was standing by the chair with a fresh G&T. I eyed her. 'Are you taking this seriously?'

Kat was obstinate. 'Are *you*?'

I chose something that felt appropriate, and slid the disc from its sleeve. *Tomb Raider II,* the video game soundtrack. The disc crackled, started to turn. The high call of a flute whined through the room, which glowed from the small flame within the sagging pumpkin, and the group of candles Kat had made me light. Gentle drums on the track. A flicker of something hot was in my belly, in the air around us; it dripped from the tap into the stainless-steel basin, it crackled in the freezer.

We turned off the lights.

'Right, let's see if this prick's still here.' She sat down on the chair, which was pointed towards the darkening windows where I crouched.

'How do you know how to do . . . things like this?' I asked, staring at one of the four piles of salt she had poured in each spotless corner of the room. I fought the urge to reach for Goblin.

'I've been reading,' she said, without skipping a beat. 'A lot. Now count.'

Kat clapped her hands together, and they seemed to rumble. A tiny storm between her palms. Enough talk.

'Close your eyes,' said Kat, and I obeyed. 'Now open them. And begin.'

I began to count, very slowly towards sixty. Each number cut through the silence in the room, breaking the cold thrum of anticipation just for a second, until I spoke the next number. Kat sat perfectly still, her face not moving. Only her eyes circling.

Nothing happened. I kept counting.

At nineteen I saw a bead of sweat fall from her hairline to her lips. She didn't move.

Onwards I counted, through the music. A clinking sound; I jumped, but it was only the ice in her drink melting, breaking apart. I picked up the count. Her knee jigged.

At forty-two she grimaced, and I thought something was happening, but nothing did. I got to sixty and she opened her eyes and huffed, frustrated.

'Fuck sake. Didn't work.' She looked me up and down for a moment. 'Right. It's your house. It likes you. Sit down.'

I didn't really want to sit in a chair with my eyes closed while she watched me, but I didn't have much choice. I took her place. The chair was warm.

'Tell me if you feel *anything*,' she whispered, and stood in the corner.

She now began to count. I stared directly at the wall, between the two windows. *'One. Two. Three.'* She took a small breath in between each number, spoke on the exhale. I burned with anticipation.

When she reached ten seconds the chair moved. *Oh Jesus Christ, it's here.* I held back a sharp gasp. The chair moved again; something had pulled it back just a little.

'Eleven. Twelve. Thirteen.'

I began to tingle all over. At twenty seconds the Björk poster caught my eye as it shifted on the wall above the sofa, the thin glass flexed with a twisting pressure. Her face warping. I heard the scrape of the wooden frame against the paintwork. Then it stilled.

Thirty seconds. Tiny bright lights in the air, like the inside of a precious stone, or a disco ball turning. Quite pretty. Then gone.

Nothing for ten seconds. I held down hot puke.

'Forty-five. Forty-six.'

At fifty seconds, a new sound. A deep, gentle groan, the noise of heavy breath catching in the throat. Close to my ear. I twisted in a quiet new fear.

'Fifty-five, fifty-six, fifty-seven, fifty-eight, fifty-nine.'

At sixty the clanging of a bell, less like a church tower and more like that round the neck of a tethered, hairy animal, chewing cud on a mountainside somewhere. And the movement of something large behind me that I could not see. *Come out, come out.*

'Are you there?' I whispered. Nothing. I waited a moment or two. The floorboards thumped beneath my feet. Another thudding, from the wall. Something at my neckline like a hot wet tongue; I stood up fast and swivelled. I was *thrumming*.

Kat was sitting wide-eyed, her crossed legs jigging.

'What was that?! What happened?'

'Nothing,' I lied.

'I saw that picture move!' she said, and I shook my head. Was that all she had seen?

'You liar! You heard something! It's in here. Don't be scared. Take your socks off.' She got up fast, looking a little nauseous.

'Why?'

'Simon, just do it. Socks *off*!' she ordered.

I slid both socks off like fruit skins, feeling their mild greasiness between my fingers. My toes left the sweaty ghosts of prints on the floor, before they slid away: stickers unpeeled. I looked up at Kat.

'I've got a verruca.'

'How old?'

'About a year.'

'Then I don't care.'

She was upending her tote bag over the kitchen table; I winced at the chaos.

'I've brought some stuff,' she said, pointing to the pile on the table. I swivelled in the seat to watch as she waved her hands over the items gathered there, among the gum wrappers and receipts. She spoke each name aloud rapidly. She was excited.

A bundle of pale green leaves. 'White sage, for cleansing. Highly effective. Crucial.'

Little gold Bible. 'Who knows if that shit works.'

An elegant yellow tube. 'Long matches. From Paris.'

A *Lord of the Flies*-style conch. 'A shell from the ocean. Well, the seaside I think. For tapping.'

My bottle of gin. She caressed this like a little pet and cackled. 'Most important!'

Kat lit a match, and her face became illuminated, both golden and shadowed, just for a moment. She held it beneath the sage until the acrid smoke was thick enough to leave a trail in the air.

'*This* is going to start the job of getting rid of that thing.'

'Isn't this cultural appropriation?' I said.

'You don't know my culture,' she said, and took a swig of gin from the bottle.

Next, Kat lifted my right foot with a warm hand, inspecting the sole, forcing me to tilt back a little further on the chair. I watched, my neck at an angle, and behind her the sky through the window was almost black. With one finger, Kat dabbed the still-smoking sage, ignoring the heat. She placed a dot of black ash on the sole of my foot. Her finger turned.

She repeated the process on the other foot. I yelped.

'It's very hot!'

Kat eyed me, and brushed a long curl from her face.

'Poor baby. You need extra protection. Now sit up.'

I sat up.

Now Kat ashed her finger again, and then reached for my face. I flinched, but then relaxed, allowing her to wipe her finger Simba-style across my forehead. It burned.

Rhythmically, sensuously, Kat began waving the sage in small circular motions, like a conductor. In her other hand, the G&T she'd picked up from the table remained steady. She took a sip as she saged the sofa. I could smell her perfume, a strong smell of vanilla mingling with the sharp smoke.

'You have to do it in all the places where dodgy shit likes to hide,' she said, her voice low as she saged a circle around me. 'And I think it especially likes *you*.'

I watched her smudge inside each cupboard, opening and closing them in procession. She did inside the fridge, too, which wafted out a vegetable smell as she opened it. Next, she did the washing machine, poking the burning sage in and out, in and out, like a penis. She looked over her shoulder and grinned wickedly, her tongue between her teeth.

A thin breeze blew in from the street, disturbing the

haze. I watched the smoke move on the ceiling above me, through the dim pools of light that each of the four candles sent upwards. I saw something there, like the movement of a long hand, playing with the smoke. I heard something on the roof.

Kat did not pause, nor turn around as she moved into the corridor and I jogged to keep up. 'Do you have a cat?' she said.

'No. Why?'

'I think this place needs a salt lamp. If a cat licks a salt lamp it could die.'

'There are no cats here,' I confirmed.

She froze in the corridor. 'Ugh, Jesus. It feels like we're being watched.'

Suddenly she shouted, head back to the ceiling so her voice echoed, dark with rage, raining back on us.

'Get out of here, you slimy cunt! He's not alone anymore! Get back to where you came from!'

She'd had a lot of gin by now.

The corridor was also dark, the tealights Kat had placed in mugs and jam jars our only sources of light, causing the whole place to wobble in shadow. We both looked towards Massimo's closed door, the only room we hadn't entered. The only room I hadn't touched. She strode forward and opened it, the draught causing some of the candle flames to flicker.

'Careful,' I said.

The room was as it had been early that morning. The

bed was strewn with tangled sheets, the cupboard doors open.

Kat turned on the light and we both blinked. I felt almost embarrassed.

'It used to be much tidier in here. Spotless.'

Kat shrugged. 'It's not too bad.' She nudged a bottle with her foot. The skeleton mask was nowhere to be seen.

'It's not as bad as when it was my old housemate's room and I hadn't tidied it.'

Kat pulled a twisted face. 'You tidied his room? Now *that's* . . .' Kat said, tapping me hard on the chest for emphasis, '. . . fucked up.'

I suddenly felt uncomfortable with how much this stranger was seeing, how much I was giving away. What she was learning about me so quickly. Rummaging through my life.

'There's nothing in here, I don't think. But I'll smudge it anyway; it stinks like boy.'

In the kitchen, the record playing freed itself, a long loud call like a wild bird filling the flat.

Kat tapped a foot, nodded eagerly down the corridor. 'Your room then,' she said, and I swallowed down bile.

When I reached my door, I pressed a quivering palm flat against it, the way you would touch a large, nervous animal. I pressed on the handle and opened it in one smooth motion. My room, tidier than ever; clothes folded, bed made, blinds up, floor Goblin-fresh. The sweet smell of bleach. In the semi-darkness it felt almost sacred.

Kat swept fast into the room, a little frenzied, muttering. 'I'll fucking find it, Simon. I will find it.' She pointed the smudge stick towards me. 'This *will* work. I'm not leaving this flat until I find it.'

Go on then, get on with it. Fucking find it.

She was trailing white smoke, surveying my kingdom. In the dim light of my own clean white candles, reserved for emergencies, she stared at the neat piles of paper on my desk, the stacks of gay mythology on the bookshelf, my shirts hanging straight on their steel rail, like knives in a block. She smiled at the queer art tacked on the wall, erotic but tasteful, and the thumb-eared photos of old pets. I waited for my review.

Instead, she called: 'Come out, come out, I know you're here. Come out and pull my arm off!'

Nothing happened, and Kat grimaced, before slumping slightly. Was she running out of steam?

'This room is too tidy, I feel like I'm in a shop.'

'Thank you,' I said.

She rolled her eyes. 'I'm gonna need another drink. You finish this room. You need to state your intentions.'

I accidentally took a frustrated breath.

'What exactly will that do, Kat?' She turned to face me.

'It's banishing. You have to tell it to leave!'

She left the room. *Tell it to leave.* I let her last words linger in the air between us. I turned them over and over as she left me in the darkness of my room. The idea of urging the beast to leave disturbed me. She wanted me to kick it out, this thing that had caused her so much horror. To never see it again, perhaps even kill it.

That's not what I wanted at all.

CHAPTER TWENTY-EIGHT

The room was silent; I only heard the muffled rustle of the freezer drawer in the kitchen as Kat fixed another gin.

I looked at the sage in my hand. It burned softly, unconvincingly. I wiggled it through the air, and left a thin trail of smoke. Nothing happened. I stepped to the corner and waved it over the clothing rack, where something had once hidden. I saged it twice, wondering if I'd need to wash the shirts.

Something moved beside me.

I shook the smoking stick, harder. I heard what I thought was a deep cough. I turned toward it.

Oh, there you are.

'You don't like this?' I said, wiggling the stick again. In response, a cadaverous breath beside me.

'Are you there?' I said, quietly so Kat couldn't hear me. I held my breath, listening. But nothing spoke back.

I smudged the fern, the bedside lamp. I turned in a circle, smudged all over the desk, the pens and pencils and paperclips, the whole time feeling like something was side-stepping heavily behind me. Breathing. I wanted to turn around and touch it, but so far, physically, I was still alone in the dark room.

'Show yourself then. Well? Are you fucking there?' I teased it, growing more confident with every shuffle and clicking throat-groan that reached my ears. It was really *here*.

'I can't hear your intentions!' shouted Kat from the kitchen, startling me. I heard a cupboard slam. 'I mean it Simon!' Was she coming back?

I bristled. The sound of her voice irritated me. I felt that deep, familiar yearn, to do what I was told. To be good, to follow Kat's instructions. I did not want her to catch me misbehaving in my room. I clenched my fists, and cleared my throat for show.

'I want you to leave,' I murmured. *Just show me your face. Just the face!*

'Louder!' screamed Kat, and now she sounded closer to my room, like she was coming to check on me.

'I want you to leave!' I said louder, closing my eyes, feeling for it. I heard it laugh. *Just touch me. Say my name or something. Please.* Soft shards of light washed across my vision, pulsing as I squeezed my eyes tighter.

I took a deep breath, and smudged faster, my eyes thin creases in my face.

I've had fun. OK I'll admit it. And I fancy just a little more.

'It's too much. It needs to stop now. You have to leave!' I swung the stick and called out loud, for Kat, who whooped from somewhere in the tunnel of the flat. She sounded drunk, and coming closer.

I opened my eyes. On the roof of the fire station, lit by the streetlamps, a boy sat cross-legged, watching me. Massimo. I blinked, and he was still there, laughing into his fingers. I looked him in the eye, across the lane of hometime traffic. He stared back. My reflection wobbled in the dark cross-section of the windowpanes, flickering in the candlelight. I could see myself, pale and hunched with a dark ash gash on my forehead.

'One more time with feeling, big boy!' Kat yelled, so close now I could hear the gin on her voice, and whatever else she had found in the kitchen.

I gripped the sage and tilted my head back and closed my eyes again and yelled.

'FUCK. RIGHT. OFF!'

Silence. Then, a shrill whine began to build in my skull, and the room got hot so quickly I struggled to breathe. I began to panic, held firmly in place while a deep pressure was forming, the heavy force of something pressing down upon me. It started to hurt. Smoke curled upward from the sage in my hand, filling my nose. I tried harder to find air from somewhere, but could only force a wheeze.

The heat was rising fast, the whine building slowly to a

scream. Through the windowpane, I looked for Massimo on the roof opposite, but the glass was inky black. The window was shimmering, flexing itself, and I realised the glass in front of me was simply filled with the reflection of whatever was standing behind me. I reached out a hand, to touch the pane.

My lungs tightened further. I squeezed out a whisper into the dark room.

'That hurts, you're hurting me.' The pressure intensified. I thought I might piss myself with fear. Or excitement.

'OK, stop. Stop! It fucking . . . *hurts*! Now I want you to fuck off. I really do!'

The glass began to pulse rapidly, rippling like water. The pain intensified, unbearable. It was too much. It was not enough. Sweat was running from my armpits as the pain grew wilder, like I might crack right down the middle.

'Stop. I really want you to *stop*!'

The whining was so loud I thought the glass would shatter; it was vibrating like crazy. The whole room was screaming at an impossible frequency. And then, as if being delivered by the window itself, a terrible voice spoke.

'No you don't.'

I gasped, finally pulling in enough breath, and dropped the stick of herbs. It smouldered gently for a moment on the floor, and then went out.

The overhead lights flashed on.

CHAPTER TWENTY-NINE

Kat stood in the doorway, mouth wide open. Drink in one hand, tub of fine table salt in the other. I spun around from the window to face her. The noise, the pressure, the vibrations, all had ceased.

'What was that?' Her face was a mix of horror and awe.

'Nothing. It didn't come.' I flicked sweat from my fingertips.

'I saw something behind you.'

'No, you didn't.' My voice was harsh.

She was shaking, the salt in her hand pouring to the floor and beginning to mound. She fanned her face with the other hand. 'It's fucking hot in here!'

'Kat, the salt.'

Her face was furious now. Her crazy hair doing its thing.

'You were talking to it. I *heard* you. Why are you lying?'

'You have to go now, Kat, I'm very tired.' My whole body was on fire.

'What the fuck, Simon?!' The salt was pouring everywhere.

'Watch the fucking salt, Kat!' I shouted, and watched spittle fly from my lips.

At this, she came to life. She looked at the salt, and jerkily started tossing it into the air.

'This . . . is what . . . I'm here . . . to do!' Salt flying through the air, landing on the clean sheets, the polished floor. Getting *everywhere*. 'Where did it go? We have to kill it!'

'You need to fucking leave. Now.' My voice was steady as I pointed her towards the door.

'Simon, please. Just tell me what happened in here!' She was so confused.

'Now!' I roared, and lurched forward to push her. She was on the edge of mania, but so was I, shoving her out of the bedroom, down the corridor and out of the front door with big hard hands, where she fell to the concrete and stared up at me, begging me to talk to her. She banged on the metal of the door repeatedly after I'd slammed it in her face.

I stood still for a moment, and waited for her to stop. I heard her gulping little sobs of confusion as she descended the stairs, stopping once to call my name. Eventually the steel clang of the main doors signalled her departure. I breathed out, and looked down the murky corridor. The whine had stopped; I felt no pressure.

I prayed she had not scared it off. Right here, right now,

that was all I wanted. To be together with my new friend. Just me and the beast, in the confines of the flat. No barriers, no boundaries.

My stomach bubbled. Not dread. Anticipation. I called into the silence.

'Are you still there?'

I waited, feeling my breath begin to regulate. The flat was still heavy with sage, and I noticed the remaining smoke was thinning and drifting upwards, disappearing into the ceiling.

'I'm sorry about her. You can come back now.'

More silence for a moment.

'Come back!'

I heard something chuckle in the bedroom.

Above me, the spotlights began to flicker, and each bulb began to gently hiss. Soon they were smouldering, a pale, chemical smoke trickling downwards towards me. I walked towards the bedroom, through the acrid smoke that became thicker until the lights popped, extinguishing one after the other, softly bursting until the final light tinkled, and a soft dusting of glass showered down onto my hair and shoulders. I stepped through the doorway to my room.

The bedroom was very dark now, candles snuffed, lit only by the whitewash of the streetlamp outside. In the corner, near the bed, something stirred. I smiled.

'You're still here.'

I stayed where I was, standing near the desk, breathing. The fern shook hard, its pot cracking and a chunk falling loose. I saw its soil spilling out in rotten wet clumps, could smell its fresh mould.

My eyes strained to see. The rug, spread at the foot of the bed, was being rucked slightly at the corner, folded inwards as it was moved. I saw at its edge, in a small square of light, the gentle singeing of a footprint, burnt into the fabric. Round, like something you might see pressed into desert sand. Then another. I felt, but could not see, a large body getting closer to me.

I smiled. Christ, I was *really* smiling now. Because here it was, what I had wanted to find. All to myself. I stood, motionless, in the centre of the murky room. I let it come to me.

I felt hot rancid breath in puffs on my face and thought for a moment I saw the glimmer of a huge chest beside me, the curve of horny bone. Feelable, just *there*, but not quite touchable. Sweet spit filled my mouth, pooled inside my molars.

And then it spoke again.

'Simon.'

The voice seemed to come from the very walls themselves. Every particle of paintwork, every bit of concrete and bookshelf and bright white bedsheet, all seemed to throb with the loud, wondrous voice. The being was beside me, certainly, but the voice was a huge, delicious, state-of-the-art surround sound.

An eruption of tingling across the plains of my skin. That *voice*, clear at last. So familiar, yet like nothing I had heard before. A cavern's song, ancient and slow. Louder than traffic, louder than drums. Like Easter, and holidays, but also like skeletons suddenly standing up and secret ice beneath thin snow that sends you cracking to a frozen, silent death. Beneath it all, that thin whine. It was good, *so good*; it was the worst sound I'd ever heard.

'Tell me what you want.' I tilted my head back and spoke upwards, towards it. I could *smell it*. That glorious, rotten stink.

'To come in.'

The enormous voice, exploding from monstrous bellows, echoing from the mattress, the shaking lamp, the small speaker in the corner. Flakes of paint drifting downwards, shaken free by the tremors.

Maybe it could come in, if that's what it wanted. It could come in and take everything, leave nothing left, fill me up like foam and nestle in my bones.

'You'll let me in, won't you? You'll let us be friends?'

'I saw you, in there, on the bed.' I gestured with the tiniest nod of my head, towards Massimo's room.

'The veil was thin.'

'You've been killing people, out there.' I lifted a finger to the window.

It grunts.

'Collateral damage.'

'Did you eat that boy?'

A soft chuckle, deep and long. I wanted to reach out and touch that sound, it was so physical, it was the air itself.

'It's you I want to talk about. My friend. I've been trying to come in.'

I clear my throat, blink my eyes hard, as I feel hands on either side of my head. A warm vice, tightening.

'You were in here, the other night. Walking around.'

It purred back at me.

'Do you live in Massimo?'

'Mostly.'

'Have you been in me?'

'Only partly.'

'What does that mean?'

It let out a growl. I saw the smallest glimpse of it, in the darkness beside me. White, waxy, huge.

'I've been inside, and had a taste. Such a small taste. I left a bit of me in there, actually. Just a drop. Haven't you felt it, my friend? Don't say no, that's a lie. You felt it, you liked it. So I'm coming in now, to give you a little more.'

What a voice, shaking the whole room. A breeze that carries bees.

'You must allow it. I am no plunderer.'

'Oh.'

'So I'm coming in?' it half-told, half-asked as I felt something pushing against the soft nest where my ribs ended. The flesh there was getting hot, and I thought maybe my whole chest was glowing, in the darkness of the room. My mouth filled with more of that spit, sticky-sweet and tinged with blood. The thing pushed harder against my chest, moving upwards, and I felt a vibration like two shuddering hands pressing hard on each pectoral, against each nipple.

My insides tingled, my whole ribcage shuddered; oh *God* the way it felt, sinking into me. *Amazing.*

I nodded. *Yes. Come in.*

Those huge firm hands now also on my ankles, my calves, the tops of my thighs. I tried to turn, but the pressure was forming above me, almost forcing me to fold in half, until suddenly I felt movement as a large hand, gnarled and scaly, slipped itself into mine and squeezed. The whine was building to a howl, the pressure throbbed like the air itself might snap, and its large face was brought close to mine, a hot tongue sizzling with spittle, deep into my ear canal.

It writhed against me, and I felt its weight, a muscular force rasping its way up my torso, scraping my belly button through my shirt, singeing those curly hairs. The clanging of another bell, pressure now on the base of my spine up under my clothes as my skin exploded into goosebumps. My shirt shifted as I twisted and fell to the bed. The air around me was hard to breathe, soupy, like fresh vomit filling my lungs. I breathed it in and felt something groping for an entrance at the back of my skull.

And then came panic, then came Simon, and I heard myself freaking out, fighting back, felt myself pushing, like a part of me was beginning to heave my full weight against a boulder. No, no. I pushed back hard against what I could not see and a barrage of voices in Swedish, Danish, Italian, Punjabi, they all spoke back. Mocked me monstrously. They told me not to bother.

'You're not coming in, actually. I've changed my mind.

You're fucking not.' My own voice thick and gritted, hands clutching the bedsheets, face twisted. My belly ached badly, as it turned to rot.

It only laughed.

'It's too late.'

Movement outside the window: a small tanned face peering in. Eyes wide. Hands against the glass. The beast was too massive, it was coming in and I couldn't stop it. I pushed harder still, hard as I could. My back bucking, my mouth a twisted knot, a little scream squirming in my throat. Hands gripping the bedsheets. I released the scream as I writhed and the scream was a muscle, pushing back with me. A roaring, loud as a train, howling around me. The weight of something on the bed, pressing down on my ribs, thick hands on my chest, and I screamed against it. I tried pushing again, losing strength. But I couldn't stop it because, also, I wanted it. Oh how I *wanted* it. It was too delicious. One last feeble heave, one last pathetic push against it.

Something snapped like bone, and then all was still.

My phone was ringing. The room was fuzzy around me but I heard it trilling. I found it near my pillow. It stopped. It began to ring again. I answered it.

'Simon, what the *fuck*?!'

The sound of Lana's voice slowly tugged me back to reality.

'Where the fuck are you, Simon, it's a fucking shitshow here!' I was late for a shift I didn't even remember agreeing to.

Lana sounded like she might explode, which made me

smile. I wasn't afraid. I was feeling good, actually. Really good.

'Simon, for fuck's sake, can you hear me?'

I slowed my panting, rubbed my watery eyes, sat up and put on my good voice.

'Yes, I can hear you,' I replied, and one of my teeth fell out.

I reached down in the half-darkness and found the slimy molar in a little crimson wet patch. I stroked it, pocketed it. That's mine. I rose from the bed, testing my movements very slowly. I found a white shirt in the washing basket, then noticed the chocolate stains all over the sleeves. I put it back down and closed my eyes. Steadied myself, my little Bambi legs. Listened to the bubbling in my gut. A sensation was growing; I felt alive.

I looked around at the same old sights, the sink scooped into the counter, the spider plant splayed in the corner. The room felt smaller, because it was, and I felt bigger, because that was also true. I leaned all the way back and laughed upwards at the ceiling.

In the bedroom, I had fought back, fought my hardest against the visitor. For a moment. But now something lingered inside me, something remained.

Because, I'd let it.

CHAPTER THIRTY

I was almost ninety minutes late and arrived to find the restaurant heaving.

I paused for a moment outside and looked at my reflection in the window while carefully gathering myself. I looked pale in the cornflower-blue shirt I'd just stolen from a laundrette. It billowed in the wind. Weird look, but good enough. I looked a little taller, my back looked broader. The veins on my neck seemed chunky, full of blood. My eyes were green, bright as new buttons. Spooky boy.

Lana appeared in my line of vision, striding to the door and pulling it open. Rosy round cheeks ballooning.

'Simon, are you just going to stand there? Are you on the same planet as the rest of us?' she hissed, through the open door.

I was extra calm and extra polite. 'I'm sorry, Lana, I'm super sorry.' I splayed my hands out like spiders to prove it.

She looked me up and down. 'You look like *shit*. You look . . . different. Your eyes. What the hell is that shirt? Where's your apron?'

'Oh damn! I forgot it.' I put a hand to my forehead. Duh!

'Christ, Simon. What is going on?' Was she actually concerned? She had lowered her voice, and she was squinting so hard, trying to work out what was causing this sea-change in me. She had no idea.

She rubbed her temples. I rolled my eyes. The *drama*.

My skin itched, too deep to scratch. I followed Lana through to the back. We paused in unison for a customer asking for a jug of tap water, no ice, actually just one cube, or a couple, do you have mint and lemon? We both grinned with practised patience. I clapped my hands together. 'Excellent choice.'

Out the back, Lana found an apron. Clean enough. She tied it tight, she had to step close to me to do it. Close enough for me to bite her nose.

'Simon, are you OK?' I had not bitten her nose, but I was looking at it carefully.

'I'm OK.' I smiled a straight white line.

She led the way back to the restaurant. I pressed past her to begin the shift. She stopped me, a hand on my back. Sniffed.

'Simon. Is that you, smelling like that?'

I stopped walking. 'Why do you keep saying my name?' I asked her. 'Why do you *always* say my name like that?'

She looked at me, a little shaken for the first time ever. I gave her my best Simon smile.

'What has got *into* you, Simon? *Is* it you, that smell?' she repeated.

'I think it *might* be,' I said. And I winked at her.

The new pot-wash guy was there, scrubbing a saucepan in the kitchen. That lovely dilf. I noticed a tiny sexy gut creeping over his belt through his tucked in polo shirt. *Huge* arms. He smiled at me and raised a soapy hand. Did I just wink back at him? He turned to get more pans and I watched his arse rolling away.

Yes, I was being a little over the top, I could see this. I took a beat in the walk-in-freezer to cool down, in case that helped. But my friend took me in his fist and dragged me back out. *Come on now, no time to waste.* There were tables to serve. Sweet customers all dolled up in their silky T-shirts and loose trousers. Witchy little boots on their soft feet. I trod on someone's toe on purpose and she squealed.

'Excuse me, can I have some goat-milk ice cream?'

'Excellent choice!'

In the corridor I felt something on my skin, or in my skin. When I looked down inside the billowing shirt, I saw hard shapes moving on my torso, a pressing from beneath the muscle, like it was rolling over, getting comfortable. Flexing. My chest was practically vibrating. I burped, bilious, and shuddered with glee at the smell. I felt the tooth in my pocket, turning it over like a sticky little gem.

I brushed a crumb from my apron, made it really neat. Looked out at our guests. Put an arm around Lana like we were married, and she heaved it off. I surveyed the kingdom. The whole rabble. Aha. There she was, at the back. The regular. Bob feathered, glasses bottle-bright, all glinting in the mood lighting. Anna fucking Wintour perusing the menu like she ever ordered anything else. iPad flashing on the table. She sensed me, raised her head. Saw me, raised her hand. I walked over and I barely felt my feet on the wood of the floor.

'Can I have another small glass?' She raised the empty glass and pointed to it.

'Of course.' *Just buy a bottle.*

'Excuse me?' She peered up at me.

'Excuse me?' I peered back.

'Did you say something? After you said "of course"?'

'I said "of course", and then I said "what are you watching?"'

'Oh. It's a romcom. Slow on the com.' She smirked at her own joke. 'So, yes, that wine please.'

'Excellent choice! Really good. I'll be right back with your wine.' I turned on my heel, spun around full 360 with my arms out. Made another half-turn. Found my point of direction and scurried to the back.

I heard my stomach rumble and realised I was starving. I felt my new friend coursing through me, alive and kicking. When nobody was looking, I pulled a cauliflower, speckled with black mould, out of the slops bin and took a hearty bite. Looked around for more and licked a sticky plate clean. Good good. Really good.

Then I was right back with the wine. I had drunk half the glass on the way but I hadn't lied about fetching it. That tasted amazing too; everything was sweeter, soaking into my fat tongue like gravy into bread. I placed it in front of her, asked if she was going to be having French fries.

'A bit later. Maybe in act three.' She *chortled*. She thought she was *funny*. She looked at my face. 'You've got something round your mouth,' she said. I saw myself in the wall of smoked mirror behind her. My hair crazy, gob smothered in sauce.

I leaned my face down towards her and whispered, 'Want a little taste?' I giggled and ran to take another order.

I stalked the restaurant, leonine, and skipped around the largest table. Delivered bread baskets, poured beer into bulbed glasses. Startled a child into a spooky little scream by whispering really close, 'There's a fly in your soup. Doin' the backstroke.' I ate a French fry from a plate. Not sure anyone noticed that so I did it again. Drank long from a bottle of fusty orange wine in the fridge. I wondered, for a moment, as I strutted proudly from the bar to the bogs and back again, the funky mood music sizzling in my ears, whether this is how Josh might often feel. So big, so brave, so beautiful.

It kept saying things to me. My friend.

Put your filthy tongue in the bouillabaisse. Snap that lady's hideous glasses. Wiggle your nasty hips. Go on, finger his foie gras! And I did. I would do whatever it said. *Now put your manky tooth in his tequila.* Good idea. I dropped it in the glass and watched a man swallow it down.

Lana at my neck. 'Simon. I've had a complaint.' *About your breath?*

'Excuse me?'

'Lana, darling, you do know you're not the fucking manager?' I stunned her into glorious silence.

I took a shot of vodka at the bar. Then two more. When nobody was looking, I went out the back and slurped a slopped tomato. Found some cheesy mushrooms that were headed for the bins, swallowed them in chunks. Could not get enough. Couldn't get the idea of earthy food from my head. Put my whole head in the bin and bit down. Emerged, gasping for air. Corny dribble-juice going right down my chin, then my hand and all the way down-sleeve. Blooming yellow against the blue. No peppers on the rack which was a damn shame. Meat would do only if slightly sweaty, a bit shiny, on the turn. Not much of that here. Why didn't we have more mushrooms?

I stepped back inside the restaurant. The fit pot-wash guy made me jump, coming up close behind me, and I howled, cackled. Grabbed his bum. Lana looked over once, twice, three times. Oh this was fun! This was something else. I was smiling because I meant it. I could feel it inside, that deep tonguing that was tickling my bad side and waking it, letting me say everything I'd ever wanted to say. To do my worst. To be my *baddest*. Such sweet escape. I nicked three gulps from a negroni sweating on the bar, and crunched the glass between my teeth.

A very small dog I had not noticed rushed out to lick at the bones of a dropped short-rib. Tiny tongue flicking out. We did not allow dogs in here. This one was bug-eyed and had slipped through the net. Lana flashed over, didn't mention the dog, near skidded on grease from meat. I was already on it. Crayons for the child, sir? The dog kept yipping at me. *Eat it.* Should I eat it . . .?

A hand went up in the corner again. I hopped over in a single leap! The Regular wanted *another* glass. Unbelievable. Just buy a bottle. It's cheaper. Less work for me. It's an excellent choice. *It works out cheaper. Buy a fucking bottle. You're throwing money away. Buy a fucking BOTTLE. Come on, baby, BUY. A. BOTTLE!*

The room was silent, pin-drop quiet. Everyone was looking. Lana was purple. Had I said all of that out loud? Screamed it? To her. The Regular. Ha! I'd drained her half-full glass into my mouth then knocked it off the table but it hadn't smashed, just skidded. Shame. So I stomped on it. Mazel tov! The other guests and the one shit waiter had their mouths wide open, catching flies. I saw the dilf pot-wash putting on his coat, sneaking out the back. That dog going mad. I should eat it. Was someone crying?

Lana at my elbow like a fucking limpet as always. 'Simon. I'm sorry, madam. *Simon*, come with me. What are you doing? Simon. *Simon*.'

I pulled my elbow back from her.

'Say my name. Say it. One. More. Time. I dare you,' I said to Lana. She pulled back her face in a haze of smoke that I had blown.

I was smoking a cigarette. I'd taken it from the pocket of the Regular, out of her big brown faux fur coat. I'd lit the fag from the candle on the table, inhaled, puffed out into Lana's face, and now she was coughing. The Regular, was she smirking? Oh, she loved a laugh. Maybe I could set off the fire extinguisher, a great big stream of chemical jizz all over the shop and the people eating their artichoke hearts and sausage soup and potted fucking *poussin*. Was it hazardous for children and dogs? Oh, we'd soon find out. What was round my mouth? Had I eaten that dog? I had downed an entire bottle of Lambrusco and I was standing on a table that wibbled beneath me. A sound from my mouth, a sonorous boom of sorts, rocking the very brickwork that contained us all, that housed the napkins and the little green cups and wide-eyed women. Tablecloth whipped around my head flinging bits of bread into unblinking eyes. What was on my hands, blood or beetroot? Hard to tell, with the room spinning like a top, blurs of pink and polished glass like a hand in a blender. Floorboards and crayons 'neath my shoes. I lifted the fire extinguisher, diddled the nozzle. A huge wide arc of spicy foam entered the scene. Heavy red cannister hurtling through the air toward the windows. Sound of smashing glass. People yelling. Alarm hooting. Was that me? Hard to tell from this far away, out on the street where I'd legged it, where I was still legging it around the corner. Before I did something *really* bad, *really* stupid, like eating a dog. Or worse.

Cars revving around me, horns honking. Small boys giggling at my clumsy jogging, at the scene of it all. Headlights flashing into my green, green eyes, spinning me round to catch the glare of foxes, shopkeepers in clouds of vapour, hard stares from elderly couples putting out their bins and sweeping their steps.

I ran on into dark alleyways and shimmering side streets, through puddles from rain I couldn't remember, my friend in my head slamming its fists, tickling my guts, full of glee at the monstrous night I was giving it. *More more more!* I was choking on it, felt it crawling through my throat, tugging at my tonsils. I stumbled in circles, disappearing down holes that should have been bricked up long ago.

I turned a corner and ran smack into something huge and hot and stinking of smoke.

CHAPTER THIRTY-ONE

I was soaking wet and someone was laughing at me.

I looked up from where I was lying on the ground. Somehow I had wound up back near the restaurant, in the back alley. I saw the dilf, now wearing a red puffer jacket and kicking the back of one trainer against a wheelie bin. He was smoking a fag with one hand and he scratched his stubble with the other, before reaching down and pulling me up. The beetle-black sky swirled. I caught a glimpse of shaving rash on his neck.

'You have fun in there?' he asked.

'Oh yeah.' My breathing was a little ragged.

'Think that might be curtains for your job.'

I gave a wry little smile.

'Are you crazy then?' he said.

I couldn't place his accent, all long low vowels and clipped Ts. Norway? Russia? Mix of both? I shrugged my shoulders up to my ears, like a cartoon. I was high as hell.

'She's a *bitch*,' I said, jabbing towards the restaurant with a thumb.

'She's nice.' He laughed.

'Yeah right.' I shook my head.

'She's after a promotion.'

I made a face.

'Are you drunk?' he was asking me.

'Wasted.'

'Fancy another?' he said. 'Before she kills us both?'

I smiled a sharp smile.

'The night is young.'

The music in the bar was terrible, but the wine was fucking amazing. I had three large glasses. You'd wonder how I was standing by this point. But I had help, remember. The dilf kept speaking in my ear. I think his name was Oskar. With a K. He drank to catch up with me, downing pints. I was on another planet. Didn't even need drugs.

'I love your eyes. Green is so sexy.' He put a hand to my cheek and I licked his thumb. Saucy little thing. The music got louder, and people shimmied their hips to the centre of the room.

'Dance with me,' said Oskar, and my legs tingled dangerously. I *never* danced in public.

'I actually love to dance!' I howled, and suddenly I could stand still no longer. I threw my head back, and I *danced*.

I began kicking up my feet like they were hooves, as if I was a calf let out to pasture in the spring. The music built. I rolled my head and flicked my hands out to the side. Oh, what a feeling. That heavy beat got me lifting my knees, shrugging my shoulders, hula-hooping my hips round, round, round.

The DJ hit us with a berserker, and I let rip. I danced like an animal attack video – 'Man bitten by croc', rolling around with my hand in a vice-like jaw, trying to get free as it death-rolls. 'Woman climbing into polar bear habitat', and I'm putting my hands up. 'Up! for help' as I'm dragged down by a massive white bear. I am 'unlucky teenager swallowed by Python in Indonesia' so I'm swaying and rolling my hips because oh no I can't breathe, the snake's got me, but the beat is so good, it's really amazing. As the song turns into a proper boot stomper I select the very best, the most special and unique to match the total euphoria – 'Grizzly bear revenge'. There's no coming back from that one.

My date was holding his gut and laughing in amazement. I touched his arse, firm as a car tyre, squeezed hard enough to make him squeal, and pushed him to the bar. Ordered shots that we knocked back. He licked salt off his hand, licked my cheek.

'We're gonna have sex,' he said in my ear and I nodded. Oh yes, please, I want it. 'Give it to me, Daddy.' I felt him grab my hand and we were suddenly on the street, calling for something. In the taxi I felt his hand on my thigh, moving up, rubbing at my groin.

The taxi drove for a while through empty lanes, past used-car dealerships, past rusting lidos and late-night tennis courts. We snogged the whole way, tongues lashing us into the middle of bumfuck nowhere. Suburbia. Streets empty and wide. I hardly noticed. I was the first up the stairs to his flat, panting, pulling at my laces and tossing my trainers aside once he had the door open.

'My kids,' he hissed, finger to his lips.

'Your *kids*?' A dilf not only in theory, but also in practice. How old *was* he? But I was too far gone to care.

We fell into his bedroom, and again I was tearing at my clothes, unbuttoning my jeans, rolling my hips. He looked impressed, just as eager, and we bashed against each other with a growing intensity.

'You can be rough with me,' he said, with a grin, but I spotted it, that little flash of something vulnerable in his eyes.

Good. I'll pull your whole head off. I'm sure I only thought this, because he remained excited while the room spun around us.

I started taking off my T-shirt. He did the same.

Inside me, the thing rubbed its hands.

We started fucking. I remembered how to do it, I was shown by my friend. We writhed and wrestled, our bodies making smacking sounds as we both began to sweat, the room around us practically steaming. He asked me to choke him, so I did. I was looking down at my hands which encircled his throat, and saw the veins beneath my knuckles standing out thick and purple in the glow of his bedside lamp. They looked good. I squeezed harder and he made a sound. I pulled back, but he said it was OK, asked me to do it again. *What a night!*

I felt his sheets slipping against my bare back, sliding down a little over my bum, and I hoisted them higher, so they cloaked us completely. Our hot bodies crawling over each other in the dark. The friend pushing hard, thumping me with glee from the inside. The hard, clean lines of my chest, his shoulders. The sexy curve of my calf muscles, the rounded hillock of his arse. His dick in my hand like a trophy. The light shifted against his face as the duvet slipped again; he smiled up at me, eyes wide open. Oh yes, this was *good*. He wanted more.

I put my hands on the man's neck again and he tilted his head back so that the bump of his Adam's apple moved against my thumbs, like a boat rolling over a little wave. He swallowed, and the wave rose higher.

He swallowed again, and I felt the muscles moving between my palms, which were now pressed flat against his throat, my fingers doing the squeezing. He opened his mouth and showed me his square teeth, and a pain burnt deep at the base of my skull, spreading through my head so that my very eyes became hot with both the sensation and the sight of him beneath me. He was grinning at me, at all of this, and I squeezed even tighter to show him that I could, and the pleasure radiated through my body, through my brain, down to my fingertips. A mix of desire, pure ecstasy, and something else pushing and pushing.

Rage.

Through the heat, and the haze, I suddenly heard choking, and felt a knocking at my back.

The man beneath me was struggling. His face was bulging, almost purple, and he slapped at my back and sides with his palms, but he was growing weaker, more feeble. I watched for six seconds, my eyes fixed.

I stopped when I realised I was hurting someone. I felt myself resisting, pushing, and I spoke firmly. I told my friend, *No. That's not me.*

The man's coughing rang through the room as I released him, although it seemed he was still trying to keep the noise down, mindful of his children even at this moment.

I lurched back and jumped off the bed, and he stared at me in shock before turning and looking over the side of the bed for water.

'What the fuck?' he croaked, massaging his throat, and looking not at me, but at the wall near me.

'I'm so sorry,' was all I could say. 'I've not done that before, I didn't know.'

'How the fuck are you that strong?' he finally managed.

I saw that the sky was beginning to glow as I left his flat, found a main road, and ran.

CHAPTER THIRTY-TWO

Everything was blurry.

'I don't like seafood anyway,' someone was saying. 'Lobster. So expensive! And it's basically a fuckin' bug. A giant red bug. Once they cook it. They're blue first. Big blue fuckin' bugs in the sea!'

I was in the back of a cab. The driver was talking to me. He turned furiously down a side street so quickly I had to grip the seat and try not to vomit.

'And prawns. I'll never eat a prawn! Feels like a dick in your mouth.'

'Yum,' I said. I wasn't feeling amazing.

The driver looked at me in his mirror.

'You gonna puke, mate?'

I shook my head, cheeks bulging. Swallowed.

The driver hit the brakes. 'I've only just had this fuckin' cleaned.' He kept saying seventy-five, seventy-five.

'Of money?' I whispered. Shit.

'Yeah. Of course.'

I took out a card that I knew didn't work, which was enough for him to unlock the doors. I yanked it wide open, that impossibly heavy black door, and legged it hard down unfamiliar streets. Where the fuck was I? I heard the driver shouting in the distance until I doubled over and puked my guts out into a bin.

Around me, the city sulked gloriously. I was somehow in the financial district. Even the tallest buildings had a gleam in their eye, and they huddled over me conspiratorially as the sky brightened. Did they know my secrets? Were they asking for titbits? My brain was pure fuzz. My phone was dead.

I walked along unfamiliar streets, kept my head down so nobody would look at me. Everyone in this city looks sketchy these days, when the weather turns. Especially in this area. They dress like rich criminals. Massive coats, balaclavas, boots, hoods up, eyes darting. *Furtive chic.* I tried to smile at a tiny nun outside a train station but it didn't feel authentic. My eyes burned too much.

I'm always looking, as you know. Eyes peeled like grapes. Watching the city groaning past, crawling beneath me. Staring into corners that are not for me, observing the slip of a smile on a lip, the cavity at the back of a laughing mouth, the clench of two fists. I stood on the street corner that morning, as the sky shook off its dark duvet, and I just watched.

I crept through the station and stared at the people around me, so busy with their days already. Filling the hours of their lives. I was jittery, everything tingled like static.

Every single damn train was delayed; I couldn't figure out the travel maths. I got on a bus instead and prayed it was going in the right direction. I was so tired. My friend was too, it was fast asleep.

On the top deck, I sat behind a teenager and stared over their shoulder as they sent endless texts, engrossed in their activity and the speed of their conversations. Only for them to open the front-facing camera, selfie ready, and catch me peering down, a black-eyed ghoul looking out from a crypt, right there large on their screen.

'What the hell, man? Fucking creep.'

I drew back, curled up against the window. Stared unblinking into passing streets. Watched a man miles up in a tower block, hanging out sheets. A small girl staring out through iron railings, unblinking. The carcass of a bike, wheels long ago removed. The odd flicker of police tape, a boarded up house, a quick snatch of broken door.

Once or twice, out there, I saw something that caught me off guard. A businesswoman falling at a bus stop, blood dripping from her nose, tears dripping from her eyes. A young man, reaching out to help her. A teenage boy in a library window, eating a biscuit carefully, smiling at the taste. An elderly lady skidding down the stairs of the underground and smashing her newly purchased eggs, trying to gather the shells. People on the phone. *I love you too, Dad, happy birthday*. Something about these raw glimpses of humanity was too much to bear. It brought tears to my eyes. I turned away.

This might surprise you. At times the beauty of the world is enough to make me burst. And the people in it, crawling through this city, desperate to survive, reminding me that all we have is this moment, and each other. What the hell am I meant to do with that information?

I tried to get comfortable, which was impossible. Eventually, I closed my eyes and slept.

I was startled awake when the bus hit a pothole. My face was wet. I realised I had been crying, dreaming about Josh. His abandonment. How he never called me anymore, how he didn't even read my messages. How his loss had punched a hole right through me. I was being dragged from a beautiful part of the dream where we were friends again, back on that pebbled beach. Skimming stones and laughing. I had been so happy, and now I was curled up on the backbench of the bus, with a monster clinging to my kidneys.

'You stink.' A small girl was looking over me.

I sat up quick, looked outside the window at houses glowing like wedding cakes in the early afternoon sun. I wiped my face, and pressed the bell three times. On the street I got my bearings, I thought maybe I knew where I was, but everything looked so much bigger than usual. I felt the thrum of another bus behind me; people boarding, jostling me out of the way so I staggered a few steps, turned, looking for a street sign or something familiar.

I saw a boy. Tall, big hair. With a slightly younger, ratty-looking guy. Arms around shoulders, super friendly. Heads back free-cackling.

Josh?

I squinted in the light. It really could be him, getting on the bus, blipping his card, leading the way up the stairs. The bus hissed at me, left the kerb, and I shouted after it.

'Josh!' I called as loud as I could. I was almost *certain* it was him.

My friend woke up and stirred.

'Josh!' I screamed, started to jog, saw him on the top deck. He heard me, looked my way. The bus gathered speed.

My friend, deep down inside, began to stretch. Shook itself.

I was somehow getting faster. My legs allowed it. I screamed his name louder still. 'Josh, Josh, Josh!' Then a bestial roar that shook the air, and caused a man to come off his bike.

His hair was different, maybe longer, and he was wearing a coat I'd never seen before, but it *had* to be him. He was peering down, and so was his mate, the younger guy with his beady little rodent eyes, his tiny square teeth. His hand on Josh's arm. I was gaining on the bus, almost. A motorbike nearly clipped me, veering off. I heard it thump into something hard. I was fast, catching up with the bus, dodging traffic, yelling his name. Beside the vehicle, looking up, and though it should have been too far away to hear,

I heard one of them speak, rat boy I think, his voice poisonous. 'Fucking psycho.'

I was going to reach the bus and climb aboard from the outside. Get my hands on Josh and whoever that rat boy was, leave the upper deck of the E20 looking like an abattoir, slipping on spleens and spinal meat, hands shaking from the murderous exertion. I was so close. I ran into a car, snapping off a silvery wing mirror with my stomach. I was winded, sent spinning. The car bumped into another. I was causing accidents. I looked down into the tiny mirror and saw my tear-streaked face, puke all down the front of my stolen shirt, saliva hanging from my lips in ropes, my eyes glimmering green. The driver slammed the horn and yanked open a door, but I barely registered her shouting. I watched the bus, getting tiny in the distance. I should stop now, I should go home.

Fuck that.

Suddenly I was running again, this time so fast I felt the concrete crumbling gently beneath my shoes. The bus was a mile away, that's nothing. It was slowing down, had stopped at a bus stop, the back door hissing open. In perhaps ten seconds I was on it, up the stairs in two, maybe three, muscular strides. I didn't even check if it was the right bus, I could smell it. There was rat boy sitting at the front, alone.

Josh must have got off the bus, though we were nowhere near anywhere he liked to go. The bus was moving again and rat boy turned to look at me with a sneer and I reached forward to grab at his hair, pull his head back so his throat was exposed and my other hand had become a fist. I saw the face of the dilf, my hands wanting to squeeze harder around his throat, but stopping. Pushing the devil down.

Now I felt my friend begin to laugh, and I did not push. I clenched the fist that grasped the boy's hair, heard tearing, smelt blood in his scalp. Someone downstairs was yelling and the boy's eyes were two eight-balls rolling in his head while my tongue grew fat in a bath of its own saliva and slopped out onto my chin. Dripping onto his frantic face, into his open mouth. His thin voice saying 'no you fucking *nutcase* no'. The way he was *looking at me*.

I hissed between my teeth. *'Eat glass you little cunt.'*

With a terrible roar I smashed his head against the glass, it made a sound like a whip cracking. I did it again. The bus stopped suddenly, I was thrown forward, rat boy's head thudding again, hard against the broken window as I was grabbed from behind and chucked so hard down the stairs I saw stars. My saliva spraying the walls of the bus as I fell. An enormous woman kicked me out onto the street and called me a crazy bastard which I was, I really was, I would've killed him, I realised as I scrabbled on the pavement for my footing.

Through my tears, the bus blurred, disappearing into the distance.

My friend wanted more, was begging for it.

Get up and go, we've only just begun. The party's just starting! Keep going, Simon. Keep going!

People were staring. There was blood on my shirt.

'Enough!' I screamed.

It was enough.

CHAPTER THIRTY-THREE

It had been fun, for a day and a night or so, enjoying a little bit of what Massimo had been hosting inside him. The thrill of sharing certain parts of myself with the wider world had been indescribable. The sweet relief! The delicious freedom of life without shackles. So *that's* how it feels.

But now, twitching on the street, cars honking around me, I assessed the damage.

Clearly I had just lost my job. For starters. And I had hurt people. Quite badly. Who knows what I would have done, had I not been stopped.

Even as I felt its pleasure surging through my veins, running on a steady charge, I knew it had to go. I almost panicked with the realisation of what I had done.

My friend tried to calm me down.

Simon, come. Let's go home. Let us go back to the boy,

and you can ingest the rest of me. This is just a little bit of me, maybe only half. Imagine yourself fully charged.

'Fuck off. That's exactly what I'm scared of.'

People had stopped looking, they'd seen it all before. No police appeared. I crept away down the road for a while, and crawled into thick bushes that hid me from view. In the dirt, I spied an old mattress with a swan crudely painted on it. I pulled it over and lay down, took deep breaths and counted to ten. I knew what to do.

My whole life, I had taken parts of myself and exorcised them. I selected those bits that I was not proud of, or saw little use for, the repulsive parts that squirmed over one another when I lifted the lid. I had removed them carefully, a relentless operation, until I was sure, very sure, that they were gone, or at least well concealed.

In this unfamiliar part of the city, in the bushes of a dirty side street, patrolling my inner workings with a cattle prod at hand, I located, exterminated, extradited. Unwelcome visitors, unsightly friends. These were things I had experience in removing. I was basically an expert. Half a demon? This was nothing.

I opened my eyes to the sky and decided to start the process of separation. Each limb: arm arm, leg leg, including toes times ten, fingers eight and thumbs times two, all need to be severed from this thing. Every hair on my head, the sandy browns and the winking greys. Also both eyes, one a bit larger than the other. Right here under a canopy of telephone wires and washing lines, I shall exorcise myself.

Dick, bum, upper thighs, all included in the detachment. All the parts inside, stomach and lungs, intestine and heart, and the spine that runs road-like behind them all. Any irregular bumps in the flesh, lumps of gristle growing willy-nilly, they're coming with me. The brain's coming too, obviously, but it's the hard part, of course, because my head is the bit that my friend loves most.

Back in my room, the beast had told me it was only partially inside me. And then, lying on the bed, I had eventually let in a little more. But not all of it. A semi-possession. I still had one hand on the wheel.

Half a demon. Nothing I couldn't handle.

I closed my eyes and searched for it. It wasn't hard to find, lying down and panting. Right there, clinging to laddered surfaces, ribs and the underside of my jaw. Laughing and laughing.

Alright? it said and I said no, all is not right, you need to go. I felt it rising up, so I summoned the fight. I lay there on the piss-stained mattress and I gathered a scream. My friend was tired from all that fun so I found what strength I still had and gave it a howling kick, a great whomping boot and it flung away, spinning, grabbing on to my guts and pulling so I felt it hot below my stomach. I looked down, and saw those hard lumps beneath my skin, straining through the muscle on my thigh, the crook of my elbow, rolling over and over. Pulling at my flesh, creating fresh agony. But one more throaty yell, one more stomp on freaky fingers and it'd be gone. It scratched at my liver but slowly lost its grip.

I kicked again, but it clawed back, and it hurt; I lay back panting. I wiped sweat from my brow that stank like black mould. I put a hand to my chest, and felt my heart cracking, the movement almost close to the skin, a bumping from the being beneath. A juddering through my vital organs, like a spiked tongue licking each in turn before moving on to the next, and then returning to the mothership, my heart, to begin again. Burning. I felt this go round three times, and I was silent throughout. The swan looked up, unamused, and watched me gasp for air like a little fish. I dug my fingers into her feathers and prayed I would not die.

I called to the four corners of the city, summoned the wind and begged for the breath I needed for one massive scream, one donkey kick to the devil dick and there it went, bursting from me and howling into the evening, a wisp of vapour that passed through steam clouds from vents in the concrete around me.

It was gone. I had sent it away.

The pain stopped.

I saw blood trickling down my arm, a wide new crack in the skin the colour of plums. I thought maybe I'd lost some toes. I saw a glimpse of my collarbone through my skin. Wow that was rough, and that was just a bit of it. I promised myself I'd never let the thing inside me again.

I breathed. The only thing I could hear was a mewing of sorts, like some timid creature calling for milk, which I realised was me.

I got up, and peeled a used sanitary towel off the back of my jeans.

CHAPTER THIRTY-FOUR

The church had always been something I'd admired; a beautiful building, with its own unique energy. If I'm being honest, I admired only the architecture. I didn't know anything about what happened inside.

For some, it's a place of sanctuary. For others, quite the opposite.

That evening, as I hobbled along my street, I stopped outside the church. A gentle sound had stopped me, the *peep peep* of a soft flute peeling through the open door, which made me step closer. The wind blew down the street, and a crisp packet skittered through the gravestones, coming to a stop against my foot. Prawn cocktail.

I had thought, for a moment, about Kat. If I could find some way to contact her, then she could help me. She would know what to do. I pictured her thick hair blowing in the wind, her kind hands on my shoulders, as she talked me carefully through the plan. She said maybe she could get rid of it. But something about the image stung, like asking for help would be giving too much of myself away.

No. What I had to do next, I could do by myself.

I heard violins, and what sounded, hauntingly, like the voices of children. I moved closer down the path to the double doors, painted American Barn Red. Beneath my feet, the leaves on the path slid a little, slick and mulchy. They tried to slip me up.

Through the stained-glass window to the left of the doors, I saw the ebbing tide of candlelight. I looked up at the window that I had always loved, and blinked back hot tears. I marvelled at its beauty – clean, calm, oppressive. This window was unique; no skeletal Christ on the cross bleeding to death, no disciples feeling sorry for themselves. Instead, a forest scene. A blue mountain rising high in the background, with the trees partly obstructing it. Smaller mountains rolled down to the foreground, where a clear ribbon of a stream flowed through round green rocks. It was through the stream that the candlelight flickered most clearly, and I stood transfixed as it sparkled. I felt the wind again, and it blew through the green glass leaves, rippled the water, stirred the trees. A crow cawed.

I moved a little closer to the doors, close enough to see through them. I could see half the choir, looking toward a tall boy dressed in black. He had golden hair, swept back and tucked behind his ears; he looked a little like me. His eyes were wide as he opened his mouth to sing with such conviction. Suddenly the rest of the choir went quiet, as if he had surprised them into silence. They stared in awe at the beauty of his voice as it rang out like a shard of ice gently melting into grass. He looked gentle and kind, so pure and good. Large hands for holding. A throat smoothly shaven, a mouth for drinking coffee and legs strong enough to crouch and load washing into the machine on Sunday morning. The candlelight wobbled around him. He must have noticed me, because he turned to look, but kept on singing his heart out, filling the cavern of the church with that incredible, beautiful noise.

Such beauty everywhere, I let out a small yowl.

The singing stopped. They all looked at the sad, mad boy in the doorway, hard, dead leaves scuttling around his feet like crabs, blown in a gentle wind. Mud and blood on a stolen shirt. All eyes on me as I stepped through the doors into the church. The choir flinching as I approached them, then turned suddenly toward a small table, and snatched up something that I needed. The tall boy with the beautiful voice blinked once, twice.

I blinked back at him, at all of them, and then turned on my heel and hurried my way out of the doors, through the dim churchyard and towards home.

To deal with Massimo.

CHAPTER THIRTY-FIVE

I could get my life back.

Exactly as it was before Massimo had turned up and fucked it beyond recognition, bringing something with him. I could find a way to get Josh home, perhaps get my job back. Or find a better one. I could reverse the terrible changes that had taken place in my neat little world. I could even redecorate. But there was work to be done first. It was time to banish this demon once and for all.

With each step I felt uneasy. The thing inside me was gone, and with it the confidence, poured out onto concrete.

Few lights burned in our flat. Each room sat quietly, well behaved and minding its own business. Twiddling square thumbs.

I found him in the kitchen, as I thought I would.

He was sitting in the darkness, at the table, doing

nothing. Clacking his teeth. A bottle of red wine in front of him, several empty glasses unstacked from the dishwasher. He was looking across the room out at the street through the open window, towards the fire station.

'Massimo. We need to talk,' I said from the doorway to his muscular back.

Over his shoulder, through the window, I could see the enormous sliding door was up on the fire station, and one of the vehicles was halfway out, being inspected by two of the largest firemen, their thick torsos washed by floodlights. He was watching them work.

Massimo turned slowly, gave me a slightly vacant look. His bruise had darkened, from where I'd punched him. He looked terrible, human. His face squirmed, the muscles working around a thought or idea, like pizza had been promised for dinner and then taken away.

I spoke to him, clearly.

'Who are you, right now?'

'I'm . . . Massimo,' he said, with a small frown. There was no sense of the cold boy, carved from granite. I was inclined to believe him.

'I got fired,' I said.

'Congratulations.'

'And it's your fault.'

He frowned.

'Yeah?'

I was surprised. I had been somewhat prepared for a fight. But here we were, chatting.

'Is that painful?' He pointed to the crusting wound on my arm.

'It's not as bad as it looks.'

He nodded, pleased about that.

'How's your eye?' I pointed to his bruise.

'Sore,' he said, and reached up to touch it.

'Where were you before this, Massimo?' I asked him.

'Sleeping, on the couch.' He gestured with his head to the sofa.

'No, before you moved in here.'

'I lived with friends.'

'Why did you leave? Why did you move into this flat?'

Massimo was still for a moment, looking at me, and then he reached a hand to scratch his chest, the black fabric of his T-shirt bunching and releasing beneath his fingers.

'My flatmate. She kicked me out, I think.'

'Why?'

He was searching for something, squeezing his eyes tight like they itched and then opening them wide, looking for an answer on the ceiling. His lip quivered.

'I scared her.'

I stepped a little further into the room, and he looked at me with sudden clarity. His voice was steady, unlike I'd ever heard it. It was lovely.

He sighed. 'Been there two years. Got lucky to find a great flat. Quiet though. Not so social. All was normal, just working, getting on with it. Going to the pub, going to the park, you know, usual shit. Looking for friends. Trying to get through the weeks, trying to enjoy the weekends.'

I nodded at him.

'I remember one night. I'm lying on my bed just drawing, reading my comics, thinking about home. Thinking about a recipe I want to make if I can get a decent fucking onion somewhere in this fucking city. Then I was crying, just a little bit, because I miss my mama sometimes. A lot. And my nonna just died. And this city . . . you're always alone, even when you're not. So yes I was crying, but I stopped because something was knocking on the window. Or . . . it knocked here.' He frowned, and tapped one knuckle on his forehead before continuing.

'It's like something says "Can I come in and be with you?" I fight it a little at first; it's so strange for something to be so horrible, so good, at the same time. You know?'

He looked to me and I smiled.

'But soon I just say "yeah", cos that sounds nice. A friend. I remember being on the floor, bleeding a bit from my ears. And then it's, what do you call it, *hazy*. I'm feeling strange. Everything tastes much better when I eat, the sunshine feels fucking amazing. But I'm so naughty. I can't behave. I'm getting fired for something . . . *really* bad . . . and then I'm kicked out of the house, and all my stuff is in the car. So then I'm at a big party, somewhere. I go a bit crazy, punch someone and break their nose, get thrown out. Your friend? Josh? He's there, he follows me. He is excited, said I can live here, easy. Said I would love it here, living with you. So I come here, and I can't keep track of the time. And, you know, I've been out there.' He points to the window that stares back, entranced. 'Doing funny *stuff*. Not sure what it was. Having fun. Some bits I remember. Some I'd rather not. Most of the time something else was doing the driving.'

As Massimo told me his story, I began to feel bad. I had never heard any of this. My mind had been so focused elsewhere, on Josh and my job, on Massimo's invasive presence, that I had never even really *asked*. I had not been a good friend. Though now I knew he had not been all there, I could at least have tried.

I looked into Massimo's eyes as he spoke, and tried to ignore the part where Josh had sent a violent party-crasher to live inside my home.

He sighed and leant back in his chair and gave a little hound huff, tired from all that talk. Shrugged.

'Then I was sleeping, today, and I wake up, and suddenly I'm . . . back.'

I cleared my throat.

'So it's gone?'

He rolled his eyes in his head, like he was looking for it.

'Guess so.'

'It was with me today, but I kicked it out,' I said.

He flashed me a look.

'With you?'

'Just part of it. I let some in.' I avoided his eyes now, ashamed to say it out loud.

Massimo rubbed his palms together, and it sounded like two snakes passing slowly in a burrow. Was that . . . envy?

'I'm sorry,' he said. 'For anything . . . when I was—'

'No. No, it's fine. I know how it goes.' I really did.

He smiled, put both hands up. Peace treaty signed. 'Good. We understand each other.'

I rubbed my blue eyes.

'I don't believe it's *gone gone*,' I said. 'It might not be inside us, but I bet it's still here, somewhere.' I circled a finger round the room. 'We have to get rid of it.' I watched carefully for his reaction.

He nodded and then he yawned, long and loud; he looked startled by the sound. Then his stomach rumbled.

'OK, Simone, we will do this together. But, will you eat with me first?' Massimo says. 'I'm fucking starving.' He laughed. Gently.

I considered this.

'Please, Simone, come.' He gestured to our table, our chairs. 'I'm so tired. You look also *very* tired. I really want to cook. All OK. I will cook you something to eat. Then we get to work. Promise.'

I relent. 'I guess we have plenty of mushrooms.' I said this like a question, remembering the last time Massimo had fed me fungus. But he just smiled, reassuringly.

I sat at the table and watched him slice the mushrooms we had picked together. I watched the back of his neck as he cooked, the smiling skin of his lower back when he reached up to the cupboard, or turned to look at me. I sat, swaying a little, drinking wine and watching him make me risotto, thick and cheesy. Somehow, the night had become *cosy*. Me and Massimo.

'Smells good.' I bent over the bowl like a dog and he sat down opposite to eat his own portion. How nice it was right there and then. How good. Almost like old times.

I listened to the quiet sound of the scrape of the fork against Massimo's teeth, a sound I usually found infuriating, but right now it was perfect, drew focus to the shape of his kind mouth. The flat was peaceful. Home. A candle burned. Then Massimo spoke, looking across the table at me.

'Tell me, Simone. Where are you from?'

'Well . . .' I swallow a mouthful. 'It's a small town. Sort of south.' I pointed down under the table, as if that is where I had been born, in a box with kittens. 'Near the woods.' My mouth was half full.

A soft glow in his eyes. 'You love the woods. Like me.' There was a warmth in his voice. It was just the two of us. How pleasant, to enjoy a Massimo without infection.

I took another forkful. 'This is really good, Massimo. Thank you. The mushrooms – they were worth the trip.'

He inspected a mushroom on his prongs. It was a bit sluggy in the light, glistening.

'What a time we've had!' I shook my head in bewilderment and raised my glass; he met it with his own.

'OK. So you want to do something? Remove our . . . little friend.'

He cast his fork around the room, pointed to all the places a friend might be. I nodded over my bowl.

'Yeah.'

'How do we do this?'

I was not sure, but had ideas.

'I don't know. But I think it's knackered. So it won't be hard.'

The candlelight flickered, his eyes were fixed points in shifting shadows on his face.

'Soon then, we will do it soon.'

He poured more wine into my glass.

'You have nice eyes, Simone. A good blue.'

'Thanks, Massimo. I always thought your eyes were a bit like emeralds.'

'You always thought?' he said, smiling eagerly, and I put a hand over my chewing, smiling mouth. A churn in my belly.

'No siblings,' he said, after a mouthful. It didn't seem like a question.

'No. You?'

Something about that amused him.

'Yes, siblings. Quite a few. Sort of.' A chuckle, wiggle of his head. A little private joke he was sharing with himself.

'In Italy?'

'No. Down deeper.' He laughed again.

Between us, the candle sputtered, burned on.

Massimo held out a hand to me.

'Come then. We exorcise.'

I took his hand. 'We need to banish it. Say our intentions.'

'If we're connected, it can't get us maybe,' he said, and I agreed. A united front. Friends.

'Fack off!' he shouted suddenly and I jumped, made a honking sound in my throat. Felt the cheap wood of the chair tense beneath me, like it was holding itself in readiness.

I reached out and took Massimo's other hand, which was warm and dry.

'Fuck off!' I croaked, then cleared my throat and tried again, louder. 'Get out of here!'

We both looked around with wide eyes and little-boy grins. Waiting for something.

'You not gonna get us again. You *dick*!' Massimo yelled this last part, and the word seemed to ring around our bowls.

'Goodbye!' We said this in unison somehow, and cackled at this. 'Bye, little bitch!'

The candle flickered, and then went out. The room held its breath with us. Then, so quiet you would hardly notice, we did hear something. A door closing softly. The wet click of a latch.

'There, it's gone,' said Massimo firmly, letting go of my hands. He picked up Parmesan instead, and grated it over his bowl.

'Like I said, it was knackered.' I smiled with relief, picked up my fork. Perhaps the nightmare was over. I was happy. Excited to finish this good food, maybe watch a film after. Curl up on the couch and drift off immediately with a full belly, my friend Massimo sitting beside me on our couch. No need for any more. I leaned back in my chair, and watched him get up.

'More wine?' he said. He was moving towards the fridge, where he removed the bottle of white he'd used in the cooking. I watched the way he moved, a little jerkily maybe. In the glow of the fridge, I saw his eye twitch. I frowned.

He brought the bottle to me, and poured it into my glass. A little violently. Wine slopped over the rim, and Massimo let out a croaky laugh.

'Sorry Simone,' he said, bending down sharply to slurp from my glass, lowering its volume, staring at me. His eye twitched again, an uncontrollable spasm. He shook himself, like a breeze was blowing through him, building in strength, then pushed the glass closer toward me.

I said nothing, continued to eat. He kept staring.

'Good boy,' he said.

I chewed slowly, and he grinned.

'*Yes.* We know you're a good boy. Aren't you a good boy then?' he said, and I felt the hairs on my arms stand up at the gruff new timbre of his voice. I watched his handsome, haunted face. His brow that was furrowing deeper and deeper.

His eyes, so green. Unblinking.

'Such a gooooood boy.' The room was suddenly getting warmer.

I hovered a forkful in the air, it quivered a little. Something was changing.

'No siblings. *No friends*,' he said, and I frowned hard but he kept going. 'And your mother and father?' I watched his face grow meaner.

'They're back in the town I'm from,' I said, almost too quiet to hear.

His whole body seemed to vibrate slightly. The steam rising from the food began to stink like a corpse. *Here we go.* I girded my loins.

'You don't talk to them.'

The air in the room was becoming warm, moving around us like vapour. That playful atmosphere had vanished in a second, replaced with something hard and frightening.

'Maybe they hate you too, like Josh?' he asked.

I almost choked. I put down my fork and watched the smile that squirmed on his lips.

'What did you say?' I locked my eyes on his.

'Do they hate you as much as Josh does?' He cocked his head, said this slowly like he was talking to a child.

A lump grew in my throat, thick and fast.

'Did Josh say that he hates me?'

Massimo was looking at me, stirring his risotto with his fork. It clicked against the side of the bowl with each rotation, striking the silence in the room. Clink.

'I met Josh once, ten minutes max. He's a fucking lumpsucker. *Josh.* Arrogant bastard,' he purred.

I saw that his other hand was flat on the table, and he seemed to be flexing it, stroking the wood rhythmically. Was he getting larger?

'He's not. That's not true. He's my best friend.' The

words were choking me even as I said them. In my mind, the image of Josh speeding away from me on the top deck of a nightbus, leaving me alone.

Massimo growled. 'Your best friend! So why did you do it? What you did. To your friend?' His voice got low, like his throat was full of earth.

'What are you talking about?'

Clink. The lamp above began to swing. The room was getting so hot. My leg jigged.

'That terrible thing.'

'I'm a good person.'

'Shall we call Josh?'

'Josh . . .' My hands were leaking sweat.

'Shall we ask him what he thinks?' He threw his head back and laughed. 'But I suppose, first he would have to answer the phone.'

I tried to speak, spluttered.

On he growled.

'Do you want to say it aloud? How *bad* you really are. Or shall I?'

My legs trembled beneath the table, they rattled the chair.

'Don't say it.'

'Poor Josh. Such a *good* friend. Taking care of you, looking out for you!'

He rolled his eyes upwards slightly so I could see the yellowy whites. He leaned back in his chair, then fixed his eyes on mine.

'Until you fucked his boyfriend.'

'Shut up, shut the fuck up.'

'But so much more than that. Such chasing, after something that made Josh so *happy*! Weeks, was it? Months! You wanted to fuck him, so you did . . .'

I was gripping the bowl, mouth wide open, tears brewing. I was going to be sick.

The shadows on his face shifting again, warping his mouth into a smile. Massimo's face, but not his voice. Not at all. The thin glimmer of hope, that it might all be over, snuffed itself out. As expected, the beast had been here all along, inside Massimo.

'And still, you wonder why he doesn't call. Who are you lying to, Simon? Remember, I've seen the whole show.' He laughed grittily and pointed at my forehead, where my hair was now plastered down with cold sweat.

'Leave,' I spat.

'You would have left a long time ago, if you didn't want it so. If you weren't the perfect house for me. Oh, you love it, to be such a *bad boy*.'

'No,' I whispered. 'I didn't ask for this!' I shouted, and threw my bowl against the wall where it cracked and slimed out rice.

He didn't even flinch.

CHAPTER THIRTY-SIX

I might as well be truthful.

Five years of life with Josh had been sugar-sweet. He brought me into his world, and in return I maintained the standards I had set when we first moved in together. The flat was always lickably clean, and I made him playlists for his morning commute. His sheets were always ironed. He rarely snapped at me, never rolled his eyes. He was a good guy. Yes, it was a little unbalanced, me the sidekick to his leading man, but it was genuinely loving and secure too – the flat was the steel and concrete that held it all together. We were having the time of our lives, perfectly in sync, and would probably have stayed that way forever.

But then it changed.

I remember the night. Me and Josh curled up under Björk, drinking two bottles of cheap red, the ping of his message alerts chiming under the music. In his brown eyes,

I watched the reflection of his phone, the illumination of boys and boys and boys, until one boy made him laugh in a new way.

Nathan. Tall, sandy-haired, broad-shouldered. Like a king.

I imagined this one would not last, like the other boys who came and went before, appearing and disappearing, drifting down the corridor at 2 a.m. to piss before leaving, jumping with fright when they met me in the dim hallway. Ringing the buzzer at odd hours for visitations, calling his name on the street after a heavy ghosting. I thought Nathan would not stick around. But he did.

Their first date was amazing, I was told. *Bowling*. Josh was *besotted*, which was adorable. Fucking adorable. Three more dates followed, and then he came over.

I first met Nathan accidentally, in the building's atrium as I returned from work. His face was pleasantly squared and he seemed almost shy, struggled to meet my eye. I smiled wide, shook his large hand, and let him through our door with my key, where I watched him kiss Josh on the cheek. I loitered, making myself a sandwich. Nathan did not say much to me, but later I heard them in Josh's bedroom with a bottle of wine, Nathan doing funny voices, Josh laughing his head off, harder than I'd ever heard him laugh before.

Nathan started coming over more. He had nice hazel eyes and big arms, and he brought them to the flat on weekends, carrying bags of exciting ingredients, big bunches of fresh carrots and chilled Dutch beer. Josh would sit on the kitchen counter while Nathan cooked fish, or spaghetti, and I would sit on the sofa and smile, witnessing the spectacle that was their growing bond and the grin that never left Josh's face as he watched this large, quiet man at work. I smiled along. In bed, I'd massage the ache from my cheeks before I fell asleep.

I learned that Nathan was an editor at a production company. Apparently that was especially attractive to Josh. Something about that large man sitting in a small room, in the dark, alone. Hardly speaking all day. Pushing buttons, watching people's faces, getting a moment just right.

'He's quiet, isn't he?' I had said to Josh in private, and he'd laughed.

'Oh, only at first. But all he needs is wine, a line and a good time, and he comes alive. Or even just a closed door. Trust me.' He'd looked me in the eye and winked, implying something I didn't want to know about.

Weeks passed and I'll admit it, I slowly warmed to Nathan. Once he started to relax, got a few drinks down him, he was quite fun. Even slightly flirty. One night as I ate my dinner and sipped my drink, he sat down next to me and whispered in my ear. I squirmed, I couldn't help it, and he laughed a big loud laugh that took me by surprise. After that, he always put a hand on my shoulder when he spoke to me. 'You're hilarious, Simon,' he'd say, even though I hadn't tried to be.

Things warmed up. Josh was enjoying it too, our

threesome, and soon we all began cooking meals in the kitchen, drinking and listening to the rain fall outside. Josh and Nathan playing footsie, me playing waiter, joining in. Meanwhile the spokes of my third wheel spun so fast inside I thought they'd come slicing through my skin. I roasted a whole chicken for them once and burnt through two layers of skin on my inner forearm but didn't drop the bird.

'You don't mind, do you? That Nathan's here a lot?' Josh had asked me after a month of them hanging in the flat. 'It's nice and private here.'

'Mind? I absolutely love it!' I had put a fist in the air instead of through the wall, to emphasise my support.

I pretended to get used to things. I watched Nathan over my plate, from the other side of the table, the lamp above making his cheeks glow. I could smell his aftershave, spicy like the black pepper he was generous with on my pasta. Sometimes, I caught him watching me back.

He really began coming out of his shell. I listened, carefully, as he grew more and more comfortable. He got drunk, and talked with more ease about himself, about his job. Even about sex.

'Yeah, my first boyfriend, I'd take a bus for an hour a week just to shag him when his parents were out.' Nathan laughed, his eyes bright. The word *shag*, his strong hands on the arms of his chair, stirring something above my thighs. Josh had just rolled his eyes.

Later, when Josh was on the phone to his mum, I'd asked

Nathan to repeat the story and poured him more wine. He looked me in the eyes and did as I'd asked. I'd counted how many times I could make him laugh like Josh did, to see how it felt.

'Nathan's a dark horse. He'll do anything for a fuck, but right now he only fucks me,' Josh had said proudly when I asked if they were exclusive. How curious. *Anything?*

I gritted my teeth as I witnessed their intimacy evolve into something to behold. How they cuddled. Nathan was there for Josh in a way that was grimly touching; leaning against the kitchen wall and listening without judgement, offering advice but not attempting to fix everything. Smiling at Josh's stories and bringing round records to play over dinner. He would bring board games too, and dessert. I was always invited. On weekends they would wake up in the flat before heading out on an excursion. Sometimes Nathan went to play football and Josh went to watch. In the bathroom I smelled the towels and tried to work out who had used which one.

One evening I had been sitting in a pub twenty minutes away by bus. I'd been reading quietly at a corner table, only to look up and see Nathan, in tight jeans and a T-shirt, ordering a drink at the bar. He had smiled widely at the handsome barman, reaching forward to point at the beer he wanted, in the fridge. Grinding his thick crotch hard against the oak cladding. The barman was laughing, taking a while to complete the transaction. Nathan laughed back, leaned forward, met his gaze and held it. I sat up, alert, and noticed the icy thrill I felt, catching this red flaggery in the act. *Interesting.*

They started using the word boyfriend. Josh would moon around the flat, batting his eyelashes and twirling a finger in his hair. Flapping whichever new gift Nathan had given him.

'He's so cute right, Simon? He's nice? Argh, he's so nice!' And of course I would agree: *he's so nice*, but I had my eye on Nathan. Both eyes, in fact.

I noticed that they'd stopped asking me to join them as much. After dinner, their coats would be on, heading to a bar. No invitation for me. I would pretend I had plans, though I'm sure they knew I was lying. I started putting a glass to Josh's door, to hear if they were talking about me and how I might feel when they left me all alone. But the wood of the door was too thick. I could only hear muffled laughter. Then other things.

One night, coming home from a terrible shift at the restaurant, I had stood in the kitchen doorway and listened to them crooning, the flicker of the TV warping the dark caves of the sink and cabinets.

Josh laughing. 'When we live together, we can get a sofa like that one.'

Nathan's voice deep and quiet. 'Yeah and I'll fuck you on it whenever I want to.' Whispers, giggles.

When we live together. A *sofa*! Where exactly did *I* fit into this plan?

I had seen the shadows start to move, and heard the

slide of underwear removed, the wet kiss of lips. I had crept around the door, but only watched for thirty seconds before going quietly to bed alone.

The ice pick had the time of its life, stabbing me right where it hurt. I did not sleep a wink, gripping the sheets and sweating, haunted by the image of being left alone in the flat forever. Or worse, ejected.

Nathan had to go.

I needed evidence of his infidelities, so I watched him like a hawk. The next time he visited, I curled mouse-like into the corner of the sofa and watched him on his phone while Josh mixed us drinks and made a chilli. I tried to make out Nathan's screen from my careful angle, and saw his thumb press down on a little orange app. Was it a flight tracker, or was it a portal of men sending him photos of their sweaty arses? Was that a spam email? The body of text looked more like an invitation, very long and rude. Scrolling his recent photographs, Nathan stalled on an erect penis emerging from a fist, smooth, long and brown. Was it Josh's, a hot little memo between two lovers, or did it belong to someone else entirely? My stare hardened. The *bastard*. When Nathan turned to ask me something I flipped my frown upside down.

That night I followed Nathan home. Just to see where he lived. Walking distance, along the canal a short stretch and then up to a leafy residential area where some of the houses have turrets. I heard him talking sexily to someone on the phone that sounded suspiciously like a man. I thought about calling out to him but instead I'd hung back in the shadows and watched him stop outside a big red building where a ginger cat mewled as he stroked its ears. I left after Nathan went inside.

Josh was oblivious: he started singing in the shower, he was so happy. I could take it no longer. I asked him outright in the hallway, as he stood dripping in his towel, whether he really trusted Nathan. His face had twisted painfully in a flash, and I felt the sweat run rivers down my back.

'What do you mean, Simon?' A look of panic on his face.

'I think he talks to other guys, maybe more,' I said, shaking only a little as Josh narrowed his eyes. I saw something in them, a little flicker of panic.

'Why are you saying this?' His voice wavered slightly.

'I'm your best friend, I'm looking out for you.'

He leaned back a little, stepping away from me, holding clean underwear, which actually looked like Nathan's. I'd never seen him this angry, or perhaps afraid, and for a moment I wished I could take back what I'd said, but I knew I was absolutely doing the right thing by him. He would thank me in the end.

He was staring me down. 'Be specific.'

I swallowed, held my nerve. 'I heard him talking on the phone to someone. And I saw pictures on his phone. He's . . . very flirty.' I realised, as the words came out of my mouth, how pathetically thin my case was. Josh clearly felt the same. His voice was ice cold.

'OK, Simon. Look, I've got something really special here; I'm not worried about a single thing. Surely you can see that?'

'I just worry that it's not as special as you think,' I said.

Josh's face was a sudden snatch of rage. I wondered if he wanted to hit me.

'I wouldn't expect *you* to understand, Simon'

This cracked me like a whip. He'd never spoken to me like that, he'd never called me out, but then I had always been so careful not to give him reason to. *Incredible.* That's what I got for being a good friend?

For a few days Josh was pricklier with me than he'd ever been, and even cosier with Nathan, massaging him on the sofa in front of me and shaving the hairs on the back of Nathan's broad neck that the barber had missed. Standing in the kitchen, fiddling with things that did not require fiddling, I had never felt more like a spare part.

But I gave it time. I did little things to heal the wound that stretched stickily between me and Josh. One rare weekend alone with him, noticing his raging comedown, I made him hot dogs and ran him a bath. I lit the fancy candle that smelled of oranges. I put on *Legally Blonde* and we watched it together. I did the bend and snap, and he laughed. He told me about his new co-worker who said they'd seen a UFO. We were on the mend. Perhaps it would be fine; I would not be forgotten.

Three nights later Josh confessed to me that he was falling deeply in love with Nathan. He reckoned he was the one. At bedtime I threw up out of my window, onto the street.

A week later I found myself in that same pub, near Nathan's house. I was sitting outside with a small glass of wine when Nathan happened to walk past, and noticed me. He said fancy seeing you here, Simon, and bought me another glass. We talked for an hour; I got a little tipsy. He kept laughing at things I said. I bought him three pints and kept brushing my leg against his, and he gave me a very long, strange look but didn't scold me. Before he went home, he gave me his number, in case he was ever near our flat when Josh wasn't home, and needed letting in.

After that I started calling him some evenings, just to talk. I told him stories about my shifts at 2 a.m. while he was pulling an all-nighter; I'd hear his keys clicking in his soundproof suite as I lay there on my lovely clean sheets and listened to the shutters rolling down on the fire station.

The next Saturday afternoon I sat watching television while Josh tried to cook a pie in the kitchen. He was moaning; Nathan had been working too much, he hadn't seen him all week. I made all the right noises in response. On the side, where Josh had left it, his phone flashed relentlessly. Nathan was texting to arrange an exciting date for that evening, to make up for his absence. When Josh was clouded in steam, putting his dish into the oven, I unlocked his phone with the code I knew by heart, and deleted the seven messages. Fifteen minutes later Nathan tried to call Josh's phone and I reached out to press the red button.

Nathan came over anyway, to see Josh. When they entered the kitchen from the hallway the two of them were looking down at their phones, comparing both screens in confusion. Nathan looked up, caught me watching from the sofa, sipping my wine and trying not to sweat. He smirked knowingly. 'It's my phone, it's broken,' he said to Josh, and laughed it off. 'It's not sending things properly.' He gave me another smiling stare, unblinking. He had enjoyed that.

I had done something bad, and it had woken those things in my belly, dark and wriggling. It had felt good, and I let myself enjoy the delicious sensation. I took a shower for thirty minutes and played with myself beneath the jets.

I kept finding reasons to bump into Nathan. I wanted to do it again. In the supermarket near his office in the city. At his actual office, looking to borrow some paper. Nathan loved the attention, and I swear he returned it. I wore a new blue T-shirt that showed my nipples. I lifted my arms to show him the patches of sweat on my running shirt and I'd watched him lick his lips. I liked that part a lot. So naughty, so bad.

One day I gave myself a telling off. This was not OK. I promised to behave, give them space, leave the flat when Josh and Nathan were home, go walking along the canals or find a quiet tree to lie beneath. It lasted a week, and then I got bored. I'd had a taste for something and I wanted more.

I plied Nathan with wine in the pub, or at our flat while we waited for Josh to get ready for a party I wasn't invited to. 'The great thing about Josh,' I said, 'is how he's so open-minded. You know? He loves to share!' and I'd looked into Nathan's eyes, and cheersed him, brushing my fingers against his, twice. Watching him grin. Naughty boy.

One night we all got drunk in the living room, after Nathan mixed us martinis with pickle juice. I thought it was the most disgusting thing I'd ever put in my mouth but I had three and wiggled my hips by the fridge. 'This is delicious, Nathan!' I'd said, walking over to ruffle his hair when Josh answered the door for pizzas. Later Josh put on Madonna and sat on Nathan's lap, and I watched as they snogged. I stayed gently bopping to the groovy track, mere feet away as Nathan caught my eye and stared back, even as his tongue slapped at Josh's.

I was drunk. Feeling my oats. When Josh went for a piss, I walked over to Nathan, got close. He looked at me, eyes on mine like it was a challenge. Slowly, I turned and sat on his lap too, facing away from him, to see how it felt. He let me sit there for a moment, and I was *sure* I felt a huge erection growing. He put a hand on my arse and we heard the toilet flush. Josh came back as I was stumbling upwards, my buttocks gently but firmly pushed away by Nathan's hands. He half-laughed, and blushed a little.

'Nathan touched my arse!' I looked Josh in the eye.

On the sofa, Nathan snorted, and put his hands up. 'He tried to sit on me!'

Josh simply put on another song, and poured himself more wine, stony-faced.

Later in the corridor, he put a tight hand on my shoulder, close to my neck. He looked furious.

'What are you doing, Simon?'

'Nothing.'

'You're embarrassing yourself.'

'*He* touched *my* bum!'

'He's just being nice to you.'

'OK, Josh. I don't know what to say.'

'It's creepy, Simon. You're fucking creepy.' He looked at me with a mixture of disgust, and something else. Pity.

They went out dancing and I stayed home to furiously hoover the pizza crusts crushed into the rug, Josh's words ringing in my head, burning me. I took breaks to remember Nathan's hands, hard on my arse. In vivid detail I recalled Josh's face, twisted in surprise as he saw Nathan touching me. That flicker of hurt. I smiled. How amazing that had felt, to be bad once more.

Nathan didn't come over for a week or so, and Josh gave me a treatment so silent I could hear my own blood boiling in my head. I went out running, and replayed the moment from the hallway over and over in my head. Josh looking at me like I was something he had stepped in. Something *creepy*. I stopped by the canal, and sent Nathan a photo of my calves. They looked good. He didn't reply until later that night, when a little love heart appeared in the corner of the picture.

Before I went to sleep, I asked myself what exactly I thought I was doing. Was I still trying to get rid of Nathan and restore the status quo? To be a good friend to Josh. Or was something more nefarious at play? Was I tempting Nathan, luring him along?

Oh, Simon, tell yourself the truth. You stepped across a line days ago. You're just having a lovely time being filthy bad. So don't stop now.

I slept like a baby.

The next time Nathan came over I sat quietly on the sofa near him, legs curled beneath me. I stretched out a foot to stroke his back and he reached around, slapped it, then grabbed it so tight it shocked me, like my foot was being charged. The look in his eye was electric, and he put his tongue between his teeth. Josh didn't see a thing. Oh what a *buzz*.

I was certain I could feel that charge growing over the space of the next week, little looks and touches until I was worried I couldn't be in the same room as Nathan without something bursting into flames. One early morning he crept into the kitchen behind me and touched my back beneath my pyjama T-shirt, as I was putting milk in the fridge. I gasped, dropped the container, exploded into goosebumps. He chuckled, and I grabbed his hard crotch, heard the delicious little moan escape his open mouth as he put his tongue close to my ear. *So, I had not been making it up.* He was enjoying this too. When Josh came into the room I passed Nathan the milk to conceal his boner.

Things between me and Josh remained sour; I was finding it hard to bring him back round. But he was all over

Nathan, he didn't notice anything untoward. The secret, the fact that Josh was so oblivious, felt good, made our little connection so much more intense. I watched Josh's dumb, peaceful face as he fell asleep watching TV, head on Nathan's lap, and something hot wriggled inside me. I was tempted to reach over and put my thumb in Nathan's mouth right there.

But it wasn't enough, these nasty little moments. I needed more.

A bleached wooden decking on Nathan's central office rooftop. An Ibiza-themed summer work party, really grim. Back in the flat, Nathan had invited Josh, and then gestured to me, where I stood by the windows, polishing the leaves of the fern.

'Let's take Simon. We can't leave him all alone, wanking off a plant.'

Josh had cleared his throat, awkwardly. Things were still cold between us.

'Come on, Josh, look at him.' Nathan had nudged Josh and pointed to my face, which I didn't realise was doing anything specific. Josh relented.

I drank beer and splashed gently in a paddling pool full of warm water, almost sexily I thought, jeans rolled up. Co-workers crooned over Josh. Nathan taking off his shirt in front of his colleagues like that was nothing, kissing Josh in the pop-up photobooth and putting the photo on the office fridge. Watching me all the while. Getting me going.

In Nathan's editing booth, the three of us did lines off

a mouse-mat, huddled close together. I grinned at Josh as the buzz rushed through us. He couldn't help it, he smiled back. The gang, back together. We danced in the kitchenette, and after a while a small crowd had formed around the pair. Nathan and Josh looked really cool together, moving in sync, their hands on each other's backs. Everyone smiling at them. I moved out of the way, and gulped down a Red Stripe until I had to piss.

I came back from the toilet and I couldn't find them.

'Have you seen the boys?' I asked Nathan's assistant.

'They went to a party. Friends of Josh, I think?' She offered me a beer, and I took it. 'Josh said you wouldn't want to come.' Right.

I got more drunk, did more lines right out on the rooftop with total strangers. I poured warm vodka, racked another line from someone else's stash. I didn't cry at all.

'I'm glad I didn't go with Josh. This is fun!' I wondered if I was slurring my words. 'It's great to be left alone. Me time!' I realised I was talking to nobody. The party was winding down, and I was quickly rúnning out of charm, so I took the bus home by myself.

When I got to the flat, cat-stepping down the corridor, I found Nathan smoking out the living-room window, his broad back filling the frame. Alone.

'Where's Josh?' I asked him, and he twisted round.

'Party.' He blew smoke out the side of his mouth. He looked very drunk.

'You guys didn't say goodbye.'

'Josh said you wouldn't mind.'

I nodded.

'You didn't stay with Josh?'

He pulled a face.

'His friends are unbearable.'

I nodded. 'They are.'

I took my jacket off. 'Did Josh give you his key then?' I asked.

'No, he cut me one.' He held up a fresh shiny key, which sent a flash of rage through me. Josh had just *given* him a key to our home.

'I'll hang out with you,' I told him, ignoring the pounding in my head. The sweat pooling in my groin. 'Do you want a drink?'

He turned around with a wolfish grin.

I watched Nathan as he looked for clean glasses, and realised that we had never been alone in the flat before. The fact that we were now was a physical presence, shuddering in the room with us.

I broke the tension.

'Hey, Nathan, want a line?'

He put both huge sexy arms in the air.

I found a gram of what was probably coke in Josh's drawer, and put some excellent music on. Nathan bucked his hips clumsily as I opened a bottle of prosecco I'd been saving and poured it into glasses, racked white lines on the table, two flat slugs I watched Nathan snort. One for me. I put some hot porn on my laptop, accidentally, and Nathan stared at the hairy men. He blinked slow blinks. Oh God, this was naughty, this was so much *fun*.

I started dancing. I think it looked good, because Nathan did another line and then got up to join me. He got really close and the music was perfect for the scene. I thought I might start levitating.

I moved even closer.

Careful, Simon, careful now.

Here we were. The tipping point. I looked down, into the abyss, and watched the dark and dirty things writhing, calling me towards them. *Come on, put your money where your mouth is. Get your fill!* I looked away from Nathan, and thought about being good. I thought about Josh, my best friend, and I thought about turning off the music and wiping down the table and drinking a pint of water and going to bed alone, as I should do. I thought about Josh, leaving me alone at the party. Because I was *creepy*. The tug of war between two fixed points, it tore at my chest, my back, my limbs. I should not do this. I should *not do this*. I looked at Nathan. I had to decide.

'You want to kiss?' I asked him quietly, and in his eyes I saw, just for a second, a tiny flash of struggle. It lasted only a second before he put his slippery tongue inside my mouth.

I would like to say he was in charge, taking my hand and leading me past the dining chairs, but I was the one who put my hands on his arse and smelled the skin above his collar. He had kissed my neck. 'You're so fucking weird,' he whispered in my ear, and then he'd put a hand up my T-shirt and stroked my stomach, and my nipple, and my body had practically convulsed. I took his shorts off and straddled him on the couch, and Jesus Christ in heaven above it felt amazing not to be good. It lasted eight minutes and I often thought about each single one.

On the eighth minute Josh had walked into the room while I was still in Nathan's mouth.

CHAPTER THIRTY-SEVEN

Let's be clear, I was not having dinner with Massimo. I knew that all along.

The kitchen was now boiling hot. There was a fat fly swimming in Massimo's wine, and somehow I could see each hairy leg up close, desperately sliding against the wall of the glass. Massimo watched it, then downed his glass and slammed it back down. The fly was gone. I saw the muscles in his face move in a circular rhythm, and his hand twitched on the table, fingernails now thick and long.

'What are you then? A devil?' I whispered into the dark.

He cocked his head. *'What's a devil?'*

'Like . . . the devil.'

He shrugged, lazy. *'If that's your word of choice.'*

The *face* of the thing, leering at me.

'What is with your fucking nails?' I said, but kept my cool.

He inspected a hand.

'Ugh. He likes them short. It freaks him out, the growing. He tries to take over.' There was fake pity in his deepening voice.

I gently slid my chair back and stood.

'Leaving so soon? Tell me, Simone,' he purred mockingly. *'Are you not having fun?'*

His fingernails now darker still, long and rough like old tin. I looked at the hand holding the fork, and that was the same – flexing a little harder as it moved through the wet gloop. My friend, here for supper. Clink. His bloodshot eyes like those of a gargoyle. The lamp swung, and he was shadowed again, but he leaned forward, further over the table, and was illuminated on the backswing.

'Are you sad, Simon? Angry?' he purred as he stood, his hand spilling the bowl of risotto onto the table, smearing it into the wood like porridge as he moved. *'I think so. Josh gone. Mother and father hate you. Not a friend in sight. They've all upped and left. Because you make it so.'*

'You don't know me,' I hissed. 'Whatever the fuck you are. You don't know me.'

His grin grew wider than I'd ever seen it.

'Oh I do, Simon. But let me in. Let me inside that stinking barrel, and I'll get to know you even better,' he said, his voice becoming harsher, unrecognisable.

'All the way this time. Give me a proper home.'

It stamped a foot, and the hollow sound echoed through the room. Massimo was warping before me, twisting into that terrible thing I had seen crawling towards me across the rug, on Halloween night.

'Why can't you just stay in *there*?' I said. 'Why isn't this good enough, then?' I gestured to Massimo's body. It stopped laughing.

'Can't. I've outgrown it. Too big! I'm breaking this one.' To prove a point, it held up Massimo's right hand that was bulbous in the swinging light, the nails growing even as it flexed each long finger. It lifted Massimo's T-shirt to show a fresh wound running down the hillocks of his abs, a network of veined cracks across his skin.

'I'm going to smash my way out, sooner or later. I've been in here too long.' It ran a hand over Massimo's chest, up to his cheek. *'This sweet boy, all the way from Rome, planes and trains and deadlines and dogwalks, all that way, all that work to end up in chunks, scattered in the street and eaten by pigeons. Won't be pretty.'*

'I don't give a fuck,' I hissed. 'Find someone else. I'm out.'

It roared in frustration, a chilling sound that filled the room. I shuddered at the sound, as a small crack formed on the ceiling above us, and a thin layer of dust drifted down.

'I have been trying! I have clawed my way through this disgusting city, squirming like sperm. Crawling through body after body, until I cannot fit any longer and must find another. But in time they crack and crumble. All wrong. All wrong! They cannot house me. Every home I try is fucking derelict!'

'You've been killing people. Tearing them apart.'

It twisted its face in mock outrage.

'Oh please. It's part of the process. I step out, they fall apart.' It winked at me. *'It can be fun.'*

It was growing petulant now, shifting about the room.

'Then I find you! What a treat. The gutters of your mind so slippery with slime. It's glorious in there. I know you can hold me forever.' That face, now twisted in a snarl. *'All those others, they let me crawl right on in. They hardly blinked. So sad, so lonely, so dull. But you, what a tease. The way you seesaw back and forth. You want something dark, and then you do not. You want to dance, and then you do not. So capricious. You somehow simply turn away, and kick me out of that delicious den, that stunning cornucopia. But I love it. I want it!'*

I stood firm, staring back.

'And if you can't ever have it?'

'I will end up on the fucking wind. And I do not wish it. I will not flicker away. You are my last chance. He cannot contain me.' It pressed a sharp nail to Massimo's temple, and twisted, drew blood. I thought it might drill right through to the bone. *'It's not enough!'*

'Well, then, why the fuck haven't you just done what you want with me?'

It stopped, and looked at my face. It seemed incredulous.

'You don't know,' it said, and the laugh it uttered was deep, almost bovine. *'You don't know how hard you're*

fighting.' This seemed to tickle it. *'How strong you are. I thought you knew.'*

It eyed me, tongue lolling. Such an ugly, monstrous thing. *'Somehow, you have a power over me.'*

I stared right back as it spoke.

'You play with me. You enjoy me, then you push me down, force me out. You let me taste you, then you throw me away. You pretend you do not want things. You act like you don't burn with longing, like all those other pigs out there. You lie to the world, about how bad you really are.'

'I've been fighting things like you my whole life,' I whispered, which only made it smile.

It cocked its head, from one side to the other as its voice grew louder, now shrill like an alarm. *'Well Simon, the fight is up. Nobody can stop me from having what I WANT.'*

It slammed down a fist and the table cracked in two, each side coming away from the other like a walnut, tipping to the floor and leaving a space for it to step through.

'Please, Simon.' It was pleading. *'Let me in. Let me leave this boy, and reside fully in you. Please, I can search no longer. I've only got one jump left in me. Let it be you. Sssstop making me work so fucking h-h-h-h-hard.'*

It shuddered, it was so large, opening its mouth to show each and every one of those beautiful piranha teeth, and then raising its left leg to move towards me as horns began to press through its skull. That familiar warmth, creeping into me. Tempted, tempted. I felt heat singe me from the inside. The devilish juice bubbling.

It stepped so close to me, I could feel its body hard and warm like summer stone. When I touched its arm, it made a sound that bodies do not make. It looked thrilled. I let it step closer still. I reached behind me, slid the item I had stolen in the church from my pocket, and held it aloft.

It froze for a moment, breathed its stinking breath. Stared at the item, transfixed, eyes green, unblinking.

'*What's this?*' it whispered.

'It's a fucking . . . crucifix!' I said, triumphant, gripping the small wooden cross tightly in my hand. Its polished wood gleamed in the kitchen lights.

'I *knew* you would be here. Do you think I'm fucking stupid?'

I took a step towards the thing.

'*No,*' it pleaded, frightened. '*No!*'

'Yes!' I said, powerful.

'*Simon. No,*' and its muscled back heaved as if it would vomit.

Brave now, feeling strong, I pushed the crucifix into its face and it recoiled, mouth wide open. A terrible scream sliding down that slick brown tongue. Less boy, even more monster by the moment. Incredible.

Then it bit the wooden cross. Took it between its teeth and crunched it. Licked its lips, opened wider, took another bite. The laugh it gave was thick, chunky with church wood, and it stepped up to full towering height, bit again, and slid a dark wet tongue between my fingers.

I screamed now, and smashed the wine glass nearest

me, lunging at the thing that looked a bit like my flatmate, ready to cut its face open, and peel the flesh from the bone to finally see what was under there in its full, disgusting glory. And it looked, just for a flash, a little frightened. For a moment, I saw the face of that terrified young man, Massimo, deep under the rot.

I used this, the sweet glimmer of something human, and I lunged again with the weapon in my hand. I almost got it, but it jumped away.

'Let me try again. Please let me try again,' it begged, and approached me, circling. *'It's niiiice. You'll like it.'*

Even in my terror, I scolded myself for being so *stupid*. For thinking I could hurt it, maybe even kill it, with nothing but a crucifix. I looked around the room for something else, anything. I thought of Kat, what would she do? Why had I sent her away? I suddenly longed for her furious energy, to stand with me and fight. But I was alone. And all the while I felt that tantalising pressure filling every corner of the room, and Massimo's teeth grew sharper still. Could I run? It was now between me and the door. I looked to the windows, and the shallow roof beyond.

I knew exactly what I had to do.

It took another lurching step towards me and I stopped, stood still, and rolled my eyes. Put both arms out in welcome.

'Oh, alright then, fuck it. Come on in.'

CHAPTER THIRTY-EIGHT

Josh was crying in the rain.

I didn't know that people did that in real life, but he wept that night, many nights ago, as a summer storm began and he took the shouting that had started in the kitchen down into the street. Nathan in his shorts and his T-shirt on backwards in the hurry, after he had punched me hard in the side of the head when I'd said it was not my fault, no way. I was a good friend! He'd been trying it on all night! I watched from the window as Josh howled on the pavement and Nathan got into a taxi. I began to sober up, fast.

Josh didn't know how to look at me when he returned upstairs alone. I didn't know how to look at him either.

The look on Josh's face as he stared at the sofa was unrecognisable. His hair plastered to his forehead in dark curls, his eyes wide, red-rimmed and unblinking. The realisation of what I had done began to dawn on me.

'Josh, please. Look at me,' I had whispered.

He did not look at me, he continued staring at the sticky cushions, still indented from my knees. But he did speak, his voice a whimper.

'Why did you do that, Simon? Can you tell me why you did that?'

Words kept catching in my throat and then dying, like tiny creatures starved of oxygen. I did not know what to say. Why?

I stared at my friend. Had I *wanted* Josh to catch us? The look on his face as he walked through the door had been priceless, the darkest treat of all. Had I known in there somewhere, throughout the deed, as my hands had explored his boyfriend's enormous back, his rolling white arse, that Josh could be home at any moment? Had it felt good, just for a second, to have a bit of what he had, although I knew it was so wrong to take it from him?

Yes, it had felt good. It had all felt amazing. I had simply let myself be carried away on that furiously rolling wave of being brilliantly, deliciously, *bad*. For a moment, I tried to tell myself it was just an accident, a slip-up. A drunken mistake. But I knew otherwise. *Oh come on, Simon, you knew what you were doing. You stepped off the ledge. With both feet.*

I had wanted something, and I had taken it; the wrongness of the act made it even better. If I really wanted to answer Josh's question, I knew what I would say. 'Because being bad feels so incredibly, wonderfully, endlessly fucking good. Because I was having the time of my life.'

But where would that get me?

So, I lied. I begged him to forgive me. 'It was Nathan! He seduced me! He's a *bad guy*! Promise we're still friends, Josh, promise.'

Josh cried again, which I was enjoying less by the second. He was sobbing. He shoved me away, hard, would not let me comfort him.

I began to panic. Our friendship could handle a blip like this, couldn't it? If I was really really good for a really long time, I could put this right. I would pull out all the stops, I'd clean his room! Slowly the wounds would crust and then heal. In the end, he might thank me, for saving him from a life of fuckboy pain. *If not me, someone else!* I had done him a favour, surely. We would toast with our cold white wines. We'd be stronger than ever. Best friends for life. Right?

I was determined.

I stood up, brushed myself off, and smiled at him. 'Do you want me to make you a margarita?' I said.

Josh began to scream. He was apoplectic. I thought he was going to hit me, but instead he took my favourite Spice Girls mug and threw it at my head. It struck my skull, then hit the floor and shattered with a brilliant sound. At this, Josh suddenly became calm and still. He walked closer to me, and then stopped. I could feel his ragged breath, but he was just out of touching distance as he leaned forward and stared right into my eyes.

'You know you're going to die alone, right, Simon? You understand that it's your fucking . . . destiny. Nobody will love you. Nobody is even going to want you near them. You creepy, slimy, *disgusting prick*.'

He did not stammer, his voice did not crack. Instead it was sharp and clean, a blade cutting through meat. He meant it.

He turned and left the room, and then the flat.

I sat still beneath Björk with my head throbbing, starting to bleed. In that moment I tried to understand whether it really could all go back to normal, just me and Josh. If he would come home, come to his senses, or if I'd killed something that night. I told myself I was a good person, I *was*! I just had to prove it. But I looked around, at the mess, the broken mug, the empty flat. Perhaps I had done something so bad, I did not have enough good in me to fix it.

Josh moved out fast, taking the first bags three days later.

All those years of being good, of keeping the peace, and keeping things down. Years of pushing things into a tightly sealed tomb, of smiling and simpering and saying the right thing. All those dark dirty parts of me, screaming to come out. Well, I'd opened the lid, all the way, and let them out.

Maybe I'm not such a good boy after all.

CHAPTER THIRTY-NINE

The beast was filling me up.

I felt it coming, as I had just told it to. Like before, on the bed. Clawed fingers pulling each tiny plug of hair from my head, looking for an opening, rushing into blood-wet holes. Massimo looking more human as it left him, sinking to his hands and knees, gasping for air.

As it entered, I stepped slowly towards the window, the broken dagger of glass still in my hand. It did not speak, it was too busy. I felt my blood get sweet as I lifted the latch, slid the frame up. Massimo panting on the floor, two boys joined by an invisible torrent of something old and stinking that was filling me up, up, up. I put one leg out onto the flat roof above the street below.

'*Wait, where are you going?*' said the voice. I flexed my fingers frantically, tried not to enjoy the feeling too much. That bulbous glittering in my chest, hardening my nipples.

Massimo's mouth agape as I clambered onto the roof. He stepped and staggered, a clumsy thing, and tried to stop me, reaching through the window. I slashed at his chest, George and the Dragon.

'Simone, don't do it!' Massimo howled, and it sounded like him.

He wavered at the window and then came for me once more. I lunged again, slashing at the air, striking his scalp, shearing a puff of dark hair. It fell to the floor, soundlessly.

All the while, I was being filled up with devil.

It was pouring in now, so thick I could almost see it in the air, like blood and gravel glittering in the lights. Something clawed my skull, got a good grip. I saw earth, trees, rock, spine, shit, blood, cows torn and scattered, birds beakless and deboned. Goats rolling in their own blood.

I blinked back through it, slow and then fast. It was *succulent*, and there was so much of it. Jesus Christ, it was torrential. I was creeping across the flat roof now, my hot skin steaming in the cold air. There was only a few metres of roof left, and an idea fixed firmly in my head. Playing over and over, loud, for it to hear. I was close to the edge now. The pouring juddered a little, faltering.

For my plan to work, the beast had to believe me as I stepped closer to the dizzying edge of the building, where concrete met the chilling wind of the city, the open air. I had to truly believe it myself. Get it all out of Massimo. Get it all into me. And then . . .

'*What are you doing?*'

It tried to tug at me, but I was strong. I kept moving.

'What are . . . you gonna . . . do . . . with a smashed up corpse?' I said, barely conscious now with the burn of it all, and I stepped further towards the edge above the street, looking down at the pavement some fifty feet below.

I stepped up, onto the ledge, and felt the wind gusting around me, the demon swirling within me. I looked out across the city, and realised the true dizzying height of the building. Saw the impact a fall would have in my mind's eye. My little blond head, split open like a juicy berry. With my friend deep inside me. If I died, it might die too. I'd seen that on the telly somewhere.

'I'm going to jump,' I told my friend. 'I mean it.'

And maybe I did mean it. It might be nice. To get it all over and done with? The days of longing and loneliness, the things I had done, the endless toil, snuffed out. All done. Would that be so bad? From inside my head, it was tugging at me, pulling me backwards from the edge. Screaming *'No!'* in that filthy, wonderful voice. *'Don't you dare!'*

I took another step.

'Please, Simon, please!' it howled, slammed its fists on my skull, and then I bent my knees, ready to soar, then plummet, and turn to pâté on the pavement. I jumped into the air.

I felt the demon make a U-turn, rushing out of me, desperate now, scrabbling somewhere in its evacuation. Making a loud sound like water down a plug. The force of the thing leaving me lifted me high, and almost in slow motion I was revolving, floating, being dragged back through cold, thin air. I heard the smashing of glass, felt it tinkling against my skin as I was pulled through the air, then through the window. I saw Massimo thrown like a daisy into the kitchen cabinets and for a second, I flew too, before my back and skull cracked against the hardwood floor and I was spinning spinning spinning.

CHAPTER FORTY

My turn now. Pay attention.

Long ago I was woken from slumber, called awake by a chorus of voices. I moved through the forest and watched the hooded red robes, the ragged flapping silk of black tents in furrowed fields. The sound of chanting echoing on rock, the pungent smell of incense. The peep of a flute. They had been seeking me. I was adored.

They brought me gifts. Many goats, for some reason. Sometimes led to me alive through mountain mists, a bell clanging, but mostly already dead. Hairy throats slit and bleeding, flies laying eggs in the mess. I left these to rot. I had no use for them. But I enjoyed the attention, gave my followers little glimmers of myself, to show them I was there.

More gifts came. The head of a man once or twice, in a golden bowl, covered in soft cloth. A little better, I suppose.

Gave me inspiration. I fingered these, tousled wet locks. Yawned and slunk away.

They grew frustrated, and called louder. They wanted more of me, and could not stay away. They became obsessed. I had that effect. 'Please, share your gifts with us!' They were desperate.

I grew tired of the open forest. Restless. Bored. I wanted to try a new home. Somewhere glorious, somewhere splendid to live. Give that to me, I told them, is that too much to ask? Give me a home!

I am a simple being. A few small things and I will be happy. Some comfort, somewhere soft to lay my horny head. Entering sleep to the sound of a beautiful piece of music, my favourite gentle flute. Growing fat on the taste of things grown in the dark and deep. Mushrooms, tubers, soaked in gore. Delicious. Puffed up, waxy and wet. The odd bite of something meatier.

Give me some ceremony! I screamed to my followers. Who doesn't like a party? A neat little knife perhaps, spilling the blood of someone special. A violent sacrifice, here and there. Babies, boys, beloved pets. A bit of naughtiness. Some sickening entertainment! Give me these things, build me a home, and I will share my gifts. I have some good ones.

But they did not understand me. They knew not the code. They brought another goat.

In my frustration, I experimented. Spoiled a few crops, maimed a few children. I did bad things. But they were riling me, calling to me, teasing me. Waking me in the woods but giving nothing of value in return. Just more goats. So, I began to wander. I entered spaces not designed for demonic dwelling.

I crawled into their terrible King. My first host, what a moment! Slipping through the channels of a madman. I snuggled down deep, but didn't stay long; I left once I saw what a pathetic little house he really was, and split him into five. What fun! His head rolling off his neck, his hands landing in the fishery, feet up on the roof. Blood on golden hallways, golden halls. O'er the carpets, up the walls.

They found a way to punish me. They found a clever man, read something in a book, performed a ceremony that snared me, dragged me kicking and biting up the hillsides, higher and higher. I was put deep down inside the mountain. Chained to a rock within a cavern.

Banished and bound I lay, deep and dirty, clamped in shining silver steel. The dark down there. It was, let us say, impenetrable. Not the home I had been looking for.

The steady drip of water over time. Tiny droplets falling from the heights of the cavern. I dragged my chains through fresh pools, watched them glide like sea snakes. My skin itched, burned for days; it was the worst part. I hunted for rough rock to rub myself on; in time, most of the stone was worn smooth and shone, a hall of monstrous mirrors.

It was some company at least, those glimpsed reflections of horn, head, haggard white skull and bone. Becoming dozens. One long leg stretched, became an octopus in appearance.

Stalagmite, stalactite, stalagmite, stalactite.

Once I heard metal hitting rock. Voices. The click of a thin wooden wagon. I saw lights across the water, figures slipping like fish through the smallest of cracks, not scared away by the thrumming of my tongue. They got closer, I grew excited. I heard their thin sounds start to echo from across the pool. I listened for goats. I sniffed for a bucket of bloodless heads. I would have gladly taken them, simply for something to play with.

The closer they came, the more it burnt in me, the knowledge that they were here, but they could climb back up and leave. They could go home, and I could not. I screamed a sound of pure rage so loud and long. Across the lake, the roof caved in, every last man turned to paste. I watched one pale hand with its golden rings, peeking from the wreckage. Lifted it, made it wave hello. I thought of my followers. I wondered if they still thought of me. I pulled the larger parts of myself around me, and slept for a while.

I kept the next man that came. Enjoy it, I whispered aloud, treat yourself. What a handsome face, the thin echo of his words into a recording machine, the twinkling of his electric head torch. He gazed in wonder at the underground world, my maze of mirrors. He did not see me.

A boulder crushed him almost in two. The trapping of that muscular arm between stone and falling stone; I took the credit. And this one was close enough for me to play with. I stroked his screaming face as it grew more bearded. Poor bastard.

He was strong! Seven days it took to climb inside that head. He tried to kick me out like a billy goat, lost a few of his vertebrae in the effort. So I waited, rocking, as lack of food and water wore him down. I made it very hot to amplify his thirst. Then I opened the door at the thinnest point, and stepped inside.

Did I believe that if he left, and I stayed curled up in that head, I'd leave too? Perhaps. But we were bound together. His arm crushed to mincemeat, pinning him down. Mine, chained to stone.

In that head, I learnt many things of the changing world out there. Everyone played with new machines. The year 2000! The world had just survived a terrible bug that never came, as promised, one midnight. I learned of a story; a man in the same predicament, crushed by rock, cutting through his own arm nerve by jangling nerve, to free himself. My new playmate played it on repeat in the most silent of hours, when the thirst came crawling. But he did not have half the guts for such a thing. So he became a handsome nest for me, a toy, a shaking-screaming pet for a while. Until he finally died. And then I got bored. A corpse is a corpse.

On a lonely night, I summoned my greatest power and I brought him back to life, for someone to talk to. I can do that. Reincarnation, it's an excellent trick. My followers love it. But then he died again. Nothing for him to eat. Later I would rumble through his bones from time to time.

Tell me, have you ever seen a human skeleton stand up from the dirt? It is a sight to see. Maybe I will show you one day.

Forgive me. Am I frightening you now?

Then tell me what you have already heard about someone like me. God? Next question please. The Devil? Satan? Rings a faint bell. Perhaps I met him on a mountain. What difference does it make where something comes from anyway? You still must deal with whatever stands before you.

Time passed until one night I simply awoke to feel the earth moving. It heaved itself from one place to another, and the ancient roots and beds of stone twisted, they popped and burst. As if stretching after slumber.

I heard a village destroyed, tiny screams carried on the wind. I felt light on my face, the slightest chink from far above. My cavern had cracked, and with it my chains. One still dangled from a wrist, but they were loose from the rock that had cracked in two. I felt strong for the first time in forever.

I could smell the world outside again, both familiar and deliciously new. Arms muscled and newly gleaming, I climbed toward the stink of promise that called me through the shale. The spiders spindled away, the worms turned.

I leaked out a little, like a pierced yolk.

I emerged.

I looked for my followers, or their ancestors at least. I could only imagine the looks on their faces! I was even keen to see the goats. I searched for the forest, but it was not there.

I found herds of cattle instead, penned in, chewing the cud, wallowing in their own shit. This was not my home.

The world had changed so much, and I found nobody to receive me. I searched further but, poking in the wreckage of the rubbled town, I was invisible. Nobody looked in awe upon me, nobody bowed down. I drifted upwards to the skies, to seek new fortune.

On the wind, I was eye to eye with a wren, a hawk, a harrier. Putrid flies pouring right through me; I felt them tinkle against my teeth like village bells. The grass was blown wet and waxy in the fields below, a train screaming through them. I peered in to see three small girls. I pressed my sunken face against the carriage windows, and not a soul reacted. I reached right in and felt the heat. I was not met with glory, just a wrinkling of the nose.

The moon shone down and I lifted my heavy head, my eyes repeated its orb. Once, twice, I blinked, and then was gone. In search of company, willing or not.

Up ahead, a city.

People everywhere. I watched you all. Did you notice? Look carefully – you may see me in the corner of the mirror, or the hot steam from your brittle egg. Perhaps when you open the front door, flecks of dust and strands of hair shall reveal me screeching on your floor. The blood from your cleaver-cut finger casting a splashed red face on your kitchen counter. But you are not looking, are you?

I grew angry. I began to relish the thought of running your minds to soft goo, then pushing you gently into traffic.

A man could pull the hand off another man, if I made it so. Teenage blood filling the stairwell of a multistorey car park. I could tell that woman to tip the pram into the fast current of the river. I think she would let me.

So I kept hunting through this hard, unforgiving jungle, where every branch was a street, every cave a department store. I watched myself disappear, in glimmers of steel and shining wet cement. I was so exposed, I needed somewhere to hunker down. In one of you. Looking for those who might look back.

A young girl tending premature piglets at a city farm, a teacher who cried in a hallway. I tested them, but did not stay long, just enough to flicker the eyelids, crack a tooth. I practised putting only a little of myself in, just a toe. All wrong, so wrong. I found others, and waded in a little deeper. A teenage boy, abs like dogbones. A woman so tall her back swayed, creaked as I climbed it. A man in a lorry sleeping with the curtains drawn, shuddering as I filled him halfway. The lonely, the alone.

Your bodies are like houses for me, but it's a rough ride, looking for a place to live in this miserable city. I booked viewings, made appointments in your heads. Your sad little studio flats, walls paper-thin. Your ugly little doer-uppers, dirty and downtrodden. I walk the corridors, check the floorplans.

We are proud to present a recently renovated waterside property! Rotting in its foundations. This three-bedroom townhouse has excellent transport links! And a lingering stench of shit. New to the market is this gorgeous family home with breathtaking views across the rotting carcass of your disgusting little life. Pathetic. Not even worth the viewing. No no no.

It is not always . . . fun, for you, my visitation. I take over, I am in charge, and it can be painful. You start to come apart, as I split your seams from the inside. Most of you cannot take it. Most of you are just too small.

When I leave, it can be messy. I might cleave you right down the middle. Or push through you in sizeable chunks. I might force my way out in a hot burst of gore, and slink away, sporting a necklace of your guts. Depends on my mood.

I kept trying, grasping for something permanent. Three days was the longest I lasted in a dwelling, before I had to split. I looked for those who might have stronger bones, better storage. I entered the body of a tired mother, alone with her fat triplets. Now those lodgings had potential! But now that house is rubble. Her head rolled down a hill and into a boating lake. Again and again I tried, bodies bodies bodies. I leapfrogged furiously from one host to the next through this sprawling city, and left a trail of wet destruction, smashing down doors, bursting folk all over the city, watching bits of them hit the ceiling as I swirled away down the drain.

I never once looked back. Only forward.

I grew weary, began to loathe crowds, the very best place to feel invisible. I found myself in a building with gleaming white pillars, a cavernous place of stolen treasures, a palace of plunder. I crept down a hallway scattered with spotlit bowls, stoneware, terracotta reliefs. I ducked behind doorways and crawled over columns, and heard the ancient whispers coming through the cracks. I stopped when I found a vase that looked cosy. I curled up inside, and got some shut-eye. Days later I was woken by bespectacled tweeds peering over me.

'Now here we have the most haunted object in the place. This article simply emits an aura of demonic essence, profound dread. None of us will touch it!'

Oh, honey, you don't know the half of it. On my way out, I cracked it in two and snickered at their screams.

I found a boy.

One particular night, hanging limply in cold night air, I saw someone who seemed rather special. I followed him home through flickering underpasses. Heard his beautiful name, his lyrical voice. Observed his gentle face, his sensitive smile, his tattooed skin. He was from a place where the sun shines hot and the vines burst with bounty. Where men once fought with lions and bulls, and sliced off heads for sport. I'm told the wine is to die for. But beneath his polished surface . . . dark depths. Something strange. I thought: jackpot baby. Here is a place I can live!

I stalked him to a tall house on a long street, colours on the doors like the insides of a fish. Long strips of paint flaking off as I moved past, blown away by the wind that I pressed myself against. Oh if you were only looking! So massive in the streetlamps, that horned silhouette in the road, my body bathed in electric light. A soft glow from the houses winking on as the mist settled, the moths and spiders turning their eye clusters devil-wards.

I climbed to the roof. The dark-haired boy inside his attic, weeping. I hissed, crocodilian, but he did not move. A bleating like a slaughtered kid-goat peppered the rooftops. Nothing still.

I thumped like a drum on the window, and he turned to look at me. He let me in, for a moment.

Then he kicked back, but just a little. Only one or two small fights, and then I was nestled there, snug and secure. It was home.

For a while, all was cosy and safe down inside him, but then small cracks began to form. I wished it could have been forever, but it became clear I would soon overstuff him. This wondrous place of brick and plenty had slowly revealed itself to be little more than a roomy bungalow, due for demolition. Such despair! I was so tired, but my hunt was still not over. I would have to find another.

But I was afraid to roam, to be invisible once more, so I stayed within him, and sent out small parts of myself to look around. Reconnaissance. It hurt greatly, to split myself this way, but it was better than riding the fucking winds. I put out feelers, tested new hosts, but always ran back, retreated to the rest of myself, inside the boy.

When he was forced from his home, for my behaviour, I went with him.

That is where I found it, in a new dwelling built of steel and concrete, squat upon a corner. In a grimy part of the city often wreathed in thin fog, where things scuttled through the streets, and all felt haunted, hungry. There I found the real bounty.

A new boy. Someone so marvellously murky, so full of secrets. I dipped a finger into him, and found mirrored hallways that echoed with soft, hissing little whispers. A slideshow of sin. Years of aching and longing and dirty dark deeds swept so far under the carpet, I knew if I lifted just a corner I would live good for eternity. In my time, I had not yet found one quite like this.

That is where I should live, down where the bad things squirm. That is the place for me. Climbing beneath the muscles of his back, right there with him as he slipped through the city. I had found a home so revoltingly perfect, so palatial, I cocked a leg and pissed upon it. Left my mark.

I tried the handle, and he opened, but only just. A meaty little taste, a titbit to keep me coming and coming. One foot in the crack of a very special door. I heard the things he pretended not to say; I knew it was my house. When he slammed the door upon me, I was appalled, enraged! It only made me want him more.

Simon. My hunt has ended.

Simon. I want it! Let me in, let me see the rest! You say you do not want to live so darkly. You wriggle and squirm. You lie. You are making this impossible. You are not going to like how this ends.

Watch out. Keep your eyes peeled, for soon I will peel them for you. All those others, one two three, ten eleven twelve, they dropped and split like apples. Unable to withstand me. But you. I will wear you like a skin. I will slip and burrow down inside to take root, part your spine like willows and step through to show them all our terrible new face.

Let me in. Just do it. A little more, a little more.

There we go. Good boy.

CHAPTER FORTY-ONE

Blood everywhere.

I regained consciousness to find carnage. Blood on the walls, the broken chair, the fridge and the floor. Glass everywhere from the window. There on my hand, a crusted gash from the wine-glass dagger. The eggshell table cracked in two. The flat silent. Everything back as it was before. I sat among the wreckage and tried to enjoy it.

I inspected my body for damage. There on my torso, a deep wet gash like bark pulled from a tree, from my tussle with the demon. Scratches all over me from the glass. I had bled a fair amount but the wounds were closing now, nobbled with drying scab. I was in a lot of pain. A tooth, a hand, my arm, my side. I was coming apart at the seams. I knew I should see a doctor. Instead I took a bunch of codeine and swigged from a bottle of vodka.

There on my phone, wet in a wine-puddle on the floor, a series of texts.

Several from the landlady.

Hey Samuel. Did you get my voicemail?

I'm on a trip to Hong Kong for three weeks (yum!) but call me when you can for rent chat.

One from Lana.

You need psychiatric help. You do not get to keep your apron. P45 in the post!

I had got exactly what I wanted. I was alone again. But I was chasing a feeling like a turtle in a slipstream. I felt for my friend, but there was nothing. It was really gone now. Along with Massimo.

I know that sleep is a cure for many things. Sleep purges dangerous waste from the brain. Unlike the bacteria that grows between my teeth all night long, the brain is lovingly rinsed of revolting slime. I must brush my teeth in the morning, but my brain has done the work for me. So, I would sleep. I took my duvet, and went to Massimo's room where the breeze from the broken windows couldn't find me. I slept for two days. I drank water, and black tea. I listened to my favourite music. I slept more. I looked after my wounds, needed to stitch the gash on my side with a needle and floss and bit so deep into a wooden spoon it splintered. I slept curled like something to be dug up in a thousand years, long dead and fossilised in the earth. The flat remained silent.

I watched hours and hours of TV. I ate bananas and peanut butter and a family size bag of M&Ms. I ordered flat Thai noodles I couldn't afford and slurped them straight from the tub. The wound on my hand started to heal, slowly but quicker than the others. It was the smallest. I washed it twice with TCP and dressed it again.

The buzzer rang, someone looking for me. Kat, saying my name. She wanted to come in, she sounded firm at first and then desperate. 'I want you to tell me the truth. Let me in.' She buzzed again, banged three times on the steel. I heard her yelling down on the street. 'Let's just be friends then, Simon! Let's be friends.'

A tiny part of me almost opened the door, but I went back to bed instead. I didn't want to see anyone, or be seen. But later that day, I took the bins out, barefoot, and loitered near the ambulance bays, just in case I might catch a glimpse of her. I was in a lot of pain. I was caught by two paramedics finishing their shift, and they stared at my cuts and bruises. But they didn't offer to help me; their work was done for the day. There was no sign of Kat.

Slowly, my head cleared; it settled like good weather. My back still ached from where I hit the floor, and my torso stung all over. My bruises flushed darker but I told myself that was good. I cleaned the flat. Bought new products and wiped everything down. Put my clothes away. Ironed my bedsheets. A man came to fix the window and he was not attractive. I told him someone threw a rock and he believed me, or didn't care. I paid him with the last of my cash.

I found Massimo's phone in his coat, and plugged it in to charge, watched the white fruit form. I couldn't unlock it, I didn't know the passcode. It rang once and the screen said *Mama*. It never rang again, until I rang it myself, just to check. I answered it and heard my voice saying his name. I cleaned out the fridge.

I realised, at 6 p.m. on the third day, that I felt good, almost back to normal.

And that I missed him.

A good walk can cure anything. I walked and I stalked, wrapped in an old black coat, scarf up to my eyes. Past the corner shop where a tall man, covered in warts, teeth like bits of broken shell, peered out from behind a stack of newspapers. We nodded to each other.

It had truly left me. There was not a scrap of it left, and I was absolutely, utterly alone as I crept through the playing fields, along the canals. The sun shone weakly through the dark clouds above and cast scudding shadows on the patchy grass around me. The wind began to blow, I let my feet take charge and found myself in the woods, paddling through the dank railway tunnels, emerging into secret dirty pockets of woodland where the leaves were falling off the trees in clumps, their arms bare and spiky. Not a single mushroom showed itself, no red fox came padding. All was quiet, the magic was gone. The wind picked up and I went home.

Then came a longing too much to bear. An itch almost physical, it crept along my arms and back, deep under the skin. It grew stronger as the days passed. I wanted to be near him, to feel that sting that transformed me. Made me better. I looked for Massimo among the bushes that, after the rain, stank of sperm. I looked for him on the lime-green bridge, hoped to see him dropping sticks into the murk beneath. I tried to catch him peeking out, popping up. He wasn't there.

The buzzer rang often. Kat again. 'Look, Simon, now I'm just worried about you, OK. Let me help you.'

Every time I heard her voice I flushed with shame for all she knew, for what she had seen, and it stopped me from letting her in. She was not the company I was longing for. Sometimes I was filled with rage, as I remembered that she had been trying to take it from me. And then envy toward Massimo, who was harbouring the thing I was slowly craving more and more.

When Kat rang again I took the handset off the wall and let it swing. Panicked, I put it back again, in case Massimo returned. He had not taken his key.

I crept along the supermarket aisles and tightroped the edge of the lido in my speedos, looking and looking. He was not swimming in the water, where the steam rose like a volcanic disaster, so I just watched the men climbing out and shivering in the winter sun, pecs and bulges goose-bumped and dripping. It did nothing for me. *Nothing.*

I ran down alleyways slippery with snails, slinking through backstreets washed blue, listening for the sound of electronic thudding. A door in a wall with a large man blocking the way. I barked something at him and he let me in; I tumbled down the stairs to a humping, pumping crowd of sweating, shirtless men. Concrete floors and flashing lights whiter than cloud. Heads swivelled to stare me down. Jawlines that could cut through butter.

The bodies parted like the Red Sea, then closed to swallow me whole as I moved deeper, through the throng. They watched the way my feet squabbled with the floor, how I put my arms up in the air and blinked my blue eyes hard like steel teeth clipping thin bone. How I tried to dance, but simply could not. I touched a man in the small of his back where the sweat pooled and licked my fingers. Somewhere in the room a naked man on a microphone howled to me, wrapped the black cord around his thigh like a tourniquet, pulled it tight. I screamed out loud, but the men turned away, they could tell I felt nothing.

The days stretched on, my money trickled away. I needed to find a new job. I had eaten all my bananas. I stopped showering, stopped watching TV. In the supermarket, I saw Kat down the cereal aisle and hid behind a tower of oats. I left without paying. Later, from the window, I saw her on the street down below, battling the wind, her loose hair a thick streamer behind her as she carried shopping bags, trying to come in. 'I won't take no for an answer. I saw you in the shop! You look fucking awful! You need to eat! Let's be friends, and just hang out! Have you seen it?'

That time my dirty hand hovered over the moulded plastic. I *could* let her in. Talk to her, say sorry, let her choose a movie. Instead, I waited for her to leave and climbed out, onto the flat roof. I looked out at the veins of traffic, the wetlands further to the east, the figures huddling and cuddling, the brothers and the sisters, the sad and the mad and the very very bad. None of them Massimo. None of them my friend.

I thought of him on a ninth-floor brutalist balcony covered in tulips, or behind the pumps of a petrol station, peeling the skin off a kitten, eyes bloodshot, barking at teenagers. Climbing the lone palm tree at the botanical gardens with a big red smile, dancing in the wind. Later on the couch, when I heard clattering on the roof, I sat upright eagerly, craned my neck through the new glass, but it was only a magpie, eating the remains of another magpie.

Some moments I felt clean and bright. Other times a familiar darkness tickled me hot pink out of nowhere; I woke up itching and furious, my body heaving with racking great yawns. Shapes at the window that I told myself were not there. The old smells came and went and I could not understand it. Was he here? Was it the friend? The heart creaking came and went, too, but was now more of an echo. Something moving in the bins on the street outside. I heard them every time I slept in his bed. Sometimes I felt whispers of that beautiful tingling. But it was just a memory.

I burned alive, sweated through sleepless nights for a week. I wondered how I would survive this horror. I began to wonder if I had successfully sent away the one thing I needed most of all.

CHAPTER FORTY-TWO

A week later I started running again, along the canals. It rained cats and dogs; the rain was freezing on my face but the rest of me was covered in plastic, and in this weather the pathways were clear of cyclists and flâneurs. I was hoping that maybe, one day, I would find Massimo stalking the tunnels.

That afternoon I had outdone myself with three laps of the waterways that ring the flat. My lungs screamed, and I pressed my hands against the wood of a riverboat, stretched my legs and tried not to be sick.

'Simon.'

I looked up to see a pale, haunted face staring out from the nippled window in front of me. Enormous hair. *Kat.* She pointed to the far end of the boat before her face disappeared. I tried to ignore how pleased I was to see her.

The stitch in my side was too piercing to run home

anyway, so I stood, puffing gently and looked at the boat. It was shabby but beautiful, smaller than most of the others in the train of barges, but actually much nicer. Moss-green, with hand-painted roses peeling gently across the side, adorning its name. *Mistress.* Smoke rose from a steel chimney and it smelt good.

Kat emerged beneath a white umbrella that glowed against the dark purple of the skies. Her hair was up, in that same old bun. She looked a little gaunt, even more tired than the last time I saw her.

The sound of the rain on her umbrella was increasingly deafening; I had no choice but to draw closer to her. 'Simon,' she said again. 'You look like shit.' I looked at the filth beneath my fingernails, smelt the breath that stank from my mouth. The burns and tears in my waterproofs.

'You live on a boat?' I asked her, but she dismissed me.

'It's not mine.' She flapped her hand. 'Are you OK?' She sounded concerned. 'What are you doing here?'

'I'm running,' I said.

She leaned against the rail of the boat. 'You're fucking *soaking*. Come inside.'

She held out a hand to lead me inside, stretching it over the gap between the boat and the towpath. Hesitantly I took it, and stepped onto the boat.

As I climbed down the steps, I narrowed my eyes. It was very cosy, if a little chaotic. The interior had been finished with care, with crimson cladding and stars painted on the ceiling, but there were stacks of paperback books, collections of dirty cups and glasses, tissues and used towels in clumps around the room. Dead flowers in a mug, a stained and undressed duvet hanging off a dark brown sofa. An iron woodburner was smouldering in the corner, and the cabin was heavy with the smell of incense and woodsmoke.

Kat handed me a stinky towel, which I used to rub only my hair. When I was finished she took it from me, dropped it on the floor, and gave me a small glass of water. I gulped it down. She filled it again, I gulped it down.

'You've been ignoring me,' she finally said.

'Sorry,' I said, and we were silent for a moment.

'I came to the flat, a few times.'

The sigh that left my chest was deep, hollow. 'I know. I didn't want to see you. I noticed you stopped coming.'

Kat switched on another lamp and I squinted harder at her. She was in her pyjamas, which did not look fresh.

'Are you still looking through my window?' I asked.

Kat barked out a laugh. 'No. I've been here. Signed off work.'

'Why?'

'Stress,' she said, and now when I properly looked at her I saw that she, too, looked like shit. Dark circles beneath her eyes, like she hadn't slept in days.

I fingered the glass in my hand. In the depths of the boat, something moved. I heard an animal grunt. I peered past Kat towards the flickering woodburner, where something was making sounds on a nest of cushions.

'What is that?'

'A puppy,' she said, and I was startled for a moment from my mood.

'Is it new?'

'Yes. I got a puppy.'

'Why?'

She looked me straight in the eye and shrugged, so lightly.

'I thought it might make me feel less alone.'

She twisted a thick strand of hair around a ringed finger, and her neck was suddenly flushing pink. She seemed so different, here in her home, from the charging juggernaut I had met only recently. I could see now the dog was a golden spaniel, with long ears curled under its chin. Like Kat, it was in need of a good brush. She lifted it up, and it opened its eyes, chapped its milky mouth. She kissed it on the head.

I had not closed the door properly, and a draught stirred the ribbon of incense that blew from a joss stick near the sink. I watched her through the haze, Madonna and child.

'Want to hold her?' Kat asked.

I realised that I did not. No, thank you. My head was beginning to ache.

'Maybe later?' I said, moving my eyes around the room. Kat studied me carefully.

'Well, I need to name her.'

'Wendy,' I said, and Kat laughed properly now.

'Wendy. Perfect.' She held Wendy in one arm and lit a cigarette with the other. Ash fell onto the puppy, and her green pyjamas. She just rubbed it in.

'Simon, you know I was only trying to help you.'

I leaned back against the yellow countertop.

She exhaled. 'What happened in there, Simon? In your flat when I came over. Why did you kick me out?'

I stared down at the floor and blushed.

'You wanted to kill it, Kat. And I didn't want you to. I didn't like how close you were getting, what you might find out.' Why was I being so honest with her?

She was observing me now, carefully. She thought for a moment.

'It was in Massimo, wasn't it? Your flatmate. That's how it arrived,' she said.

I nodded, and Kat kissed the dog on her head. I noticed the dark shadows under her eyes as she lowered her face. She looked up at me.

'You can take your wet jacket off. You can relax.'

I remained stiff as a door.

'Simon. Maybe give me a chance?' she said. 'It's not like I'm fighting off friends.'

I breathed out.

She watched me remove my jacket, wincing as I moved.

'Do you want me to take a look?' she asked, gesturing at my injuries, and I shrugged.

'Take off your top.'

I just did it.

She put the puppy down and took a green bag from a chair by the door, opening it to reveal dressings, swabs, little white packages that crinkled as she rummaged. She wet a cloth in the sink and dabbed at the crusts on my body. Tiny red crumbs fell away from my shoulder and the wound turned soft, but I didn't wince. I could smell the iron when she inspected the gash on my side.

'Fuck, that doesn't look good.' She rubbed it with something orange.

Kat's eyes widened and narrowed as she worked, like the squinting tic I'd had as a child. I felt myself relaxing.

'I got a new one every time I kicked the demon out. I'd let it in, then fight back and kick it out.' It was a relief, to speak the words aloud to someone, to name what had been going on.

'Why did you do that?' she said.

'Because first I wanted it,' I admitted. 'Then, I didn't like some of the things it made me do. When it was inside me.' I paused, and looked at her. 'Or, I didn't like how much I liked it . . .'

She shuddered visibly.

'Tell me, Simon, what does it feel like?' she whispered, her finger tracing the thin crack in my skin.

I paused, looking for the words.

'It's . . . like riding a bike down a hill.'

Her tongue poked out of her lips as she listened.

'It's dangerous though, Kat. I've been seriously out of control. I got fired and everything,' I said, and then I laughed. Kat smiled, and gestured for me to put my top on.

'Does it feel good then? Or really bad?'

I spoke from beneath my T-shirt as it slid over my head.

'It's both. Neither. I hurt someone. It makes me do stuff.' *Or lets me.*

She closed her eyes, like she was imagining how that might feel.

'But now I can't stop thinking about Massimo. I've been looking for him everywhere. It's like a craving. I feel like I'm going to burst into flames.' A tear had escaped from somewhere, it was crawling down my face.

Kat just stroked the puppy for a moment, before she poured it into my arms and spoke again, carefully.

'Is it Massimo, or the other thing?'

I felt the animal in my lap, and held her gaze as we both breathed into the room. I noticed my back was itching.

Kat reached out and touched my arm. 'Remember. I've seen what it can do. It's a killer.'

The wind began to howl around the boat.

'I hate it. But I understand it, that craving,' she said. 'It has a . . . lure. Enough to drive you mad.'

I met her eye and nodded, hard.

'Help me, Kat. Help me find it. Just one last time. I just want one more ride.'

She looked down at the dog. 'I don't think that's a good idea.'

'Then you lied.' I stared, furious, stroking the puppy harder in my lap. It twitched a little.

'No, I didn't.'

Outside, the rain was still falling into the canal. I could

hear the pattering on the roof, and now something else, coming from the corridor at the back of the boat.

I shook my head, confused.

'You said you wanted to help me.'

'But not like that.'

My face turned to stone.

'Look, Simon, listen to me. I came to this city to help people, that's what I wanted. It's who I am, for my sins. What a joke. I'm a fucking paramedic, but I run around talking paedos from jumping off buildings half the time.'

She looked up, as if there was one right there above us.

'Then this *horrible* shit starts happening. I'm taking pulses off corpses over and over again, I'm absolutely useless. Something is killing people, day after day. It kills someone I *know*. I'm surrounded by it, by sad, mad, *desperate* fucking horror and nobody takes it seriously, we just clean up the disgusting mess and then I come home and I'm just alone with it all.'

Her voice was wobbling but I didn't look at her, I kept my hands moving on the puppy.

'Then I met you, and I thought maybe it was my chance to do something good, to stop something bad happening to someone else. But it sounds like, it got you too.'

She sighed, and closed her eyes for a moment, before smiling warmly at me.

'Simon, that thing, it's not what you need.' She put a hand on my knee. 'Look, I know a lonely bastard when

I see one. What do you think about letting *me* in instead? Maybe we can be friends. Huh?'

I looked right at her now, hot with anger.

'I am not lonely, and I don't need a *friend*.' Why was I crying?

The wind was blowing harder outside, the log burner screamed as its smoke was sucked away. A wind chime above the kitchen sink began to tinkle. Kat touched my hand.

'Come on, Simon, aren't you tired?'

I *was* tired. And I liked it there on that cosy boat. And I liked Kat, I had to admit. An image began to form of hot tea, the door bolted against the rain. The telly on. Or, the two of us in a restaurant, both laughing at something the waiter had said. I felt myself on the edge of surrender, my head forming a nod.

'OK.'

Kat grinned, and suddenly her eyes were dangerously wild.

'Great. In that case, Simon, maybe we can do it together?'

I sniffed hard.

'Do what?'

Something started banging from the back of the boat, and Wendy began to growl.

CHAPTER FORTY-THREE

My head had begun to pound.

'OK, Simon, I'll take the dog.' Kat's voice, like in a dream. I felt the puppy's head in my hands, and the breath from its mouth, its wet nose leaving a snail trail and slicking the fine hairs on my arms down dark. Such fragile bone, I found myself thinking. If I moved my hands just so . . . I watched my fingers flex slightly against Wendy's head, my grip tightening just a little.

I could just start pulling bits off, like sections of a pine cone, and fling them into the wood burner, if I wanted to. My fingers worked their way into the curls of long spaniel ears, picking through the strands.

'Simon, the dog. Simon, what's wrong with your face?'

I was snapping my teeth, for some reason. My eyes were twitching. My heart was thumping, groaning. I could hear it. My skull suddenly throbbed with pressure. The puppy growled again.

Something was scratching on wood, deep in the navy corridor behind Kat where pictures of flowers and forests hung on the walls. Or was it behind my eyes? A little wicker cow-head began to quiver. The incense in the air became frantic, looking for a way out.

'What's that?' I said. I put down the puppy and it opened its eyes.

'Don't be scared, OK?' Kat whispered.

I wasn't scared. I was excited. I got up, and pushed past her.

I could feel that thin whine at the back of my brain, building. That delicious hot soup brewing in my belly. The meal I had been longing for. Was it *here*?

Kat was touching my elbow. 'Simon. I just wanted to know . . .'

I ignored her, kept walking down the corridor as the scratching got louder, followed now by loud banging. I was heading towards a dark-green door, and as I got closer I could see that it was bound shut to a hook in the wall by a thick, studded belt. The buzz in my head intensified.

'What is this, Kat? What's in there?' But I already knew, and every limb I owned was itching, jangling, burning. I hardly dared believe it was true.

She didn't answer, and she wasn't trying to stop me. I reached the door. With some difficulty, I unbound the belt, turned the little brass handle, and opened it. The darkness beyond was shifting. I could make out a black towel, draped over a small porthole, open just the smallest of cracks. Beyond, the rain poured down. In the room, a stink like week-old bacon. Kat's voice a whisper behind me.

'Be careful. Don't let it out.'

The sky ruptured with thunder above us, but I hardly heard it, the buzz in my brain was all-consuming as a shape emerged suddenly from the gloom, a hollow, gasping face pressing out of the shadows.

Massimo. He stared at me, trembling. Looking like I'd never seen him before, like he'd been dug from a grave. He opened his dry lips and I saw the tiny triangles of his dirty teeth.

Behind me, Kat was panting.

I said his name, and he stepped forward three inches, his eyes rolling.

'What the fuck,' I whispered.

'I was just trying to help him.' Kat's voice quivered.

'Help him?!'

'I couldn't do it though.'

Kat was wide-eyed. My voice got louder.

'You said you wanted to be *friends* with me. You fucking liar. You just wanted to get to *that*!'

Kat was stammering, getting flustered.

'He was very hurt, he's all fucked up! I saw him one day, following you out there.' She pointed through the grimy window at the towpath I'd been stalking for days. 'It's still inside him, and it's very very weak. I tried to get it out!'

Massimo shook violently as a strong wind blew through the boat.

'I had to lock him in there.' Kat was sheepish. 'He kept trying to eat the puppy.'

I looked at Massimo's sunken eyes that seemed to throb in their sockets. He looked feral, a creature transformed, nothing like the tanned, healthy boy who had arrived at my front door not so long ago.

Kat's voice was growing reedy, almost tearful. 'I thought if he was in here, everyone outside would be safe! It's in him, and he's in here. That fucking parasite. Jesus, the shit that it's done. And *I'm* the one going out there and having to clean it up. So I've been watching it for a week, trying to figure out what to do.'

Now I turned to her, so she understood that, besides her fury, I knew how excited she had been by the friend. How terrified, how stimulated. How *obsessed* just like me.

'And did you like it, what you saw? Be honest, you wanted a taste.'

'It's terrifying.' She squeezed her eyes like she was banishing memories of things she'd seen. 'And it didn't care about me,' she hissed. 'It would not speak to me.' She was standing, back against the wall with the puppy to her chest. 'It just kept saying your fucking name. I think it only wants you.'

She stamped her foot and, as if in response, Massimo lifted a quivering arm, reaching out to me. I turned, almost lifting my own hand.

'You've just had him locked down here, rotting.' *Keeping it to yourself.* I breathed in the stink. 'What the fuck, Kat?'

She breathed out.

'Oh, please, Simon, you're not the only one with secrets. Besides, I was enjoying the company.'

Massimo whimpered. I felt the deliciousness cooking in my belly.

I looked at Kat once more. Now I really saw the dryness of her skin, the nails bitten to the quick by frantic teeth.

Her voice became dark.

'So will you help me?'

'Help you *what*?'

Kat put the puppy down, which ran to the kitchen with a whine. In the dim light of the corridor, her eyes in shadow, she looked crazy. She put a shaking hand on my shoulder.

'I was getting ready to kill it.'

Suddenly, the bedroom door burst fully open, as Massimo lurched forward and sprinted through the cabin, scrabbling after the puppy. Kat screamed and flinched, pressing herself tighter against the wall. Massimo ran, and I followed, to find him hovering in the living room, eyes wide. He stared me down, now a look of terror on his face. Kat behind me, reaching for a knife.

I said his name, and he turned to claw the door open, before leaping barefoot from the boat.

Without a thought, I followed, running after Massimo through the clacking door, slicing through the rain. I saw him scrabbling on the canal-side, and I jumped too, tried to catch him there on the flooding towpath, but he slipped out of my hands. I swung a punch and stumbled, hit the concrete with a pain worse than razorblades. All I was left with was that rotten stink I ran through, trying to catch him as he ran from me. I saw him through the rain, disappearing into a tunnel, and gave chase. I followed his trail like a chum bucket.

My wounds ached, the fresh dressings peeling away beneath my soaking clothes. As weak as he was, Massimo was very fast. I surely had no chance, but then there he was, crawling on all-fours and then stumbling up onto his feet, entering a tunnel through the white sheet of falling rain. I followed him, slipping on the wet brick, righting myself as I entered the darkness to find nothing but the faint echo of feet. I ran on, narrowly avoiding the water's edge, emerging from the gloom into more downpour. I found myself on a short stretch of towpath with tall brick walls on either side, the sky thundering above me, something flashing in the tunnel ahead. *There!* Massimo hunching in the shadows, looking back with green eyes ablaze, illuminating the graffitied brick, running from me as I chased him through the tunnel, and up stairs streaming with water. 'Give it to me! Give it back!' I screamed into the rain. I fell again, cracked a knee, but finally made it to the top to see a tiny Massimo disappearing across the playing fields, running from me like he could run forever.

I'd never catch him like that.

CHAPTER FORTY-FOUR

An urgent treasure hunt took place inside the flat. I had a plan.

I opened every drawer and tipped up every wicker basket. I called Josh three times. He did not answer.

I sat sodden in the mess and thought hard. On my hands and knees now, frantic as you like, I entered the crawl space that ran the length of the living room, and moved past sleeping bags never used, a tent covered in mildew. Black bin bags with the air sucked out stacked on top of each other, full of Josh's old clothes; I moved these aside and found two large plastic boxes with clips on their lids, like those that housed the cape. I dragged them both out into the living room, and pulled a spider's web from my lips.

The boxes were full of junk and nonsense. Unopened letters for Josh, old knick-knacks. Plastic fruit, scented candles. And then I found what I was looking for. A single car key, winking in the spotlights.

I knew how to drive. I did not have a car.

But Josh did.

The sliding door of the lock-up rolled like summer thunder, and I peered into the gloom. There she was. A yellow Volvo estate, three years old but practically brand new. She'd hardly been driven at all. Three parking tickets on her windscreen, for some reason. She was a gift from Josh's crazy aunt, but he hated driving in the city, he'd bashed her on a bollard, so here she waited, for someone to love her. For her moment.

She was filthy, but so was I, and there was no time to wash either of us. A button on the key flashed her to life, headlights illuminating the brickwork around us, the smashed window at the back of the room. Mouse shit on the floor, the spine of a bird that crunched underfoot as I got into the car. Her interior smelt strong and wild; the seat creaked beneath me.

I started the engine and reversed out slowly. The rain fell onto the windscreen. I turned the wipers on and the old yellow parking tickets were released. They flew into the sky, baby ghosts, free at last.

The yellow car emerged through the city gloom, headlights aglow, bottles and bent needles crunching under tyres. I stalled twice, remembering how to drive, then lurched forward down the alleyway, sped up. Turned onto the main road too fast, searching for Massimo through the wet windscreen. Desperately. A flash of white trainer, a glimpse of bright green eye. *Come on, show yourself.*

I sped up, gunned it down side streets and over bridges, circling, circling. Eyes peeled. I'll find him, I'll find him. And when I get him, it's mine again.

I hit something in the road and sent it spinning.

I slammed the brakes.

Fuck. A child? The mother of a child? The rain was still falling and I did not want to get out and find out what I had killed.

The street was empty, a narrow back-passage of sorts between large buildings and warehouses that stared down on the body in the road. The rain on the rough tarmac made it shine in the artificial lights from the car, like the skin of an orca.

Door open, feet out, peeking round the bumper. Something red dribbling from a once-breathing being, blood leaking into rainwater.

Orange hair, on something large. A boy? No. Not hair, fur. A fox. Absolutely dead. Curled up, huge, a male. Ragged black ear, scarred and torn. Amber eyes already turning glassy. I crouched down, and touched its wet head. Something slimy was leaking from its nose, but the fox was otherwise intact. I waited, as if the creature might come to life suddenly, but it did not. Something about its poor, beautiful body. Even in my desperation, I could not leave it there.

I scooped up the fox, slipping a little. He was heavy. I pivoted, pressed the boot release and placed him at the entrance which rose to claim him. I did not push him back into the darkness, he might not like that. I left him near the lip.

For a moment I sat, and began to cry. For the fox. For Massimo. For my old life. My job. Josh. For me. For sanity. Head hanging low, hands over eyes, quietly crying. Three minutes. I stopped when I heard movement in the street around me, hard thuds and splashing. Something bumping against the car. When I looked up, blinking through the blur, there was nobody there.

I had been driving for an hour, with no sign of Massimo.

The rain had stopped. The sun was setting, the sky beginning to blaze. I thought about Kat, who I had left gasping on the boat. I bet she loved a sunset, I bet she said the fact aloud every time she saw one. I breathed deep, and looked at the road ahead. I had found myself on an A-road, a main artery that would lead me from the city. I watched the fields and forests in the distance, spread like spilled ink, illuminated by the sun's last rays.

I could drive north, towards them. Onwards, out of here, into the rest of the world. Keep driving and never come back. Along the roadside, the streetlights were coming to life, where road met grass that sloped up to a thick line of trees. I saw rabbits, twitching in the grass. I saw them on the road too, half-mush, bright eyes turned dull if still in their heads. I saw their velvet legs, sticking up from the mess, swaying gently in the breeze of every passing car. Pointing north.

I slowed down and someone blared their horn.

I turned the radio on. A sparkling song, a chorus of voices in the background, a deep sonorous bass. I sang along, loud and clear. I closed my eyes, and thought of Massimo. I felt there was a spider's web, somewhere in the city, pulling me to him. To my friend.

Up ahead, getting closer, I saw the large green sign telling me to turn off soon, turn right, back to the heart of the city. Continue your hunt among the parks and glossy white columns, in the cafés and construction sites. Don't miss your turn, Simon.

The sunset burned brighter; the fields ahead began to glow, golden and green. Calling.

The music blared. Tiny nails scratched at the base of my spine, climbing up the bumps to stroke the heel of my brain. A buzzing began.

Massimo? Are you there?

On the road around me, the cars seemed to be speeding up. A black Jeep in front of me wasn't looking where he was going, switching lanes without indicating. I felt a burp of danger rising in my chest, slammed my palm on the horn, hit the brake. He beeped his own horn. The warring sounds wobbled me, a wet slap. The car behind me was going too fast.

The car was getting hot, and I felt bilious suddenly, a putrid soup in my gut that burned to bubble over. The music grew louder, the cars thrumming around me. A huge car right behind me, and another to my right. Are you going to let me in? Cocksucker.

There's the next turning now, the city lights blinking down the turn-off. The last rays of sun winking away. *Decide, Simon. Make your move.*

I whacked into the lane and hit the turn-off, narrowly missing a screaming lorry. So close. Horns honking like frenzied geese. I couldn't breathe, I couldn't see. I was going to crash, and I was fumbling for the window because I needed air, I really needed air. I swerved, steering wheel going the wrong way, and I was going to hit that small green car that didn't see me coming and kill the whole teenage gang inside it who are just singing along to something cool and not ready for this death that I was going to deliver to them shit shit *fuck* shit sorry.

I pulled over, and finally got the window down, a cold blast of air hitting my face. I took breaths so big I could almost chew on them, and turned off the engine. Silence. The car ticking, my chest rising and falling. I took a moment to breathe, felt each limb and eyelash and ripe round ball between my legs. Intact. I looked left, at the city. Warehouses, office buildings, a business park. Rows of houses, lines of trees. Telephone wires strung between them – a cat's cradle connecting it all. Home was in there somewhere, across to the east.

I should go home, I told myself. I wished that I wanted to.

In the boot of the car, something thumped.

CHAPTER FORTY-FIVE

The fox was alive.

I had seen its guts leaking from its arsehole, but it was alive.

For a moment I didn't move a muscle, just listened and breathed, one hand still on the key and the other on the handbrake. I was focused, in control. The noise had stopped.

Outside, the road was empty, and the night was getting darker by the second; the sparse line of streetlights illuminating the wooded road snaking ahead. I slowly twisted my body to turn in my seat and look towards the back of the car, and strained to hear the noise again.

There. A thumping, followed by a shifting, the fox turning over, or feeling its way around. It must've been in agony.

Had it really not been dead? It had seemed very dead.

The thumping sound moved to my side of the vehicle, followed by a deep wet crunch. I held fast, and looked out the rear passenger window. Outside, the trees wobbled gently in the wind, unhuddling after the rainfall. The lone streetlamp I had stopped beneath filled the car with a soft yellow glow, and I was grateful. The world outside was touchably dark.

I focused my gaze on the armrest in the middle of the backseats; it was tucked in, closed. When opened, I knew it would create a gap that looked into the boot. I thought I saw the edges twitch. Heard the gentle scrape of fibres.

Another hard thump.

As I watched it, the armrest moved forward, inch by inch until it stopped, resting on the seat. The cave of the boot now had a tunnel, an entrance. A hot, rotten smell dribbled through, a violent mix of blood and cheese.

I covered my mouth and nose with one hand, and flashed out the other to grab the door handle, but the hole gaped open wider still. I willed my eyes to adjust to the darkness of the boot, desperate to see, waiting for the fox.

Then it came.

One eye. Squinted and bloodshot, emerging through the gloom so slowly, fixed directly on me. The pupil contracted, a little black dot surrounded by vivid green, becoming smaller and smaller as it stared out. Not the fox. Something else. A face pushing itself against the wall of seats. Cracked skin, broken capillaries, pointed teeth.

Blood on lips, some crusted, some fresh. A tongue dashing out to taste it. Massimo. *The whole time.*

I assumed that next the seats would be pushed forward, or be torn apart, whatever it took to get at me. This was terror now, it had finally come. Did it want revenge? Did it have the strength to kill me?

I did not want to die this way, dirty and uninsured in a lay-by, but realised I probably would. I was trapped. The eye twitched once, and then the lights in the car went out.

My scream seemed to echo around the vehicle, and I left it there as I wrenched the door open, heaving myself out and onto the gravel. The seatbelt, still clipped, wrenched me backwards, and I grappled for the release in the dark. I ran to a grass bank, up and away, choking on my own breaths. I managed about twenty metres before I tripped, spilling onto some rough ground, gravel ripping chunks from my knees and palms. I twisted around to get up, and the sky tilted above me. The wind was moving fast now, hard, changing direction suddenly. The motorway hummed nearby.

The headlights flashed on, washing the road in brilliant light, dazzling me in terrible splendour. He was desperate, out of control. The car's horn blared, a brilliant and horrifying trumpet filling the air and snatching my breath with it. I cowered, hands slammed over my ears. Then, it stopped, the headlights flicked off. The boot opened, with the tiniest pneumatic hiss.

What was that? A shape slowly creeping from the boot,

lit gently from behind by the moon. Lowering itself to the ground, I braced myself for the attack. But it didn't come. It did not have the power; the beast was ebbing away.

Instead the shape went crawling, limping up the grass and on into a line of birches. Before it disappeared completely, the light of the moon shone down, illuminating two dimming green eyes and one bloodied Reebok trainer. A face of ragged desperation, of hunger and pain. He made a pathetic animal sound, and the wind snatched it. He was *afraid*.

I should have returned to the car and driven away. But this was my chance to catch it.

I took the keys from the ignition. Locked the doors. Felt in my pocket for the box cutter, cool as a fish. I left it there, it would not be enough.

Standing at the open boot, I peeked inside. Something lay in tatters, shredded like red cabbage across the matting, tufts of orange fur. One lone string of purple matter dangled onto the roadside, brushing the wet tarmac. Feeling for the catch in the flooring that would allow me to lift the mat and give me access to the well beneath, I brushed aside the wetness.

There was the tyre in its hole and next to it what I needed. A long, thick, silver wrench.

Now that thin whine was starting to creep up on me, building at the back of my head, near the base of my skull, and rolling towards my ears. Pulling.

I watched the inky darkness beyond the treeline. I felt

the forest shifting, leaves moving against each other. All the creatures of the night were right there, lined up just beyond the treeline, claws wiggling, teeth clacking, eyes rolling, spit frothing. Waiting for me.

I was ready for the hunt. Time to catch a demon.

I let the trees take me in. I kept steady, trying to get my bearings. My grip was tight on the wrench. Far to the right, the odd snatch of lights flickering, the passing of distant cars. This could have given me comfort, a reminder that I was not alone, but in fact I felt the opposite. The darkness happens under your nose. You're always next to it, trying to pretend that it doesn't exist, because maybe then it won't happen to you. But it's there. The body dragged from the canal, the addict next door chopped to chunks, the man tapping on your basement window at three in the morning. The boy, torn to pieces in the woods by a devil, metres away from the road.

I saw flashes of the thing, in pockets of memory. The terrible, pale face, the ragged hand on the bedpost at Halloween. Massimo's teeth stretching to a curve, soft like the hoof of a newborn foal before hardening in the air to something jagged. *Click*, *click*, *click.* The click of the clipper on his fingernails. *Click. Click. Click.* The clicks became the snaps of branches under my feet, whole limbs rotten through, sharp angles breaking. I felt more clear-headed than I had in weeks, and more enraged. No fuzz, no fug, no fucks to give. I've come to get you.

'I know you're there,' I called into the trees and scrubby bushes.

No reply, only the wood-creak. Silence.

'My friend. I saw you in the fucking car. You look terrible. Very weak.'

Silence. Nothing but the faint rumble of a truck on the road ahead. The strangled peep of a night-bird.

A wolfish whine, a whimper thin as a blade, almost indistinguishable, through the trees. My ears pricked up. I moved in the direction of the sound, and I called out Massimo's name; it was the only one I knew. Another sound from the same direction. A crunch of bracken, heavy in tread. I watched the trees grow thinner around me, slender speckled birches bowing their heads against one another, exhausted from their growing. The ground grew sodden.

The marshes appeared ahead of me, dark and spread like an oilslick. I stood at the edge, looked across the tufted waters, the wrench in my fist tight enough to burn. In the distance, two tower blocks rose, twin middle fingers in the sky, their lights burning bright. Watchtowers. Tiny inhabitants in the windows, strange guardians moving high above. The moon swam fat among the rushes.

I called again, across the water.

'Come out!'

A new sound in reply. Very close. Something huge moving deliberately through the trees on the water's edge. So much bigger than a man. The heavy shifting of weight on dead leaves was slow, rhythmic. Cloven.

The pilot light of rage was flickering fast, dimming, the ice pick stabbing, squirming into my gut, releasing wet slime into the cavity of my body.

I reminded myself what I was dealing with. Massimo? Frail and thin. I could handle that. But this . . .

The smell that came rushing, rich and peaty, stronger with each huge footfall. Revolting. Delicious. That stink from somewhere deep, old, tugged through a membrane, but now worse, like corpses, like a foot pressed down into a drowned man, releasing hot gases.

Another thick crunch, that whimper again. The gentle clinking of chains. The forest was moving around that sound, the worms squirming deeper into the soil, bats creaking leather wings over eyes, not daring to look. But somehow I was looking. I was waiting to see what was coming.

A spin of the wrench, my hand began to shake, shackles up, breathing in and out, puffs of steam dissolving in the night air. It had stopped, but it was there. All in a moment, a lorry swung along the road far behind me, washing the woods in a wall of white light. It was gone in mere seconds. A lighthouse beam, but in that flash, I saw a glimpse.

Walking, hunched between the trees, fifty yards away through the bracken. So big. An angular head, huge hands, tapered fingers grasping bark. A long back roped with muscle. Over seven foot tall, maybe more. The sight of it turned my last droplet of courage to vapour that puffed away, into the night.

The devil turned my way. Eyes round and hollow like thumbs pressed deep into meat.

That earthy, sulphurous, flesh-rot smell intensified on the wind, burning my nostrils. I began to gag as it stepped closer. Now its voice, which seemed to echo across the marshlands with the deep and furious sound of rock moving against rock. Just one word that rang out in a voice loud and terrible enough to churn butter.

'Sssssssimon.'

I spun away from that sound, ran towards the water. Suddenly the clouds parted, birthing again the yellow moon, meekly offering itself in aid.

It was coming closer, and now I was terrified. The wind shook the grasses as it raced across the water, licking hard at the surface. I would have to swim, I knew. I waded out, into the water that gripped my thighs, clung on tight. I prepared to dive, but something stopped me.

The lake was thick with small bodies. An enormous gull, inches away, dozens more. Seagulls, moorhens, thirty chinese ducks. Huddled on jetties, gliding on the water. Birds everywhere, all staring in one direction, towards the reedbeds. Their gaze followed me, watching what walked behind, and then they thundered upwards. I flinched, dropping the wrench into the water.

There it was. The whole being, in all its glorious horror. Stalking through the reedbed, head lowered so as not to catch a twisted horn in the branches above it. Limping slightly, feet dragging. A big, tired, terrifying thing. The head was . . . unbelievable. Skin tight and ridged like lumpy bone had been pushed through a skein of stretched putty. Dagger-toothed, eyes at first like a shark's, both blind and seeing, before the moon caught an iris as the head righted itself, and the eye was more crocodilian. Burning green but flickering above a mouth I couldn't describe. The eye flickered again.

Yes, the feet were cloven. Yes, the hands were clawed. Arms like He-Man dug from the grave, a clinking chain dangling from one wrist, trailing the earth as it came closer, reaching the shore.

I stood in waist-deep stagnant water, staring up at bleached bone and shagged twists of hair, sockets deep and cavernous, a tongue slipped out of white lips. I saw slices of birch bark on the trees behind us silently buckle and peel in its heat, revealing fresh white flesh beneath. The *size* of it. The way it shimmered, the way it stank. Those pleading, blinking, bright-green eyes.

It began to speak, exhausted. Its voice more terrible than ever, out here in the woods. '*Simon. We could be good together. Sssimon, I . . .*'

I took one last look, and sank beneath the water.

I was down for seconds only, sinking my hands into the mud. Couldn't breathe. Wanted to get up, but stayed down. One more desperate plunge into the mud and there it was, cold steel in my fist again.

When I emerged it was looking right down at me, and I gasped in not fresh air but instead the steam of singed guts, rotten bone, the stink of teeth that should have been cracked out years ago.

It began to say my name again; I stood upright. I brought back my arm and struck with the wrench, straight to the ribs, swinging up and under with all my might. I thought maybe my arm would go right through, but the wrench smashed into the beast, hard. It buckled a little, so I took another swing to the knee that cracked like thunder. The fat head went back moonwards in what must have been pain, and the heavy wrench came up sharp, straight into its monstrous chin, which poured hot blood down my arm, onto my face.

It was even weaker than I thought. It was pathetic. I smacked it again, direct to the horn, and the water churned red around me. Another smack, sounds of splintering bone filling the night, blood spurting into my eyes. Made me blink. Made me stop smashing. It fell back, crashing into the reedbed, and disappeared from sight.

When I waded over to inspect the body, it was not the same. Now it was a young man, about my age, covered in blood. His filthy T-shirt had ridden up to expose a beautiful line-drawing of two men kissing. He was on his back, crimson and carp-gasping, but his chest was already beginning to slow. I watched it slow until it didn't move anymore.

He'd stopped breathing, I think.

CHAPTER FORTY-SIX

Empty streets in the middle of the night, as if evacuated. The building was confused, a little concerned at the sight of us. Me, dragging Massimo under his arms into its hallway and up the stairs. Both of us were covered in blood, our movement into the flat leaving a dark streak down the corridor.

'It's fine. I'll clean that up.' I said this to the rug, and kept pulling.

I had dragged Massimo's body through the woods. He had been breathing, but only just, and leaking more blood by the second. It took twenty minutes to get him to the car, and the woods seemed to part before me furiously, urging me on. I did not know if I had smashed the devil out of him completely, or if it might be circling the forest. I'd put him on the backseat and drove us both home, ignoring the copper tang of fresh blood soaking into Swedish fibre.

In his bed at home, Massimo lay still and, for the second time, I wrapped him in bandages. I turned him over, inspecting his injuries, the dents and gashes I'd made in his skin with the wrench. The blooming bruises. His wounds were bad enough, but not fatal. He did not resist or make a sound as I nursed him, but something did. A thump from within, a lump pressing through the skin of his lower back. Groaning.

Ah. *Hello.* Still there then.

Dead bugs appeared in the room over the next two days, inexplicably. Some sort of small cockroach, tiny woodlice, a centipede. I rolled my eyes and fed them to Goblin, who emited a vomity smell to tell me his bag was full.

I lay next to Massimo, poker straight in the bed; I heard it trying to whisper to me.

'Sssssimon. I'll get stronger. I'll be back.'

'Yes, well. I'm in charge now,' I said firmly. 'I know you need me. If he dies, I reckon you'll die too. The state you're in! Right?'

The water jug wobbled on the bedside table. The nice one I had put there.

I stroked Massimo's brow.

'I have a plan. Do you want to hear it?'

A low murmur in response, a flicker of the eyelid.

'You are very unwell, both of you. When he's a little better, when you have the strength, I'm going to let you in. Into me.'

The jug splintered at the rim, a crack ran through it.

'Not all the way, calm down. We'll start slow. My rules.'

The water in the jug changed to rusty pink.

'I will let you in, bit by bit, from Massimo and into me. I will enjoy you, and you can have one more look. Inside this.' I gestured to my whole body.

A thin voice crept from Massimo's open mouth.

'And then?'

'We'll see.'

The water in the jug turned brown and bubbled. I gave it to the spider plant as I got up and watched it wither.

'It's teamwork, but led by me.' I turned out the light.

Over a week, I washed Massimo's pits and groin, and dried him down, and then he curled up puppy sweet in the sheets. I fed him roasted red peppers from the jar and watched them slip between his lips until his teeth caught hold and began to bite. His tongue came out to catch the juice, a good sign. He started to purr in his sleep, or at least, something did. A great walloping tractor sound that made the walls vibrate and the headboard wobble, though Massimo lay corpse still. I put a finger under his nose to check for breathing, and it came back stinking.

A cold flannel, wiping the crust from his nails. I fed him more. Mushrooms, steamed and leaking, pressed into his mouth like a disc into a slot. Small, rhythmic chewing. The thumping sound of banging on a door. Coming back, bit by bit, ready to give me what I'd been missing.

One morning, Massimo opened his eyes for longer than five minutes; that was sign enough.

'Come on then,' I said, putting a hand on his greasy head.

The demon was still weak, huddled inside Massimo. It couldn't do much in this state. I was stronger; I would decide how much I took it in. I called the shots.

Kiss by kiss, gulp by gulp, I swallowed it down like cold Guinness. I had, in the past, wondered often how it would feel to have Massimo's lips on mine, but now it did little for me. I knew now that the desire had always been about something other than Massimo. He was simply a vessel for something more exciting.

Even so, a kiss is a kiss.

It tried, at first, to rush in, but I put out a firm hand on its horny little head and stopped it. I set the limit. The beast felt different as it wiggled down inside me. Because I was in charge. A forced entry is no match for the gentle warmth of a slow immersion. Now I was a steak gently searing, a gleaming Tesla on charge. My body tingled with it, my skin alight. I lay down on the floor of the living room and moved in circles, Massimo's gym shorts sliding across the wooden floor as it climbed through me with deep joy.

'The size of it in here! The taste of your tongue. I am happy it's you and me, boy.'

It was ecstatic, momentarily. It wasn't enough.

'I cannot do this for long. So you know. Cannot live between two like this, it hurts a lot, Simon. Can I come in all the way now? Please. I know you like it. Please let me in.'

'No,' I say.

Heaving Massimo through the forest, I had come up with my plan. Or rather, my idea. I did not know if it would work. But I knew that, over the past weeks, I had learned to control this thing, to kick it back. I'd had some power over it, like I did with all the dark and dirty things that squirmed inside me. And now, with it being so knackered, even more so.

I would keep the demon safe at home, and take little bits of it into me, when I wanted to. It wanted to live inside me so badly, I knew it would not say no. In the end, when I'd had my fill, I'd kick it back out, into Massimo. Then I'd find Kat and, together, we'd find a way to kill it. I only hoped it would not see this plan, when it came walking in my head. But still, it had little choice.

Each day, I let in a little more, tripping and tripping until one night I was absolutely buzzing on the thing. I stepped out all dressed up. I wore big fuck-off boots that I'd found online, and bought expensive wine with Massimo's card, from the Turkish cats who kissed my hand with a rough lick. The blue paper on the bottle crinkled in my jiggly hand which was, yes, more muscular than it used to be. I crushed a bottle with one fingerflex. I found a wild party and swished the cape around me in rooms full of sexy strangers. Everyone talked to me, and I talked back with easy charm. Oh how we laughed! I was having the best night ever. But the beast grew exhausted. The longer I was away from Massimo, where the rest of the devil lay shivering in cotton-poly, the more it faded away from me, out of me. I felt it leaving me in the morning light, leaking out and travelling homeward as I shivered on the street.

I considered, for a moment, just letting it all in, getting my fill and going with it, but the fear of losing myself, of being swallowed whole, was too much. Of what I might do. And I knew this couldn't go on much longer, this shared custody.

It was time to say goodbye.

The sun was setting pink on the purple blanket I had laid out on the flat roof. A gentle wind lifted the tassels as I led Massimo through the living room window; he staggered a little but grinned. I'd let him wear the cape.

'Are you cold?' I asked.

'Not really,' he croaked. He still looked like shit, tired and twitchy.

My body was giving off impossible heat, and as his arm brushed against mine, birds filled the sky above us. I watched them twist as one, a black cloud, moving above the city.

I poured us both big whiskys and we chugged them down, chased them with hot sausage rolls. We cheered as the sky grew dark around us, and the smell of bonfires was delivered on the wind. We grinned and moved closer on the blanket, then I kissed him, hard, because I could. He kissed me back, the two of us naughtily grinding our erections together so hard I thought we might create sparks. I bathed in the feeling; who knew when I'd next have the courage to kiss a beautiful boy from Rome, and be kissed back?

An explosion hit the sky and we gaped upward at the bursts of red and gold. The city watched too, and glowed at the spectacle. Down on the street, children screamed with horror, then delight. Dogs called to each other in fright. The fire station was having a party, and music pumped through the open windows. When we stood and downed more whisky, we could see their hunky bodies moving to the beat. We held each other.

On top of the building, on top of the world. Two boys, embracing, sharing a demon for the last time. The city throbbing with its own power, wide awake, watching. I prepared to exorcise myself. I was getting ready for the final exit, to kick it out, all the way back into Massimo. I had the ropes and tape ready, in the kitchen, to hold him down. I knew where Kat's boat was moored. I would find her later, ask for help. She would come. All was prepared. But as I felt its warmth in my belly, and tried to imagine its absence, I began to get cold feet. When it spoke, using Massimo's mouth, it sounded eager, confident.

'Simon. Is it not good? Is it not great? To feel me so purely.'

I stepped back, and told the truth. 'Yes. It's very good.'

'Do I need to convince you further, to let me stay?'

I considered this. Again I pictured giving it up, this beautiful thing. All it gave to me. The joy, the rage. The freedom. I imagined myself sat staring at the clean walls of the flat, with a horrible new flatmate. Or alone. Serving drinks to glamorous teens, forcing a smile, squeezing out a laugh. Roaming the city once more, friendless and empty.

'Have I not done enough to show you?' Massimo's eyes were pleading as it spoke.

I felt tears in the corners of my eyes. I watched the fireworks fizzing in the sky, and they looked exactly how it felt. To have my friend.

'Well?'

'You've done enough,' I said. The sky split above me.

'You know this body won't take the exit?' Massimo put a hand on his own chest. *'It will likely fall apart.'*

I nodded. 'I know.'

'And you know, once I'm all the way inside you, that's it. After that, if I leave, if you force me, you will die a horrible death.'

'Yes. I know.'

'So, shall we?'

'Let's.'

'Good. Well, there's just a little bit more to go. Take my hand.'

I reached out a hand.

'Good boy.'

A hand met mine. The air crackled like cellophane. I felt my trainers on the loose gravel of the flat roof, and heard the whine of a flute. I tilted my head back and felt the first speckle of rain in the wind, landing on the thin skin of my face.

I let the rest of the demon in.

I was full of a burning sensation that was wound and salve at once. I looked down at my feet and was amazed to see them touching the ground, I felt so impossibly *light*. I looked at Massimo. He watched me closely with a searching, shuddering look in his eye.

It was filling up the gaps like foam sealant in the bricks of my house, the cracks in the walls. It was ten times anything I'd had before. Ten times the previous experiences. So much stronger, so much more wondrous. And I was still there with it. I had not disappeared.

'Oh. But there is so much room in here! Even more than I thought. It's disgusting in here. It's amazing.'

I rolled my eyes and giggled at its glee. It was pouring out of Massimo, but he was not bursting, he was not dead. Perhaps it had lied to me. He seemed fine! It began to rain, chucking down cats and dogs as I led us to the window. I pushed him in first, to keep him safe.

I'd barely slid down from the frame after him when Massimo started screaming.

I turned to look at his face, and noticed one brown eye was hanging from a thin wet thread, bobbing softly on his stubbled cheek. It looked down at the floor, the eye, to where three beautiful fingers rolled slightly in their own sticky blood. They'd fallen from his hand. On his white T-shirt, a small rose of blood was blooming, larger and larger, covering his chest. Another near his navel, dripping to the floor. Added to the screaming, which got louder, came a sound of tearing. The cape across his back ripping, the muscles beneath it beginning to shred as the last bit of devil, the last ounce of wondrous friend was leaving him, and stepping into me.

I told you so, my friend purred, as Massimo crumbled to the floor.

CHAPTER FORTY-SEVEN

It's almost spring.

The flat is looking amazing. We painted the living room green and got some new plants. The mould has all cleared up and the fridge is full of new and exciting snacks. The rooms get too hot now and then, but we just crack a window. Sometimes, when the place begins to stink, we light a fancy candle.

I found a table on Gumtree that they said was once used in a movie. I polish it every night so, when we eventually sit around it, everyone will admire the gleam. Through the window, in the churchyard, daffodils are sprouting through the graves, nourished by the long dead and bringing colour to the street.

I've been lying low. I go out mostly in the night, but I'm feeling more confident by the day. I don't have much to fear these days. I do pretty much what I want, and I try not to hurt anyone. It works, most of the time.

The sound of tinkling bells wakes me from a nap I've been taking. Someone carries a tray full of jars and dishes from the kitchen to the hallway. A girl in a ripped red nursing cape and purple crocs, a waterfall of hair straight and sleek down her back. Kat comes over a lot now, bringing her bandages, bindings, creamy thick plasters. Red peppers, jars of jam, mushroom soup. We're becoming good friends. We have sleepovers, she tells the most revolting jokes. She listens. Really listens. She's an amazing dancer.

I've had some wild experiences recently, if you know what I mean. Chaos in all its forms. But Kat looks out for me. If I stray too far, if I step too close to a violent edge, she comes to find me. If I climb too far up the monkey-puzzle tree, get too close to the firemen inside the station, she calls me back. To begin with, I made some big mistakes, but together, me and Kat, we've figured it out.

When I go out, I always take my phone with me. It's unconditional. Find my Friends is permanently activated. When I stole a police horse and took it cantering down the motorway, Kat was there to end the joyride. She brings the beast home. If I find trouble, get into a bar fight or a midnight brawl, the yellow car soon comes gliding through the streets, its headlights washing me white, and I'll stop whatever I'm doing. I'll put down whatever I'm playing with, and Kat will take me home, back to the flat, where she can keep an eye on me. On us.

She's good to have around. She's funny. She's kind. She gets it. I will see her watching me, and know she's dreaming of what it feels like. She'll rest her hands on my back some nights, like my friend might press out to meet her.

I've started giving her little bumps of demon. She sits very still and I perform a trick; something flips through the air like a golden coin, finding its target in her open mouth, and she shudders, her eyes squeezing tight as she's sent briefly spinning into a new world. But it always comes creeping back to me.

Kat's little dog brings joy to the building, new life! I promise I will not hurt her, not Baby Wendy. She howls at the moon sometimes and it's the sweetest little peep you ever heard. I follow suit and it's like a trumpet from the depths of hell.

That little puppy follows Kat *everywhere*, even into the spare bedroom where something lies deep-breathing in the bed. The lights are dimmed all the time, his one remaining eye is very sensitive after all it's been through, and often closed.

I was in there this morning. Stroking his hair, scraping the crust off his eyepatch, whispering in his remaining ear. 'You'll be up on your feet soon and we'll take the dog to the marshes and buy ourselves new knives for a great and glorious mushroom excursion, I promise. It'll be a fresh start and maybe one day we'll move to a bigger house, all together, a big one up in the woods!'

Really, we don't even know if he'll live. He's already been dead once.

There's a bloodstain in the kitchen where Massimo fell to bits. Where my friend pieced him back together again, my own little Lazarus, bringing him back to boyness. It was conditional, I said. 'If you're going to live here in me, I want Massimo up and walking again. He's my friend. I gave you a home, now use your power.' The mark won't come out, I've tried. I've put a new rug over it; that's the best I can do. Anyway, at least the bathroom is gleaming; I've cleaned it three times today.

The landlady rings me twice, and I cancel the call both times. She texts me soon after, inviting me to a gong-bath and begging me to call her back. They've been offered money for the building. Someone thinks it could be a hotel, but I've changed the locks, and painted the front door black. I don't think she'll find us.

Today is a big day. Massimo lies in the bedroom, bandaged and bleating. 'He wants a pizza!' said Kat, which is an excellent sign. The sun is shining like crazy and Baby Wendy yawns to show us the brown-pink roof of her mouth. I don't have time to enjoy the scene, I'm running late.

We're going out tonight. I've made a reservation at the karaoke bar. All three of us, if Massimo is up to it. We might go dancing afterwards.

I asked Josh; I think he's thinking about it.

But right now I have a job interview. Managing a

restaurant with a big glass ceiling and a fiddle-leaf fig tree. Something of an institution. Flat little fishes you gotta de-bone yourself, pink napkins. Espressos poured over fresh gelato. Delicious! On the bus heading west, I mouth my lines. I could have run the distance in a heartbeat, but it's not a good look.

I'm standing tall, my chest is broad and my hair feels thick and glossy. I'm wearing a shirt that I stole from Burberry. Don't ask me how, I don't want to repeat it. It's ruby-red and really brings out the green of my eyes.

The tall woman in front of me has a weapons-grade bob and she shuffles my CV, takes a sip of coffee. Her little tongue peeks out to snatch at foam that doesn't want to let go. Oh, it's gone.

'You've had almost six months off, from the last job. What have you been up to?' she asks, looking at me over the single printed page. I straighten up, shoulders back, smiling sweetly. Little black brogues aligned beneath the table. I look her in the eye.

'Well. I suppose you could say . . .'

I pause to rub my eyelid that's started flickering like mad. *Behave.*

I clear my throat.

'I suppose you could say I've been working on myself.'

ACKNOWLEDGEMENTS

My first thank you goes to John Ash. A very special person, and a very special agent. Thank you for seeing something in my unhinged manuscript, working closely with me to make it even better, and sending it into the world with care and passion. I rest safely knowing I have an agent who not only has a wild and wonderful imagination, but also handles everything with speed, style and kindness. I will be forever grateful.

Thank you to everyone else at CAA, too. Julie Flanagan, you matched me with the best US publisher I could have asked for, and did it with such panache! You're a dream. Thank you, Yasmin McDonald, for your enthusiasm and wisdom, it's such a pleasure to work with you – the way you handle everything with humour and integrity is amazing. Thanks to Gabby and Erika too, for getting me published in foreign languages, and keeping the ball rolling.

Thank you forever to Katie Bowden at Fourth Estate. For knowing exactly what I wanted to do with the novel, and pushing me to get there. Your taste is impeccable and so I still pinch myself – I cannot believe you pre-empted my novel at a party underneath a grisly Caravaggio. I am honoured to be in your classy brood, and feel lucky to have your guidance on this adventure. Thank you also for championing and publishing queer horror, and allowing it to shine on a very special platform. It's a wild dream come true to be published alongside some of my very favourite authors. Thank you also to everyone at Fourth Estate involved in bringing this book to life, to Kish, Lola and Eve for your generosity, diligence and assistance! It truly takes a village. Very special thanks also to Georgie Proctor for the incredibly sexy, head-turning cover that really made everything feel very real indeed.

Zack Knoll at Abrams. Your enthusiasm and insight was magical from day one. Thank you for bringing me in to such a special US publisher, and for being so excited about my book. Your joy for books is infectious and the way you spoke about *He's the Devil* never failed to move and inspire me. Thank you for talking about it so eloquently, for having such excellent ideas, and for making it all so fun.

Jamison Stoltz and Ruby Pucillo, your excitement, ideas and efficiency already make me feel in the safest hands. I cannot wait to go on this journey with you both! And thank you Eli Mock for the absolutely gorgeous US cover design – it's a true work of art.

My husband Christoffer, who told me: if you can't find it, write it. Thank you for having such easy confidence in me. You made me feel like I was already a writer, and I just had to get it done. Your humour, your enthusiasm, your love, they all made this happen. You are also in this book, all the way through it. I hope you love it.

Alex Kendall, I owe you so much. You read and read, then challenged me in the early days when this book was not close enough to the bone. It would not be the book it is today without your generosity and insight – that will always mean the world to me.

Thank you so much to Natalie Young, for introducing me to *The Artist's Way* in January of 2020, encouraging me to take it on, and opening a door that would lead to the creation of this very book. I needed to find a way to become unblocked, and you gifted it to me.

To early readers – Luke, Rona, Naja, Helena, Lilly. Thank you all for your words of encouragement that kept me believing, and writing! To Sharmaine Lovegrove, for always pushing me in the right direction. To all of my friends, every single one of you – one million thanks for your endless support. There are chunks of you all in this book. Sorry.

To my family. My mum and dad, and my brothers. I love you! For always allowing me to try whatever I needed to try. For accepting all the parts of me I unleashed upon you, and then encouraging them. For teaching me resilience, tenacity and strength. For having a home filled with books and terrifying films that I should definitely not have been watching, but am so glad I did. Thank you for laughing at my stories and my made-up characters and listening to me when I needed it. My imagination is what it is because of all of you. My humour and darkness and emotion is made up from little bits of all of you. Thank you so much.

Finally, thank you to my late grandma, who made me fall in love with books right at the beginning.